Leading Voices

a novel by Bill Ellis

PublishAmerica

Baltimore

First printing

ISBN: 1-4137-3075-2
PUBLISHED BY PUBLISHAMERICA, LLLP
www.publishamerica.com
Baltimore

Printed in the United States of America

In memory of Edith Hailey Ellis Preddy

To Ashley!
Enjoy!

Bill Ellis
May 8, 2007

To my children, John, Matt and Susanna: the future.

How a President Should Be

"A good president should be smart and kind. He should always tell the truth. A good president should lower taxes, lower rent and other things. He better be nice to his wife!!"

—Susanna Ellis, Third grade

One

Winter, 1950: an unnamed battlefield north of Seoul, Korea.

Artillery and mortar fire screamed overhead and thudded into the dull brown hills around their position. Thousands of Chinese charged blindly into certain death from the withering machine guns of the US Army. Yet Charley Company was pinned down, and its men were being picked off. Captain Johnson sank back into his trench shivering. His hands covered his head to hold back the pounding sounds of the shells decimating his troops. He was at a loss; no escape plan came to mind. This situation hadn't been covered in the ROTC classroom where he'd been until two months ago. He had been suddenly jerked from his sedate campus environment where he'd barely learned how to drill troops, and rapidly promoted to fill in the gaps in this ungodly "police action."

His men popped up their heads between explosions and searched for his guidance, any sign of leadership, anything to relieve them from this hell hole. Instead the captain remained squatting, unsuccessfully trying to hold back the noise unleashed by the dogs of war. But his make-believe sanctuary was abruptly torn apart when his first sergeant, a tall Norwegian named Conley, jumped in beside him.

"Sir, you need to call in an air strike and have artillery shell our location. That's our only way out of this quagmire. There are too many of them even with our superior firepower. We can't hold them off much longer." *Why does the sergeant look so calm? The man is a ferocious fighter and I rely on him to make most crucial decisions. The men think highly of Conley.*

They'd follow him to hell and back. Probably wouldn't follow me though. How can a Norwegian be named Conley?

"Ca–can't d–do it. Don't know. D–don't know." Captain Johnson looked up into the Norwegian's ice blue eyes for solace and found none. The defeated captain saw no pity or understanding, just disgust. Johnson hung his head and sobbed.

First Sergeant William Conley tore the radio from the back of the dead corporal slumped beside the captain and cranked it for transmission. "Comanche to Rover, Comanche to Rover. Fire on coordinates three eight dash one by six six dash seven. Repeat. Coordinates three eight dash one by six six dash seven. Over."

"This is Rover. That's your position, Comanche. Verify with second in command. Over."

"This is Sergeant Conley, damn it. There is no command or second to verify. Fire on the goddamn position before they overrun us. Do it now! My wife's expecting. Got my orders. My tour is up and I'd better be there for her or your ass is grass!"

"Roger that, Sergeant." The radio went dead and Conley gave the high sign to the men of Charley Company.

"Hang on and keep blasting those bastards," he yelled down the line. "Be ready to hunker down when our guys start firing on us." He got thumbs up signs from all the men as the news was relayed. They had fought beside and under him most of this war. If there was a way out, Bill Conley would find it.

Captain Johnson came alive and crept up over the lip of their fox hole into a standing position. Before Sergeant Conley could jerk him back down, the man calmly stepped out from cover and raised his hands to surrender. He took two steps, grinning like a fool, before the impact of a hundred rounds slammed him backwards. "Stupid, stupid, stupid," the sergeant muttered to himself. Snapped completely. Nothing left inside, just a shell when enemy fire put him out of his misery.

The distraction delayed the sergeant's recognition of the high-pitched whine of Navy jets swooping low over their hill. Conley stood and yelled to his men, "Down, down, incoming!" He presented a tall, six-and-a-half-foot target, waving his arms that drew everyone's attention on both sides of the fighting, and caught a bullet high on his left shoulder. Still the man continued yelling and waving to warn his men. He dropped down under cover as the first blasts from the air strike and artillery zeroed in on their position.

"Good morning, Sergeant Conley. Step inside for a minute." Colonel James Hunsinger was a veteran of the Big One against the Japanese, and he now commanded the battalion that included Charlie Company. Much of his command had been fractured and demoralized by the recent suicide attacks from the North. He stood behind his desk, an empty ammo box, and returned the salute of the gangly fellow at attention across from him.

"You wanted to see me, Sir?" Conley carried his left arm and his orders for home in a sling.

"Yes, at ease, Sergeant. I understand from pretty high sources you have important personal business to attend to back stateside. General Kramer wanted me to speak to you personally about it. He couldn't be here to see you off and wanted to make sure, uh, I'll quote him directly, that, 'his ass wasn't going to be grass.'"

Conley chuckled. He'd been kidded for weeks about this and wondered who he'd cussed at. So it was a general, eh? Didn't matter, most of his men escaped, some had died, and many had wounds, but they had escaped.

"Please convey my sincere apologies to the general, Colonel Hunsinger. Guess I got a little steamed out there. Didn't look too good for a while. This is Elizabeth's first, our first, and I plan to be there start to finish."

Colonel Hunsinger scanned the tall man's folder refreshing his memory for the general's next question. "Uh, Sergeant Conley, General Kramer also was curious about another matter in your personnel file. The army asked you for some kind of ethnic identification and you put down Norwegian-American."

Conley grinned as if anticipating the next question and interrupted the befuddled colonel. "Sir, my grandparents processed through Ellis Island as immigrants straight off the boat. As Grandpa used to tell it, some smart-alecky clerk asked for his name five times and never understood the answer. The fellow mumbled something about too many syllables and wrote down 'Conley.' We've been stuck with it since. My parents were afraid of long names after that so they gave me only two, a first and a last. That also confounds the bureaucrats." Both men laughed.

Hunsinger searched the face of the big man in front of him. He didn't speak like a sergeant. Didn't act like one either. There was a self-confident air that put him on an equal footing automatically. Rank and position didn't impress him, only results and mutual respect. There was a natural mantle of leadership, an aura coming from him, and the colonel could understand what the reports were saying about this man. He nodded for the photographer, waiting off to the side, to step around to the front of the tent, then he walked up to Conley, smiling.

"I think the general's feelings weren't hurt too much, Conley. He's authorized your promotion to lieutenant. Congratulations." The colonel pinned a gold bar on the sergeant's lapel. Second Lieutenant Conley received a battlefield promotion that was followed by a silver star pinned to his jacket. The camera's flash caused the dumbfounded new officer to flinch. But he recovered quickly.

"Thank you, Sir. This was unexpected and it is much appreciated. Sure will help on the expenses once I get the wife and baby home." Conley peeked down at the gold bar. He had intended to apply for a commission after Korea and make the Army his career. He also had plans for night school to get his degree. And he wasn't stopping there.

"I do have one question for you, Lieutenant." The colonel returned to his desk and rummaged through some reports. "A few witnesses say the captain deliberately stood up and walked into enemy fire to commit suicide. But your report says he was signaling to his men and was shot being a hero. Or, something to that effect." The colonel fixed the newly commissioned officer with a steely glare. "Which is it? Did the man give up his command? Did he quit or did he die a hero?"

Lieutenant Conley returned the colonel's glare with a confident smile, blue eyes steady, unblinking. "My version is correct, Colonel. I was right there with him."

"Thank you, Conley. Dismissed. And have a good trip back home." Colonel Hunsinger watched the young officer about face and part the tent flaps to exit. He had ten reports to the contrary of Conley's, all swearing the captain had lost it. And all swore that Conley had saved their butts. He would believe the new lieutenant on the first score and his men on the latter. The colonel felt in his bones that this would not be the last promotion for William Conley.

"Major, you cannot go in there. Labor and delivery procedures are restricted to medical staff only."

Bill Conley stood his ground. This was going to be their fifth and final child; they hoped for a girl after four rambunctious boys. He had insisted on being there—barged in, as many maternity ward professionals termed it—

for each child's birth, and he wasn't going to miss this one.

"Nurse, it is my right and privilege, and my responsibility to be there with my wife and to see that child born. I will not faint and have not caused a problem in four previous births. My wife needs me in there and frankly she expects me to stand by her as she always stands by me. Now," the lanky major towered over the intimidated nurse, "please, step aside and let me tend to my wife."

The harried nurse turned in exasperation and went to her station down the hall to call the doctor on duty that night. The out-manned doctor would not have any better luck persuading Major Conley from his rights and duties. The doctor called the hospital administrator, a full colonel. He would stop this maniac from disrupting their maternity ward. But that man failed too. All had failed it seemed, as examination of medical records of Mrs. Conley's four previous deliveries had proved. Even MPs had failed as they attempted, admittedly half-heartedly, to arrest the devoted husband and father. He was bigger, stronger, and outranked all of them. Plus he simply refused to go.

Tonight he had walked past the nurse and gone to his wife. While the superior officers and doctors pondered what to do about him, Bill Conley massaged Elizabeth's feet, her arms, her hands, her shoulders and whatever other part of her straining body required it. He neither asked for help from the nurses, nor did he get any voluntarily. This disregard had become the nurses' usual practice once he had gotten his way, and he accepted it. It was unprofessional on their part, but he took it in stride. He knew enough about birthing babies to warn the nurses when the head crowned and Elizabeth needed to be taken to the delivery room. He knew enough to cover his uniform with a surgical gown and get himself ready as if he were the obstetrician. He also knew how to coach her through the increasing pain from the contractions.

Most men of the 1950s, and probably for a few decades to come, would not understand how a man like Major Conley could be such a success in the military, yet always put his family first. He often told younger officers under his command that the most important thing they could ever do, and he meant ever, would be to bond with their children from the moment of birth. No one doubted his bravery; he had the medals backing that up, and certainly not his masculinity, with four boys and now a daughter from this latest delivery. Yet the combination of male toughness and being a devoted father and husband escaped most men until long after Bill Conley retired from the army as a two-star general.

This was leadership on another dimension far from the battlefield. Yet it wasn't everything in the man's bag of talents. His mind was an incredible mechanism. He simply remembered people, places, events and reams of information that enabled him to out-think most humans. And he worked hard alongside officers and enlisted men and women, disregarding military protocol in order to get the job done.

"We expect you to be at the cocktail party tonight, Colonel Conley. The Commanding General requires it. Command performance, don't you know. Won't bode well for your career to miss it." The command's Chief of Staff, a brigadier general, puffed up with this profound directive and then deflated at the junior officer's response.

"Sorry to disappoint you and the general, Sir, but my daughter's soccer team is playing their last game tonight and I promised I'd be there. Afterwards, I have a case full of reports to look at so I can put together my analysis of the situation in Heidelberg. Something is out of whack in our European command and I intend to find out what it is. Elizabeth hates those parties, so we probably wouldn't go regardless."

Before the Chief of Staff could muster a strong reprimand, Colonel Conley was up and gone from his office. Young Sara Conley's team won the game and her father placed a report on the Chief of Staff's desk Monday morning that blew the lid off a spy ring operating under the nose of the army's European commander-in-chief. Several years later Major General Conley would go undercover himself to ferret out yet another illegal operation in Germany, this one a drug ring operated by naïve Army officers who thought they could avoid military law while all attention was centered on the Vietnam war half a planet away.

"Bill, come inside, it's the governor on the phone," Elizabeth yelled from their back deck to her amateur golfing husband. He was sneaking onto the ninth fairway from his home to get in a few holes before dark. The man rarely called in for tee times, preferring to play bits and pieces late in the afternoons.

They loved living in Colorado Springs. The general had retired shortly after the Berlin Wall came down, saying the free flow of spies would undo his work for the last decade. He had managed an undercover operation in the shadows of the Brandenburg Gate that was unparalleled in military history. The general's men and women had infiltrated Soviet and East German networks with ease, gaining him an international reputation. Even these days, not six months into retirement, he still received unmarked packages containing sensitive information with cover letters begging for his expert analysis. These packets came from a vast network of friends he had in CIA, FBI, NSA and any other acronym gathering intelligence for Uncle Sam. There had been so much material he'd gone out and bought a safe for its storage. For sure it was unmarked and not officially classified, but he knew just how delicate were the contents. Someone had told him early on that once you were a spy you could never fully avoid dealing with undercover operations.

But the governor calling? What could that right winger want? The general had registered independent mainly to keep away from people like Marvin Granger; keep them all from recruiting him for blue ribbon commissions. He would say no to whatever the man wanted. Bill Conley wanted no part of either party's agenda, no matter the goal.

"Hello, Governor. What can I do for you?" He answered in a tired voice, hoping his lack of initial enthusiasm would put off the officious bastard.

"Afternoon, Bill. I have some terrible news and the State of Colorado needs your help." *Bill? Since when did we get on a first name basis?* "You may have heard about Senator Garth Mattox. His plane went down near Telluride, killing everyone on board last week."

"Yes, I heard, Governor." It was a terrible loss for the man's family. But in the Senate, Mattox had blocked any legislation dealing with health care, welfare, and just about every domestic initiative. The senior senator from Colorado was an avowed war hawk and voted to increase the Pentagon's budget every year. Garth Mattox would not have gotten the Conleys' votes in next year's general election.

"My advisors have been tossing around some names of possible individuals who might be a good fit to complete the rest of Garth's term in the Senate. He would have been up for reelection next fall and had personally confided in me that he was bowing out. There are several fellows anxious for me to appoint them, but I'm caught between a rock and a hard place on this."

Bill didn't need to use much brain power to figure out where this was going. It was widely known that the governor, most of all, coveted that Senate seat. If he appointed someone who was a competitor, the man might beat him out for the party's nomination and send the governor into early retirement.

Granger wouldn't dare appoint someone from the opposition party and give those liberal scalawags the chance to upset the balance of power in Washington. That left the notion of a caretaker as his choice, namely an independent, a retired military man like Bill Conley. No one would question his appointment. Conservatives would rejoice in a presumed smooth transition to a man who, it might be supposed incorrectly, had similar political inclinations as the deceased incumbent. He chuckled to himself. What they didn't know would surprise them. And, any moderate to liberal opposition wouldn't object too much since it was only a temporary job, lasting less than eighteen months. If they checked carefully they might find the general stood closer to their side on some of the issues.

Bill Conley had always reversed the military's edict to place the mission first over his soldiers' welfare. He had watched closely as experts preached this dogma with a wink. Sure, complete the mission but never without supreme consideration of the people involved, instructors hinted with body language aside from the Pentagon's script. He had read numerous combat reports detailing fragging incidents, wherein soldiers rolled grenades into junior officers' tents. Why? One hundred per cent of the time it was because those officers generally ordered their men to charge into certain death disregarding alternative safer options.

The retired general had become an expert in human relations. His subordinates remained steadfastly loyal to him and he returned this loyalty always. What's more, Bill Conley always accomplished his mission. Now he mentally paused, anticipating the governor's next move and thinking about what his life's mission might be.

"You might guess that your name came to the top of my list, Bill. You're a military hero. Highly regarded nationally as well as in Colorado. I doubt if you have any political aspirations after almost a half century of service in the Army. Bet you want to spend time with your lovely wife, maybe play some golf. I kind of have my eye on Mattox's job myself, but, uh, well, I need somebody to hold it for me until the election next year. You understand, Bill?"

He understood perfectly and the conniving governor was playing his cards well. But Conley wasn't giving the man any immediate satisfaction.

"Let me talk it over with Elizabeth, that lovely wife you mentioned. She runs the show around here. I'll give you a call in the morning. Goodbye, Marvin."

Later than evening, he made their usual margaritas on the rocks, no salt, and dragged Elizabeth out to the deck for a conference. They had avoided assignments to Washington for many years. He'd always wanted to be closer to the action and she couldn't tolerate the cocktail circuit, where it seemed most political connections were made.

"So that's the deal. You know me and politics, honey. I never wanted to run for office. Hell, we don't like politicians. Lot of hot air and arm waving. But I want your opinion." He relaxed with a big slurp of his drink and waited for her to squash the notion. Yet his thoughts delved into the possibilities as a member of Congress.

She surprised him though. Elizabeth scooted forward in her chair and came knee to knee with him. She searched his eyes for the truth. Her own eyes gleamed with woman's intuition when she found it.

"William Conley, you are not the retiring type. I can count on my two hands the number of days you have done nothing since you quote unquote retired. Daily some package comes in here for your perusal. I hear the gist of your phone conversations from people back East asking your opinion. You haven't retired, you just moved West."

"Aw come on." He tried to stifle his grin, knowing she had found him out, probably knew from the start. But she interrupted his feeble attempt to make an excuse.

"I like the idea, Bill. We can keep this place for getaways and rent something up on Capitol Hill so you can walk to work. Maybe even come home for lunch or a nooner." Her hand tickled the inside of his thigh, suggesting he might get lucky tonight. "It's only for eighteen months, a short tour in the Army, and those guys take a lot of time off to travel." She had inched both hands up to his middle now and was close enough to tease his mouth with a kiss.

The general noticed this tactical maneuver though and countered with his own strategy, one that had served him well in their lifelong partnership. He scooped his arms under her, lifting her as a newlywed carrying his bride across that initial threshold. Next he kicked aside the screen door and marched to their master bedroom. He let her down next to the bed and they both undressed. After more than fifty years of marriage and countless times making love, it still thrilled them. There was romance and gentleness, more now as both enjoyed their seventies, but at times like this they were as excited as teenagers at a drive-in theater. Except each knew where to touch, and when, and how much to massage and when to just go for it like sprinters the last few yards of a race. Fingers played an excited rhythm this night like a stirring Rossini overture rendered from memory by the hands of a concert pianist.

They lay side by side, captured in the afterglow. She would not let him escape. She would keep him cuddled close to her until he nodded off. *Funny*, she thought. Making love exhilarated her, woke her up. Whereas, her magnificent lover always dozed off gradually. Still, she knew she had a moment yet.

"You are the most wonderful lover." She paused one beat. "Let's go to Washington and do it up right."

He half mumbled now. "I love you. I am a lucky man."

"Yes, you are," she whispered as his eyes slid firmly closed. To her utmost satisfaction, he grinned in his sleep. And she reflected on her prize. Her husband had too much to offer to stay put here. His mind went everywhere for answers and she believed he had better ones than were coming from their nation's capitol. Oh sure, he might think of this as a temporary assignment of eighteen months, but she had seen the excitement he'd failed to hide. He would have turned down the governor on the spot if the job hadn't intrigued him. As always he deferred to her, and she had given him *their* opinion. The country needed to hear from Bill Conley. Her man was a leader, unafraid to stand for his beliefs. Elizabeth Conley firmly believed that if JFK had lived, the next chapter in his *Profiles in Courage* would have been about her husband.

Elizabeth laughed at the inflammatory headline on the front page of the *Denver Post*. "Colorado's Maverick Senator Stuns Congress Again."

She scanned the article recounting the defeat of a conservative initiative to reduce the budget for Medicaid. Why didn't they believe him when he gave that speech against this proposal last week? The people came first, he'd said. But the party had considered his words nothing more than a cover for the voters, something to be published in the *Congressional Record* that wouldn't be backed up by his actual vote. Surely, some of the quoted but anonymous senators were reported to have said, the man would come to his senses and stick with the tide.

Chagrined was a mild description of the defeated senators. And this after his vote last week helped squash an additional obligation of funds for a new super jet fighter for the Marines. It didn't matter that test flights had proven the plane inadequate and a waste of money. Both senators from the state where the aerospace company was located had lobbied hard to continue throwing money down the rat hole. Too many jobs were at stake, they clamored. Their state's economy would suffer. In response, Colorado's Junior Senator had dropped a bombshell proposing the complete abolishment of the project. Blasphemy! screeched the war hawks. Yet not one senator dared question Bill Conley's patriotism. He had told them outright what he would do and he did it. And apparently this was an oddity inside the beltway surrounding Washington.

They had been in Washington only a few months and already her husband's record was a national news item. It was typical for him, yet the people outside of Washington found his views refreshing and Coloradans were starting a campaign to get him elected to his own six-year term. She noted her lifemate had not immediately spurned the attention and the talk of another term in office. He made it clear he would not accept any donations from anyone, wealthy individuals and corporations included, that exceeded ten bucks! That was her signal. She had known it that night out on the deck alongside the golf course. News media made a joke of it and said it was political fantasy. No one succeeded in politics these days without millions in contributions. But the money started dribbling in and increased after each staggering vote the interim senator made.

Bill Conley was a renegade, one everyone wanted on their side. He walked to work and took the Metro subway to meetings around town. There would be no special perks, never had been. He didn't just show up for every vote on the floor of the Senate, he spoke his mind on every issue regardless of either party's standard line. He was independent and no one could budge him from that spot. Numerous lobbyists had tried. He would meet with none of them. He accepted no favors, no lunches, no plane rides, no honorariums for speeches—he was paid two salaries by Uncle Sam and owed it to the people, he'd said. Neither would he accept tickets to sports events, and no fact-finding trips to foreign lands, especially the latter—they had been stationed overseas most of his career and had traveled the world. That, plus he still received anonymous packages asking for his analysis of world leaders. Elizabeth figured he knew more about foreign affairs than anyone in the Senate. Bottom line: he accepted nothing.

Meetings at the White House? If it was a nice day he walked, usually passing by the line of limos waiting to disgorge VIPs. On the way up Pennsylvania Avenue he chatted with people, shook their hands, and heard their complaints, their views. Her husband was having a ball. He was out in the open, no longer a master spy working undercover. And raising hell. The people loved him.

The press was ambivalent. He had invitations every weekend to appear on the Sunday news talk shows and debates. He turned them all down. His weekends were spent with family and trips back to Colorado. He refused requests for personal interviews by the TV news magazines. He was quoted as saying he and Elizabeth were not celebrities, they were public servants. If his family wanted to be in the limelight, that was OK. Just keep him out of it.

It was the same when they went back to Colorado. They paid extra for first class seats themselves so he could stretch his long legs. Offers from contractors, defense types mainly, were rejected. Governor Marvin, as Bill called him, was incredulous. He called their home often, their answering machine proved it, but the Senator and Mrs. Conley were never there. It wasn't a matter of avoiding the man who had appointed him and hoped to become the next senator himself. No, Bill Conley just wasn't an office person. He and Elizabeth drove around the state and met people. They would pull up in little towns and go "main streeting," as he called it, walking into shops and offices, banks and schools, just to meet the people and hear them talk about their lives and their communities. They avoided party caucuses and conventions. Senator Conley did not represent parties and politicians. He represented the people of Colorado.

Elizabeth observed an interesting phenomenon in those visits. Folks understood her husband would take the time to listen to them and he would always remember them in a follow-up note. She thought his secretary, Alice, was an overworked angel to keep track of his numerous pieces of correspondence. Yet he was never caught in a crowd because he took time to be with regular folks and his reputation for doing so spread quickly. People respected the Conleys. They were a handsome couple, both tall and attractive and openly friendly, never in a hurry to move on to a next appointment. As a result, there was no pushing to get too close. The Conleys were given space to breathe and never threatened.

Another three months went by and both major parties in the state courted the interim senator to run for election. But there were always catches. How would he vote in this issue? Would he support that proposal? Each party had a list of issues and its candidate would have to stand up and speak for them.

"Would you look at this garbage?" Bill passed a sheaf of papers over to his wife one evening out on their deck. She leafed through the vague legalese then glanced up to ascertain his demeanor.

"Not very good," she said. "This is not us, not you. Nobody seems to get it."

"No, they don't. The governor and his hacks want me to compromise to the right. The other guys expect me to be their white knight and save their sorry butts. They have no program, only criticism."

"You'll run in the fall, won't you?" It came out more a statement of fact than as a question.

He gazed off towards the steep slope of Cheyenne Mountain to the west and became lost in thought. Elizabeth followed his line of sight and kept quiet, waiting. She knew what was coming; he just had to say it out loud for both of them.

"I owe it to this country, to the people, honey. We both do. We see it in their eyes on the main streets walking along. I read it in their letters every day. Folks want someone to represent them, and don't feel the little guy has that anymore. These are not dumb voters. They tell us they write their members of Congress and get back the same old party line. They don't have the money to pay for a night in the White House or a tea with the First Lady. Small business owners aren't invited to closed-door meetings with the vice president to talk about health care or energy policy or foreign trade, or anything."

He turned his chair facing her and reached for her hands. Her smile was set in affirmative reinforcement. He had known it would be.

"Let's give it a ride, Elizabeth. But there have to be some rules. We do this together and we do it our way. I'm sick of the campaigning the way it's done anymore. What are your thoughts?"

"I like the contribution limit of ten dollars. Whatever comes in goes for literature, buttons, posters, and maybe a few TV commercials if there is any left. We take no money for ourselves; make it a cheap strategy."

"I'll check on the balance of the trust fund down at the bank on Monday. Alice keeps up with that stuff with help from your district office in Denver. I have no idea what has come in and thought it was taken as a joke from the get go." He paused a minute. "We will certainly stay independent and unattached to any organized political structure. I don't want some spin master interpreting our message for us. For that matter, I don't want any paid consultants or campaign managers either. Typically those folks want a job later on. I'm not handing out patronage. We don't believe in it."

"I agree completely. That may be what's wrong now. There are so many people being paid off, no one is actually running the government."

So it began. The two major parties held conventions and nominated their respective candidates, Marvin Granger being one. There followed the Green Party, the Libertarian Party, and even the Communist Party. Still, there was no word from the incumbent and supposed lame duck interim junior senator. While campaign money flew like geese, Senator Conley stayed in Washington and attended every Senate session. He voted on every piece of legislation, continuing to make news by his forthright stands on issues from health care to military spending to the simple needs of an aging population. It was ironic that Bill Conley overshadowed the candidates back in his home state because of his low profile. He changed nothing. His style, if anyone dared to describe it as such, never varied.

The dog days of August arrived in the swamp where Washington bedded down. That was when Bill and Elizabeth flew to Denver and reserved Civic Center Park downtown right across from the state capitol building. Alice sent letters to the TV stations and the major newspapers around the state inviting the public to a barbecue. There followed the biggest love fest ever experienced in the state. The crowd was estimated at several hundred thousand and all had come to hear Bill Conley announce his candidacy. He didn't disappoint them and neither did the food and music.

At high noon he stood on a platform in the center of the park and held up one hand for quiet. He didn't yell for attention or slap the microphone a few times and count to four. He just held up a hand and the people shut up. TV camera crews faced him from across the street and roving minicams snaked through the crowd getting a flavor of the mood of the voters. But the image of their man standing tall, holding his arm aloft and smiling out to the crowd, hit the front pages of every newspaper and was rebroadcast time after time on television. He said few words, but they were good ones.

"Thank you for coming to our little picnic. Also thanks to the many restaurants who donated the food. It's nice to see the American spirit moving, coming alive. I'll cut this short because everyone knows I don't like to make boring speeches. I will run for the United States Senate this fall. I would be honored to represent you in the Congress. I will continue to work for the people of Colorado, but as has been my practice, I'll make no promises other than to do my best. My policy for contributions continues to be a maximum of ten bucks per person. Anything more and we'll send it back. Thank you." The expectant crowd erupted in cheering and applause.

Bill Conley stepped down from the platform and gathered his wife by his side. They made their way through the crowd shaking hands and visiting just like always. The people allowed a respectable bubble of space around the happy couple. They understood this had been an historic moment. These voters and many others across the state, who would watch the evening news and read the Sunday paper, felt this was a couple sincerely representing them. They sought no privileges and accepted none. They were regular folks.

The Conleys went to each food stand, intending to thank the owners and chefs personally. But the first problem of their campaign faced them at the first location, Antonio's Pasta Kitchen. Tony himself wiped his hands on his apron and came around to the front of the booth to shake hands.

"Sir, Senator, Mrs. Conley, uh, we got a slight problem back here. What do you want me to do?"

"Tell me what you need, Tony," the new candidate said.

"Well, see, it's like this. We were glad to donate the food and the drinks but I put up a tip jar for the workers. Me, I can write this off easy, but my staff has to stand here all day and take the orders. They work very hard and they all donated their time today. But the tip jar is a problem."

"Tony, we can't thank you enough. All of you." Elizabeth's smile dazzled the rotund man. "But please keep the money. It's yours."

"Ah, well, there's too much. Let me show you." Tony reached back under the counter and brought out a clear glass gallon jug allowing them to see the many ten-dollar bills packed inside, top to bottom. "And there are five more like this one. Pete counted it up and said there was enough in one bottle to compensate him and his crew. The rest is for your campaign."

Elizabeth took charge. It was she after all who managed the household finances.

"OK, Tony, here's what we'll do. Take the extra money and deposit it. Then send a check to our Denver office." She handed Tony a business card with the address. "Tell us how many voters this represents, figuring you'll divide ten into the total to get that number. That's how we'll report it."

But the same issue arose at each food stand. Tip jars overflowed with the desire of the voters to participate and of course get some good food. And Elizabeth advised each vendor to take what was needed to compensate their workers, then deposit the surplus and send a check with a calculation on the approximate number of voters. As dusk settled on downtown Denver the picnic continued as the Conleys made the rounds to well-wishers.

Two weeks later, in their Capitol Hill office, Alice whistled softly as she finished adding up the latest figures from Denver. She took the tally into the senator's office and waited for him to hang up on another lobbyist who had sneaked through her guard. She slumped into the closest chair, exhausted from the rigors of the campaign.

"No, I won't support more aid to Myanmar, the legitimate name for Burma. Not as long as they have a dictator denying freedom to his people. It is time this country stopped pandering to despots. And don't call here again." Wham, the phone hit the holder and a red-faced Bill Conley turned to glare at Alice. But her smile softened his feelings.

"Sorry, Alice. Lost my cool there. I heard the other line ringing and figured I'd help out. Next time I'll let it ring. We probably need to hire another person, huh?"

"She'll be here tomorrow, Senator. I've been under siege since you announced. But I thought you'd like to see these figures." Alice pursed her lips then smiled broadly. She passed her financial report over to her boss and waited.

The Junior Senator from the Great State of Colorado stood with his mouth open. Never a man for many words, he had nary a one at the moment.

"Denver says about $5,000 comes in every day now from around the state, but you got about $500,000 from the picnic and all I did was send a letter out. It cost us nothing other than the money we sent to the City of Denver for security and the cleanup. So, adding the picnic money to our existing balance brings the total in your campaign fund to a smidgeon over one million dollars!" Alice bent double laughing. Her boss stood, gulping air. His naturally white hair gave him the appearance of an albino rainbow trout. "Senator...Bill, snap out of it. This is real money. It represents about 100,000 voters and more comes in daily."

"Holy cow, Alice. What are we going to do with all this?"

"Well, there are some rules, but yours are much stricter. Maybe you can use some of it to pay for those first class seats back to Denver." But she knew that was out of the question right away.

"No, no, no, Alice. You know better. Think I'll go have lunch with the boss and ask her what to do. It's about noon anyway." He turned pink and Alice covered her mouth stifling a giggle.

The campaign was not so much a contest as a whipping out behind the shed. The incumbent interim senator agreed to one debate and the remaining candidates opted out after that debacle. Bill Conley knew foreign policy, domestic policy, and the will of the voters. He owed nothing to political financiers, to lobbyists, to anyone except the people, and their monetary support continued to flow unabated. He spoke straight from his heart and from his steel-trap mind without filters from party platforms. His answer to one question set the stage for the entire debate.

"How would you deal with Burma, Senator?" That was one specific question probably fed to the moderator by that lobbyist he'd slammed the phone down on back in DC.

His answer was, "You really mean Myanmar. I would give them no support whatsoever, cease diplomatic relations, and recommend economic sanctions by the United Nations. It's past time for this nation to stop being hypocritical. We cry democracy for everyone except where malevolent dictators give us a military base or with whom we do lots of trade. Do you not believe that lobbyists have paid for influencing members of Congress to vote for continued support of the dictator in Myanmar? In Pakistan? In a whole slew of South American countries?"

The other two candidates made it clear they weren't sure just where Burma was and neither had heard of Myanmar. Who was its leader? They had no clue. Plus, Senator Conley had specific responses to local issues: school funding, taxes, highway construction, and water rights. His answers turned into a lecture series of facts and solutions, while his two opponents could only touch the tip of the surface while spouting politically correct, committee-developed party lines.

Elizabeth ran the campaign with help locally from the Denver office staff, and strategically from Alice. She refused to pay the exorbitant rates for TV and radio advertising, bumped up just for the election season. The money so generously being donated by individual voters went for literature, buttons, stickers and signs. Bill Conley received almost continuous free publicity from his news-making, voting record, and military background. Never before had an international master spy run for office in Colorado.

Elizabeth's only concession to TV and radio was to Rocky Mountain Public TV and Colorado Public Radio. The nation tuned in as well. Her husband had struck a tremendous nerve. He spoke clearly and without allegiance to special interests. He was not bought and paid for. More importantly, neither did he give the appearance of such. He was an honest man, and although in favor of a strong military, he knew where the waste was and seemed to be more moderate on human rights than any previous general running for public office. In a word, Bill Conley was unique.

He won in a landslide. The remaining money in the campaign treasury went to Colorado charities decided upon by an oversight committee of volunteers from around the state.

The independently elected senator from Colorado had served two months in office when his wife met him at the door with exciting news one afternoon.

"I met the neatest gal today, Bill. You'd love her. Her name is Hailey MacMurray and she was just elected to the House of Representatives from southwest Virginia. Turns out she's from Blue Ridge, where Sara and Joe live. Sara gave her our number and I talked to her several times during the fall campaign, sort of told her what we were up to. Hailey called me this morning and invited me to join a group of women to, well, er, stir up trouble it sounds like. She'll be over at seven for supper and her son, Adam, will be with her. So, go get cleaned up."

He uttered not one word and went straight to their bedroom. When Elizabeth got this excited, she was either pregnant or about to start a revolution. He was certain this was the latter. *That's a good thing*, he thought. *Wasn't it?*

He answered the door promptly at seven and opened it to one of the most beautiful women he had ever seen. Hailey MacMurray had smiling deep brown eyes in an oval face. Her mouth was set in a friendly smile. She was tall and had silky, chestnut brown hair down to her shoulders. Bill's gaze stopped at that point. He made an effort to maintain eye contact before embarrassing them both. He did happen to notice a small boy shyly half hidden behind her with his arms around her waist.

"Hello, Senator. I'm Hailey and this is my son, Adam." She shook hands firmly like a man only with soft skin.

He found his voice at last. "Hello, Hailey, and I'm just plain Bill. Now who is this hiding back there again?" She nudged Adam out to her side and he came forward now grinning. Bill shook the boy's hand too and showed them inside.

"I take it you're anxious to start a revolution, Hailey. Nothing else can get Elizabeth so up in arms. What's your agenda? Oh, come have a seat. Elizabeth will be right out. Get you something to drink? What about you, Adam? Soda, water, glass of milk? Have any hobbies?" Cripes. He was chattering on like a kid on his first date. Where was his wife? He needed rescuing. Small talk was not his suit and this woman just returned his smile with such warmth and sincerity. He turned to look behind for reinforcements and found none.

Hailey answered his initial question. "My agenda is women, Bill. Just that. I want to meet strong women here in Washington and find out what their priorities are. Hoped to make some new friends now that I have to work in this town. I've admired you and your wife for years and just had to meet you both." Bill looked puzzled. "We're from Blue Ridge, the same town where Sara and her husband Joe Wolf live. Small world, isn't it?"

Then his memory kicked in. He had read classified reports when he was stationed in Berlin that contained excellent analyses and were signed by "H. MacMurray." His confidence returned.

"Smaller than you think, Hailey. Did you sign all your work out of Moscow using only a first initial instead of your full first name?" She nodded, perplexed at his recall. "Excellent work." He beamed and Hailey's mouth dropped. He explained that as a spy—a term he used jokingly—he had access to most all classified material relating to Europe. He remembered hers in particular.

Elizabeth returned and took Hailey off to the study to talk. Bill latched onto Adam and the two worked up a good game of Scrabble. The boy had a surprising vocabulary for a first grader. He also spoke French and Bill allowed the boy some words that left him dazed. Dinner went quickly and their guests left early. Adam had school and Hailey had an early committee meeting in the morning. Bill stood at the window watching them drive back to their home in the Virginia suburbs. Elizabeth came to his side and found him in deep concentration.

Elizabeth gushed with enthusiasm. "She's a jewel and the boy's a diamond in the rough. What personality he has; smart like his mother. Did you hear her say she has a knack for languages? She speaks Russian and French and is learning Chinese of all things. Took that up in the State Department when she couldn't fly jets anymore. And she's a single mother. God, how many points does she get for that? And the boy. Tall for his age, but then Hailey is tall, so that figures. A little shy but he's only in first grade. Hailey practically home-schooled him during their overseas assignments. And he's his mother's escort to all official confabs. What a story, Bill."

Two

"Setup, Hailey!" The tall, athletic brunette drifted under the volleyball Mary Jo had placed in a perfect arc leading down to the top of the net. Two defenders rushed to block the suspected slam from Virginia's all-state spiker. She was just under six feet tall with jumping ability that had gained the attention of top-flight college basketball programs in the region. Hailey jumped and the two defenders leapt with her, but she only got off the floor a few inches. She landed in a crouch and shot straight up, her feet nearing the bottom of the net. She swatted the ball at its pinnacle, sending it just over the heads of her opponents with a resounding thwack! crushing it to the floor immediately behind them, where no other defender could possibly reach it. Game, match and state championship came with that final blow.

"We did it! Woo-hoo!" Ecstatic girls jumped in the air and created a pile of bodies out on the court to celebrate their victory. The Blue Ridge Lions had made it two years in a row, beating the Rambling Rebels from Chesterfield again in the state finals. Hailey and Mary Jo, the best setter on the team, hugged and screamed.

Two men sat at the top of the bleachers in the James Monroe Stadium in Charlottesville observing the excitement, yet keeping their eyes on one girl in particular: Hailey MacMurray. They did not join with the parents and students who now rushed to the court to help celebrate the Blue Ridge phenomenon. A town of just under 10,000 inhabitants in southwestern Virginia, made up mostly of coal mining families close to poverty, had just beaten the team from one of the state's biggest schools in the suburbs of its capitol city. These men had watched only one player who was being hoisted on her teammates' shoulders for a victory lap around the stadium.

"Well, Congressman, there she is. What do you think?" Adam Knowles nudged the important man, breaking his reverie. He had written to Merton Alexander months ago about Hailey and had invited him to this tournament.

"She's beautiful, uh, a great athlete, Mr. Knowles. I'm sure she'll do well at Tennessee down in Knoxville. They have a great basketball program."

"She might, Mr. Alexander, but Hailey wants to fly. Already does in her cousin's little two-seater. Learned when she was old enough to drive. She wants to fly jets for the Air Force. And that takes entry into the Academy out in Colorado Springs." Adam waited a beat as his guest was lost in thought again. The congressman couldn't deal with his daughter's good looks, something Hailey didn't appreciate. Adam and Marie had taken her into their home after her parents died within a month of each other more than ten years ago. Father caught a lung infection in the mines and mother wasted away quickly from a broken heart and deep depression.

"I'm not sure I can help you, Mr. Knowles, because there's plenty of competition for slots into our military academies, mostly for young men, a policy I endorse, frankly, and allowing women into the Air Force Academy hasn't been too popular back in the Pentagon so far, you see, and I doubt there would be much support for the young lady." Adam looked away. The imbecile kept adding clauses to his sentences so no one could talk or converse with him, or try to make sense of his addle-brained and ancient conservative perspective.

"Sir, did you look over her transcript? The girl has never made less than A's. She's valedictorian, National Honor Society. She volunteers in the nursing home after school and weekends. Made it to the state forensic finals last fall in Norfolk. She's team captain, a natural leader. Yes, she is an attractive young woman but try to see beyond that." Adam stopped. He didn't want to whine or beg. He thought this sporting event might dent the fuzzy thinking of their district's representative, a man who almost always ran unopposed and seemed to hold office as if it were his inheritance. He had no record of accomplishment to speak of, but the voters had little to choose from.

"Naw, Mr. Knowles, can't help you. Been a mighty nice diversion for a Sunday afternoon. Good to get out of Washington with all those liberal scalawags ranting up there, wanting to pass legislation to fix everything under the sun. Mighty pretty girl, though." He stood and shook hands and waddled down the steps to his chauffeur waiting below.

Jerk, Adam thought. First thing the man had wanted to know was how many MacMurrays lived down in Blue Ridge. He was fishing for votes and was disappointed when he'd found out Hailey was the only one. Now Adam would drop back to plan B. His petition was circulating through town and he had close to a few thousand signatures on it. He would send it straight to the Academy and beg them in writing. It wouldn't do much good to approach either of Virginia's two senators. Both men had adamantly opposed women in the armed forces. They were carbon copies of Alexander, products of the old Byrd machine that had run Virginia politics since the Depression. Qualifications were staunch conservatism and loyalty to the system. Play by the rules, meaning vote down anything resembling progress, and go up the ladder when it was your turn. Most were old men without a fresh idea amongst them.

However, the following Sunday Adam's prayers were answered by an unexpected source. *Parade Magazine* published its annual All-American selections for high school volleyball and picked Hailey as the best in the country. The town of Blue Ridge was overjoyed and treated the award like it was a prize for best small town in the country. Adam remembered some reporter who came out of the stands one night and asked to take a picture of Hailey and her teammates. The fellow had asked her a few questions and of course she'd said she wanted to fly for the Air Force. Now that personal background appeared under her picture in *Parade*, a picture bigger than all the rest. Her GPA was there too, and calls started coming in to the Knowles' home that evening.

A week later THE LETTER arrived from the Air Force Academy. It held incredible news. Their registrar had received a letter of nomination for Hailey from a retired Air Force colonel living in Richmond. The man had watched Hailey beat his Chesterfield team two years in a row and had written the letter after reading the Parade article. *She was the best player he had seen at any level*, he wrote. *And she wants to fly.*

Senior Cadet MacMurray groaned when she looked at her watch. She had stayed too long working on her engineering design project and didn't see any male cadets around who could escort her back to the dorm. Hailey risked a class one offense if caught by the AF Police. Female cadets had been warned they flirted with assaults out at night alone. She glanced outside and saw only dark. Not good. She had to have an escort, but it was only a few hundred yards back to her room and she'd hustle now.

She slung her book bag over one shoulder and double-timed up the road. This would be the night she had brought practically her entire library from the dorm to finish that engineering diagram. The wind increased up and down Colorado's Front Range, gusting hard and forcing her to lean into it to make headway. Fortunately there were no cars and no signs of the police patrolling. But lights shone from behind and she heard gravel crunch as tires left the pavement and continued along the walking path towards her from the rear. She glanced back and was blinded by high beams.

The car pulled close beside her. The driver opened his door and kept going, knocking Hailey down. She lay stunned and tried to get up but strong hands grabbed her arms and legs and began dragging her back to the car. *This was it*, she thought. *Must be three of them, and too strong to fight off.* She yelled and kicked out and received a hard slap across her jaw.

"Stop fighting, bitch. Better just lie back and enjoy it. We got you now." The voice was low, almost a growl. She twisted to her right, freeing one leg and kicked at the closest groin. One attacker doubled over and let go, grabbing his family jewels. That freed her other leg and she flailed away at another set of legs just before a fist smashed into her left eye. She groaned in pain and began to lose consciousness.

Tires screeched to a stop on the road and she vaguely caught the sound of a door opening.

"Let her go. Get off her now, Murphy." Hailey was half-conscious as her attackers dropped her to the ground and faced a fellow cadet charging towards them. She rolled to her side and got to her hands and knees in time to see the fight between her savior and two men. Her third assailant still lay in the fetal position with both hands hugging his middle. Fear and anger kicked in now, bringing Hailey to her feet. Damn, this pissed her off. One semester to go and this happens. She knew who would be punished regardless of the circumstances. But there was no time to worry about the future as her protector landed on the bottom of the pile and was taking the worst of a beating.

She picked up her thick engineering text and slammed it into the back of the nearest man's head, knocking him sideways. Her next swing caught the last man behind the ear and sent him limping off into the scrub brush and out of sight. Another car pulled up. The police had finally arrived.

The nurse swabbed at the cut over her eye almost angrily. "Ouch, that hurts."

"Sorry, miss. I just get so mad. It's almost spring and the sap is rising. You're our second rape this weekend. Did they, did—"

"No, they didn't get that far," Hailey said. "Three of them grabbed me and one fellow named Murphy hit me where you're scrubbing. I almost went out, but then another guy came to my rescue. How is he, by the way? And where is he? I need to thank him."

"You can do that later, Cadet. Finish up, nurse, I need to question Cadet MacMurray." A lieutenant "lite bird" colonel stood just inside the door to the examining room looking unpleasant at best. His attitude exuded distaste for the entire scene before him. The nurse visibly froze and stopped her ministrations to her patient. She gathered her medical kit and left quickly. Hailey slid off the table and stood at attention. She was dizzy and disoriented.

"What were you doing out by yourself, cadet?" The man's voice was threatening, intimidating. The colonel looked her up and down suspiciously. His eyes settled on her chest. Hailey glanced down and saw her blouse had been ripped, exposing her bra and skin above it. She turned away from the officer and did her best to cover up. At least her sweater still had buttons. She pulled it closed and fastened it top to bottom.

"Lost track of time, Sir. When I finished working at the library it was dark and there were no males around. I thought I could make it to my room safely." It sounded puny in the face of his accusing glare. *Why was that? She had been attacked. Beaten up by three men and this callous man made her feel guilty.* Hailey fumed and confronted him.

"What about the men who assaulted me, Colonel?" Her voice caught fire and gained strength. "Did you catch them? One is named Murphy. I heard his name mentioned. Their car must have been left there because they lit out running when the police arrived." Her breath came in huge clumps. The confrontation left her empty of energy. She was hyperventilating and her insides were jittery. *Must be nerves and maybe a bit of shock from the attack*, she thought. Hailey slumped back against the examining table, exhausted, ignoring the officer's unspoken command to stand at attention when he entered the room.

"No one was positively identified. There was no car at the scene. The police found you alongside another cadet, a male, and you were partly undressed." He spoke to her as if she had rolled in the dirt and flung herself against a tree to simulate an injury, then passed out next to a convenient male to feign an assault and hide an illicit rendezvous. "Report to my office at 0800 hours tomorrow, Cadet." He left the room. Hailey dropped to her knees and vomited into a plastic trash can.

Next morning she waited her turn outside the colonel's office. She had been directed to the Office of Military Protocol and had no clue as to its mission, much less how this particular office related to her assault. Shortly after her appointed time the door swung open and a man exited who had obviously been in a recent brawl. He had blond hair and was taller than Hailey. *He might be good looking*, she thought, except for the bruises and swollen black eyes. She recognized him as the gallant hero who had protected her last night.

She stood and met him before he could hurry out. "Thanks for last night. You saved my bacon, uh, Cadet Burgess." She read his name tag while he squinted through swollen eyes at hers.

"You're welcome, Cadet. Looks like they did a good job on your eye. Sorry, I have to rush to class. I'll try to contact you later. Compare notes." He was off and she felt as confused as she had been last night under the unfriendly interrogation in the infirmary.

"Cadet MacMurray, please come in, won't you?" A female colonel stood in the door smiling and Hailey gained back her confidence.

"Yes, Ma'am." She entered the friendly lady officer's dimly lit room and felt safe and secure, perhaps for the first time in 24 hours.

"Have a seat, Hailey. Ooh, that eye doesn't look very good. Did the nurse give you any painkillers?"

"No, Ma'am, I took a couple of aspirin back in my room. It throbs some but it'll go away. I've had worse slamming onto the gym floor for a loose ball."

"Yes, I know. I've seen all your games and congratulations on that first team All-American pick. You have made the Academy proud."

"Thank you, Ma'am. I'm flattered and appreciate your thoughtfulness. But, what about last night? I was interrogated like a criminal after being attacked and nearly carried away by three men. That colonel, can't remember his name, was nasty to me." She shut up. Maybe she'd said more than she should.

Worry lines creased the colonel's forehead and she leaned over her desk in obvious concern. "I've spoken to your interrogator, Hailey. He won't do that again, and there won't be any charges placed against you. Heaven's sake. Yes, you were attacked and hit pretty hard it looks like." The lady officer sighed deeply and swung her executive chair around to peer at the steep roof of the Air Force Chapel that dominated the immediate view. Hailey waited for her to speak and begin to answer some of her questions. Finally the colonel turned and faced her wearing a serious expression.

"There is an ongoing investigation, Cadet. We don't have any identification on either the assailants or their car." She held up both hands to stop Hailey's interruption. "I know. You say they ran off and left the car and that one man was called Murphy. But the police report has no information pertaining to a vehicle and your white knight couldn't recall naming any of the men." She stopped Hailey again. "But, we're still investigating, so don't worry. We have had some trouble from soldiers at Fort Carson down the road. And some leads are being followed up concerning several other cases like yours."

Her ears burned. It was a cover up. Bad cop last night, good cop this morning and a change of sex among the cops to lull her into complacency and compliance. But her face must have shown her anger.

"I don't blame you for being upset, Cadet. It's fortunate you are in your last semester here and not far from graduating. We've had other incidents and the girls dropped out immediately. You're at the top of your class too, I see. You also have a good shot at fighter training school. Your instructors and classmates alike have written some nice things about you and there is a good chance you'll be selected. However, a lengthy investigation at this point might stall the paperwork and bring up unnecessary questions." The colonel hesitated a beat. Hailey nodded her understanding.

"Thank you, Ma'am, for your time and consideration. Is that all?"

"Dismissed, Cadet."

Edwards AFB, California: Two years later.

Hot wind gusted across the Mojave Desert, canceling all training flights for the new class of fighter pilots. These were now experienced pilots who had tested out of flying planes from around the world: Migs from the Soviet Union, Vipers from China, and Harriers from Great Britain. Of course they found even outdated USAF fighters the best still. Hailey was proud of her accomplishment, but there had been no time for socializing. Now would be a good time to make some friends, especially with Lt. Chad Burgess, who'd transferred in to her unit and was walking just ahead. Hailey tapped him on the shoulder and beamed her best smile.

"Morning, Chad, good to see you again. Remember me?" This day the tall blond Air Force officer could see her clearly. He didn't have to squint through black eyes. *He* was *good looking*, she thought. A few inches taller than she. Slim. Broad shoulders. Strong hands. With long fingers like those of a surgeon, or better, a concert pianist. Ummmm, where had her thoughts wandered?

"How could I forget you, Hailey. I never could get around to talk about that night. My squadron leader kept us all pretty busy and then we were sent to different flight training schools. Anyway, looks like we finished at the top of our classes." They had ranked in the top five and he had beaten her by one spot, but that wasn't what Hailey thought about at this moment. His gaze covered her from head to toes and Hailey warmed inside. She had been observed, ogled, by men before, but something about Chad's look sent a flutter down through her middle.

"Buy you a drink? Soda maybe, downstairs in the lounge?" Both chuckled at this. If they wanted to get test pilot status, drinking was not an option.

"Sure, let's go," she said. "We have time on our hands for once." They walked side by side down the hall and passed several male pilots along the way. Each nodded at Hailey and exchanged manly smirks with Chad. One even gave him the thumbs up sign and she couldn't stifle a giggle.

Over iced tea they got down to the issue that had been hanging over her for the past two years: the night of the attack and the following morning. Hailey recounted her side of the sordid affair and waited for Chad to fill in some blanks.

"Pretty much the same thing happened to me when I reported to the lady colonel's office. She praised me and assured me there would be no charges for fighting. The jerk lite bird had threatened those the night before." Hailey sadly shook her head at this tactic. Yes, a definite cover up. "I was offered a slot in flight school and told further investigation wouldn't look good on my record. I was also informed that their files didn't show anyone named Murphy at the academy." He paused and let Hailey settle down. Her face had gone red like she was breathing fire.

"But to assure you that we didn't see a mirage, yes, there was a car parked there when the police showed up, and I did know a cadet named Murphy; never saw him again. But I'm sure glad to see you out here." Chad smiled and Hailey began to forget about the incident. She let him cover her hand and massage the fingers. He was smooth. She was a novice. It felt right though, and she certainly was attracted to him.

Over the next few weeks Hailey and Chad had dinner often and went out to clubs and movies a few times. He kissed her on their third date. He let her know he'd be patient; didn't want to frighten her after what she'd been through. She let him know of her inexperience. He just smiled and found another gear, a slower, gentler one. Hailey felt no pressure from Chad, but her body and her mind instilled their own forms of stress. She knew Chad was the one; he was everything she had hoped for. She was in love.

In the air Chad excelled and quickly soared to the top of their class. Hailey was near the top, too, but no one had the verve and, possibly, the reckless edge that came automatically to Chad. Hailey felt his affection, love maybe, but recognized that flying was number one. She accepted that order of life's events and accommodated herself to stay close to this man who had rescued her. They became lovers after a couple of months.

They saw no daylight on the weekends. Immediately after being dismissed on Saturday mornings, they left for their rendezvous at the nearest hotel. Hailey was enthralled with feelings of contentment, having a lover who showered so much affection on her. However, circumstances left her no choice but to reveal an intimate bit of news to her man. She judged the time as right as could be. Both lay sated from an initial bout of lovemaking that always occurred as soon as they entered their room. Clothes flew off and they entwined naked bodies, throwing caution aside. Perhaps this impulsive habit had led to her current state.

"Chad, darling, I love you." He smiled his affection in return. He never said the words but she accepted him like that. She felt certain he would accept her as she was. He rolled away and stood to go shower. Hailey pulled him back to bed. "Honey, sit here a minute." She paused at the instant furrow that sprang between his eyebrows, a sign of impatience she could quickly identify now. Regardless, her news couldn't wait.

"I'm pregnant." Hailey waited for his reaction. What man wouldn't be shocked as Chad apparently was now. He jerked his hand from hers and stood like a statue, stony without life.

"What do you mean? I took precautions. This shouldn't happen. It's not happening. It can't." She pulled the sheet up to her throat, no longer feeling uninhibited from their lovemaking.

"You didn't that first night or the whole weekend. When we enter the room together every Saturday we just go at it like animals. And I'm regular as a clock. Never late, never miss. Dr. Smothers verified it yesterday." But she spoke to a vanishing image as Chad left her to go shower, slamming the door on the way. How did she feel about that? Women who tell their men this news always hope for shared feelings of joy and excitement. It is a most vulnerable time and they need reassurance, compassion, and love above all. She understood Chad was a different being, but he'd come around.

He burst from the shower with a towel wrapped around his middle. He was at the bed side in three strides. "Get rid of it. I'll lend you the money." Her hopes fell. Commonsense took over, mostly.

"No. We will get married." She shook her head to cut off his interruption. "This stops my career as a fighter pilot, but I have no choice. I stayed up all night thinking it through. I want our baby to have two parents, Chad. This child is in my body and it will stay there until it's time for it to be born. So don't argue with me. But I want it one hundred percent legal. My medical records are already updated and I'll not go through life with the guilt you'd pressure me into." She wasn't nervous at all and spoke with an internal strength Chad could not overcome. Hailey MacMurray was a determined woman. To her this was no mistake. It was meant to be and her upbringing led her to no other conclusions.

They had leave coming around Thanksgiving and flew back to her hometown, to Blue Ridge, Virginia. Amelia, the town clerk, fixed up the proper license and sent them upstairs to see Judge Anderson. Hailey looked green around the edges but she smiled regardless. Chad was resigned but disparaging. He kissed his bride after the civil ceremony but didn't hold her hand leaving the building.

Back on base, Hailey found a small apartment. Her attempt at making a love nest failed after two more months. Chad moved out one Friday. He needed air, he said. He felt like he was suffocating, he complained. So he left. He had not spent many nights with her since their return from Virginia anyway and Hailey knew he was logging more and more time at the officers' club bar.

She went to the base chaplain, a Major Scandling. He seemed a nice man, a nondenominational minister used to counseling wives of pilots. He soothed her feelings but made no promises about Chad. Pilots were a different breed, he informed her. She probably knew that, he said in a calming voice. The major held her hand and hugged her when tears came. He was comforting and gave her a grounding she needed at a time like this. She would need Major Scandling's support again in her seventh month of pregnancy, on the day Chad waited too late to pull the ejection lever and drove his F-15 into the tarmac. Flames and the tremendous blast from the explosion killed him midair. An autopsy showed he had been drinking heavily the night before. Friends at the bar confirmed that was his usual habit lately.

The kind major came to tell her the news personally. He hugged her close and received her sobs, soothed her shaking. Then he did more. Hailey was too upset to notice at first, but her swollen breasts were too sensitive not to send a warning. Next there was a projection against her stomach, against her baby! Damnation, the man was trying to feel her up and his erection poked at her. Her combat training kicked in and her knee went up between his legs, sending the fervent counselor to the floor in agony. Were there no good men? She was pregnant; just a few months from delivering a child, and this ordained lecher wanted some action. That cinched it.

She cancelled paperwork changing her last name to Chad's, but kept her married status intact on all subsequent government forms. A few friends thought this a rash action taken in a time of severe grieving. She knew the marriage had never been true, yet wanted her unborn child to know its mother had been married. Hailey took the Foreign Service Officer's test two weeks after Chad was buried. She had mastered French at the academy and had been told her ability to learn a language was exceptional. Only then, she had wanted to fly jets. Then, she had ignored her instructor's urging to go to the language school at Monterey. Now, a week after Adam was born, Hailey reported to Monterey to learn Russian. The State Department was happy to expedite her transfer from the Air Force, and Hailey was finished with the military.

French Embassy, Moscow.

"Mademoiselle MacMurray, would you be so kind as to introduce me to your escort." The French attaché for trade spoke only French while Anatoly, Hailey's date, spoke only Russian. He was a handsome man of equal rank to the Frenchman, at least superficially. Anatoly had confided to her something about being an information officer but she knew he was a spy. However, serving as an interpreter for these two men presented no problem for her. Hailey had sailed through the Monterey foreign language school and been shipped to Paris. From there she transferred to Moscow where her facility in

French and Russian proved rewarding to American interests. Still, she remained puzzled at how many sensitive bits of information were passed through her as interpreter, French to Russian, Russian to French. It was like she vanished as an American diplomat and became a vessel to fill up with one language and make deposits in another. Her *clientele* forgot that she was foreign to both countries, and if they noticed her it was for her beauty and not for any ability she might have in understanding complex international issues.

She listened to the French attaché rattle on about trade agreements with Middle Eastern countries. She noted where the man had reported different information to her State Department, then translated to the Russian. Dutifully, that character came forth with equally duplicitous statements vastly different from Moscow's latest fax to Washington. Their conversation completed, the Russian pulled her aside.

"Hailey, can we get out of here? Find some secluded spot? Hmmm? Be alone together, just us?" She let him reach an arm around her waist and nuzzle her ear, holding her ace for the right moment. She was tempted for only a second. He was a good looking man and she was a single woman.

"Oh, Anatoly, you're quite a charmer. How can I turn down such an invitation? But unfortunately, my sitter goes home at eleven and it is too cold to bring Adam out after that. Tomorrow, maybe a walk in the park? I have a backpack to carry my baby and we could take a stroll." His eyes went wide with fear. Another one, she reckoned and watched him backpedal.

"You have a child? But you are single, yes?"

"The father died in a plane crash. Yes, I am single and I do have a child, not quite four. Do you mind?" Of course he did, she just wanted to point out his avenue of escape. She sidled closer to him and flirted outrageously, adding a soft breath into his ear as a tease.

"No, of course not. I don't mind at all. Oh wait; there is something I must do tonight. I forgot. Please excuse me." He did not run but it was a fast shuffle across the parquet dance floor.

Now it was Henri's turn. The Frenchman saw his opportunity and moved in fast. He was not dismayed by her motherhood. She was a beautiful woman and single. He simply wanted to give her a tour of the embassy. These Europeans were real smoothies.

"This is our library, Hailey." He opened huge floor-to-ceiling, ornately hand-carved wooden doors. Hailey was a sucker for libraries and waltzed in nonchalantly. But the lights went out right after the doors shut with a thud. Henri came up behind her, encircling her waist with his arms. He began kissing her neck and shoulders as a distraction from his hands that crept upwards near her breasts.

She caressed his right hand and gathered his index finger firmly. Then all it took was a quick wrenching backwards and Henri was on his knees. "You don't even know me. Do you all think you can just cart me off to bed without so much as offering food, or a movie?" Moonlight filtered through the tall windows and allowed her to see the beads of sweat rolling down his face. He was ready to beg.

"Ah, please. That hurts. You are so beautiful and alluring. Why waste time? Life is short. Ah, DON"T!" She added another twist and left the man bent over his finger and huffing for breath on the library floor.

She stayed in Moscow until Adam was ready for first grade. In that last year she became a trusted advisor to the ambassador and served as interpreter to the President on his trips to see the Premier. Thus it came as a shock to the State Department when she resigned that summer.

"Why, Hailey? You have become indispensable to my staff, to me too, and what will I tell the Secretary. The man has a crush on you. You could sleep your way up in no time." Both laughed. Charles Morgan was the only man who could talk to her this way. He was a personal friend, and an aging widower who always claimed that if he were thirty years younger he'd sweep her off her feet. In truth, he was her mentor, and a surrogate grandfather to Adam. Hailey confessed that she had finally found a good man, only one though, sadly, and he was an old fogy.

"It's time for Adam to go to school, Charles. That, and I have some personal business back home I can't let slide any longer." She looked away and Charles recognized an unspoken sigh with the shrug of her shoulders.

"He must be very special, my dear. I envy him."

"*She* is special. Marie is losing her memory and I've got to see to her. Her husband, Adam, died several years back and she's gone downhill since. They took me in, Charles. Brought me up as their own, and left me everything, including a house." He knew the details and thought it a wonderful story. The whole town had adopted her when her parents died, yet Adam and Marie Knowles reared her to be a strong, self-sufficient woman.

"I'll probably teach school or something. I have some friends back there and it's a perfect place to raise Adam."

Three

Judge Bradford Anderson banged his gavel to restore order in his courtroom which served as the town meeting hall tonight.

"OK, Hailey. Speak your mind."

"Thank you, Judge." She faced the packed seats filled with old friends and some new ones. This should be easy, she figured. "When my parents died, Adam Knowles set up a trust fund for me to cover my education and upbringing in general. All of you contributed money for me and straight off I want to say thanks, again. Luckily, we had a great volleyball team," she smiled over at Mary Jo Tyler, her personal setter, "and I got a free ride through school at the Air Force Academy. I didn't need any of that money then. I didn't need any of it later when I worked for the State Department in France and Russia. I also managed to save some and I don't need any of that money now, personally, for Adam or for me."

A voice chirped from the back row of seats. "Well darn, Hailey, we'd be mighty pleased to take it back. With interest of course." Laughter chorused through the courtroom and the judge had to rap his gavel once more.

"James Burton, you'd just drink it up down at the Caddyshack. Let's listen to the rest of Hailey's speech."

"Yessir, Judge. I'll keep my appointment next Monday. Hope to see you there." Again laughter broke up the meeting. James Burton was almost always arrested for public drunkenness every Saturday night and was arraigned every Monday by Judge Anderson. He slept a couple of nights in the city jail and got fed three squares a day. They let him out by Friday and the whole scheme

42

repeated Saturday.

"Nice to see some of the old customs haven't changed," Hailey said. This time the laughter dwindled down quicker. "As some of you know, I came back to town to take care of Marie Knowles. Sad to say, I found I couldn't take care of her. Marie needed to be in the Willows long before I got here. I hadn't been out there since I volunteered for them in high school and the place needs some fixing up."

"Tearing down and rebuilding is more like it, Hailey." Jane Carothers spoke from the front row. "Most of us have put relatives out there and some in this room will end up there." Murmurs affirmed this point of view.

Hailey searched the faces looking to her, expecting answers. "I thought a lot about the Willows on my flight here from Moscow a few weeks ago. I'd hoped not to have to use it, but see no alternative. In fact, I want your permission to spend the trust fund to help fix up the Willows." Her pronouncement met silence for a second. Until Sara Wolf stood up.

"I second that motion, Hailey." People began to stand around the room and applause erupted. Sara spoke again. "How much money is in the fund, Hailey?" Hailey nodded to Frank Thompson, the local banker and executor of the fund. He was nervous as always when someone threatened to spend money from his bank.

"Harrumph, uh, er, let me see here. Last figures Emily came up with showed an outstanding balance of $98, 512.32." The murmurs raised a notch. That was a lot of money for this small town. "Emily found some nice tax shelters and municipal bonds awhile back. Did right smart on that." There was more laughter. Everyone knew Emily ran the bank and wrote out what Frank was saying. They also looked the other way when she'd moved into his house after Frank's wife passed away. Frank had more to say. "But it will take a court order to break the trust and use the money for other than its original purpose."

Hailey turned to Judge Anderson and gave him his cue.

"It is so ordered," he said, and banged his gavel to seal the decision amidst loud clapping.

"Judge, judge. Hear me out a minute." Doug Wade stood about middle ways back waving his hat like a wild man.

"Don't hold us up too long, Wade. Some folks got work to do. Go ahead man, talk."

"Well, I looked around this room and recognized just about everybody's here who contributes to the community. I'd say we have a quorum for a civic caucus same as for the trust fund. Y'all agree?"

Sara seconded his statement and shot a sly grin up at Hailey, whose expression turned quizzical.

"Therefore, I'd like to nominate Hailey MacMurray as our candidate for the Congress in this fall's election. All in favor say aye." Before she could protest, the halls of justice reverberated with a loud "YES" and Hailey found herself running for office.

"But I don't belong to any party," Hailey complained to Sara Wolf after the crowd had dispersed, rather quickly she noted. She looked at her lifetime friend, Mary Jo, and saw guilt and complicity lurking on her expression. "OK, out with it, Mary Jo. What have you cooked up now?"

"Just think of me as your permanent setup partner, Hailey. A bunch of us got together and talked about it when we found out you were coming home. Finally. You always were the smartest of our crowd, and now you've gone off into a man's world and beat them at their own game." Mary Jo drew her breath in sharply when Hailey grimaced. "Sorry, Hailey, we understand it hasn't been easy, losing your husband, changing careers, and raising Adam while working overseas."

Hailey remembered the countless sexual advances and the near rape. She was still looking for a good man who would remain honest and not try to grope her on the first date, or run off as soon as she admitted to being a mother with a small child. In State Department circles she had a reputation as the "Ice Maiden of Diplomacy." Men referred to her as a one-date tease. Mary Jo would have difficulty understanding what she had been put through, but Sara would know since she had been in the Army.

"I'll say it again, Sara, Mary Jo, I'm not a politician and I don't belong to a political party."

"That's not a problem, Hailey," Sara chimed in. "This was not a caucus of any party. It was plain folks here in town speaking their minds. Most voters in this region don't register with a party, they vote independently. Heck, from what Joe says—he teaches history and government over at the county high school—people in these hills fought against both sides in the Civil War and they switch party allegiance every four years, according to Joe, 'To get rid of the bastards.' Problem is, our current representative runs unopposed every time because no one will challenge him and his party backing.

Now Mary Jo added her two cents worth. "Even worse, Merton Alexander retired and just handed over the job to his son, Merton Alexander III, and still no one opposed him. It was like, whoa Nellie; we don't have royalty in this country."

Hailey remembered the name. For one agonizing week Merton Alexander had quashed her dreams of getting into the Air Force Academy. Adam Knowles had been distraught back then, but he hadn't given up, then came the *Parade* article. And here she was, selected by her community, chosen to serve. She needed a job but hadn't given any thought to working in Washington. Or being a politician, yet she had been a diplomat and members of that profession had their own foggy *diplospeak*. It was similar to the convoluted bureaucratese politicians employed: never come right out and say the obvious; leave wiggle room in all cases.

"OK, I'll run." Mary Jo and Sara whooped and grabbed her in a threesome, jumping up and down like they'd beaten Chesterfield in the state volleyball championship again. Hailey steadied herself first and her stare bore down on these two co-conspirators. "But." They stilled and waited for a big shoe to drop. "I need a campaign manager and a treasurer. Thanks for volunteering, ladies." However, their reactions surprised her.

"We already decided that," Mary Jo spoke up. "Sara will be the campaign manager and I'll handle the money. Her twins are in school and my four are still running around the house in diapers."

"Four?" Hailey was shocked.

"Yeah, well, it took awhile to talk Mike into getting fixed. I told him it was about time a man took the lead, except by then we'd already repopulated our part of the county." Mary Jo grinned with pride and looked ready to go for number five. Hailey turned to Sara, who had been quiet a few minutes. The mother and author—her romances sold well and she typed them up while she cooked and cleaned house—was pondering, and Hailey didn't want to push her.

Sara said, "We have to find a way to get you on TV down in Roanoke. I'll call Daddy. He'll tell me what to do."

Hailey had been in Moscow too long to keep up with current affairs. She said, half laughing, "You'll call Daddy? Who's that?"

Sara broke out her biggest smile. "My maiden name was Conley. Maybe you heard of Senator Bill Conley out in Colorado. He's running for another term and he's independent too, just like you." Hailey certainly knew of Bill Conley. His reputation as a master spy was still talked about in embassy circles. Yes, General Conley had retired right after the Wall came down. It would be interesting to see the ideas Sara got from her father.

Crisp fall air blew in for this special August weekend in Blue Ridge. City Square Park had been converted into a gigantic craft sale and pot luck extravaganza with all proceeds going to Hailey's campaign. The park sat in front of the old court house with its four white columns resting on locally mined marble steps. Main Street had been closed to traffic and it didn't matter, since almost everyone could walk to the center of town within a few minutes. Two stone soldiers saluted each other in the center of the park. Originally representing honor between the men who had died for both sides in the Civil War from this small town, they had evolved into a universal memorial to all servicemen and women who had sacrificed their lives.

The Blue Ridge High School band marched down Church Street in their dark blue uniforms trimmed in confederate gray with red and white striping. They played Souza numbers while marching and switched to their preferred classical style after taking their seats on metal folding chairs arranged to the side of the speaker's platform.

The band and the schools held precedence in this town. Education took priority over just about everything else, including football. The only person to supersede the band and the school was Hailey. And today the folks of Blue Ridge came to praise her.

Sara ginned up a press release and sent it out to TV, radio stations, and newspapers in the southwestern Virginia congressional district. As a result, several minicam units from Roanoke were on hand for the pot luck. But few reporters from newspapers came. Sara didn't care. She was certain that as soon as people saw Hailey and heard her speak, things would change. She had convinced her friend to let loose a little bit, and Hailey had reluctantly agreed for just this once. The two women had a heart to heart talk one night and Hailey discovered that Sara understood too well why she wanted to be elected because of her brains.

Sara had lectured her younger friend in plain English. "You are a beautiful woman, Hailey. So why try to deny it? Come on. All women have this problem, not just the good looking ones with super bodies. Men can't help looking at us, anyway. They're programmed from their days in the cave to check out everything from the neck down. Poor dears. So I say use it. Not saying sleep your way around, just stop obsessing over the fact that guys notice beauty first. The good ones fall in love with who you are, not what you look like."

Criminies, Sara figured, *Hailey had a great body, why not take advantage of it? Just this once. After all it was a picnic and everyone would be in shorts and tank tops.* The romance writer sure would have her main female character do this in a book. And Hailey had agreed. She had also felt relief from an invisible burden that she had imposed on herself at an early age.

Examining her appearance today, Hailey wasn't so sure Sara's ideas for dress were best for her. She checked her reflection in the hall mirror and grimaced. Sara had suggested the shorts to expose her gorgeous legs. They exposed her legs all right and were so tight anyone walking behind her could tell if she had a 1945 dime in her back pocket. Also, Sara had insisted on a blazing red tank top with a scoop neckline that exposed a good bit of cleavage. Good gracious, her breasts had always been large and she was sure the tank top exposed too much. Men loved to stare at women with large breasts and had no idea of their burden. For most of her life she had kept them hidden. Just not today, implored Sara. It was not like she was flashing the town every time she bent over. There was the bra her friend had picked out. Yet, it was so flimsy her nipples showed even if there wasn't a chill in the air. At least it covered her, well, mostly. But she had stood firmly on displaying her stomach. Too much, she argued, even though the younger crowd wore their shorts and pants on their hips and let their tops ride another six inches above, often with a ring piercing their navels.

She had stood firm on the stomach issue and declared to her campaign staff, now grown to twenty-something women and men, that if elected she would immediately return to pant suits and ankle-length skirts. She would be no pin-up politician.

"You're beautiful, Mom." Adam sat on the stairs and peeped through the banisters bug-eyed. "You should dress like that more often. You look great. You're some dish, Mom." Oops, it had slipped out and he caught the full force of his mother's glare, the one that demanded the whole truth and nothing but. She waited for his answer with her arms crossed, her smile evaporated.

"Guys at school said that. Sorry, I won't say it again." He paused long enough to see her shoulders relax. "Still, it's true." He ran for his room as she chased him upstairs. Hailey got a foot in his bedroom door before he could shut and lock it, and caught him around the waist just as he tried for the closet. She tossed him onto the bed and began the tickling torture.

"OK, ok, I give up. I'm really sorry this time and I won't say it again. Honest."

Hailey gathered him in her arms and crushed him in a ferocious bear hug.

His arms went around her neck and they regained their breath together, laughing. Hailey and Adam were best pals as well as mother and son.

"Ummmpf. You're getting too big to hoist like that anymore. Just watch your language. At least you didn't use any bad words." She set him down on the bed and saw the embarrassing red creep up his neck. "You don't use bad words do you, Adam?" It was a rhetorical question. She read the answer on his face. "Just remember. I don't want to hear them in this house." He nodded assent. "Also, I'm running for public office and how you behave is a reflection on my ability to be a good representative. Got that?" He nodded harder this time. "Think on it, Adam. I'm a single mom and some people will say that I didn't do a good job raising you, or that I spend too much time out campaigning when I should be home taking care of you. Now, you know how we did it in the past. We are partners and always think of each other first. Right? And it worked. So we just have to stick with the plan." Her son lowered his head and she felt bad immediately. Hailey kneeled and took his arms in her hands.

"Look at me, honey. You'll make mistakes. All little boys do and all big people too. I make them and so does everybody else. You have to remember to tell me the truth. Always. OK?"

"I love you, Mom." He wrapped his arms around her neck and kissed her. Adam left and Hailey tore into her clothes closet. If her six-year-old son had that reaction to her costume, Lord only knew how older men would react. She selected a pair of culottes that came down to her knees and a sleeveless blouse. To placate Sara, she just maybe wouldn't button the blouse all the way to the top.

Tom Woodley, mayor of Blue Ridge, spoke. "It is wonderful to see all you folks out here today to honor one of our finest citizens. It is my pleasure to introduce her. Now, folks hereabouts know all this about Hailey MacMurray, but I'm gonna repeat it for the out-of-towners and the TV cameras anyway." As if on signal, a minicam operator edged up right in front of Tom, who put on a huge grin and fiddled with his floppy bow tie.

Martha Woodley shouted from the side of the stage, "Stand up straight and quit hunching your shoulders, Thomas." The mayor turned beet red and waited for the laughter to subside before he went on.

"Seems there's a lot to say, so I'll hit the high spots. For two years runnin', Hailey led the Blue Ridge Lions, that's our high school," he leaned toward the camera for emphasis, "to the state championship in volleyball. Hailey was picked an All-American in high school both years and was named the best player her senior year." Applause interrupted him and he waited patiently. "But we all knew that her first love was flying and so she went into the Air Force. Oh, almost forgot. Hailey was valedictorian of her class and graduated with a perfect GPA. Now then, uh, dog gone it, if she didn't do the same thing in the Air Force. Made All-American there and was tops in her class." There was more applause. "She got to fly fighter jets but had to quit when little Adam came along. Went into the government and worked in Paris and Moscow. Whew, that's pretty far off, eh, folks?" Everyone laughed and applauded. Tom ran unopposed every year because people generally liked him. They also understood that Martha kept him in line.

Hailey took the microphone from Tom's shaking hand and gave him a hug. He hadn't completely introduced her but the nervous fellow had run out of words. She turned to the crowd and was met with thunderous applause, cheering and not a few whistles from the males. She noticed the minicam roving closer and reached to button the blouse all the way up. The TV guy was grinning ear to ear.

"Thank you Tom, and Martha. We love you both. Thanks also to you folks who came here today to support me. I'll make this short. I accept your call to run for Congress." Applause, foot stomping, cheering and many more whistles broke the air. One minicam scanned the crowd, now grown to several thousand. "This town raised me when I lost my parents, and I want to give something back." Hailey grew serious and the crowd quieted down.

"My priorities are health care, senior citizens, mine safety and education. I stand for the right of a woman to decide, or choose, but personally, I am against abortion. That makes me pro-life, pro-child, pro-women, and pro-family. It's time the two sides of this issue found middle ground and stopped calling each other murderers and scoundrels." Applause interrupted her and Hailey caught her breath. She was on a natural high and forgot all about the camera.

"I served in the military. Shot every kind of gun in our arsenal, and yes, flew fighter jets until morning sickness set in. I am for a strong military, but I am pro-peace and anti-guns. On this issue I don't want to take away your right to own a gun, but Lord Almighty, we need to keep them locked up. We need to honor our local police and state troopers and the national military. We don't need to fear our government; it is us after all." The response was deafening and she paused to let it come back to a quiet level.

"This country is aging and millions are without healthcare. But from what I have seen out of Washington, our country's leaders are more interested in increased spending that will raise the deficit, and going to war. So I will work for seniors, and especially for the miners who risk their lives every day." Shouts and cheers came with a male tone and she noticed some women wiping their tears.

"In the time left before the election I will come to you and listen. Tell me what you want in a representative. I want to represent all of you, not just the few special interests. And as for my challenger," Hailey stared straight into the nearest minicam, "Mr. Alexander, I am ready to debate you anywhere, anytime. Thank you folks, now enjoy the food."

Sara got her wish. The Roanoke TV stations aired a significant portion of Hailey's speech over the weekend. The minicam operator got good close-ups of the shapely brunette with the beautiful face. An anonymous voice-over gave a synopsis of her background and made special note of her status as a single mom. One particular shot pictured Hailey and Adam holding hands up on stage. Sara called the public TV station and got Hailey on the following week to discuss issues. That half hour also brought in a different kind of support for her candidate that had not been expected.

Hailey answered her door one morning and found her front porch full of young women. Radford University's Women's Political Action Group had decided to get involved. They had seen her on TV and were there to help. When the last student left her living room, Hailey had a network of volunteers that covered her entire district. Some were collecting signatures on the petition to have her name placed on the ballot. That wouldn't be hard. they said. They had to collect a percentage of the voters who actually voted and since Alexander ran unopposed there hadn't been a big turnout. Some sought to remedy the turnout. A group of five or so sat under an ancient oak tree in Hailey's backyard and developed a campaign to get out the vote. Others vowed to begin an email campaign and would scan Hailey's position papers into a web site. All of this work was free and without promises for payback.

Four

During the next week, Hailey went to Roanoke, Radford, Dublin and Pulaski. People smiled at her on the sidewalks and some introduced themselves and shook her hand. Inside stores and offices she introduced herself and made time to visit and sit a spell, and to listen. It was a simple technique Sara Wolf had told her about, one her father used successfully out in Colorado that he called "main streeting." Before she left Roanoke a public television reporter found her in a mall lobby and asked to tag along with her minicam. She was a one-woman crew, meaning she took the video and did the voice over to narrate the happenings to the viewers. Her name was Katlyn Arnold, and she was a fresh graduate from Radford University in journalism. She had short fiery red hair that seemed to spring off her head when she talked. Katlyn was animated to the bone and very excited to meet her idol. She peered through large frame, bottle-thick glasses and had to walk fast to make her short chubby body match the long strides Hailey took.

Hailey grew curious as she drove the Interstate over to Radford. "What are you going to do with all those tapes, Katlyn? It must get expensive."

"I asked my boss if I could do a documentary on you. You know, follow you around as you campaign, do whatever. Capture you driving real fast, like right now going 85 in a 65 zone, like it's your old fighter jet or something."

Hailey laughed at this. She was a notorious speeder. She liked this young woman on the spot. She had so much energy and enthusiasm. And she wrote down everything Hailey did, every name of every person she talked to, and the stores and offices, citing dates and times. The end result could serve as a diary for both women. But who would want to watch it? All she did was listen to people and walk around. And her driving. Wait until the state troopers found out she routinely drove so fast. Still, Katlyn stuck with her the remainder of August, never tiring of Hailey's exacting pace.

Hailey answered the door one morning and found Katlyn standing there with a big smile bursting from her face. The sun was just past the top of the Blue Ridge Parkway off to the east, so it had to be earlier than 7AM.

"Surprise, Hailey. Figured you were staying put today and I wanted to do a personal interview with you and Adam here. What do you say?" The young woman's hopeful look beat that of a new puppy eager for a tummy scratching. To deny her would be heartbreaking.

"Come on in and have some coffee. I'll have to roust Adam from bed. You're up early. What's the rush?"

Katlyn followed Hailey to the kitchen and dropped heavily into a chair. "Big news. My producer loves this whole deal. She's going to vote for you and thinks what you're doing is fantastic. So, we're running all the main street walks as a series. Each show will feature a different town. I'll have to edit some stuff like, oh, I don't know, stuff like when a candidate for high public office makes a pit stop or admits to speeding."

"Great news for you, Katlyn, and I suppose I'll owe you my soul for cutting out the speeding bit."

But the bubbly reporter got serious and leaned forward, resting her arms on the table. "No, never. I said you were my idol. And that's the truth. People identify with you, women and men. You're the real deal and honest. You raised your child and gave up your life's passion to do it. Lots of folks read your issue papers and know you'll be speaking for them in Congress. You try for them and they love you for it. But mainly they know you'll represent them, not special interests."

"Thank you, Katlyn. That makes me feel good."

The pert redhead turned red in the face before she continued. "There is one fault some bring up though. I found this out by talking to people away from the camera after you had gone on to another person nearby." She hesitated and seemed ready to keep her secret.

"Better tell me now, Katlyn. I need to hear the good with the bad."

"Well, this is hard to say straight out. Uh, and it comes from men and women about the same. Now don't get upset and let me try to say it diplomatically. You see, well, people like you for yourself and your ideas and they appreciate your hard work. But, uh," she paused and then let out the rest in a spurt, "they think you ought to date and get married."

Hailey groaned and put her head down on the table. "Impossible. It's just impossible."

"You're not gay are you?"

"Ha, did some of them think that? No. Definitely not. The impossible part is finding a fellow who will be straight with me." She recounted her history to the intrepid reporter and required it to remain off the record. Then the interview began.

Katlyn: Mrs. MacMurray, many people know about your personal life from newspapers and TV news. Would you like to tell me in your own words what it was like growing up here in Blue Ridge, as, some would say, the town's adopted child?

Hailey: Sure, but you have to call me Hailey or I'll look around for my mother and she's been dead a long time. My father died from a viral infection he caught in the mines when I was five. My mother had wrapped her soul around him and most folks believe she died of a broken heart. They had left families behind to come here so no one knew of any relatives who could take me in. Adam and Marie Knowles came forward and adopted me. They gave me a home, but many people in town knew me and contributed to a trust fund for my education. This was often the case around here when children survived the loss of a parent, usually from a mining disaster.

Katlyn: So you were taken in and raised by the Knowles. Did you name your son for Adam Knowles?

Hailey: Yes, I did. Adam Knowles was a father and mentor. He guided me all the way to the Air Force Academy. Marie was the homemaker and always there when I needed her support. They were two loving people and I came to think of them as my real parents.

Katlyn: What happened to Mr. and Mrs. Knowles?

Hailey: Adam Knowles died about five years ago. Marie is a resident at the Willows, the local nursing home.

Katlyn: Tell us about school here in Blue Ridge. Did you play sports?

Hailey: Yes, we had a state championship volleyball team two years in a row. Playing volleyball helped get me into the academy.

Katlyn: Were you a good student, grade wise?

Hailey: I was. I loved reading and learning about everything. Later, in the Air Force, I discovered this knack for learning foreign languages. That was the career path I followed when I became pregnant with my son.

Katlyn: What foreign languages do you speak?

Hailey: I speak three: Russian, French and Chinese. I lived in Paris and Moscow, so it was easy to polish my skills in their languages. I got curious about Chinese while in Moscow and started picking it up my last year there.

Katlyn: Tell us about your husband. Where did you meet him?

Hailey: We were both in fighter training together and were attracted to each other from the start. We had only been married a few months when his plane crashed and he was killed. He was a talented and gifted pilot. I never had contact with his family after his death.

Katlyn: So you lost contact with the MacMurray side of the family at that point?

Hailey: I never knew of them. My husband never mentioned them and my maiden name is MacMurray. I decided to keep my own name when I got married.

Katlyn: Tell us about Paris and Moscow. Wasn't it romantic being a single woman overseas working as a diplomat?

Hailey: No. It was work, but interesting and educational. The romantic part usually stopped cold when foreign embassy staff discovered I had a curfew and had to go relieve my baby sitter.

Katlyn: So you didn't date much?

Hailey: I had a lot of first dates. But I would say confidently that 100% of those men scampered when I said I had a child and couldn't stay out past ten or eleven at night. And, let me add this, because I know it'll be your next question, that pattern hasn't changed since I returned to the States. I know folks are curious about my personal life, which I guard for my son's sake. But, men do ask me out and then disappear when I suggest an outing with my son. Adam has been fortunate to have several special grandparents wherever we've lived.

Katlyn: What about you? I'm sorry, but this next question will sound too much like popular gossip TV. Do you ever get lonely?

Hailey: Ha! I'm too busy. Oh, good morning sleepy head. Here's my son, fresh from about twelve hours sleep. Why don't you ask him some questions while I scrounge up breakfast?

Katlyn: Good morning, Adam. I've been interviewing your mom for a TV show. What can you tell us about her?

Adam: She's the best mom in the world, and I hope that gets me blueberry pancakes for breakfast.

Katlyn: Tell us more. What about school? Was it hard to keep up moving around?

Adam: Mom taught me. She bought some books and we did homework at night when she got home from work. It was fun. I even learned to speak French. Not Russian though. It sounds funny.

Katlyn: Do you miss your dad?

Adam: *The boy looked puzzled at this question as if no one had ever asked him this before.* I never knew him. I was born after he died. Mom and I are always together. Uh, guess I don't really know what having a dad would be like.

Hailey: Let's break for something to eat. Unless you want burned pancakes

Katlyn left the camera running but set it on the counter across the room. Hailey served their plates and the camera recorded silence for the next few minutes. Katlyn came up for air grinning. "And you cook, too. How did that come about?"

"Self-defense, Katlyn. This little guy eats like a horse and we couldn't afford to eat out; wasn't healthy either."

"Did you ever cook for a date?"

"We're back to my non-existing social life I see. No. None ever got that domestic. I'd usually meet a guy somewhere for dinner or a party at an embassy. And, as I said before, any notion of doing something with Adam kind of scared them off. There is another factor when single-parenting is involved. Honestly, I am attracted to some men, but can't help judging them as potential fathers for Adam. Having a child and being a single parent gives you tons of responsibility that single people just do not have. The game changes and I suppose I am more comfortable thinking of my child first. Does that cause loneliness for me? Sure, sometimes. But look at this boy." Hailey hugged Adam to her side. "He is the delight of my life."

The public TV station ran the personal interview and the main streeting walks throughout southwest Virginia's Blue Ridge country. Merton Alexander III laughed at the entire campaign, one he termed a charade of silly women. He refused to debate Hailey and was quoted as saying she was the challenger. He would stand on his record. His sponsors contributed heavily and developed a large advertising campaign that failed majestically. Why? It was obvious. Alexander's campaign strategy did not consider Hailey a serious candidate. She had no experience in politics. She should be home raising her child instead of parading around the Virginia hill country in shorts. This theme continued even though Hailey had appeared just one time in public wearing culottes, not shorts. Daily she thanked her gut feeling that caused her to change out of Sara's costume. Everything the ads said was an attack on Hailey and brought her a ton of free publicity. Sara avoided any mention of Merton Alexander III in her press releases.

Adam accompanied his mother everywhere and the charge that she was abandoning him to run for office fell flat. When she took him out of school for a trip to a town in an out-of-the-way corner of her district, his books and homework went along for the ride and photographers were anxious to capture such scenes on film. Actually, she had become a favorite for photographers since her initial speech. But many voters were tuning in to her message: she would represent people, not interest groups.

Merton attended hundred-dollar-a-plate fund raisers with the upper crust. Hailey went to barbecues wherever she was invited. Merton was driven to campaign stops in his limo with a phalanx of aides in mammoth SUVs front and aft. He went straight from the limo to the speaker's platform, gave his standard message and left. Hailey drove her compact with Adam and sometimes Sara or Mary Jo, and walked through the crowds shaking hands. She rarely made speeches but preferred to hold town meetings and listen. All was not pleasant though.

It happened one evening in a high school gym full of white-haired conservative voters from a precinct that had always bent far right.

"I hear you're in favor of killing babies. That makes you an abortionist in my book. You'll not get my vote." The craggy-faced man glared at her just before he was pulled back into his seat by his red-faced spouse. Hailey was tired and ticked off.

"I do not favor abortion. I have said that maybe a thousand times in the last month or so. I am pro-child and pro-family. But I am also for women's rights. And it galls me to the heavens why you think you have the right to pry into the privacy between a woman and her doctor, peek into her personal medical condition where you have no business and act like a God. How can you stand there and say the government has no business telling you how to run your life, yet you insist that you can tell me what to do with my body?" She glared back at her tormentor. "I was flying jets and got pregnant. I quit and had my child and that was my choice. My choice! You stay out of my business and I'll stay out of yours. If you want to vote for someone who'll tell you what you want to hear, go ahead. My challenger will tell you anything to get elected. But I'll tell you ladies something. If you get pregnant and something goes wrong, don't look for any mercy from your current representative. He has voted down every measure that would support women's health as, and I quote him, '...it is God's will for women to bear this burden.'"

A few got up and left in protest. More, the majority women, stood and applauded. Cameras flashed continuously and then the moment came that many considered the turning point in the race. Adam ran on stage and hugged his mother. He turned an angry glare towards the hecklers in the crowd and stood between them and his mom, as if protecting her from further verbal abuse. There was no political strategy more powerful than to have a good loving child by your side.

The award-winning picture covered the top half of the *Roanoke Times* Sunday edition just days before the election. And for once the headline sought the high ground:

"MacMurray Against Abortion; Defends a Woman's Right to Choose"

November 3, Pulaski Civic Center. At a political rally here Saturday, Candidate Hailey MacMurray recounted her decision to forego a career as a military pilot and have her baby. MacMurray adamantly defended a woman's right to make her own choice, even as she strongly reiterated that she personally did not choose abortion. Although some hecklers in the crowd at Pulaski's town meeting attacked Mrs. MacMurray for her stance, most applauded her honesty. Proof that her decision was right for her was demonstrated by her son, Adam, shown giving his mom a hug after the rally. The first grader campaigns with his mother and is her official escort to many campaign functions.

For the first time in many elections, southwestern Virginia voters had a choice themselves. Women registered in large numbers and most cast their ballots for Hailey. Men fit Sara's description of their prehistoric programming, appreciating her beauty at first. Hailey was young, nearing 31, tall, slender, and energetic, with an athletic tone to her body, head to toe. Her hair was a shiny chestnut with natural streaks of reddish-brown that framed an oval face. Her complexion was smooth, light, and unblemished by worry. Deep brown eyes held an openness that bespoke sincerity, interest, and welcomed friendship. Thus, visually, most men pictured her, as the trite country expression went, as a long cool drink of water. But when she spoke of her passion for service, men listened. They came around to her strong positions on the military and health care. Not many women, they admitted, could equal her record of success in the military. Not many men either. But another category carried the day for the single mom: independents. Like Bill Conley in Colorado, Hailey was not affiliated with any party and refused to join one during and after the election. She also had a low budget, no-favors-promised campaign. She worked for the people and for no one else.

Merton Alexander III was a sore loser and did not make the customary courtesy call to concede the race. "She's just a pretty face," he was quoted as saying. "Wait until she gets to the big show in Washington. They'll eat her alive up there."

Five

"Elizabeth, you're a savior. Thank you for watching Adam today. I got caught in a bind without a sitter and had to bring him back into town to finish that darned committee meeting."

"Hailey, it was my pleasure. I haven't had a young man pay me so much attention in decades. And for our meeting tonight, I have our usual professional sitter lined up. In fact, it does Bill lots of good to have a companion he can play with." Both women chuckled at this. Adam MacMurray and Bill Conley had become close buddies. The senator helped the boy with leftover homework some nights, then they got down to their favorite video game, Blaster.

Elizabeth checked her watch. "Grandpa Bill will be here promptly at eight or I'll have his hide."

Adam watched the two women talking back and forth and tried to decipher their meaning. He didn't want a sitter; didn't need one as long as Grandpa Bill was there. But where was he? The senator usually gave him a big hug when he arrived and took him into the study so they could play Blaster on the computer. Funny. Adam knew his new grandpa had been in the Army, but he sure was a lousy shot playing Blaster. Adam always won.

Just then the front door opened and Senator Bill Conley walked in. Adam ran to greet him and the two swung in a circle, arms tightly wound around each other.

"Sorry I'm a little late. Alice made me sign all this paperwork. What a slave driver." He grabbed Elizabeth and gave her a juicy kiss, moved his head back a fraction, then kissed her again, this time going for a record-breaker.

"Ouch! Hey that hurts. No pinching; that's the rule. Oh, we have company. Hi, Hailey. How goes the war to liberate the Congress from the two major parties?" He gave her a friendly squeeze.

"It's a battle, Senator. We have just a handful of independents in the house. Most newcomers went into political debt just getting elected, so it's too early to get them to break ranks. On the plus side, Elizabeth is a great help with her networking and we're growing stronger." Any further conversation came to a halt as the doorbell rang announcing the arrival of the first guests to Hailey's Women's Connection, an informal social group of political troublemakers she and Elizabeth had created.

The senator took Adam off to play Blaster while the women greeted their arriving members. It was an eclectic mix of congressional secretaries, members of Congress, senior executive managers, executive assistants from various agencies, and one Secret Service agent. Her name was Jennette Marshall and she and Hailey were becoming close friends. Both women had lost husbands: Hailey's to a plane crash, Jennette's to the Gulf War. Both were tall and attractive women who had remained single afterwards. And Jennette always lingered after their Connection meetings to chat with her new friend.

"What's on your mind tonight, Jennette? You were very quiet the whole meeting and I can usually count on you to argue with somebody. So what's up?"

"I came to a decision tonight and it's all your fault." Jennette wore a relieved expression and grinned, letting her friend know *her fault* was a positive thing.

Hailey assumed her own faux stance of exasperation and said, "OK, spill it, lady. What did I do now?"

"I've sworn off men, just like you. Should have done it years ago before I got to the point of forgetting their names the next morning." This last bit of personal information embarrassed both women and Jennette looked away. "Sorry, Hailey, you didn't need to hear that. But I feel better that it's out in the open." Her pretty green eyes filled with tears and Hailey pulled the tall blonde into a comforting embrace. They stood together for some moments until Jennette regained control and wiped her eyes.

"OK, Jennette, my friend, let me tell you something. You were vulnerable and guys took advantage of you. You're a gorgeous woman and attract men like bees; I've seen the looks. My advantage was getting pregnant and having a baby to be responsible for. In hindsight, I forced Adam's father into a marriage he didn't want and he abandoned us." Hailey paused to let her friend shut her mouth, fallen open in surprise. "So you see, I was by myself months before Adam's birth. I had time to deal with a possible future as a single mother with an estranged husband. And then—" It was Hailey's turn to lose composure and her voice at the same time.

Jennette gathered her friend in a hug, returning comfort, and said, "Take your time. Sounds like you never told anyone about this and maybe you need to spill it too, like I did."

Gradually, Hailey regained her breath and voice. "Wow, I didn't realize that moment was still stored inside. But yeah, you're right. I need to get this out one time and be done with it. So, here it is, I had gone alone to the base chaplain for marriage counseling. He was so friendly and consoling and we always ended our sessions with a hug. I thought he was such a nice man to be so understanding. He provided just enough affection to tell me I was OK as a person, even though my stomach was sticking out a ton, my face was blotchy, and I felt a wreck with my hormones gone crazy from carrying a child around. Then he, gee…this is hard, he, this chaplain, was the one who came to the door to tell me my husband was dead. He came in and held me and I felt secure and free to let go my emotions. Next thing I know the guy is feeling me up, and poking at my belly with an unregistered weapon below the belt."

"Hailey, that's so disgusting! I hope you turned him in."

"No. I used it to build up my determination to leave the military and do something else. But I read a study that talked about this phenomenon. It happened during Vietnam, and wives got taken in by smooth talking counselors. They were vulnerable, see. Just like you and I were."

"I just started going to bars and picking up random guys, Hailey. I'm ashamed of it, especially compared to what you did. But no more."

Both women turned to gather their coats and leave. They passed by the study where the senator had been watching Adam and noted Hailey's son fast asleep on the couch, covered by a quilt. They also noticed the senator and his wife in a tight embrace in his recliner. Elizabeth lay across her husband's lap and framed his head with her hands while she drew out a marathon kiss. The senator had one hand on her hip while the other roamed up and down her back caressing with gentle affection. It was obvious that in another minute both young women would witness more than they wished for. Yet they couldn't stop watching as the two septuagenarians continued to make out like newlyweds.

The reverie broke when Bill Conley opened one eye and spied his witnesses. He nudged his wife who broke off the kiss with reluctance and turned to smile over her shoulder at Hailey and Jennette. She sat up, straightened her skirt, turned back to her husband for one more smooch, and then rose to say goodnight. But she caught their looks of amazement and understood why neither woman had moved.

"Some day the right one will be there for you, too. When he comes along, grab on and don't let go. Not all men are slobs."

Hailey shook Adam awake and they said their goodbyes. Outside the two close friends stood by Hailey's car for one last word before going their separate ways.

"I believe her, Jennette. I haven't given up on men entirely. It just seems that way. The ones I come across either run when I bring out Adam, or want a roll in the sack with no strings attached."

"Well, I'm sticking to my original statement. No more men. I've done the sack bit and it stinks. Good night, my friend." They hugged again and each went home alone.

Meredith poked her head into her boss's office. "Hailey, Speaker Nederthal called and asked for you to come over to his office. He said it was important."

"Thanks, Meredith. I'll bet you a buck I know what he wants. I argued with my subcommittee members yesterday when they talked about cutting out my amendment for healthcare legislation. Since my proposal for expanding coverage wasn't on either party's agenda it was like tossing a monkey into the punch bowl. Or whatever the saying is."

She rushed down the hall to meet her boss. Everyone had one, she thought, a boss, that is. It didn't matter if thousands of people had elected her to high office; someone was higher and would always want to flex his muscle. Today that someone was Cantwell Nederthal, Speaker of the House. She had not received a warm welcome from him or any of his hired hands, the lobbyists that clung to the halls of Congress like lichen. Cantwell kept sending smooth talking men down to meet with her and Meredith turned them all away per Hailey's instructions. On that score she was following her mentor's example. Bill Conley held lobbyists far far away and so would she.

Hailey got just inside the door to Nederthal's office and was met by the man himself and one other person, a handsome chap, dressed like someone who just stepped off the front cover of *GQ Magazine*.

"Should have told you to bring your rain coat, Hailey. Judson and I are taking you to lunch and it's drizzling. But his limo is right outside so you won't get too wet. Oh, yes, Judson Mackensie, this is Hailey MacMurray from Virginia."

Judson Mackensie held Hailey's hand like it was filled with gold. "Delighted, Ms. MacMurray. I've heard such nice things about you." He was suave and honey-tongued. His hand was soft, softer than hers, and exquisitely manicured. His golden blond hair was coiffed to perfection, not a stray could escape the slicked down locks held firmly in place by the latest gel. His hawkish features reminded her of Major Scandling, the chaplain at Edwards AFB, and the glint in his eyes told her this man's objectives would be similar. This one had been brought in with a specific goal: charm the recalcitrant lady from the Virginia mountains during and after working hours. Anything achieved beyond a positive vote for the majority's legislation would be icing on the cake.

"Sorry, Ned, but I go to the gym during lunch and eat some yogurt at my desk between votes. And Mr. Mackensie, whom do you represent? No wait, let me guess. Would it be the health insurance industry?" A huge smile creased his face. "Yes, I thought so. Well, Ned," she turned to face the Speaker directly, "I don't talk to lobbyists and I do not appreciate being jerked around by you in order to get one near me. Remember this in the future. I do not care what your position is. I represent the voters back in the Blue Ridge country in Virginia, and this man's industry won't offer coverage to most of them. Do not play games with me. You don't have my vote and you won't get it." She left both men staring at her back as she sped away down the hall, high heels clicking an angry rhythm.

"Hailey, wait up, please." It was the smoothie from the industry. She stopped and turned halfway to meet him face to face as he jogged up. "This isn't business now. How about dinner tonight? I know a nice four-star French restaurant over on K Street where we can escape this rat race. What do you say?" He was all smiles and so confident she could have sworn the man had never been turned down. He reached a hand to her arm and she shook it off.

"Would you be able to write off paying for my child's sitter, Mr. Mackensie? Along with the food and wine?" Got him. Mackensie gulped visibly; just another lecher who wanted no part of her child.

"Uh, I was told you were single, and I, uh—"

"Forget my child, Mackensie. I do not go to dinner with lobbyists under any circumstances. That's my policy, but I just wanted to see your reaction when I told you I was a mother of a seven-year-old boy. Good day." This time the man did not follow her. But he did appreciate the view from behind as the beautiful Congresswoman glided down the hall.

"Stop drooling, Mac, I'm hungry so you might as well write off another lunch and feed me." The Speaker smirked as Mackensie kept looking back over his shoulder, hoping for another peek at the Virginia beauty. "Nice try. She turns everybody down. Some of the guys call her the 'Ice Maiden.' No one has seen her with a man and the word is she and some blonde, a female, are real close. Get my drift?" Both men frowned and came to the same conclusion spoken aloud by the lobbyist.

"What a waste. She just needs to get laid. That'll settle it; get her back on track."

Hailey found a close friend waiting by Meredith's desk. The senior senator from California, Burch Magnum, greeted her with a warm smile. Hailey was delighted to see him.

"Hello, Burch. What's up?"

"I see you escaped once again from the clutches of our capitol city. Who was it this time? Military-industrial complex? AARP? Health Insurance? Ah, yes, the vivacious Ms. Calloway, no doubt."

But Hailey returned a puzzled look at this guess by her friend and said, "Evidently they send the good looking women to take you to lunch and I get the fashion plates with slicked back hair and manicured hands. I was greeted by Mr. Judson Mackensie. He even followed me down the hall, begging for a dinner date until he learned I was a mother." They walked into Hailey's office and sat on facing easy chairs. "What is it with you guys, Burch? Mention a child and red alarm lights go on."

"But, Hailey, my friend, you would have turned him down anyway. Right?" Hailey shrugged her shoulders, a signal it was time to get to work. They had become friends soon after Hailey arrived in Washington. Burch was serving his third term in the Senate and discovered the two shared many of the same domestic policy ideas. They also got along famously because Hailey didn't ask him about his estranged wife, Marcella, who had recently shacked up with another lover in the Hollywood Hills. Likewise, Burch respected her feelings about men, and only wished he could lose about twenty years so they could become more than friends.

He was a golden Californian, handsome, rich, and smart. The rich part came from Marcella though, and her father's fortune had paid for his initial campaign for a senate seat. Prenuptial agreements demanded by Big Daddy ensured that Burch would receive nothing if he divorced the rich princess. Meanwhile both partners dallied with various lovers. Burch was discreet and Marcella threw caution aside. Neither had the energy to make their separation legal.

Burch and Bill Conley were sponsoring legislation to expand healthcare in a senate bill that matched hers in the House. But it was an uphill fight all the way, there were too many interests twisting arms threatening to kill their proposals. Yet the three members of Congress had jelled into a formidable political force and independents had started listening to their logic and begun voting in a block to support them. Still they were stymied as long as the White House and the Congress went with the tide of the interest groups that fed their campaign coffers.

Today Burch and Hailey wrapped up their brainstorming session on a down note. They didn't have the votes to bring their proposals out of committee hearings. Ever the optimist, Burch had another idea.

"Do you like football, Hailey? Ever see a pro game?"

"Yes and no. I dated a football player once in high school. Didn't last and he was the school hero, too." She offered a faux sigh of regret. "But Adam and I watch the games on TV. They're too expensive though, and you know, of course, I won't take tickets from the interest groups."

"I own a box at the stadium. Marcella paid for it when she brought one of her gigolos to town and wanted to impress him. She hasn't been back for years and I have the rights to it. Comes with tickets of course. Why don't you and Adam join me when you get back in town after the August dog days? First regular season game is the first Sunday in September." He waited for her reply and found her gazing off to a far corner, lost in thought.

"He was really buff, I remember that much, and all the girls envied me that I was going to homecoming with him. Randolph Purdy was his name. Of course he was the quarterback and had a big ego. Big feet too. All the girls giggled that everything about him must be big as well. We never got to the dance after the game. He faked running out of gas and we wrestled in the front seat until I got out and walked home." She let go another sigh to the past, then remembered Burch's offer. "Sorry, Burch. Yes, I'd love to go."

Six

Burch Magnum had an SUV full of women and one boy. Hailey and Adam met him at the Smithsonian Metro station. Jennette lived in a condo on his way down Connecticut Avenue. And his secretary, Rose, always drove to his house and attended these games with him. She was more his age and his best friend in this town, someone he confided in after work. They never went out socially. Burch never understood how that arrangement developed, but it seemed to work for Rose. She ran his office with extraordinary efficiency so he wouldn't argue.

Today heads would turn when he showed up with Hailey. She and Burch were alike in some ways. Of course there were the political agendas that were similar. Both were moderate and put domestic policies foremost. Burch belonged to the minority party and Hailey was independent, making them close when it came to issues. But the real talk would be about being seen together socially, which had come to mean more to the power elite cocktail circuit about town than actual substantive ideas. A stupid turn of events if you thought about it, Burch pondered. If so and so was seen conversing with such and such about this and that, well then, the media was on it like a bunch of piranhas. They'd gnaw it down to the bone, placing social connections above the difficult work that was done in committee meetings and Capitol Hill staff offices.

Today Burch figured he and Adam would pair up and watch the game while the ladies chatted about whatever women chatted about. He wouldn't pay much attention. He was a Redskin fan to the death and would watch the

'Skins' ultimate dynamic duo of Cramer and Daniel to see if they were as special as last year. Sometimes it took a few games for the pros to get it going, but not those two. Cramer was the top quarterback in the league and Daniel was an extraordinary tight end with the blazing speed of a wide receiver. And block? Talk about crushing defensive backs, well, the man was awesome.

"Burch, the man wants your car keys." Rose jabbed him on the shoulder to roust her boss from his daydreaming. She knew his mind had drifted off to the coming season. That's why he brought her along. Burch needed someone to keep him on track when he wasn't on the senate floor. She grinned at his embarrassment as he handed the keys to the valet parking attendant.

"Everybody out. Just follow me and we'll take the elevator up to the box." He was back in charge and leading the way. The attendant was gone with the car, and his entourage faithfully tagged along. Only Rose realized he'd lost contact with the real world for a moment.

Once inside the sky high executive boxes, Burch's group divided up pretty much as he'd expected. Rose, Jennette, and Hailey huddled to discuss some kind of connection while Adam came to his side and began to ask about the players.

"Who are the best players, Senator Magnum?" The boy couldn't take his eyes from the scene below as thousands of fans filled the mammoth stadium and the Redskin band, the only one in the NFL, struck up Hail to the Redskins. Pandemonium reigned everywhere he looked.

"First of all, Adam, I hope we can do this on a regular basis, so why don't you call me Burch?" But he could see this didn't set well with the young boy. Maybe it was too informal to start. "OK, what about Uncle Burch?" Now Adam smiled. "Fine. Good. Now, here's the scoop. On defense we're pretty down. We didn't do so hot last year and need help at linebacker and defensive end, and possibly a few safeties. In short just about everywhere. But when it comes to offense we're tops. Keep your eye on two guys: Jason Cramer at quarterback, he's number 6, and Mark Daniel, tight end, number 27. They have become the best passing combination in the league. Cramer's from Ohio State, and," Burch checked to see how close the women were, but they were still huddled together, paying him no regard, "he has the reputation of being a playboy around town. Something of a ladies man." Adam looked puzzled. "I'll explain it in more detail next season. Anyway, he can hit a dime fifty yards down field and his receiver is usually Daniel for a TD."

The senior senator from the Golden State was on a roll with his audience of one. "Now that Daniel is a real anomaly. Nobody heard of him in college since he went to this little podunk school out in Gunnison, Colorado. Place called Western State. He came into the 'Skins' training camp as a free agent and blew everyone away. Started his rookie year and made the pro bowl. He's been to the pro bowl every year since."

Adam pointed to a group of rather large women in flouncy flowered dresses wearing floppy hats. Each had enormous noses and they were all very much overweight. "Who are those people, Uncle Burch?"

"Ah, the famous Hoggettes, Adam. They are really middle-aged men dressed like women and they're the wildest and most loyal fans in town. OK, pay attention. The kickoff is coming and the Skins get the ball first."

Rose had filled in her companions about the Cramer to Daniel combo during their huddle. Hailey was pleased to see her son and Burch close together on the opposite side of the penthouse suite. She loved football and it looked like Jennette and Rose did too. What a nice diversion from reality before the fall session of Congress started.

The Skins huddled at their ten after their kick returner had almost lost the ball from a vicious hit. Their quarterback took charge with confidence.

Jason Cramer called the play. "Just like coach drew it up, guys. X27 post on three. Break!" The offensive line and the backfield jogged to their positions appearing anxious to run the play. Mark Daniel, however, casually strolled toward the sideline as if he was going off the field, becoming uninvolved. Cramer hollered THREE and the ball was snapped. Mark took one more leisurely step even as chaos erupted around the line of scrimmage. The corner back assigned to the Skins' tight end bit on the fake by the running back into the right side of the line. Then Mark took off and hit top speed within a couple of strides, passing first the befuddled corner back, and then the safety, easily streaking down the sideline wide open. He caught Cramer's laser pass over his outside shoulder at the fifty and never broke stride. It was 6-0 Skins and only thirty seconds had expired.

Hats flew in the air. The Hoggettes loosened the floorboards jumping up and down. The band played. Cheerleaders pranced. Rolls of toilet paper rained throughout the stands. But Adam watched Mark Daniel and nothing else. The terrific tight end had burst into the end zone, slowed to a walk and handed the ball to the referee. He did not slam it into the ground and he did no victory dance like Adam had seen so often on TV. This guy was different; it was easy to see and appreciate. Mark Daniel acted like he had done this before. Next, he and Cramer, who remained understated as well, slapped high fives as the team huddled for the extra point.

Burch knew the boy was impressed. Hell, everyone was. Cramer to Daniel was not only a superstar athletic show; it was a demonstration of sportsmanship. The rest of the league could dance and showboat. These two were a class act.

Mark Daniel was a mountain man and a Renaissance man rolled into one extremely talented football player's body. He lived in the beautiful village of Crested Butte some 30 miles north of Gunnison. The altitude of about 9,000 feet helped him maintain his superb physical condition and his summers were now occupied with friends from around the league who came to town to work out with him. These were professional players who tried to beat him every Sunday but were friends in the off season. Many stayed in his lodge high up the side of Mount Crested Butte, which was not far from the ski runs.

Mark appreciated the physical and creative gifts he had inherited from his parents, for he gave them the credit. He dabbled in many things: his sculptures were in galleries in most Western states and brought high prices; he played a mean jazz piano and sang, imitating several rock stars to the delight of patrons at his restaurant; and he cooked alongside his lifetime pal, Morgan Cutcher. Morgan really ran the kitchen staff, since Mark played football half the year.

He was a ruggedly handsome man standing six and a half feet tall and weighing a rangy two forty with little body fat. His smoky gray eyes and reddish-brown hair attracted women, and he had dated quite a few. But only for short periods of time. He left many saddened when they discovered he could not commit to a lifetime relationship until his playing days were over. And who could argue with his reasoning? He'd been quoted often in the local press as saying he didn't have the time necessary to be a good husband and father—goals he admitted to—and the ladies would have to be patient.

He compensated for his lack of time for a family by sponsoring a summer camp for kids at his expense and that of his special friends who came to visit. Mark and his guests taught basic conditioning and football techniques to groups of underprivileged kids from around the state. Their goal was to teach sportsmanship and team play. It was a success story all around, and the press in Colorado wrote it up each summer. Yet few outside the state knew about it. When Mark put on the pads for football season he went back East—Westerners didn't distinguish between North and South, or Northeast and Southeast, regions as unique as the Pacific Northwest and the Texas Panhandle. Back East he focused on playing football at its highest level.

Jason Cramer was something else. He nurtured his playboy image to the hilt and made a fortune. He was the highest paid football player in the world and lived a jetsetter lifestyle. His fortune, however, did not come from football directly. Jason had majored in marketing at Ohio State and parlayed his stardom on the field into a sports management empire. Along the way his company produced men's cologne—Mark, his best friend, claimed it smelled like used shoulder pads—and arranged appearances for the star and company CEO. Money rolled in effortlessly, and a hefty portion went to Mark's summer camps.

Jason was movie star handsome and was often seen around town with a new woman, usually a gorgeous fashion model. But none of the women made it past the goal line. Jason was too busy making money and playing ball. And, like Mark, he said he'd wait a bit.

Bottom line: Only Mark and Jason would admit, and only to each other, that the right woman had not come along for either.

Adam and his new friend, Uncle Burch, had a lot to cheer about in this game. The Cramer to Daniel combo scored three touchdowns. Mark caught ten balls of the twelve thrown his way and Jason went over the 300-yard mark in passing yards. But the Skins' defense allowed opposition running backs through gigantic holes for over 200 yards rushing offense, and by the fourth quarter, the defeat was assured.

"Just proves a team has to do more than pass the ball, Adam." Burch had drifted into a silent mourning around the middle of the third quarter, but Adam had hung on to the last second, hoping his team could pull it out.

"Too bad, Uncle Burch. The coach ought to build the team around that Cramer guy. He needs better players. The other team sacked him too much, one time when Mark Daniel was in the open and could have caught another TD."

Burch studied the boy's face. Adam was smart and savvy for a seven-year-old kid. He appreciated the good players and was even a bit stoic about winning and losing. Didn't dwell on losing and started looking for ways to improve right off the bat. *Why not reinforce those positive characteristics?* he thought.

"Rose, you know how to get back to our car. Why don't you take Hailey and Jennette down when you're ready to go while I introduce Adam to a couple of the players."

"We have more to discuss about Hailey's group anyway, Burch. We just got on to discussing legislation for improving nursing homes. Take your time and we'll meet you in about half an hour." Rose turned back to her two friends and their huddle reformed.

Hailey came over and gave Adam a hug and a kiss. "Thanks, Burch. This is really nice of you. Adam, behave down there, OK?"

Burch led Adam to the elevator outside their booth and punched a button for the lower level. When the doors opened Adam went bug-eyed with excitement. The hallway led straight to the team's locker room. He kept close by Senator Magnum, who seemed to know everyone and had no trouble walking right in amongst the disgruntled and downtrodden football players. Most were half dressed and were still in the process of pulling off tape and pads. All had their heads down. The scene could have been mistaken for a butcher's meat locker with big sides of beef hanging listlessly, except these hunks of flesh still had arms, legs and heads attached. It was not a fun sight and Adam got a good feel for the sour atmosphere around grown men who had lost something important.

"Over here, Adam. Let's visit number 6 and his buddy Mark." Burch pulled the boy along to a corner where several reporters held microphones up to Jason Cramer to interview him. One minicam got right up in his face, leaving only inches for the man to breathe. Adam and Burch stood back a ways and let the press have its day.

"Jason, tell us how it feels to have your offensive line do such a lousy job of pass blocking." The reporter shot a nasty question at the beaten down quarterback.

The seasoned QB gave the reporter a withering look and paused to think about his reply. "I thought they did a good job, Bert. The Lions have one of the best pass rushes in the league. Give the other team credit for once. They played hard and beat us. We'll get 'em next time."

"But your left tackle left you out to dry and then got flagged for holding at a crucial point. Doesn't that burn you up?"

"Jones is a good player and he'll get better. Why don't you go tell him what you think? I told all you guys I'm not going to badmouth my teammates.

That's what you want to happen so we'll give you a hot story and then we'll start a pissing contest talking to various reporters and the team will crash and burn. Now beat it. This interview is over." Cramer turned back to his locker and finished removing his pads, shoes, and the tape from his ankles. He slammed his gear into the locker and looked ready to punch the reporter's lights out.

The intrepid reporter moved one locker over to Mark Daniel, who had his back turned. "Hey, Mark. Bert Jones from the *Times*, nice game today." The big tight end slid around on the bench and faced the reporter. His expression was neutral and he did not return the greeting.

"Tell us what went wrong out there, Mark."

"The other team beat us, Bert. They played better and we'll get them next time, like Jason just said. We're a young team and we'll come along as the season progresses."

But the reporter seemed intent on baiting one player to criticize a teammate. "You had a good day at least. But there were a few times when your quarterback didn't get you the ball right on time or the Skins might have won. What do you say about that?"

Adam looked from Mark to Jason and back again. This was scary and the tension was thick, so bad he felt it. The locker room got quiet and he noticed other players looking towards Mark and waiting for his reply. It was true. The reporter wanted to stir up dissension to create a sensational story, so a lot was riding on Mark Daniel's response.

Slowly Mark stood and the reporter backed off, bumping into his cameraman. All the players were quiet now and heads turned to one of their leaders. Then the big man spoke loud enough for the entire locker room to hear him.

"OK, Bert. Repeat your question so all the guys can hear it." Mark gently grasped the little man's shoulders and turned him to face the team. "Go on, ask me again." Adam got frightened and reached for Uncle Burch's arm. These were big men and most were getting angry at this scene. Then he saw Jason Cramer's face and relaxed. The all-pro QB was smiling and nodding his head at his friend.

Burch whispered into Adam's ear, "It's OK, watch this." The senator wrapped an arm securely around the boy and felt his young body inch closer.

"Uh, I said, you had a good day out there, Mark." The microphone shook and the man's voice cracked like an adolescent's going through puberty.

"No, no, no, no. That's not all of it." Mark grinned down at the nervous man. "Say the rest in a nice clear and loud voice so the guys can hear. I promise we won't eat you for dinner." Deep-throated chuckles erupted all around and the reporter grew red in the face.

He gulped and continued, "I said there were a few times when your quarterback didn't get you the ball right on time or the Skins might have won." Mark stepped beside the man and wrapped a long arm around his shoulders like they were best buddies. He got serious and looked around to his teammates eye to eye.

"Fellows, listen up. We lost the game today. All of us. Jason Cramer is the best damn quarterback in football and I know he did his best to win. All of us did. It is not a question of maybe if this had happened or that had transpired and we could have beaten the Lions. They beat us. They played harder and they won. We will get better. This is a good team and each of us can do better than we did today." He scanned the room once more then shouted, "Am I right?"

"You know it, Bro," Maurice Johnson, all 350 pounds of him, stood and yelled back. Others began to stand and shout and chaos broke out, transforming the once beaten-down locker room into a reformation and a rekindling of spirit.

Mark and Jason went around the room slapping hands with all the players and building them up for next week's battle. The reporter packed his gear and sneaked out the door before Mark could grab him. Burch looked down at his new nephew and grinned.

"Adam, if we had more people like Mark Daniel in public office there'd be fewer problems. What you just saw was leadership of the highest caliber. Come on, let's go meet him." They stood near Mark's locker and heard Jason speak quietly.

"Thanks for backing me up. The team needed that. You were hell on wheels today, partner."

"Mark, Jason, I want to introduce a new fan to you. This is Adam MacMurray, Congresswoman Hailey MacMurray's son."

Both men stood and greeted the senator and Adam. "Good to see you, Sir," Mark said. He shook hands with Burch and then with Adam, who had lost his voice. The big man sat down again and came to eye level with the boy. "Too bad you didn't see us win, Adam. But did you enjoy the game? Was this your first one?"

Adam forgot the rest of the room full of carousing players and looked into the kind and smiling eyes of a new friend. He sat on the bench beside Mark and found his voice. "Wow, I'll say I did, even though you lost. Uncle Burch brought me and Mom and some of his friends and we sat in the booth on top and it was just fantastic. I could see you go out on patterns and watch the ball sail right into your hands and see you outrun those guys." Jason and Mark got a laugh from the boy's enthusiasm and nonstop description.

Jason said, "Well, Adam, what do we need to do next time to win?"

"Well, gee, I didn't see much of a running game and everyone knows you need a balanced attack. Plus you threw to Mark most of the day and the wide receiver was open down the middle a couple of times too." He paused and looked up to the ceiling for his next piece of analysis. "And, uh, well, those guys on the line need to work on their pass-blocking, but I understand why Mark did what he did to that reporter."

"What did I do to the reporter, Adam?" Mark said, struggling to hide his laughter.

"You used him to build up the team. It was great, Mark. I liked that part almost as much as the way you handed the ball to the ref instead of spiking it." The small boy looked into his hero's eyes and declared with a serious voice, "That was sportsmanship, just the way my mom tells me."

The three adults stared at this special child, then exchanged amazed expressions. Mark reacted by grabbing Adam in a bear hug and tousling his hair.

"You can come in here after every game, Adam. We could all use your words of wisdom." The tight end reached back into his locker and pulled out his game jersey. "Here, take this home, wash it and then you can wear it." Adam clutched the jersey to his chest, then threw his arms around Mark's neck and hugged him fiercely.

"Wow, thanks. Gee, wait until Mom sees this."

"Next time you can bring your dad back here to see us, Adam," Jason said.

The boy grew quiet. "He died a long time ago, but maybe my mom could meet you guys down on the field after the game before you take your clothes off." Burch, Jason, and Mark howled with laughter.

"Come with me, Adam. These guys need to get cleaned up. Good luck next week, fellows," Burch said. He glanced back to find Adam and laughed again. The boy had already shrugged into the large jersey, ignoring the dirt and grass stains, and was rolling up the sleeves.

Mark watched the boy stroll out of the locker room on a cloud. "Nice kid, Jason. I wonder what happened to his father. But he seemed to take it in stride. Smart little guy, too. You ever hear about his mom?"

"Nah, probably some pompous politician. I can picture some fuddy duddy in a suit, too straight-laced to enjoy life. Politicians are not for me."

Mark shook his head. "I don't think Adam's mom would be like that. That boy is special. Somebody special raised him and is doing a great job. I know, I'm around too many kids who don't have one loving parent at home. This kid does."

At home that night Hailey had to wrestle Adam out of his jersey. "Just take it off long enough for me to wash it, please. Then you can wear it to bed if you want to."

"Ok, Mom." But he followed her to the washer and stood by it until the shirt came out mostly clean and with a few great grass stains as proof of battle on the field. Hailey just shook her head and held the garment up for his inspection before she tossed it into the dryer. And again her son stood guard. When the buzzer sounded he jerked open the door and pulled out his prize. It was still hot but he wriggled into it regardless.

Hailey finally got her son calmed down and into bed. She sat on the edge and smoothed his hair. "Your football player must be some guy. Do you think you can get to sleep now after all the excitement?"

"You have to meet him, Mom. He gave this pep talk to the other players and didn't let this awful reporter bother any of them. Uncle Burch said he's a leader on the team." His eyes glazed over and for a moment Adam drifted off. Then quickly, his eyes popped open. "Promise me you'll come with me next week to meet him. OK?"

"I promise, honey."

But next week didn't happen for the rest of the season. Hailey was snowed under by meetings, briefings, and legislation drafting on the side by her Women's Connection. This politically "subversive" group crossed party lines. It also mixed legislative and executive branch agendas. There were no men directly involved, only women members. Yet, several men indirectly influenced the group. Senator Bill Conley was primary, and Burch Magnum ran a close second in suggesting areas where the group could influence legislation and policies. Foremost was the area of health care, and in that arena, specifically women's health. Yet neither of the major parties had run their latest election campaigns with this issue as part of its platform. Special interests controlled the congressional agenda.

Hailey's record of success proposing new legislation was practically a big fat zero, and the Redskins faired little better, breaking even on the season at a record of 8-8. Adam continued to attend the home games with his Uncle Burch and visit with his new pals, Mark and Jason, for a post-game analysis and review.

In January Mark returned to Crested Butte to run his restaurant full-time. He worked mornings and weekends during the day on new sculptures. Adam approached his eighth birthday and traveled to Blue Ridge with his mom to hear what the voters had to say. Jennette kept her oath to swear off men and grew into a successful Secret Service agent, largely from the positive reinforcement from her best pal, Hailey.

Seven

A new administration came into power in the same general election that saw victory for Bill Conley and Hailey MacMurray. During the early months of the new year, White House officials presented the president's budget for the fiscal year that would start the following October. For several months leading up to the compilation of the mammoth federal budget, agencies glued together requests for money from their various components and major programs. For the duration of this exercise, despised by most budget officers outside the Beltway, there were many outside influences that swayed the budget makers within Washington. In particular, two agencies, the FBI and the National Archives, located diagonally across Pennsylvania Avenue from each other, were representative of the fiscal games held this time each year.

Ronald Kraft had been appointed Director of the FBI during the defeated president's administration. Today, he met with his older brother, Kent, the Senate Majority Leader, for advice. They chose the Vienna, Virginia Dogwood Blossom Private Club to share a full day of golf and information.

Ronny hit a successful chip shot from the deep bunker onto the green that stopped less than five feet from the hole. "Yesss! Looks like you're going to owe me lunch on this round, Kent."

Kent smiled with sarcasm. He had never beaten his younger brother in sports, but in the world of politics he ran circles around the relative he'd worked to get appointed to a plum position. "Tit for tat, Ronny. I'll buy lunch and we'll talk about that new task force squirreled away in your budget."

The brothers looked an odd pair as they trudged up to the club house.

Ronny was a handsome man, trim and fit in his mid-forties, and rumored to be involved with a socialite connected to the party machinery. Kent knew about the connection and had even suggested it to the lady in question. If he was going to groom his brother for higher office, this woman would make a much better partner, politically, than Ronny's plain vanilla spouse who managed to birth babies, keep house and do little else. Ronny was pleasant and made friends easily, but had always been missing a few key cells up top. This fault, for Kent did consider it a fault for his sibling to be less than brilliant, was both a plus and a minus. His brother's personality and friendliness would gain him many voters when it came to that, and contributions would be easy to collect. The minus side meant that Kent would have to pull strings to gather the right people around Ronny. After all, someone needed to tell him what to do.

Kent Kraft was the older brother by a decade and purported to be the power behind the throne, or the Senate, depending on which party held the White House. He was a wiry sort and the opposite of Ronny in looks and demeanor. With these characteristics, the senior senator from Kansas easily outmaneuvered more stolid senators and managed to push through a majority of his proposals and block the opposition's. However, he knew he lacked the spit and polish to make a run for higher office, thus the grooming of Ronny at an agency that practically ran itself chasing crooks, yet provided high profile exposure across the nation.

Kent laid out Ronny's budget strategy on a napkin. He drew a simple picture of basic figures his brother could fetch to his staff for action. "Here's the line item, Ronny. Don't worry about the details. Your staff will understand what offices are affected. See this amount on the right? That's the money earmarked, or that the White House wants to earmark, for the task force on computer security. You'll simply direct your people to swap the funds from one fund to another designated for organized crime."

"Swap all of it? Kent, you got to be kidding. I got a call yesterday about that money. Some guy called from OMB and said the president was personally involved in that issue."

"You didn't say how much was allocated did you?"

"Naw, gave him a ballpark estimate though. But my guestimate was close to what you have written there. Pretty good guess I think."

Kent ran his fingers through his balding hair and sought to smooth some back on top to stave off the cold air pouring down from a vent right above their table. Damn this environment. Rooms were either too hot and stuffy, or air conditioning got turned on in the winter by ignorant HVAC people from hell.

"We need those funds over in this other program, Ronny. We have immigrants pouring into major cities and setting up criminal networks. Nobody gives a fig about computer security. Just order your people to move those funds. Do it today, this afternoon. I'll back you in committee hearings. We'll be rid of this guy at 1600 Pennsylvania Avenue in four years anyway."

The National Archives' final budget document landed on the desk of Justin "Smokey" Cole, Chief of the Office of Records Retention. He expected the Executive Officer, Nathan Alsbach, momentarily. Alsbach's staff prepared the budget but Cole had approval control over every dime in it. This authority was not written down in agency directives; it had just evolved over time. Cole's program garnered most of the money parceled out to the minor independent agency, and the historian at the top, Dr. Dalbert Forrester, Archivist, only looked at his own pet projects revolving around Indian treaties in the nineteenth century. Justin Cole knew to put barely enough money in those programs to fund current staff with no promotions. However, his operations—storing millions of cubic feet of rarely referenced old documents— grew steadily year by year and were covered by one humongous line item the Congress rarely questioned.

Nathan Alsbach joined his sponsor, who didn't fail to notice the worry lines creasing the paper pusher's forehead.

"You cleaned out the program we set up last year to provide training to other agencies, JC. What gives?"

"So who's going to complain, Nat? I can show facts, actual numbers, where my programs save money. That's all those bumblers on the Hill care to know about. Jankowski's little money-grabber training program puts on these dog and pony shows and blows hot air, if you ask me. Caroline Jankowski is a pain in the butt, Nat. An attractive pain, but a pain nevertheless. What does that woman know about our mission? If she questions you, tell her the Archivist did it. He won't remember and he couldn't care less about her stupid ideas."

Nat kept silent on this issue. JC didn't bother to hide his dislike of women in general, especially those in management positions. The man never promoted a female above a male if at all possible and Nat knew this unofficial policy had wrecked morale in several programs. Caroline Jankowski had just left his office furious at this last "edit." He was caught in the middle once more, but his loyalty was to JC first. The man ran the agency and had promoted Nat over better qualified men and women who had been in his office much longer.

"We have a request for assistance from the White House, JC. Who do you want to send over there?"

"Our best, Nat. This administration let us know how much the President appreciated that little package our research branch put together. So I'd say choose Marshall in the Disposition branch and let him handpick the rest. But send him through me before he goes over there."

"What about Norton Roscoe? He sent me a formal request again, the fourth one, almost begging to help out the President. The man is an expert in presidential papers."

"Hell no, absolutely not. Look up loose cannon in Webster's and you'll find a picture of Roscoe." JC pointed his index finger to the side of his head and made a circling motion to indicate the expert was daft. "We'll save Norton for some administration we don't like so much, Nat."

"What'll old Dalbert say about this budget shift, JC?"

"Nothing. He'll never see it. Fix a cover sheet that shows the entire amount we're asking for and highlight his little history projects specifically. Mention the rest is for overhead, supplies, you know, stuff like that. He'll sign it then go back to checking out the Trail of Tears, or some such bullshit."

The final budget document was reviewed the following week at an executive staff meeting. Caroline Jankowski trailed her finger down the column of figures for the second time. Her program was not there. Somewhere someone had dropped it. Must have been a mistake, one she'd correct right this moment.

"Dr. Forrester, my training program is missing and needs to be put back in this document. Funds to cover two people are gone. I need that money, Sir."

Dalbert Forrester peered down the table at the tall attractive woman, the only female on his management staff. She was obviously upset and he had no earthly idea what she was talking about. He turned to his executive officer.

"Nat, can you enlighten me about this matter?" Heads turned up and down the thick mahogany table, a gift from the Indonesian Archivist. Those in the know trained their sights on the token female troublemaker. Few dared glance at JC, yet all present understood what he'd done to Caroline's prized initiative.

Nat's voice was unsteady. "Uh, sir, you took out those funds when you signed the budget last week. I believe you said something about the lack of demand for such an outside activity since this was a research facility and we should just let the papers come to us for a decision on their permanency." The professional bureaucrats recognized this euphemistic gobbledygook as a cover the archivist would understand. Forrester chewed on his pipe stem, repacked it with fresh tobacco, relit it and followed the swirling smoke for a moment, keeping everyone in suspense, as if they mattered less than the smoke now dissipating over the high transom of the matching mahogany floor to ceiling door. Forrester blatantly ignored regulations forbidding smoking in all federal buildings. He'd been known to say it was his building and his office.

JC sneered behind steepled fingers, ignoring the resentful look Caroline shot down the conference table. He knew the old fart would cogitate and appear to understand, gain everyone's undivided attention with his ignorant stare at the ceiling, then quash any thoughts the dreary woman ever had of spending their money. There, Forrester rocked forward and fixed Jankowski with a bored, ivory tower glare.

"Waste of money, Caroline. Saw no use for it. I believe we put those funds towards further research, didn't we, Nat?"

"Believe so, Dr. Forrester," Nat began an unrehearsed reply that was interrupted by Caroline Jankowski.

"No you didn't, Nat. I see now the increase went to JC's program, grown larger by exactly the amount of my training funds since I last checked this document. Dr. Forrester, I want that money back. Nat agreed with me only two weeks ago on this." She turned and fixed the floundering executive officer with steady blue eyes. "You know you did, Nat. But we all know who switched the money." Her gaze turned to Justin Cole, who valiantly tried to keep from licking his lips as if his latest canary was the best ever.

"Discussion is over, Caroline. I made my decision and that's final." Dalbert spoke neutrally but his staff knew her arguments were fruitless. JC had won again. Without a political sponsor on the Hill, Caroline would always lose. That was the game, the only game in town. Logic and common sense mattered little. It was who had the connections, the backing, and in this case, a member of Congress willing to argue for a measly amount of money to fund two whole positions. It hardly seemed worth the effort.

Yet Caroline Jankowski was fed up. She had devoted her career to improving government operations. Her outreach programs helped every government office in town and saved millions by streamlining bloated paperwork pipelines. But every time she tried to improve her program by adding a function her customers asked for, she was thwarted by JC. Justin

Cole was the emperor who pulled strings for friends, vendors who received contracts to provide the agency with supplies and services that were eternally overpriced. Each contract held a slice of management oversight that somehow—she was certain of it—ended up back in Justin Cole's own pockets.

Caroline slammed the door to her office. She was the only manager without space on Mahogany Row, the euphemism for top management offices alongside the archivist's executive suite on the main floor. She reasoned she had several options: blow the whistle on JC to the agency's inspector general; sit back and do nothing; or, find a sponsor on Capitol Hill who would back her programs. She had no proof of JC's cozy connections to vendors and didn't have the time or resources to dig out the information. Nat wouldn't cooperate with her anyway, since the man owed his job to Cole. But she was too upset to forget about this trick. It seemed every year the man used some mechanism to steal her funds.

Finding a sponsor seemed the only alternative, and it meant owing her soul to some politician in return for possible failure. Plus, she had nothing to offer in "payment" to such a sponsor. She cursed mentally at the images of the simple maps in every school room showing how a bill went through Congress to become law. Those poor kids had no clue about the shenanigans in this town and their teachers probably didn't either. What did she have to lose? JC had stolen her money and she'd lose sleep and grind her teeth for a month.

Caroline wheeled around to her credenza and opened her Government Organization Manual. It was an updated edition and listed everyone in town in all the federal branches. She needed someone she could talk to, woman to woman preferably. Her search of female members of Congress was short; there weren't many to choose from. Wait, who was this freshman from Virginia? MacMurray, and she was young. Caroline remembered an article in the *Post* about the incoming Members of Congress. Hailey MacMurray had stood out as the only single mother. Caroline grabbed her coat and left the building to catch a cab. She'd wait in the woman's office and beg to be heard.

"Mrs. MacMurray, there's a Mrs. Jankowski from the Archives to see you. She doesn't have an appointment, but your calendar is fairly empty at this late time of the day." Meredith liked the woman instantly and felt sorry for her obvious state of frustration. She could tell by the tone of her voice that this visit was some sort of last gasp. She received the OK from her boss and sent the visitor on in.

"You aren't a lobbyist are you, Mrs. Jankowski?"

"No, not at all, Ma'am. I'm a mid-level manager for the Archives and need to bare my soul. I feel, I'm, uh, oh hell; I've never appealed my case to a member of Congress before. Never, and I know I sound desperate because I am. All my work for the last ten years is being flushed right out of my agency's budget and I'm helpless to stop it. I'm a career civil servant and I came to you for help. I don't know what else to do."

Hailey led the distraught woman to a comfortable chair and invited her to sit and relax. "I have almost an hour before I have to catch the Metro and pick up my son from his after-school program. I'm all ears, and call me Hailey." She liked this woman instantly and saw her as a potential recruit for the Connection.

For the next hour Hailey did what she did best, she listened. Caroline laid out the whole saga in detail. Yes, she responded to one of the few questions Hailey posed, she had statistics, reports and letters commending her staff from agencies all over town. Yes, she saved money. The reports proved it. No, she was not staffed adequately, and had virtually no flexibility to increase service regardless of the increasing demand. When Meredith buzzed to let her know it was time to catch the Metro, Hailey reached into her center drawer and passed a card to Caroline.

"If you like, I'll make you an instant member of our little group. We meet this Tuesday night, seven PM at Senator Conley's at the address on the card. My home phone number is there as well. Yours is exactly the kind of situation we welcome."

Caroline looked up from the card and searched the friendly woman's face. "What do you want in return? I have no connections, no pull whatsoever. I don't even live in your district. Isn't this how the game is played? You scratch my back, I'll return the favor."

"You mean like the good old boy network, Caroline?" Hailey stepped closer to her and grasped her hands gently. "I came here to represent my district. They tell me they want things to be done differently in this town. I don't have sponsors to pay back for anything other than the people who elected me. I promised them I wouldn't work for anybody else. Understand? I'm independent, Caroline. And as of this moment, I work for you."

Tears rolled freely down Caroline's face and Hailey embraced her new friend to let her relief express itself. She was determined to unravel the gnarly network of connections and payback that had prostituted much of public service. But the biggest feeling she had was that here was one small step she could take to begin fixing the system.

Hailey had felt stifled when she learned she'd been assigned to the House Government Operations Sub-committee on Housekeeping. Meredith had reported back from the secretary's grapevine that it was the lowest of the low as far as freshman jobs. Virtually nothing was unsettled before the sub-committee held official appropriations hearings. Committee staff even wrote scripts with allocated questions and their expected answers for members to use.

Now though, her boring assignment to the sub-committee from hell was comical. It was Brer Rabbit being thrown into the briar patch, only this time Hailey held the thorns that would puncture the false budget from the nation's history repository. She observed the three stately executives at the witness table as they droned through their presentation. Caroline had briefed her on these men. The one to watch was Justin Cole. He was a real snake and had an obvious disdain for women. She waited her turn to ask questions, deferring to seniority and protocol. But to her surprise, the chairman brought his gavel down to close the meeting and declared the presentation well and good.

"Excuse me, Mr. Chairman. I have some questions for the gentlemen from the Archives."

"But we've covered all the pertinent issues for this small agency, Mrs. MacMurray."

"Maybe according to your script. But I have some specific areas to ask about that the staff report either ignored or overlooked."

The white-haired southern gentleman from Georgia was in his last term and had never been stopped by such an ignorant disregard for protocol. Yet, she was a rookie. What harm could she do?

"Proceed, Madam."

"Thank you, Mr. Chairman. Mr. Alsbach, where is the funding for assistance to agencies? I don't see it anywhere."

Justin Cole spoke. "It is a minor item and we lumped it into the funding for records retention."

"Tell me how much is there, Mr. Cole, since you seem to be running the show and Mr. Alsbach has lost his voice. No, just a minute. Mr. Alsbach, did you prepare this budget and did you not receive input for programs to provide assistance to other agencies?"

Justin Cole interrupted and spoke for Nat Alsbach. "I repeat, that money is in my—"

Hailey cut him short. "No, it is not. Stop interrupting, Mr. Cole, or should we just invite you to these hearings and ignore the gentlemen who are supposed to be here? What about it, Mr. Alsbach?"

Hailey waited for the man to speak but he sat in silence. She waited a beat and spoke for him.

"Mr. Chairman, committee members, I am passing out a document that demonstrates the value of a program which has been eliminated from the budget of this agency. My analysis of it has been verified by executives from around town and I'll call them as witnesses here in a moment. But in short, these men sitting before us have swapped money from one pot to another to eliminate an invaluable program. Mr. Cole, who seems to be in charge, has the biggest line item and claims to include the supposed funding in with his operations. That is not true. However, I will assent to overlooking this petty maneuver with the presentation of a revised budget that earmarks money specifically for the program I have cited. That revised document should accordingly decrease the funding for Mr. Cole's operations."

Justin Cole was red in the face and shaking with anger. Nat Alsbach had turned a chalk white. That left Dr. Forrester to mutter feebly in response, "The program you speak of is a minor concern to us. But we'll send up a revised document tomorrow for your approval."

However, the current budget document was now in full sunshine. The chairman, who had seemed bored, suddenly became dislodged from years of antipathy, startled at the report Hailey had passed around.

"Hold on, Forrester. It says here, and with documentation from quite a few agencies, that actual millions are saved annually by this outreach operation. MILLIONS, Forrester! How could you let something that important slip away? My God, man, double the amount. And we want to hear from this fellow Jankowski about his work." He turned his craggy face down the table to meet Hailey's beaming smile. "Thank you, Mrs. MacMurray. Good catch."

"Thank you, Mr. Chairman. It's *Mrs.* Jankowski, and I'm sure the archivist will be most pleased to get her up here tomorrow."

The sub-committee did hear from Caroline Jankowski and also from several witnesses representing major agencies. Justin Cole's budget was reduced yet again and the reverberation would hit several long-time vendors where it hurt. Hailey had done more than make a good friend. She had done the people a service. She also recognized that Caroline would have to watch her back. But Hailey vowed to be there for her.

"Tell me how you define this so-called 'Potomac Fever,' Bill." Elizabeth questioned her senator-husband one night after Hailey's meeting had broken up. She was thrilled at Hailey's success on one hand, and was dismayed at the effort it had taken just to set up funding for such a small operation that was doing so much good. When she told Bill about it he said it was just another example of "Potomac Fever," thus her question.

"I have my own theory but it probably isn't too far off the mark. It all has to do with power. Way I see it, there's two kinds of people who come to Washington: those who want power, we'll call them empire builders, and those who want to serve. The first group includes jackasses like that Cole fellow Hailey butted heads with. That man doesn't care if another program in his organization is doing something beneficial. He just wants his program to get bigger and that means a bigger budget. For him that translates into power. He'll take what he can get and the means don't matter.

"There are also people who have a fixation on power and glory in combination. Those people believe they have been called to get to the top of the heap. You can call them delusional because most are. They wait for a signal, an external happening not of their making, that calls them to rise up and run the country. They are certain it is only a matter of time before they'll get a call from the White House to come advise the President, or in the extreme, the people themselves will call them to BE the President.

"This latter group belongs in an institution while the former is more detrimental and becomes a barnacle on the ass of progress. Their reasoning is skewed as well. I once knew of a man who got his position in government by the *sword*. He was a political appointee and the people under him loathed him. Nothing happened that he didn't have his finger in it and he was always there to have his picture taken and of course to gather the credit. In time he believed he was the only person who could serve in that position, even though he had been put there because he contributed to his party generously and ran a shopping mall, thus making him a qualified executive to run part of the government. But, when his president lost he was kicked out and replaced by another man with identical qualifications: party contributor and business manager. The last day he was in office he called his managers into a big auditorium and whined and complained about his unfair treatment and how he had been let go with no regard for his ability to do the job better than anyone. Fortunately for his agency, he died by the same kind of *sword* that had put him there."

"That's a total waste of money, Bill. All this game playing and who does the people's business while these maniacs scratch for power?"

"Fortunately there are three million workers below this political rat pack. People like Caroline Jankowski, who want to do good. Their allegiance is to the Constitution, not to a party platform. Most are smarter than the people above them and they constitute the folks who come to town to serve. But back to Hailey. What she did will circulate and more people like Caroline will surface and seek her out for support. Before long the press will report it and her popularity will extend beyond Virginia."

Eight

The word spread inside the Beltway. Government workers and voters alike learned that certain Members of Congress paid attention when they had a complaint. It made no difference how large or small the problem either. Hailey's Women's Connection became known, as did the maverick senator from Colorado. Their efforts got quick results and proved more effective than official channels of complaint. One example that made the front page of the *Post* and *Times* involved James Buchanan. Mr. Buchanan was not related to the bachelor president preceding Lincoln, but he got more done.

The initial scene in Mr. Buchanan's saga occurred in his agency's human resources office.

"I'm afraid you're between that proverbial rock and a hard place, James." Wilfred Hamilton, expert in employee relations, droned in a monotone voice as if discussing his choices for lunch. "You have been given an order by your supervisor, thus to disobey it would be insubordination, punishable by fine and perhaps severance from government service. However, as you claim, you consider Mr. Crandall's directive illegal, thus following it may perhaps, and I emphasize perhaps, be breaking the law. This infraction would also result in a fine and possible imprisonment. Either way you lose. You have recourse. The Inspector General was appointed to hear complaints like this; however you tell me he hasn't seen fit to give you an appointment. That's absurd and hard to believe, James. The Inspector General position was created for just such a situation as yours. Perhaps you're mistaken."

"There is no *perhaps* to it, Hamilton. Compiling a list of employees with addresses and home phone numbers and providing the list to any outside source is illegal. And you know it. You also know the IG is related to somebody important in town, we won't say the name out loud, but the man is as high as you can go in the upper chamber of Congress. Let's also say that our most capable director depends on this anonymous member of Congress for his lunch money and is trying to raise campaign funds for the next general election for all his buddies." Buchanan stood and raised his voice. "Saying I have recourse is total bullshit, Hamilton. Last year you were a clerk in personnel and somehow you got promoted above people more competent. It happened right after the election results came."

Hamilton stood and raised his voice to match Buchanan's. "Leave my office before I call security and have you thrown out." But he was speaking to the backside of James Buchanan, who slammed the door on his way out.

"Senator, Mr. Buchanan is here." Alice chuckled to herself. The visitor couldn't sit still and no attempt on her part to calm the man down had worked. He didn't want coffee or tea and hadn't even noticed Chrissie standing by the files and sorting papers. That meant this was serious business because everyone noticed Chrissie. She had cautioned the lady her first day on the job to lengthen her skirts and start buttoning her blouse above the ample cleavage. If she had said any more than that then Alice would have stepped over a line. She didn't want an employee grievance. Chrissie was a super worker and Alice couldn't get along without her. She would just ignore the attention the woman collected from all the male visitors to Senator Conley. All males except James Buchanan.

Bill Conley rose to shake hands with the nervous bureaucrat standing in front of his desk. "Mr. Buchanan, welcome. What can I do for you?"

James looked around and nodded at the open door to Alice's outer office, hinting that he'd be more comfortable if that door were shut. Bill got up and shut it, then sat on a sofa joining the man informally to get comfortable. The senator listened as Buchanan dumped his worries in a rehearsed speech that lasted no more than two minutes. He also produced a memorandum from his supervisor documenting the request he'd talked to Wilfred Hamilton about.

Through this revelation Bill Conley said nothing. He was amazed, and pleased really, that people had the guts to come forward. It didn't take an attorney general to determine the memorandum called for an illegal action and that some low-level political appointee had picked on the wrong bureaucrat to execute the illegality.

"Alice," he hollered, forgetting his door was shut. She came anyway.

"Yes, Sir?"

"Alice, could you get me the IG's office over at FBI? I'd like to visit with him if the man is there. Just ask if he's in. I don't want an appointment. Oh, and make me about ten copies of this memo, please. And, Alice, leave the door open. I was watching Chrissie do her filing before." He grinned and laughed out loud as his faithful secretary bristled and left in a huff. He'd pay for it later when Alice tattled on him to Elizabeth, but he enjoyed stepping out of character to razz his secretary.

James turned and looked over his shoulder and finally noticed Chrissie. "Oh my," was all he could say.

Alice was back in a minute. "He's there. Want me to call you a cab?"

"My car is across the street, Sir. I'd be glad to drive you." James was excited and not just about Chrissie, as realization hit that a United States Senator was on his side.

"Fine, let's go. And Alice, fax a copy of this to Dan Roberts over at the *Post*. Tell him to have fun with this and to call me if he has questions. Oh yeah, Mr. Buchanan, give Alice your home phone number. I promise we won't hit you up for a contribution."

The fortress-like FBI building was diagonally across Pennsylvania Avenue from the National Archives. Its location might have been perfect except for the oversight by engineers who constructed the monument to J. Edgar Hoover directly above the underground river that had drained the swamp that had become the District of Columbia. Initial excavation had gone well until the sub-basement level was reached. That's when the river came into play. It no longer drained a swamp, yet persisted in a continual ooze that created havoc for the construction crew. The builders were forced to sink enormous concrete pilings deep into the soggy earth to support the monster crime-fighting institution. Still, decades after its completion, sump pumps operated 24/7. Across the street, archivists joked about this misfortune because there was a permanent pool in their own sub-basement not far from the vault that would protect the original Constitution in case of a nuclear attack.

The guard at the front desk asked Bill Conley for ID. "Sure thing, Sergeant."

He pulled out his Member of Congress identification and showed it to the man who stood immediately.

"Just a minute, Sir, and I'll have someone from the Director's office come escort you."

"No thank you, Sergeant. I'm not here to see Mr. Kraft. My new friend here is showing me his office and he'll be happy to take me up. By the way, Sergeant, all other IG offices are in other buildings to provide employees some form of confidentiality."

"I don't know about that, Sir. This fellow moved here right after Mr. Kraft was appointed."

James Buchanan held up his ID badge and the two men walked into the closest elevator. They got off at the third floor and James proudly led the man he now thought of as his senator to the door of the IG. Both men entered a semi-darkened outer office. It was absent a secretary and anyone waiting to file a complaint.

Bill Conley headed for the inner door and opened it. He found darkness there as well and thought the room empty until two heads popped up from a sofa strategically placed with its back to the door.

"Get the hell out of here immediately! Who told you to come barging into my private office while I was working?" James hung back, chastened by the gruff voice of political power. Senator Conley walked to the light switch by the door and flipped a whole row up, fully illuminating the IG and his secretary, whose afternoon *nap* had been interrupted. Again James turned away, embarrassed at the plight of the poor secretary who had misplaced her skirt and pantyhose. In a panic she grabbed the nearest piece of clothing, the IG's trousers, and wrapped them around her waist. She then fled to the sanctuary of her outer office and on into an adjoining private bathroom.

The IG was a balding man with pudgy love handles. This fact was easily observed because he had somehow lost both his shirt and trousers and wore only a sleeveless undershirt. He retreated behind his massive executive desk as if sitting there would magically instill decorum. Bill Conley took an easy chair, rolled it to the side of the desk, and stared.

"We've come to file a complaint, Mr., uh, Harris." He turned to read the man's nameplate and noticed the absence of a single slip of paper on the surface of the ornate desk. "That is if you're not busy working."

"I can explain everything, Senator—"

"No you can't, Harris. Fucking on government time is against regulations. Fucking up is another matter. And that's why we're here." He slammed a

91

copy of the memo down hard with a resounding slap that made Harris jump back in his chair, then just as quickly, jump forward to gain cover for his lower body parts. "Read that now." The senator's voice sounded more like that of a commanding general giving a direct order that was not to be disobeyed.

Harris fumbled for his glasses in the center drawer of his desk and came up empty. James picked them up from the sofa and delicately handed them over. They were slightly bent and so cockeyed only one eye was provided improved vision at any angle. Harris held the fragile frames up to his face in both hands and perused the memo from hell.

Senator Bill Conley removed his pen and motioned for James Buchanan to approach. "I suggest you write at the bottom of this memo that you are filing a formal complaint to this official and that you are refusing to follow this illegal order. Sign it, date it and hand it to Mr. Harris." James did as he was told. "Mr. Harris, you will sign and date this memo below Mr. Buchanan's signature and note that you have received it." Harris did so with a shaking hand.

"Where's the nearest copier, Harris?" But no sooner had Bill Conley asked the question than James pulled the memo from Harris and walked over to a convenient copier in the corner of the office.

"I'm sure you know that Mr. Buchanan is protected by the Whistle Blower Act, Harris. But if I get one breath of a hint of retribution against him, or you fail to see him on this or any other matter, I'll run you out of town after you've been tarred and feathered by the press. Now, I want to know precisely what you're going to do, and when you are going to act on this matter."

"I will call his supervisor and have him retract this memo, Senator."

Bill Conley inspected the man as if he'd shown up for roll call in the Army without his uniform. "Put on some clothes first. Let's get out of this shit hole, Buchanan."

The *Washington Post's* top political reporter, Dan Roberts, did have fun with the memo. As it turned out, it had been drafted by the Director's office and handed out to every component at FBI headquarters, not just to James Buchanan. Senator Conley reported the ignominious IG's actions to the reporter and let the fur fly. He was thoroughly disgusted with the man and followed up until both Harris and his willing secretary left government employ. Their exit was sped up by a local tabloid photograph showing the couple cozying up at a local restaurant.

The floodgates opened with this publicity. Civil servants began to step forward from other agencies, all with copies of similar memos. The rout was on and the current administration fell into damage containment mode. Senator Conley became known as the man who took problems head on. He did this for voters in Colorado and for anyone who stepped forward to identify where their government had taken a wrong turn. As he performed these tasks, the word spread that this man worked for the people. Bill Conley had become a statesman.

Many of his informers sought confidentiality in the form of large brown envelopes stuffed with inside information. Thus, he was always kept informed as much as he'd been running a spy network.

Hailey followed his example, however with a woman's perspective. Much of her network was the group of women known to the members as the Women's Connection. Outsiders, those who had become deserved targets for charges of gross malfeasance in office, referred to her members as "angels of death." Those individuals and groups who sought relief said the ladies were "avenging angels."

Nine

That summer the mid-term election campaign began for Hailey. She was getting a late start because there was just too much work to do. Her constituents were letting her know via mail, email, and phone calls that she was appreciated. Still, she had to get back out there and campaign, and that took energy. And money. By the middle of July Hailey had neither, so she drove home to Blue Ridge to rest and think of a way to get reelected. First though, she'd go to the Willows and see how Marie was doing.

The appearance of the nursing home was greatly improved and she had to thank Wendy Tucker, the administrator, for that. The grounds had been landscaped and a walking path curled through flower gardens. Dogwoods and crepe myrtle trees were scattered about, giving a fresh perspective to the once drab "old folks home," as the community was used to calling it. But no more. Today, Hailey appreciated the repaired front porch, screened and locked for the safety of the residents. New storm windows cut down on utility bills and the outside had been painted a crisp white with rust-brown trim.

Hailey punched in the access code to the porch door and walked inside. The cookie lady must have baked a fresh batch, she noted, as the heavenly scent of baked cookies wafted down the hall. Before Hailey got too far, Wendy came out to greet her.

"Morning, Congresswoman MacMurray. It's an honor to have you with us today." Wendy was nothing if not prudently professional.

"Hi, Wendy. Please knock off that formal stuff. We've known each other since junior high. I'm the same person who pulled you into the deep end of the pool not knowing you couldn't swim. Now say after me, 'What's up, Hailey?'"

Wendy laughed. "OK, I'm just so thrilled at your success. What's up, Hailey?"

"I'm home from the big city and came to see your place. Wendy, you have really turned the Willows around. It is gorgeous. I like the new carpeting and the little rooms with different stores depicting the main street of an early twentieth century small town." The women strolled down the Willows' Main Street and Hailey scanned the entryways to a library, a post office, an old fashioned ice cream parlor, and an exercise room. Each small room was furnished with comfortable chairs and sofas where relatives could visit with residents. Wall coverings, paintings, and knick knacks reminded Hailey of life as it was decades ago when most of these residents were growing up. She also passed by a small theater where residents could watch TV or see a movie.

"Thanks, Hailey. We really owe it all to your initiative to let us spend that trust fund money. Plus, much of the labor was donated by craftsmen and small businesses around town. It was really a super community effort. Ok, now, here comes Marie. Be prepared for anything."

Hailey watched a gray haired little woman shuffling down the hall behind an aluminum walker. She stopped at the cookie lady's station and took the warm cookie with relish and chewed it like it was the first time she had eaten one. With half the tasty morsel gone, Marie wrapped the remainder in a tissue and slid it into her dress pocket. This task complete, she began her journey towards Hailey and Wendy. When she was about five feet away, Marie pulled back on her walker like she was guiding a horse-drawn buggy. She peered at Hailey through thick lenses and her eyes scanned every facial feature over and over.

"Aunt Louise, is that you? Lord what a pleasant surprise."

"No, Marie," Hailey said. "Aunt Louise died long ago."

"Oh my heavens. No. Tell me it isn't so. Oh child. Mercy sakes." The little woman appeared to shrink in size and she felt for the tissue in her pocket to wipe eyes freshly grieving for Aunt Louise. The cookie dropped to the floor and she quickly bent to pick it up. Her grief forgotten she smiled at the delicious morsel as if it had never been seen and gobbled it up. Then her head turned once again to Hailey and she stared as before.

Recognition lit her face. "Janey, I knew you'd come to see me. Gracious, honey. How have you been?"

"Marie, Janey is dead too," Hailey said. Identical shock registered again and Marie was plunged deep into grief.

"This is too much. Oh my." She searched her pockets for another tissue and parts of another cookie from days past crumbled to the floor. This she ignored. Suddenly angry, Marie turned her walker around and shuffled down the hall. Hailey was crestfallen and her eyes filled with tears. Wendy pulled her into an office off the main hall.

"Sit down, Hailey. Have a cup of hot tea and let me explain a few things to you." Wendy efficiently poured hot water and steeped the tea, taking her time to allow her friend to collect herself. "Here, sip on this and listen to me for a bit." Wendy slid her chair closer to Hailey and patted her arm. "This is the way Marie is now. She is in no pain and if she does get hurt the pain is forgotten almost before we can give her medication for it. Her mind slips from one memory to another, one decade or generation to another, and, as you just saw, from one person to another. Don't feel bad. Many folks here do the same thing. They have no control over the memories that pop up from the recesses of their minds."

Hailey sniffled and wiped her nose. "This has progressed so fast, Wendy. I wasn't prepared for what just happened. I've been away too long. Tell me how to deal with this, please."

"Next time accept where she is and go with it. Don't try to bring her up to the present by telling her all these people are long gone. I guarantee you she'll suffer grief anew as if it were the first time she has ever heard of a loved one's passing. Introduce yourself and make sure she understands who you are. Sometimes she'll understand it's you and there may be a short spell in which you two can talk about old times. Then again, she may not remember or recognize you at all. Also, don't feel guilty about taking a long time between visits. Most relatives are so depressed and saddened when their parents get like this they don't come back except when it's time to bury them."

"Where did she get those gigantic glasses? Her eyesight has always been perfect."

"Borrowed them from another resident," Wendy replied with a smile. "They go into each other's rooms, take a nap in the wrong bed, put on clothes belonging to someone else, and wear glasses they never needed, or lose the ones they rely on. It really gets funny sometimes. We have to take their jewelry before they wrap it into tissues like Marie did to her cookies, and next thing you know they flush the tissues down the toilet." Wendy paused to see if her friend was getting in a better humor before she dropped her next bombshell.

"Marie has a boyfriend. She claims he's her first husband and they are so cute when they walk side by side and hold hands."

"That's rich. Marie was married to Adam right out of high school and never even dated another soul. They were so close you never saw one without the other."

"Well don't be surprised if she tells you about Edward and her children. She says she has two boys and two girls and they all moved away last year."

"Marie and Adam never had children until they adopted me, Wendy. She sounds schizophrenic, like she has two different lives and one is a fantasy.

"Could be. We'll never know. How could a psychiatrist ever talk to her?" Wendy stood and drew Hailey up with her. "I suggest you come again in a few days. This has been a shock and I can see it on your face. Take some time to deal with your feelings. Be prepared next visit to go with the flow. And remember, she is secure here. She's not going anywhere and the bad stuff is forgotten almost immediately."

Sara appeared at the front door Saturday morning looking sheepish. "Can I come in and chat, Hailey?"

"Sure, come on down the hall and have some coffee." Hailey sensed trouble and decided to relieve her friend right away. The two women sat across the kitchen table and Hailey interrupted what must have been a difficult speech keeping Sara awake most of the night in its preparation.

"I don't expect you to be my campaign manager, Sara. It's too much work for a working mother, and you really went out of your way last time."

Sara slumped in relief. "You are a special lady, Hailey. Thanks for rescuing me from saying that. Joe and I talked last night and I was plain worried sick. You need help, the professional kind this go-around. Both parties are running candidates against you, two slick lawyers who are rich, good looking, and married with the requisite two point three kids and so on. Other words, they look great and have big bucks paying for TV time. I can't compete with that."

"Not your problem, Sara. Now tell me about those twins." The two friends chatted for an hour and Sara left to spend a relaxing weekend with her family. Hailey checked the *Roanoke Times* and got a front page look at her opponents.

They were from solid Virginia stock, having names like Raleigh Comstock and Randolph Macon. Virginia families had a penchant for giving a poor child two last names, taking a variety of middle and last names from both sides. She couldn't argue with the practice, since her own name was a mix of the Pittsburgh MacMurrays and the Virginia Haileys. But where they'd gone off to she had no clue.

Hailey grimaced as she read the brief campaign platforms of the two men. Every word was straight national party proclamations, but each man had tailored his campaign slogan to fire a warning shot directly at her. Both men promised to work full time for Virginians and let their wives take care of their kids. *Here we go with more family values and many irrational arguments why single moms had best stay home.* Would people ever get over this bump in the road? Would she?

She and Adam played hermit the rest of that weekend. He was content to watch some videos and sleep, claiming his school schedule was tiresome. Hailey could only sigh at his minor gripe. The boy had boundless energy and had friends all over Northern Virginia. She drove him to school in the mornings. When school was over, Adam went home with friends and called his mother to let her know where she could pick him up. Although this freed Hailey so she could work longer hours in the House, it was making her still-very-young son gain more independence. But he thrived on it, until today. There had to be another reason. Her mind drifted to so many thoughts she was unable to focus. That told her she needed to take a nap too. She pulled a blanket over her and fell asleep on the family room sofa.

A door opened in the kitchen. She startled from sleep, disoriented. Where was the noise? Had someone come into the house? Now her supposed thief was rummaging in the fridge moving bottles and packages, opening the crisper, checking the freezer. Hailey tiptoed to the doorway and peeked around the corner. Her thief was only a little boy with an armload of food desperately trying to close the door without dropping anything. Growth spurt! That's it. Her son was eating more and sleeping more because he was suddenly blooming into a big boy, transitioning from little boy status.

Mother and son shared a snack. Hailey nibbled on an apple while Adam downed an apple, a banana, a piece of chocolate pie, and two glasses of milk. Where did it all go, she wondered? But he wasn't through. The fridge door opened again and he removed the leftover macaroni and cheese and a can of soda. He retrieved a large serving spoon and piled three dollops of the macaroni and cheese onto a dish and brought that and his soda back to the table. There he spooned the food into his mouth and swallowed some soda as a chaser.

"Don't you heat that up? It must taste awful cold."

Adam chewed like a cow lazily working on her cud out in a pasture and threw his mother a funny look. He slurped more soda and cleared his throat to answer her. "It's better this way, Mom. It's a great combo. Eddie eats it like this when I go to his house. Only his mom cooks it an old fashioned way with lots of chunks of cheese in with the noodles. She doesn't use a box like you do." He didn't notice her smile fade and went back to devouring calories only two hours before supper time.

Brother, what to do? It looked like she needed a campaign manager and a cook. Or she could get up earlier and prepare their supper before leaving for work. Or go out to eat more. Or, or, or. Guilt hung over her like Shenandoah Valley fog. She needed to solve at least one problem this weekend, or drift and feel useless.

Hailey stood and Adam looked up. "Get your shoes on, we're going shopping." This was an every aisle trip and she let Adam do most of the choosing just to see where his appetite led them. They stayed in the fresh fruit section longer than anywhere else and that pleased her. Neither had made a habit of chips and sugary junk food. Next he pointed to broccoli and cauliflower and the host of fresh veggies undergoing a thunderstorm from their overhead sprinklers. More good choices. Milk was next and he pulled out two gallons. Fish, steaks, chicken and pork chops made it into the burgeoning cart. Then he reversed course and headed for the bakery section. His timing was perfect, as the store's baker was unloading fresh containers of oatmeal raisin cookies. Adam tossed a package into the cart and beamed at his mom.

"That should do us for tonight. Geez this was fun, Mom. Next time just send me down here with a list and I'll do the shopping." Hailey reached for him and hugged him tenaciously. She kissed the top of his head that almost came to her shoulders. How she loved this child. He was all hers and quite happy with how they lived. Her guilt forgotten, she could only think of the hours, days, weeks and years they had been constant companions doing everything together. So what if she used a box for stupid old macaroni and cheese?

Back home they found company for supper. Katlyn Arnold, the intrepid public TV journalist, was sitting on their front porch rocking and fanning her bright red curls, trying to keep cool. Hailey was delighted to see her after her months struggling in Washington. Each had gone separate ways right after the election and Hailey had lost sight of her main streeting partner.

The two women hugged. "Hey, lady, come eat supper with us. Adam, go fire up the grill, we're putting on the dog tonight."

Both women were done and sat in stunned amazement as Adam finished pieces of their steaks and gobbled his fourth ear of corn.

"If I ate like that I'd be a cow, Hailey. Where does it go?"

"He's been like this since early April, Katlyn. Eats like it'll be his last meal. Today I let him shop and he bought food to last me a month and for him maybe a few days. He is the biggest kid in his class and getting into an awkward stage. His body can't keep up with his brain and he's always tripping and stumbling over things. Check out his feet. Adult size 9! One more than his age."

Adam wiped the vestiges of corn from his face and looked up at his examiners evaluating his eating habits. "Can I go to Jack's house, Mom? His mom made lemon custard pie this afternoon."

"Go and take these dishes to the kitchen on the way." The boy started piling plates and Hailey put a hand on his arm. "Don't make yourself sick eating pie, and wait to be asked, OK? Also, be home by nine and stay out of the fields back of their house." Mother and son exchanged a solemn look. Then he hugged her around the neck and took off.

Hailey sighed and shook her head. "His friend Jack introduced him to smoking last week. They rolled rabbit tobacco and took turns puffing, making them both sick. Adam came home and threw up most of the night and vowed not to smoke anything the rest of his life."

"Looks like something bad turned out to be a worthwhile learning experience," Katlyn said. "But now that he's gone off to devour your neighbor's food, I want to pass an idea by you." The take-charge journalist seemed nervous around her good friend and took a sip of iced tea as if to gain courage before continuing. "I have developed a network of friends and colleagues since I documented your last campaign. The series we did on your main streeting was quite a success, and won me a full time job at the public TV station. It also gained me access to channels of communication that have proved very interesting." Katlyn peered directly into Hailey's eyes and waited for her reaction.

"That's wonderful for you, Katlyn. I knew you had a talent for this business. I get letters and email all the time about the series. It did me lots of good, that's for sure. What's your next step, heading up the ladder for a bigger market? Is a major network offering you a position?"

"Actually, I just quit, at least temporarily. You see, I had this idea of going to work for a good friend of mine who needs my kind of expertise. The station let me take a leave of absence until right after Christmas. Or, if this friend won't bite on my suggestion, then I'll go back to producing videos."

"It must be nice to have that kind of flexibility with your boss. Is this other offer a better paying job?"

"There is no salary, Hailey. I'm doing it gratis except for the need for a place to sleep since I would no longer be able to afford my studio apartment back in Roanoke. The last time I looked, this friend of mine had a spare bedroom facing the street, she had a child eating her out of her house and needed a part-time cook as well as a campaign manager/publicist/fund raiser. She also had no time to campaign for reelection because she put all her time into that precious child and serving her constituents." Katlyn drew breath and let it out slowly. "So what do you say? All we need is another phone line to the bedroom and I can work from there. I'll do a web site, set up a contribution account at the bank, network to all those connections I bragged about, the works. Once you win, I'll go back to my day job at the station being held open for me by a woman who tells me she knows the genuine article when she sees it and she thinks quite highly of you."

Hailey cried and didn't bother to wipe the tears. She hugged her new campaign manager, her shoulders shaking with emotion. She sat back and opened up to Katlyn.

"It gets so very hard being single and doing all this. Thank you, thank you. But I have to pay you something. Geez, I haven't even asked anybody for money to run a campaign. There is just so much to do and I feel like I'm losing touch with my son some days. Then today we went grocery shopping and I knew whatever I'd done had been right and good. But you, oh, Katlyn. You're saving my bacon." Hailey stood and hugged the chunky redhead again. "Let's go check out your campaign headquarters. And there are two bedrooms, not one, but there is a door between them."

Katlyn moved in right away and set up a campaign to match the values of her new employer. Those values matched the ones used by Senator Conley in his successful bid for the senate. Voters still liked and appreciated Hailey for owing no one except them. Like Senator Conley, her limit was ten bucks per family or corporation. Her positions on every major issue in the Congress were published and distributed to Katlyn's network of media connections, and posted on her web site. Katlyn had transcribed her notes from the main streeting documentary and sent contact letters to key people Hailey had met along the way. The Radford University students were reconnected and they began another "get out the vote" campaign. Hailey's own Women's Connection gave her free publicity via interviews and press releases. Soon, public service announcements popped up throughout Hailey's district and a trickle of money began to flow. Public Television aired segments of Katlyn's documentary. Katlyn's old boss sent free tapes to the major TV stations that ran abbreviated segments as news bites about Hailey.

But her opponents were well-funded and generated big profits for the networks with expensive political ads. Most attacked Hailey as unfit to parent and represent the voters. Reporters quizzed her at impromptu press conferences after her renewed main streeting visits.

Reporter: Is it true you send your child to school and don't see him until late in the evening as Mr. Comstock has charged?

Hailey: No.

Reporter: Care to elaborate on that Mrs. MacMurray?

Hailey: I take Adam to school and he attends after-school activities with friends, then goes to their house before coming home. I see him around supper time after I pick him up. We sleep in the same house every night and are together all weekend. Is that sufficient?

Reporter: Why have you not remarried and provided a father for your son? To quote Mr. Macon directly, 'It is a woman's duty to find a suitable mate to build a strong family with strong family values.'

Hailey: My campaign manager has given the press the numbers for the amount of correspondence I have received questioning my so-called inability to provide a father for my son. It is fair to say that I get a hundred letters a week and perhaps one of those asks that question. I tell those constituents the right man hasn't come along. Many men are only interested in me and shy away when they realize I am a mother. Others are interested in nothing beyond one night, if you get my meaning. And to answer your next question and save you the embarrassment of asking it, I do not have sleepovers with my infrequent dates. Frankly, I do not have them anytime, anywhere.

Reporter: Have you had any serious relationships that have come close to being the right man?

Hailey: Do you have a single question that relates to this campaign?

Reporter: Mr. Comstock did wonder about your stance on abortion, seeing as how you believe in women choosing what to do and all. Care to comment?

The same tired questions abounded, and Hailey struggled to keep her sense of humor. Each town, each community read the local papers and asked the same things. But she needn't have worried. Her opponents were busy shooting their own feet. Comstock had ties to several defense contractors and couldn't give valid answers to questions about his law firm having lobbied for said contractors. His campaign treasury was audited and donations exceeding federal limits for corporations were widely reported. He dropped too many points in the polls to remain a serious threat.

Macon, it turned out, was married to his third wife and didn't have a good record of making regular child support payments to the previous two Mrs. Macons. His arguments about Hailey's family values were forgotten. But the debate with all three candidates was the icing on the cake. Hailey answered all questions related to foreign policy, those directed at her, and at her opponents who weren't sure of their party's stance on Russia, China and the United Nations. Macon vowed to get the United States out of the United Nations as his first act upon being sworn in. Comstock vowed he'd vote against allowing China into the United Nations, then stumbled to recover when informed that decision had already been taken.

On domestic policy, Hailey's opponents demurred to party line, and vowed allegiance to whatever their caucuses allowed. They became known as the bobble-head duo as each nodded to the wisdom of a committee of campaign contributors no one in southwestern Virginia knew. Hailey had specific recommendations on health care, Social Security and education, based on what the voters told her during main streeting. She acknowledged being unaware of the specifics of the major parties; but scored kudos for stating political party positions were irrelevant; it was the mood and will of Virginians, especially those in her district that mattered most. The polls taken immediately after the debate showed her judgment, relying on her constituent's feelings and needs, counted.

The polls were also a reflection of the ability of one child to make a difference. Katlyn received calls the following morning after the debate, congratulating her on a masterful stroke of campaigning based on the appearance of Adam on the stage with his mother. Both mother and campaign manager did their best to keep the boy out of the news but they couldn't keep him from running to Hailey before the cameras clicked off and hugging her, then turning to the two challengers and shaking their hands and the hands of their wives and children. It was a lesson in manners and courtesy no viewer would forget on Election Day.

Hailey received a majority of the votes and retained her seat in Congress. After receiving calls from Comstock and Macon conceding defeat, she asked Katlyn to join her in the family room.

"Dear friend, thank you for pulling this election out of the fire for me. I'm really grateful."

Katlyn beamed with success and accomplishment. "I did it for Virginia, Hailey. This state needs you. Heck, the country needs you. Next stop, the White House!"

"Whoa, not so fast. I need something else first. Now listen carefully to my proposition. I called Meredith right after you came to live with us and work gratis. I told her what you were doing and asked her to check into my administrative budget. Well, it turns out I have money for an assistant job if you want it. You can work in Roanoke in my district office or Washington, or switch back and forth as the need arises. The pay is pretty good; those staffers on Capitol Hill must have a good union."

The fiery redhead's eyes glistened and for once she was speechless. All she could do was sit up straight and pat her breastbone with both hands, vainly trying to breathe in and out.

"I take that as a yes," Hailey said with a chuckle. "And I have one other recommendation. There is room in my condo in northern Virginia for you to stay. Again, the deal is the same. Free room and board; cost of living is high in the DC megalopolis. You'd just have to help cook now and then. If you decide you need more space and privacy for your raging love life," she paused and both women rolled their eyes, neither had gone out socially with a man in months, "then you'll at least have food and shelter to help you transition to the big show."

"You're a good person, Hailey MacMurray. Thank you, and yes to both offers. I'd love to commute occasionally and I'll keep a lookout for some eligible fellows."

Hailey had promised Adam she'd take him to visit Marie, and Katlyn was invited along too, but without her camera. She made it clear the Willows and Marie Knowles were off limits.

As before, Marie shuffled down the hall and pulled up short when she spied them. But her attention stayed on Adam and her face was all smiles.

"Come here, child. It's so good to see you again. My how you've grown."

Adam looked to his mother for guidance and she nudged him forward to greet his grandmother. "Hello, Grandma, it's me, Adam. You look pretty good today all dressed up."

"Yes, I know you, Adam. Couldn't forget my precious baby boy. Come on with me and I'll get you a treat." She placed his hand on the top of her walker and led him off to the cookie lady. Hailey and Katlyn stayed behind. Katlyn turned to ask Hailey a question and saw tears flowing freely down both cheeks.

"What's wrong, Hailey? She knew him right off. She seems to be OK to me." But then Hailey recounted her first visit just weeks ago and Katlyn began to understand why this subject was off limits.

"It's OK for you to know about Marie, Katlyn. Just keep it confidential. The public has no need to know she has Alzheimer's. One minute she knows me, then another time she is lost in another world."

Hailey wandered down the hall to join Adam and Marie while Wendy Tucker gave Katlyn a short tour of the facility. The journalism graduate was curious about everything and anything to do with Hailey MacMurray. Ideas were beginning to form in the back of her mind as to what use she could make of her documentary on main streeting.

The voters reelected Hailey during the middle of the new pro football season. Adam continued going to games with his Uncle Burch and they visited with Mark and Jason after each game. The season was going well. It looked like the Redskins would have a winning record, and perhaps make the playoffs for the first time in several years. Their rebuilding program was working, and the Cramer to Daniel combo led the league in passing. However, Hailey turned down Burch Magnum's invitations to the games so she could work for her constituents and strengthen the Women's Connection.

Adam decided to act on his own. He waited until the last regular season game to do it, on a Sunday morning before his honorary uncle would pick him up to ride to the stadium. "Mom, can I have one of those pictures Aunt Katlyn took for your campaign posters? You know, the one where you're at a barbecue over near Radford wearing shorts and your hair is kind of blowing away from your face and you look really good."

Hailey stopped with her coffee cup in mid air and set it down. "Are you kidding me? I must have packed them up or Katlyn has them stashed in her room. Go ask her. No, wait. What did you want with it? This isn't another show and tell with your friends at school is it? Like, check out my mom, the hot chick in Congress and all that?"

He had practiced his response to this exact question and kept his eyes on his mom's. "No, a good friend asked me for it. You know about Mark Daniel the football player, the one you promised to meet after a game and never had time to do." Neither mother nor son had used guilt before to get something from each other and Adam knew this was stepping over the line. But he had calculated for several nights about how to do this, and his mother was delivering a deep sigh now that proved he'd figured correctly.

"OK, sure you can have a copy, but you'll have to find it."

Adam brought his right hand from behind his back with the photo and held a black marker in his left hand. "Just say, 'To my friend, Mark. For being a good sport.'"

Hailey shot her conniving son a shrewd look that meant this was a first and last opportunity and he'd better not try this technique again. Then she caught the look in his eyes and changed her expression to love and concern. Adam could not conceal his feelings about how important this photo was.

"You must really like this fellow, honey."

"He's a super guy, Mom. He leads the team and encourages everybody,

106

even me. He's my friend."

This was something new. Mother and son understood instinctively that Mark Daniel was not one of those typical fellows who flitted in and out of their lives on a whim. Hailey wrote the prescribed greeting and added her own words to thank the football player for being a good friend to her son. Still, she wished he'd picked out a photo where she had worn more clothes.

Burch Magnum looked at his young friend with pride. The boy was so likable and was obviously taken with the big football player who was shucking off his game uniform and answering the same withering questions from the sports reporters. Mark Daniel was sincere in his friendship with Adam. Burch was positive about this or he'd have stopped bringing the lad down to the locker room last season. He also struggled to keep from laughing as Adam played out the final scene in his little charade. This occurred when the final question was asked and answered.

"Hey, Mark. Good game today. Where do you guys play next week?" Adam shook hands with his hero and with Jason Cramer, who had set a new record for touchdown passes.

"Hey yourself, Adam. Looks like either Chicago or St. Louis. Our record is not good enough to get home field advantage, so you'll have to catch us on TV from now on. But here's the photo your mom asked for." Mark rummaged into his cluttered locker and pulled out a manila envelope. He handed it to Adam and received in exchange an envelope with the boy's 8X10 black and white of his mother at the barbecue.

Jason said, "Open it, Daniel. Don't keep us in suspense. The team has money riding on this."

"OK, big mouth. Don't pay any attention to that blabbermouth, Adam. He's betting your mom is a fuddy duddy in a gray suit like the other members of Congress. Oops, sorry, Senator." Burch gave his friend a slap on the shoulder, indicating all was forgiven.

Mark slid the photo out as if it were made of fragile material that would disintegrate when exposed to air. Adam stood back grinning as other players crowded around the big tight end's locker to get a peek at his mom.

"Pay up, Cramer. Adam, your mother is beautiful." But Mark had to hold on to the picture as teammates tried to take it and get a better close-up view. "Back off, guys." Whistles fluttered around the room as Mark held the photo up for long distance viewing. Adam beamed with pride as all the players admired his mother. But he only cared about one of them. It was just too bad there were no more home games.

The crowd had left. Mark and Jason lingered, to share a peaceful moment, letting the air finish drying them after their showers.

"Call her up, Mark. You want to, I can tell."

"I don't know. It is tempting, but she probably has guys asking her out all the time: diplomats, politicians, fancy lawyers, Members of Congress. I can't compete with those guys."

"You're just chicken, buddy. She asked for your photo and even signed hers with a nice little friendly note as your friend. Hell, you're already to first base."

"You know that's not what I want, Jason. You can tell the boy is first class and he gets it from his mom. She would not go for some guy messing around without a commitment. Look at the boy. I can tell he is her universe and I'll bet you another twenty he rigged this whole deal. No, I'm not ready. Maybe next year. We have to focus about playing the Bears in Chicago for the first round of the playoffs."

"Here's your photo, Mom." The boy stepped back and took a deep breath. It was exactly like he'd ordered: Mark Daniel in normal street clothes. How else would his mom see what the guy really looked like? He waited for her reaction and kept his fingers crossed behind his back. But she said nothing, just stared. Finally she smiled and gathered him into a fierce hug.

"He's a nice man, honey. Did the locker room get a kick out of my picture?"

"Oh no, Mom." But his cheeks burned and he was caught. "OK, some guys whistled and Jason Cramer lost a bet with Mark, but he did say you were beautiful, and you are."

"Thanks, honey. I love you. Are you going to continue playing match-maker and set me up with a date?" Her joke was misinterpreted though as Adam's eyes went wide with expectation. That was what he wanted. She knew. "Come sit with me a minute." They sat on the sofa in the family room and held hands.

"Do you want me to find you a new dad, Adam? Are you lonely?"

He took his time answering and seemed to be considering a wealth of input. "That's not it, exactly. I like Mark. He's my friend and he treats me like I'm a grown up. He doesn't talk down to me and listens when I make suggestions about football. He, he's just my friend and I thought, well, you know, I hear you always telling reporters and Aunt Katlyn that the guys you've gone out with always shied away when they heard about me and they were only interested in you for one night." Mother and son both blushed: Adam for venturing onto an adult topic; Hailey for ever replying to a reporter in such a fashion.

Hailey recovered first. "OK, if he calls me I'll agree to go out with him. But he has to call. I'm old fashioned that way."

Her son wrapped his arms around her neck; his ultimate dream had surged into its second act. Then he sat back into the cushions and got a sheepish grin on his face. "Mom, I hate to bring it up, but, uh, it's time to have the talk."

"What talk is that, Adam?" But she had a good guess in mind.

"You know, talk about all that stuff guys do with women and such. Talk about things like what those guys wanted just for one night with you." He rushed on before she could object. "It's a goal at school. We all have to ask our parents about it before school is out next summer."

"A goal at school? How old are you, buster? Eight, eighteen, twenty-eight? And who came up with this goal? Not you I hope."

"I'm almost nine and Jack told me some things last summer but he didn't make much sense and then the kids in my class are always snickering about it. So please tell me and I promise I won't do any of it."

Mother and son huddled around a book that evening. Hailey had to thank Elizabeth Conley for lending it to her. Pictures did speak a thousand words and Bill Conley had gone through this with four boys already and his daughter had delivered twins. So Elizabeth reckoned Hailey had better use for the book now. And she was right. Yet Hailey doubted the Conleys ever had the same kind of discussion that followed with Adam.

"So you and Dad made love and that made me?"

"Yes, we did. And then we got married, which is kind of backwards from how it ought to be, and that fact is our family business."

An innocent one, the next question was logical although too personal at any age. "Did you make love with other guys after Dad got killed?"

Her son was without guile and Hailey felt her heart tug. "No, never, honey. Some people do. I never felt close enough and I was truthful when I told those reporters about the men I'd dated. And furthermore, that's not an appropriate question for you to ask at any age, to anyone, especially your mother."

But he had more questions. "Did you ever want to?"

"Time's up. Go finish your homework. Come back to me in another ten years and I'll answer more questions, Mr. Curiosity."

Ten

Above the Kazakhstan/China border: One year into Hailey's second term.

Captain Mikhail Federov felt the sleek new prototype jet fighter shudder. This was bad news. He'd taken the jet up to test its stability over the Himalayan Ranges south of Novosibirsk and had found it wanting. In clear air the plane was a smooth ride, yet the dangerous turbulence over the highest mountain peaks in the world befuddled it. And now he was in serious trouble. Not only was the plane functioning poorly, but he had inadvertently flown first into Kazakhstan airspace and now teetered just over the bristly Chinese border.

The tipsy jet jerked and this time not from a faulty steering mechanism. The Chinese were firing on him as the plane plummeted to the ground. The experienced Russian pilot had two choices: he could put the plane into a suicidal dive and eject, or try to land and explain everything in a language he never understood. That is, try to explain if he could land safely.

Her nightmare recurred: Her hands are clenched, knuckles white on the witness table. Her long chestnut hair hangs over both shoulders of her modest business suit. Her knees are pressed together so hard they ache. She holds her head up ready to face the onslaught of questions from the Supreme Court Justices. Her robed accusers are all dour-faced men. Women justices had been barred, yet another constant in this nightmare beyond her control. Worse is the first-time allowance of cameras in the chambers of this private institution. Her life may be ruined by the unprecedented proceeding, but she had sworn an oath to uphold the Constitution. Darn it, she has worked hard for this, harder than most people. Many thought her beautiful, yet those also wonder how she could be smart enough to do, what? Any job? This job?

The Chief Justice and his male cohorts leer down. He begins the questioning arrogantly in a strident voice, thundering with disapproval. The scene is straight from tea with the queen and the Mad Hatter.

"You're just a pretty face, young lady. What makes you think you can do a man's job?"

Her answer is childish, Alice tumbling into a hazardous wonderland. "I'm a smart person, Sir. Really I am." Her voice sticks in her throat. There is no glass of water and no microphone.

"Preposterous! You can't expect us to believe that?" Then the questions become extraordinary.

"Why did you kill your husband?"

"How many men have you taken to bed?"

Applause rings down from the gallery. In her dream she thinks, *Gallery? When did the Supreme Court add a gallery? Wasn't that in the Capitol Building across the street? Why were spectators allowed?* But the absurd questions continue, stripping her pride. Her head sinks lower with each innuendo, each accusation posed without recourse.

"Who did you sleep with to get elected?"

"Where did the trust fund money go?"

Before she can frame an answer to these false accusations the gavel slams down. The verdict is always the same.

"Guilty as charged of high crimes and misdemeanors. Bailiff, take her away."

Murmurs from the audience are a self-fulfilling prophecy:

"Too good to be true."

"Knew there was something fishy about her."

"Too perfect if you ask me."

"Uppity female."

Hailey found herself in a small cell. But this time her twisting anguish over the unfair Supreme Court debacle was interrupted by the jangling phone beside her. It had to be early. She checked her radio clock and noted that it was to be 3:15 AM.

"Hello," a yawn broke her angry reply to what must be a crank call about her refrigerator running away again. Adam's friends had discovered telemarketing and his number was one of their favorites.

But an old friend was calling for help. "Hailey, this is Charles Morgan. I'm very sorry to bother you, but we need your help." Charles, her old mentor from Moscow, was the current Secretary of State and the only bright spot in an otherwise dismal administration.

She swung her legs off the bed and planted her feet to the floor. "Ok, I think I'm awake enough to understand you, Charles. What's going on?"

The United States Secretary of State described the latest international incident involving a Russian jet getting shot down over Urumqi, China. "I offered to broker the negotiations, Hailey. It's a good opportunity to settle a testy dispute and make friends simultaneously. I also had you in mind when I made the offer."

"Just great, Charles. And how do you expect a representative from little old Blue Ridge, Virginia to solve an international dispute between two countries chomping at the bit to tear into each other?"

"An old flame of yours happens to be involved, Hailey. Remember Anatoly Tushenko, the gallant young diplomat? He wanted to show you his private dacha on the river front one night, but you had to relieve your sitter. I believe you said he had been interested until the boy was mentioned and then rushed off to apparently forgotten last minute meetings."

She remembered too well. Anatoly had called to apologize the next day. He was an anomaly as a Russian diplomat; he spoke only Russian. Yes, she remembered. Things had gone well that evening...up to a point. It was a good thing the French weren't involved. Henri would not be inclined to negotiate after she nearly broke his finger.

"Can you come down to my office and let me fill you in on the details? Please."

This was wonderful timing. Katlyn, her live-in sitter, was down in Roanoke and Adam would just have to tag along. She told Charles she'd see him in less than an hour and to expect her son to be with her, so please inform the security guards to let them both in.

She was greeted warmly by her old friend who had fixed up his plush sofa as a bed for Adam. Once the child was settled, then both tiptoed into the conference room adjoining his office for her briefing.

Hamilton Thrust, a lawyer and presidential advisor, did most of the talking, making it clear the administration was not totally pleased to have her fly solo as the potential combatants demanded. Mrs. MacMurray was not on the President's team after all, and who knows what kind of compromises she might concoct. Hailey ignored the man; Charles Morgan was incensed.

"I'm disgusted with your line of reasoning, Thrust. Mrs. MacMurray is a seasoned and professional diplomat. She speaks both languages involved and has volunteered for this assignment. Her political views as a representative from Virginia are irrelevant, especially since she is known by the Russian, who, by the way, is quite in favor of her selection. When this meeting is adjourned I will introduce Hailey to Fang Shau, the Chinese negotiator, who I'm certain will approve of her selection as well. And as to your request that Mrs. MacMurray contact the White House before making any commitments on the part of the United States, try to keep focused on what is going on here. We offered to broker as a neutral country. We are not in any position to offer anything except good will and a highly skilled diplomat who speaks Russian and Chinese."

Hailey had never seen her friend so worked up. He was not getting along with the political operatives in the administration that saw every event and action as a ploy for gaining votes. Charles Morgan had always been a super patriot and a professional diplomat. His international reputation alone had gained his country a role in this potentially disastrous circumstance. She patted his arm to calm him.

"I'll keep the Secretary informed, Mr. Thrust. All I ask is two plane tickets to China."

The top political advisor was puzzled. "Why two tickets, Mrs. MacMurray? I thought the main advantage you brought to the table was your ability to deal with both countries without support."

"I'll require a male companion on this trip, Mr. Thrust. My sitter is out of town. Christmas break starts in two days. My plane leaves today and my son will be flying with me." Hailey leaned over the front edge of the table and stared directly into Hamilton Thrust's eyes. "That, sir, is not open for negotiation. I want to add that Secretary Morgan has given you a delicious win-win proposition. If this works, your administration gets major points on the international scene. If it fails, you can always blame me." That said, she got up from the table. "I have to go pack, Charles. Wish me luck."

Fang Shau liked the voice of this American. Her dialect was more academic than he was used to, but they understood each other. Strange request though. She asked that her son be given a room where he could study since he would need to make up some homework assignments. Her son was coming? Still, his record search on her background found this Hailey MacMurray to be a worthy person. He would have his own translator along though, just the same.

Anatoly smiled at this news. Hailey MacMurray was coming to the negotiations. Perhaps she would favor his country since she'd enjoyed an assignment in Moscow. It couldn't hurt. That, plus the work would have to stop for meals and some after hours' entertainment. Hopefully she would not have to relieve a sitter this time. Based on his previous relationship with the American beauty, Anatoly rejected the offer of his own personal translator.

Urumqi was not an easy destination. Hailey and Adam transferred to a Chinese military transport in Beijing and were jostled halfway across Asia to the northwest corner of the country. There they were met by Fang Shau and shown to their spartan room containing two single beds, an adjoining bath, a radio and a desk that would allow young Adam the opportunity to catch up on his homework. Fang was startled by the beauty of the American and resolved to bargain even harder to compensate. Anatoly was again crushed to discover Hailey's child was an ever present factor in her life.

Negotiations began before schedule over dinner. Hailey had suggested Anatoly, Fang Shau and his translator join her and Adam at her expense at a restaurant off the military complex. Both men acquiesced graciously, neither desiring to offend the diplomat who had begun brokering on her terms.

Speaking Chinese, Hailey said, "Ambassador Tushenko, Ambassador Shau, my son and I are honored to be here tonight with you." She raised her glass of plum wine. "I offer a toast to the continued prosperity and good health of your countries." She repeated her toast in Russian for Anatoly and motioned for Adam to raise his glass of water along with the diplomats. The boy was a consummate actor, having been rehearsed through this scene back in their room. Next she would take it a level higher.

Hailey said in French, "Adam, honey, please start the meal by passing the rice around to Mr. Shau." Her State Department background folder noted both Mr. Shau and his translator spoke French and she was determined to begin a friendly relationship between them and Adam who had learned the language during her Paris assignment. It worked and the Chinese and Adam kept up a conversation the entire meal. And, as coached by his mother, the boy wrangled an invitation to see the Russian plane the next morning.

With this initial breakthrough, Hailey brokered with the Chinese to allow her and Anatoly to tag along with the boy. Thus with one simple meal, she pushed the negotiations forward by weeks as neither ambassador considered the visit more than satisfying the idle curiosity of a young boy. She took on the issue of the pilot with the same degree of suavity, explaining Adam's intense curiosity to see the man and her desire to assure the Russians their pilot was being treated fairly. But Fang balked at this suggestion.

"I can assure you the man is safe. He was injured only slightly from errant shrapnel before he signaled for help and is in hospital. You need not visit. The military warmonger is being treated as a prisoner of war." Fang's voice rose at the end of this pronouncement and heads turned all around the restaurant.

Hailey translated for Anatoly. "Mr. Shau compliments your pilot for landing without damaging any civilian facilities and assures me Captain Federov is resting well in the hospital." She paused to let Fang's translator note her change to his statement, making it far less strident. When he was done she fixed Shau with a steady look. "You understand, Mr. Shau, that Russia and China are not in a state of war and thus, prisoner of war status is irrelevant. Mr. Tushenko only desires to visit the man, not steal him away from the hospital." Before Shau could respond, Hailey turned to Anatoly and translated her statement for him. Then before Anatoly could respond she spoke in English reproaching Adam on his use of chopsticks and wiped his chin with her napkin.

The uncanny mix of cultures, languages, and family values befuddled both foreign ambassadors. The fact that a young and attractive woman scripted the remaining negotiations with this opening scene drew their admiration. Hailey demonstrated that she sincerely appreciated each country's position and proved to be an accomplished broker. The next morning their little group saw the jet and talked to the pilot. Hailey spent time listening to the man's description of his plane's haphazard performance, and translated for Fang Shau and his interpreter. On the spot, she asked to be taken to the air controller's tower so she could corroborate the flight pattern and sequence of events as described by the Russian pilot. Once there she listened just as intently to the Chinese side. Then she translated for Anatoly.

Adam was escorted to his room to study and catch up on his sleep, having flown halfway around the world in the last 24 hours. Hailey and her male entourage adjourned to the conference room. There she asked Anatoly and Fang if she could offer her perspective on the situation. Both agreed, having gone along with her script so far. The men looked bemused in anticipation of her next act.

Deferring to the host, Hailey began in Chinese. "In my country we sometimes assign arbitrators to make an objective decision when two sides disagree. Many times the arbitrator comes down right in the middle, say in a salary negotiation between a baseball player and the team's general manager. And I see that as my role here. My government selected me because I spoke your languages." She translated for Anatoly and returned to Chinese. "However, my former colleagues in the United States State Department forgot that I was once a jet pilot. During my training I had the opportunity to fly many types of jets, some, uh, procured from other countries. So I bring an additional skill to these meetings." Fang nodded, having gleaned this from her background report. She translated for Anatoly and he sat straighter at the table.

"In my previous life as a pilot, I flew a plane much like the Russian jet. I believe the pilot when he says he lost control over the mountains due to turbulence. I did that myself and it was no fun." She translated for Anatoly again and his expression turned grim. Fang smiled in perceived relief at her statement, which he believed strengthened his position to demand reparations and to keep the plane.

"I also believe the air controller who says the pilot radioed for help and indicated he was in trouble and unable to avoid Chinese air space. These facts, plus the obvious fact that the plane was a prototype and unarmed, prove to me the Russian pilot had no intention of attacking targets within China." Again she informed Anatoly who grew more confident while Fang Shau's previous exuberant expression drooped. Neither man spoke or tried to interrupt her, as if she held all 52 cards in their poker game.

Hailey challenged them to discount her analysis by looking down at her notes and waiting a full minute before continuing. She had them now and hid a smile. "I would like to offer a quick solution," she spoke in Fang's language to start. "Give the plane and the pilot back to Russia. I can assure you that your latest fighters are much better and you will gain little from dissecting Captain Federov's broken jet." She translated for Anatoly and his smile widened. She continued in Russian for his benefit. "Mr. Ambassador, offer an apology to Mr. Shau and pay his country for the time and expense of facilitating the transfer of your plane and pilot back to Russia." She quickly turned to Fang and repeated her suggestion. Both translations over, Hailey excused herself and left the room. She joined Adam who was asleep and soon claimed it for herself.

A timid knock brought Hailey out of a deep slumber containing no nightmares. She draped her robe around her shoulders and opened the door a crack. The translator stood smiling. He was a young man who wore black horn rim glasses and was dressed in stylish American clothes. He could have been someone from California or Missouri, a student or an E-businessman. Yet he was near the top of power in the Chinese diplomatic service. He now spoke in flawless English with a tinge of a Southern accent—a student at a Southern university in the United States?

He shook her hand. "Mrs. MacMurray, your work is exceptional. The ambassadors request you and Mr. Adam join them for dinner."

Hailey said, "Vanderbilt?" He shook his head. "William and Mary?" His face expanded into a wide grin and he nodded in the affirmative. "Fang Shau picked you because you studied in Virginia, correct?"

"Yes, it is a beautiful place and I have been in your mountains, even your little city of Blue Ridge. Mr. Shau wanted to know why a woman was chosen and why in particular a mother who would not abandon her child with such an opportunity. I knew of you and I told him what to expect." The young man straightened his shoulders with pride. "He was pleased. You have, uh, the American expression is 'swept them off their feet.'" He laughed.

"Please tell me your name, sir."

"Lin Tao, at your service. I return to Georgetown University next fall for their graduate program in political studies." They shook hands again.

"Then you have a standing invitation to dinner at my house, Lin. Please tell the ambassadors we'll be ready in one hour."

Their dinner was more like a family reunion, only this time Anatoly picked up the tab in several ways.

Anatoly said, "A toast to Hailey MacMurray and her associate junior diplomat." Fang Shau and Lin raised their glasses to Hailey and Adam. "While you caught up on your sleep we have been in communication with our governments." Anatoly nodded to Fang who listened to Lin Tao convert the Russian's words. Fang withdrew a slender folder from his dispatch case and passed copies of a thin document to Hailey and to Anatoly.

Fang said, "We wrote your words, Mrs. MacMurray, with Lin Tao's assistance. Though simple in appearance, your, how do you say, 'quickie solution,' intrigued Moscow and Beijing. Our ambassadors at the United Nations will hold press conferences and bluster about for a few days, but in the end, what you proposed will be done." Hailey translated for Anatoly, who nodded his head with vigor and returned a huge smile.

Quiet fell on the table as each read a copy of the proposal. Adam looked over his mother's shoulder to get a peek at her English version. As he read the two-page document, his body slid closer to his mother and his arm slipped around her shoulder.

"Mom, that's great. Wait 'til Jack hears about this."

Before either ambassador could interject, Hailey spoke their minds. "Jack will have to read about this in the paper, honey. It will be up to these gentlemen and their governments to announce a settlement." She made eye contact first with Fang, then with Anatoly. "I suggest your premiere make a short state visit to Beijing, Anatoly. Hand over the check in person. And your premiere, Fang, can turn over a set of papers transferring the plane."

After translations, Lin Tao scribbled notes and both men seemed in agreement. Hailey understood more than jet planes and their respective languages. Russia needed markets; China needed goods. Global economics superseded warmongering.

Adam broke the ice on the last item up for negotiation. "Mom, how much does a plane like that cost to make?"

Hailey answered her son in English and then translated for both men. "I'd say $5 million tops, Adam. Although a new stabilizer and the proper navigation equipment would put it well over that. Considering use of the Chinese facilities, repairing the holes from the shrapnel blasts and the medical care of Captain Federov, plus transportation to the border, I'd add another $5 million. Let's say $10 million tops plus reimbursement to our country for plane fare, which is pocket change in comparison. Our good will is free." Mother spoke again to her son, repeating her cost analysis in Russian and Chinese, glancing occasionally at the ambassadors. Then she picked up her chop sticks and finished eating.

Hailey and Adam spent three more days in Urumqi and toured the countryside with Lin Tao. During this time, as Fang Shau had predicted, the Russian and Chinese ambassadors acted out their roles in the United Nations Security Council. After three days both governments announced a vital breakthrough and Hailey's quickie solution was proffered as if from intense Sino-Russian negotiations. Charles Morgan was not surprised when Hailey called him immediately after that second dinner and before taking off to do some sightseeing. However, the White House bristled.

Hamilton Thrust yelled into the speakerphone. "I told you the President wanted to know about these negotiations. Why didn't you tell us there had been an agreement?"

Charles Morgan hung up and thought about his career. He used the intercom to inform his secretary to hold all calls, especially those from Mr. Thrust. At some point every man banged his head into a brick wall for the last time. He had served his government, his country, in spite of political operatives like Thrust. He knew there would be a backlash, but keeping Hailey's promise to the Russians and Chinese had been paramount. He'd emphatically agreed with his special envoy on that issue. Hamilton Thrust would have exploded literally if he knew Hailey had secured an agreement within 24 hours. He did not tell the White House because the agreement was a matter of honor and dignity for both Russia and China. And honor and dignity were not in Thrust's vocabulary. Credit, however, was another matter. Now the White House clamored for the lion's share of it, and to hell with sensitive international relations.

The esteemed Secretary of State had tried to explain diplomatic negotiations, especially those regarding the threat of war, but to no avail. Hamilton Thrust wanted blood, his blood it appeared. Charles turned to his old manual typewriter and wrote out a one line letter of resignation, dated and signed it. He left the State Department and strolled to 1600 Pennsylvania Avenue to meet with the President.

Hailey and Adam flew back home indirectly via Beijing and Moscow, where they met both Premieres and received their thanks. They made a stopover in Paris for a short rest before continuing on to Washington. The news hit them full force at the American Embassy where they'd spent the night. Two headlines flashed across the *Washington Post* front page:

"President Claims Major Role in Russian-Chinese Negotiations"

"Secretary of State Charles Morgan Resigns"

Hailey got off the phone with Charles who said he had, "decided to retire rather than watch any more political types screw up a wet dream." She called Fang Shau and Anatoly to personally assure them she and Charles Morgan had kept their promise. Their answers were identical: Yes, they believed her and their own politicians were spinning the truth as well. Thankfully, the plane and pilot had already been secretly transported back to Russia and only the formality of the political handshake in Beijing remained. Their premieres would ignore the bombast from Washington. All things considered, ten million for the plane plus pocket change for airfare for the two negotiators from Virginia was a small price to pay to avert war.

Hailey changed her plane tickets so they'd arrive late at night out in the Dulles Airport countryside some thirty miles from the District of Columbia. It made no difference. Katlyn took the transport bus from the airport central terminal out to meet them before they deplaned.

"It is a typical media zoo back there, Hailey. We need to tell them something. Do you want me to handle it?"

Hailey slumped back into her seat and cradled Adam's sleeping head to her breast. She motioned Katlyn to a seat and they sat in silence until they were the only passengers remaining. "I'll deal with it, Katlyn. Thanks for coming out to get us." They joined other passengers on the transporter and received several glances of recognition and smiles. When the bus emptied they waited until the last and Hailey led the way out.

Voices shouted and flashes glared from what seemed like a thousand cameras. The cacophony would have been funny seen in a romantic comedy or read in a book, but this was reality for someone in politics. Hailey pushed Adam and Katlyn off to fetch their bags and wait for her at the curb. She endured the demanding shouts for another few minutes, looking for a familiar face in the crowd. There! Dan Roberts from the *Post* stood quietly to the side waiting patiently. She winked at him and motioned the mob to be silent. It took another minute or two before she could speak above the rabble. She nodded to Dan and ignored last minute shouts from the others.

"Can you tell us your role in the negotiations, Mrs. MacMurray, and what do you make of the Secretary's resignation?"

"OK, Dan. Yes, I had a role in the preliminary talks." Several stringers dropped out of the pack and raced to phone in the next day's headlines. "Mr. Morgan asked me to help since I spoke the languages. However, Charles and

I both promised the parties involved that we would not disclose the nature of those talks and that it would be up to them to come to an agreement, which they did." Another reporter shouted to interrupt with his question. Hailey held up a hand and continued to answer the second part of Dan Robert's question.

"Charles Morgan was one of the very best Secretaries of State this country ever had. He was ambassador to Russia when I served in the embassy in Moscow. His reputation for honesty and integrity alone carried weight internationally. Russia and China knew him and trusted him and that is why he volunteered to help. Mr. Morgan and I kept our promise and I will continue to do so. I will not discuss the talks further. Thank you and good night." She turned away from the horde after signaling Dan to walk with her.

"Have you talked to Charles about this, Dan?"

"Yeah, I did. He said he's had enough and was going back to Minnesota to do some ice fishing. What did you do over there? You know it will come out and someone in town will take credit regardless."

She stopped at the curb and noticed Katlyn and Adam cozy together in the car, waiting. She wrote two names and phone numbers on a piece of paper and handed it to the reporter. "Call these men. I promised them and they will have to release the story. If they tell you what happened, give them credit. Both took extreme risk to go along with my suggestions. In decades past they would have been shot for even listening to me. But they will have to tell you, Dan. I promised. Charles promised. The White House broke that promise. And, everything I just said to you was off the record. I trust you."

Eleven

Katlyn answered the umpteenth call the next morning. Her answers were the same to each caller: "No, Hailey had nothing to add to the *Post's* sensational story this morning. Yes, she was still asleep." But Katlyn's answer changed with this caller.

"Good morning, Senator Conley. Yes, sir, she's right in the next room. Hailey tried to sleep in but the damn phone is ringing off the hook. In fact, after you hang up I'm unplugging every phone in the house and fixing a late breakfast, so come on over."

Bill and Elizabeth Conley arrived in a short thirty minutes and came with appetites. It was a chilly December morning and the fire felt good as the informal group gathered for coffee after gobbling up Katlyn's pancakes. The Conley's relayed the news of the day from their perspective as close friends.

"I've never seen the likes, Hailey. Dan Roberts got releases from those two fellows who gave you all the credit. Of course their governments gave them permission to talk, since neither Moscow nor Beijing has an appreciation for the foreign policy of the current administration. And after Charles Morgan's resignation they have even more dislike for the White House." Bill Conley paused. "But you they love. And Adam, too." He tousled the boy's hair and grabbed him for a grandfatherly hug. He nodded to Elizabeth to state their business.

"Honey," she grasped Hailey's hands and stared into her eyes, "We decided to make a run for the White House and we want you as our vice president."

Hailey's mouth dropped open and her brain struggled for a reaction. She looked from Bill to Elizabeth to Katlyn and finally to Adam, whose eyes were popping wide with excitement. "I can't possibly do that. I—I just got into this game of politics three years ago. I'll barely be old enough to serve if the people are crazy enough to elect me." Her hands shook as she counted fingers desperately attempting to calculate her age only a year from now when a potential Conley-MacMurray administration might be sworn in. Sleep deprived from traveling around the world on her recent mission, Hailey stared straight ahead and felt behind for a chair to slump into.

Elizabeth moved quickly and knelt in front of Hailey. "No, wait." With affection, she touched two fingers to Hailey's lips to stop her objections. "You're no longer a secret weapon inside the Beltway and down in Virginia. Today the nation discovered you. Bill's network has been calling him all morning confirming something he and I agreed on last Thanksgiving when we went down to visit Sara and Joe in your hometown."

Bill Conley spoke. "The people want a change, Hailey. They want change in many ways and you and I represent a lot of what they want: independent spokesmen for the average voter. Charles Morgan agrees with us. I talked to him yesterday and he told me how you handled everything. Dealt with two foreign superpowers and took care of your precious Adam simultaneously. No one has seen the likes of it. I know I haven't, and we want you with us. Same rules as always, just like the campaigns you and I have run before."

Hailey sat a moment and let the offer simmer. But only for a moment. "Yes, I'll do it. We'll do it." Her friends and family whooped and hugged each other. She let the excitement slide into an afterglow of satisfaction before speaking. "Senator, Bill, Grandpa, this country needs an honest man, one who isn't a front for special groups and money. You have been my example from the start and I'd be proud to take on this race with you."

Katlyn listened to the newest candidates for high public office and her mind drifted to another dimension. It would be a dream, no, a fantasy to see them win. Both were smart and worked hard. They owed their allegiance to the people and to the Constitution. Bill Conley was a respected military hero with connections around the world and across the nation. His record was spotless, never having taken a dime from a lobbyist or special interest group. He had mastered the technique of main streeting and the people respected him so much he was never submerged into a crowd and threatened. No one could forget his brilliant mind. The man might be in his seventies, but his memory and thinking ability ran circles around most. He served the common man without ego. By picking Hailey to run with him he showed the American people he was brave enough to buck the trend and point to the future.

Hailey was such a bright star that Katlyn was thrilled to be her friend and associate. Her assets were as strong as the senator's and ranged from being a marvelous single mother to striding the world solving thorny diplomatic problems like the Russian fighter fiasco. Katlyn knew her friend and boss was defining a new role for women in politics. There had always been a certain mystique about the difference between men and women and what that would mean to national leadership roles. Women, it was theorized by some, were more nurturing of life and would automatically encourage peace rather than war. Critiques of this perspective warned that opposing nations would see the election of a woman to the top office in any country as a signal to attack, to bully. Katlyn wondered why. Did some cultures perceive women as weak? Perhaps so. But Hailey didn't fit that description. She had graduated from the Air Force Academy and trained on the world's best fighter jets. She supported the military; was outspoken about it. Yet, her son was always cared for, Adam came first, even taken to work as far away as Urumqi, China. Katlyn smiled to herself, reflecting on a conversation she and Hailey had last night driving home from the airport:

"I'll tell you a secret, Katlyn. Men cannot deal with an attractive woman who has any brains, especially one who is a mother. I could sense that as soon as Anatoly and Fang Shau met me in Urumqi. Their eyes went wide and they struggled to keep from checking me out. It was one of the only times in my life that I consciously used, uh, what shall I call it, my feminine wiles, to get something done."

"Since we're having this conversation off the record, define 'feminine wiles.' Would that include, oh, well, give me a clue here, since I'm short on that score."

"Dear friend, it's just, well, men try to hide that they're looking, but I have eyes. I can see what they're doing. So I accept it; let them. Wait for their minds to catch up with the subject matter. And a little friendliness short of an outright tease can smooth the way, so why not smile? Of course you have to know what you're talking about and be determined to focus on the objective even if the men have gotten a bit fuzzy about it while they're admiring you. Yet it becomes easy to guide the agenda."

"I never heard you talk like this, Hailey. Is it something you have needed to get out? If so, I'm privileged to be the one you tell it to."

"You're right, Katlyn. Guess I'm old enough to talk about it objectively, leaving emotions aside. But there are drawbacks. I think many of the right kind of men shy away from attractive women. They feel like, oh, I don't know what they feel, but I know some don't call or ask me out figuring I'm attached already, or that my ego must be outrageous and they couldn't measure up."

"So you overcompensate by dressing down, hiding that wonderful figure, wearing loose clothing so men have to deal with you from the neck up. Is that it?"

"Well, it does help keep them focused. Even our next president had the problem. Elizabeth told me he had to work at concentrating on what I had to say when he first met me. She laughed about it, secure in their relationship, never doubting her man."

"Let's call it the 'beautiful woman syndrome.' What an awful problem you have. But wait, there is a solution. Lend me your body and you can take mine, that'll even the playing field."

Katlyn felt a jolt and realized Hailey was poking her in the side and expecting a reply to some question in the current dimension.

"What do you think of that, Katlyn? Hello, Katlyn, come back to earth." Hailey and the rest of the room stared at her anticipating a response, and she hadn't the foggiest idea what had been said.

"Sorry, I drifted off. Repeat the question."

Bill Conley spoke for the group, "No. You're too late. We'll pick someone else to manage this campaign." But his wide grin belied that statement.

"Wait, wait, yes, I'll do it. What did you propose? I didn't hear it. My mind wandered for the last time in this campaign. Whatever it is, the answer is yes. Now, what did I agree to, and I hope it has nothing to do with a blind date like the one I had last weekend?"

Senator Conley wasn't letting her off that easily though. "We chose you to lead us to victory. What do we do now?" Everyone laughed and Katlyn understood her career had shot up to the highest level. However, she was not speechless. She couldn't make the excuse that she'd never done anything like this. No one in the room with her had either. Regardless, Katlyn forged ahead.

"I'd definitely wait until after the Super Bowl to make an announcement. Our Redskins are favored to slice through the playoffs and win. The town will be crazy about football until spring at least. But that doesn't mean we sit still and do nothing." The idealistic group smiled as the feisty redhead naturally took charge. "I'll need lots of help. Both of your Congressional offices will have to pitch in. We'll need to write up position papers and get them distributed. Pick a place and time to announce. Find cheap labor to help; I'll call Radford University this afternoon. Those women are avid admirers. Uh—"

Hailey stifled her with a hand over her mouth. "Enough already. Tomorrow is soon enough to get frantic."

Burch Magnum drove a full compliment of football fans to the game this Sunday. His long-time football buddy, Adam, was riding shotgun. Rose and Jennette sat with Hailey in the back to discuss her triumph only a few weeks past and the upcoming presidential campaign. Adam seemed pumped about the playoff game with the Bears that afternoon. He had provided a continuing analysis of his team's prospects the whole ride to the stadium.

"I don't think it matters that the Bears beat us last year in the first round. We have the best record in the whole league this year, Uncle Burch. Our guys have the best passing attack and a solid running game. The Bears play good defense and run the ball."

"I agree, Adam. But while you were busy negotiating with the Russians and Chinese over world affairs, the Bears soundly thrashed the Giants last Sunday, and are on a roll. And our guys had a bye week and might be rusty with the lay off. However, there is another bit of news I heard about this week from my inside sources around town. There will be a surprise announcement at half time and I think you'll be mighty pleased when you hear it."

"Tell me now. What is it?"

"Patience, lad. Wait and see."

Once in the senator's penthouse booth, Adam forced his mother to watch the game with him and stop talking about politics for once.

"Watch him, Mom. Mark is fantastic. He led the league this year in receptions and touchdowns and total yards. You gotta see him." Mother and son were not disappointed. Mark caught two touch down passes in the first half. Jason Cramer threw another to his running back and the Skins led 21-0 by the half.

"See what I told you? The guy's great and he's my friend." Adam jumped up and down he was so excited, and Hailey recognized hero worship. Just before the end of the second quarter, Burch tapped her on the shoulder and passed her his binoculars.

"Don't go away. Focus on the fifty yard line and watch what happens."

The grounds crew lugged a huge swath of outdoor carpeting to the center of the field and stabbed a big microphone in its center. Several men in suits walked to the podium now placed there as well, and Mark Daniel walked with them.

"What's going on, Uncle Burch?"

"Hush and you'll find out."

Hailey trained the high-powered binoculars on the man wearing number 27. His photo in regular street clothes disguised how big he was. She checked the program: six six, 240. But she had watched him play. She had to or her son would disown her. The man was fast. With his long, easy stride he was outrunning the Bears' linebackers and defensive backs. He also made bone-crushing blocks downfield. Adam had a friend anyone would want in a battle.

"Ladies and Gentlemen," the speaker was the Commissioner of the NFL according to Burch. "Each year the players and coaches and management of the NFL choose one of its own as their Man of the Year. This award goes to the person who we feel exemplifies the best of sportsmanship on and off the field. This year we are proud and honored to present the award for the NFL's Man of the Year to the Washington Redskins' All-pro tight end, Mark Daniel." The huge stadium swelled in thunderous applause that lasted several minutes. But the commissioner wasn't done talking.

"Mark never asks for credit for his accomplishments in the community so I'll tell you about some of them. Each summer, in the off-season, Mark sponsors a football camp for kids here in the Washington area and out in his hometown of Crested Butte, Colorado. He also strong-arms friends around the league into donating their vacation time, to contribute money and their personal skills in running these camps. These athletes, with Mark's leadership, work without compensation and the kids attend the camps at no charge." The commissioner paused as the applause, whistles and cheers drowned him out. "Some of you know that Mark is an accomplished artist and musician. I know my wife was impressed with his impression of Frank Sinatra, but we won't get into details about that." Laughter filled the stadium this time. "But back to Mark. He conned, er, talked other players with musical talents into cutting a CD and the proceeds of the sale go for inner-city kids." Again the applause rose.

"There are more accolades and praise I could mention, like his artist scholarship program and owning the best jazz restaurant west of the Continental Divide. But, personally, I want to say that I wish all young athletes could model their play and behavior on the field after this man. Mark Daniel is a sportsman and a leader. I am proud to have him for a friend."

And he was an attractive man too. Hailey kept the binoculars honed in on the big man. Her son had a terrific friend it would seem. Someone was tapping her shoulder, interrupting her gaze.

"Mom, mom, stop hogging the glasses. I want to see."

She handed him the glasses and looked around the booth to her lady friends. Jennette and Rose had their arms crossed and wore knowing expressions concerning her lapse of consciousness.

"This man is a gorgeous hunk, Hailey, and he's your son's best friend. Why doesn't he call? Better yet, why don't you call him?" Rose taunted her affectionately, while Jennette seemed in deep thought. Fortunately the end of half time ceremonies brought their attention back to play on the field. Mark had seemed embarrassed and shy in accepting his award. He gave no speech, saying only, "Thank You," and then turned and left for the locker room.

The second half seemed to fly by and the Redskins crushed the Bears. The end of the game was the cue Burch had waited for.

"Let's go down and congratulate the players. Come on everybody. Jennette, Rose, Hailey, and Adam, let's get a move on."

Hailey felt nervous. Why was that, she asked herself? They would shake hands and congratulate the players and leave. But an honest appraisal of her feelings revealed there was something more. Her son liked this man, Mark Daniel. She had not been able to take her eyes off him during the award ceremony. Strange, but it had been like spying to check him out through those binoculars, like an inspection up close and personal before a date. Date? Now she felt like a high school senior getting ready for the prom.

The turf was green and spongy and it smelled like a field plowed before the spring planting. And it was dug up just as much. Clods of dirt with stringy filaments of grass lay here and there as if giant golfers had refused to replace their divots after taking massive iron shots from the rough. The pungent odor of sod and dirt mixed with a musky, sweaty masculine smell from the giant-sized players who stood around the field receiving the congratulations of their fans. *My God, but they were huge*, Hailey thought. And there was blood all over them. She saw bandaged hands, arms, foreheads and legs with crimson stripes and swaths of blood on practically every player. She stopped and gazed at the carnage. If this was the winning team, what would the losers be like? No wonder ambulances were on hand and a full service emergency trauma unit installed under the stands. This was authorized war and mayhem.

She recalled watching a pro basketball game with Adam one night, and play had been stopped cold when a player suffered a cut lip. The camera had zeroed in on the poor fellow who continued to run the court and suck on his lower lip to hide the bleeding. But he was spotted by the referee and walked off to a trainer. That man donned surgical gloves and treated the giant basketball player as if an AIDS epidemic were imminent. How could that happen in the sport of football? Everyone was bleeding down here, a fact unrevealed by her high-powered glasses used to keep track of Adam's best friend during most of the second half.

Mother and son held hands to keep from getting separated in the crush of the crowd, but Adam broke loose when he gained sight of his hero and dashed to greet him. Hailey felt a tinge of what? Jealousy? Or was that it or something else? Her son leapt onto the big man and hugged him with all four limbs. Mark grabbed the boy under his arms and hoisted him above the crowd in triumph. Hailey recognized the correct feeling now. It wasn't jealousy; it was thrilling, exhilarating. It was wonderful to see that this great man liked her son. She waited for the two to enjoy their own personal celebration until Adam dropped to the ground and searched the crowd for her.

"Mom, come on. You gotta meet Mark." They were no more than fifteen yards apart and it should have taken only five seconds to walk over, but she just looked at the man and he returned her stare. Anyone interested, such as her son, whose head turned from one to the other, had to notice a connection.

Why didn't she move? Now she didn't have to as Adam held onto one of Mark's big hands and dragged him to her. Adam was saying something, probably introducing them, using his manners as always. But she didn't hear exactly what he said. They shook hands and her voice bubbled up from its hidden location.

"Great game, Mark. Congratulations on winning that award." His hands were soft. How could that be? These men had been in combat and Adam's friend had made contact on practically every play. Yet his hands were gentle, soothing. She felt secure. Secure? From a handshake?

"Finally we meet, Mrs. MacMurray. Adam talks about you after every game. He's a great fan, a great friend too." Mark smiled down at Adam and crushed him to his side. He looked back at her. "You are even more beautiful than your photograph. Why haven't I called you?" Hailey turned red and lost her vocabulary in every language she spoke. She was acting like a teenager. A moment followed in which neither spoke and their spot on the field became the eye in a hurricane, calm, silent.

"Adam, go check on Jason Cramer. Tell him to come meet your mother." The boy took off looking everywhere in his excitement and was lost amongst the redwood trees in uniform standing on the field. Mark turned back to Hailey. "I'm sorry to embarrass you. That just popped out. But I feel like we know each other through Adam. Let me start over. May I call you?"

"I'd like that, Mark. Here, I saw a girl do this in a movie once." She got a pen from her purse and wrote her number on the palm of his hand. She turned his hand over and saw the scratches and scars. "How do you keep your hands from getting butchered out here?"

"Gloves. Best invention ever for pass catchers." He reached behind his back and pulled out a pair of sports gloves from his waist band. He did this with his left hand because Hailey still had possession of his right hand. Now she noticed and dropped it as if it had burned her.

"Listen, I have to go get cleaned up after I transfer your number to a permanent surface. I can't call until after the playoffs and hopefully the Super Bowl. There just isn't time."

"I know what you mean. This is an election year and I have a big campaign to run. But, uh, call, OK?" She knew it was being too forward, but she felt compelled to say it. "I don't, no, let me start over. I'm not seeing anyone if that concerns you. And please, call me Hailey." This was like clearing the field of play and going steady before having an actual date. But everything felt right. Refreshing.

He nodded and winked. "Thanks, Hailey. Say goodbye to Adam for me." He reached for her hand, squeezed it gently, turned and ran to the entrance to the team locker room. Adam returned hauling Jason Cramer along this time. He introduced his mother to the quarterback.

"Nice to meet you, Hailey." The man spoke with the confidence and ego of a national leader. "Did you meet Mark? Did he get up the courage to get your phone number? I've been bugging him forever it seems."

Hailey laughed. "He didn't have to ask. I wrote it on his hand." She excused herself and went in search of her son. Jason was left gaping.

Burch's SUV was unusually quiet after such a glorious victory. Adam sat up front as usual but wore a big smile of satisfaction. His honorary uncle thought he knew why. Jennette and Rose were silent in their own ruminations and left their good friend alone. Hailey gazed out the side window and saw nothing.

She had waited so long to feel this way again. More than that. Most times she didn't think she was meant to like a man so much after just shaking his hand and talking to him for a few minutes. She knew he wouldn't fit any of the categories she conveniently used to group men. But, what to do? They were both extremely busy and she was about to venture into the biggest challenge of her life. Katlyn had already mapped out a travel itinerary that would stun a mule. Mark was still playing football and always lit out for Colorado when the season ended. She'd waited a long time. If it happened, it happened. But it would be nice to have those strong arms hold her just once.

Twelve

Katlyn took a page from past independent runs for the White House. She sent Bill and Elizabeth Conley through key states on a bus tour. Hailey and Adam blitzed the country on a chartered jet. This strategy started off slowly due to a shortage of money at the beginning. But the American people responded to the opportunity to contribute ten bucks, the limit, to the Conley-MacMurray campaign. The people also were attracted to the main theme set by the intrepid independents: no strings attached.

Both candidates gave simple short speeches with the same message. They were listening to the people and merely summarizing what they heard along the campaign trail. They did not duck hot-button issues; neither did they promise quick solutions. They did promise to work hard and to remain accountable only to the voters. They also never mentioned their two main opponents: the incumbent president and his minority party challenger.

Negative ad campaigns developed quickly, especially those attacking Bill Conley's age—he was considered too old. More negative shots were fired at Hailey's youth and inexperience. She was barely old enough to run for the office, and, as some ads dared insinuate, was really a part-time mother and a part-time politician. Regardless, Katlyn had her orders and never once suggested an attack ad to stifle the hot air of the party hacks. She relied instead on Bill and Hailey, on their special personal appeal and clean records.

The American population was aging and Bill Conley appealed to that and most other segments of the voters. One had only to listen to him speak to realize this was no senile old man. His mind was sharp and it was easy to see why he was not invited to any of the debates scheduled by the League of Women Voters. The league itself always tendered an invitation to the Colorado Senator. But both major parties and their candidates nixed it. They were smart enough to deny a platform for Bill Conley's no-strings-attached agenda. Also, it was a fact that neither candidate, including the president himself, had the knowledge and background information the senator possessed. He simply forgot nothing and continued to receive a pipeline of information from his network that grew exponentially every day.

His shirtsleeve speech in New York City's Central Park summarized his vision for the country.

"It is no longer true that anybody can grow up to be the President of the United States. Without gobs of special interest money, that is. There is now more office space in Washington dedicated to special interests than to government operations. The highway to Dulles Airport, once a deserted greenbelt, is now littered with headquarters for every kind of group in the country dedicated to gaining the ears of elected officials.

"So, I am asked every hour, how do I propose setting the course right? How do I, a person without a party, without control of either chamber in the Congress, and not beholden to any attachments, or strings pulling me this way or that, how do I propose to fix government? You notice there is never the question, is government in need of fixing?

"I'll give you a simple answer. One night last winter I was sitting with my honorary grandson, Adam MacMurray, while my wife and his mother schemed up trouble for the status quo in their Women's Connection meeting. As was our custom, Adam and I were tuned in to *Startrek: The Next Generation*. And in this episode, the spaceship was in deep trouble—not as much as the government, but trouble nevertheless. A deadly virus was eating away at the brains of the engine, and the computer software was unable to counteract it. System after system failed and there were doubters throughout the wondrous vessel, doubters that their Starship *Enterprise* could survive an obvious downward spiral. Breathable oxygen declined. Folks were slumped against corridors and some were on the floor bereft of hope.

"The captain waited for input from his engineers and found it wanting. There were no ideas left. So he did what anyone would do when their computer was all fouled up; he turned it off. He waited a full minute until the virus died from lack of anything to destroy, then turned the engine back on. And of course it worked.

"Now you can attribute actions and characters in my little parable about a spaceship to whatever you desire, but essentially I will shut off the current system. Your government will continue to operate though; it just won't have the special-interest virus running amuck. Your next question is, How do I do that? Well, that's an easy one. I owe nothing to big contributors. In fact, all my contributors are equal, none having more than the pull of ten bucks. I have no network of job seekers out there campaigning for us in hopes of a plum job in Washington. Traditionally, many of the better volunteers and contributors politically appointed to federal jobs, work just long enough to find a public office for which they can begin to campaign. Those folks will not be in my administration. None of them.

"By my own estimate this act alone will save taxpayers five percent right off the top in wasted time and energy, and in duplicated payroll. There will be an outward migration of displaced political appointees from both parties the day I am inaugurated. Why both parties? Well, political appointees tend to grow fond of getting paid for overseeing the actual work of civil servants, making sure everyone follows the party line or the policy of the White House. And they find ways to burrow into the bureaucracy to keep getting paid even when their party loses an election. When their party comes to power again their own onerous virus is reactivated and they fill higher jobs while appointees of the defeated party slink downward into the system and await their turn to rise again.

"You might wonder how much time it takes to shut off this pipeline of political appointee viruses. My estimate is three months. All will be directed to resign. Many will. Some will ignore the order. Others will try to burrow. We will find them. I'm sure about that. Permanent employees have already begun to identify them and to let us know. But three months to rid the system of them is short. Some administrations take two years to get their people in place and that is only for the first go round. There is a continual revolving door of people seeking higher positions and leaving to go get elected. Or, they sign on with companies associated with the agencies they just left. That will not happen in my administration.

"The results will be a new start, a clean slate waiting for your input. It will be up to you to evaluate how responsive your congressional representatives are. You get a chance every two years to restart the political computer, so to speak. To sum up, my vision is yours. I work for you; everyone in Washington should. My job is to manage the ship, keep it on course, and make it run better. Thank you."

A crowd of thousands rose with shouts and tumultuous applause. Pollsters surged through the throng that refused to leave the park, and asked a very simple question: Will you vote for Conley-MacMurray, and why? The unanimous response was echoed by many and it matched polls taken across the nation. The two independents made no promises except to work hard for the people. Voters wanted results, not empty promises. Other questions were posed to measure honesty and credibility. The overwhelming response showed the retired Army general and his young single mom running mate rated far above the traditional level associated with politicians.

In other parts of the country, Hailey faced different questions. Attack ads daily insinuated rumors without sources and found fault with her as a mother and as a politician. She found that her experience main streeting and coming face to face with tough, personal questions helped. By now most voters knew of her personal history and her career path. Some wanted more details.

"I am asked why I take my son out of school to campaign with me. If any of you are single parents you'll understand why I do this. Oh, there are some times when I leave Adam with a sitter for a few hours, or rarely overnight, and always with an adult. But I decided when he was an infant that I would have him with me always. I am his only parent, his guardian, and he is my treasure. I changed careers to be able to do this. I wanted to be his main influence in life, and to set standards that would last him into adulthood. I didn't really want him out of my sight. I still don't.

"I home school Adam when I take him on trips. When I went to China last year I asked my Chinese host to provide a place for him to catch up on his homework. We take his school books along and he is in the habit of actually using those books outside of class. When we lived in Paris he learned French and that came in handy when we dined with the Russians and Chinese. Adam conversed with the Chinese at one end of the table in French while I talked to the Russian Ambassador in his language. It was a unique way to further his education.

"Some folks, on the other end of the spectrum, say I don't spend enough time as a member of Congress because of my son. Tongue in cheek, I might counter that perhaps more members should do the same. But I don't take vacations from the voters. When Adam and I go home to Blue Ridge we go main streeting. Our time off and away from Washington is time listening to voters, just like we're doing throughout this campaign during the town meetings."

Television provided free publicity their spare campaign treasury couldn't afford during the first months. One such opportunity came on a national cable news network interview program.

Host: Good evening and welcome to the News Channel's 'Challenge to Newsmakers.' I'm your host, Lyman Trevolt, and my guest tonight is the independent United States Senator from Colorado, Bill Conley. Welcome, Senator.

Senator Conley: Thanks, Lyman. Pleasure to be here. Appreciate the free advertising. (Conley smiles and looks directly into the camera.)

Host: (Chuckling.) Just so our viewers understand, Senator. Let me remind them of your campaign promises to avoid big donor contributions.

Conley: (Interrupting.) Let me correct that last statement, Lyman. I haven't made any campaign promises. I've given my word of honor.

Host: Of course, Senator. But for our viewers' information, Senator Conley is running for president and will not accept campaign donations above $10. Is that the correct limit, Senator? (Trevolt barely hides a sneer behind his raised hand.)

Conley: That's right. I never accepted them as a Senatorial candidate and I won't start now. Besides, campaign promises have a way of coming back to haunt office seekers. I don't want to build up a list of obligations that might sway my thinking as president. Or worse, give the public the impression that I might make decisions based on past donations.

Host: You'll pardon the pun, Senator, but that's like saying you'll create the politically correct Immaculate Conception. (Trevolt snorts at his own stab at humor.)

Conley: (Face remains stoic, unsmiling.) About time, don't you think, Lyman?

Host: You're being naïve, Senator Conley, if you think you can aspire to the highest office in the land—in the world for that matter—and not end up owing something to somebody. (Trevolt frowns his disbelief, challenging his guest.)

Conley: I will owe no individual or corporation a thing. I will owe the American people my honesty and integrity. They should expect nothing less.

Host: Oh, come on, man. You have to have people working for you in every locale, every state. Those folks will want a payoff certainly. It's expected and required for any man to succeed as President.

Conley: What part of the term "no obligations" confuses you? Seems pretty straight forward to me. People working for my campaign don't want a president elected who has to pay them off with a phony job on the public trough. They're all volunteers. Students, professionals, blue-collar workers, housewives. People from all backgrounds. People fed up with special access to the White House and Capitol Hill granted only to those who can pay for it. (Conley remains unflappable and turns again to look directly into the camera, ignoring his host.)

Host: I see an impossible situation brewing, but let's move on. The candidates for the two major parties are holding debates, and you're not invited. Again, for our viewers' edification, recent polls show Senator Conley with well over ten percent support among the voters. That's enough to trigger Federal Election Campaign funds to the Conley-MacMurray campaign. Still, the two parties have used a myriad of excuses not to invite the senator to the debates. What do you have to say about that, Senator?

Conley: Not a thing. To repeat, for the edification of your viewers, I make no campaign promises. I won't tie my hands needlessly. I have only one position, if you want to call it that. The American people have my word of honor. And it's closer to 20 percent, Lyman. I got word back in the dressing room.

Host: (Trevolt shakes his head dramatically.) OK, moving along. Maybe I can put this in a simple statement. Senator, just what kind of presidency can the American people expect from you?

Conley: (Smiling, turns again and looks directly in the camera.) I will be a public servant working for the people. My administration will be open. I will tell the truth and appoint career public servants to cabinet positions. Those people will not be politicians running for future office, but managers and executives. I will bring congressional leaders together to hammer out compromises—to my thinking, compromising is the main job responsibility for politicians anyway.

Host: (Hurriedly grabs a paper thrust at him from the side and reads to himself.) Looks like about 20 percent of voters favor the senator according to our latest polls. The Republicans have lost five points this week and the Democrats lost even more. But back to our guest. Senator Conley, you have no party structure, no base of support on the Hill. If elected President, how do you expect to get any of your legislation passed?

Conley: I covered that already, Lyman. I'll invite members of Congress to my house to discuss matters and we'll compromise. That's what I did in the Senate and it worked well.

Host: (Dubiously shaking his head in silent response.) What about advisors? You'll have to have an extensive staff under you. Where will those people come from?

Conley: The President of the United States has over three million "advisors," employees on his payroll at any moment. They are some of the smartest and best informed people in the world. I don't see why I need to take up parking around the Ellipse with an extra bunch. Too many presidents haven't trusted the hard-working civil servants under them. Once the political appointees leave, I'll go directly to the source for answers. My Vice President will oversee the work of the agencies and help get me the best advice possible. Mrs. MacMurray and I will continue to listen to the concerns of the American people as we are doing in this campaign and have done during our service in the Congress. We consider the people our advisors and partners in this government.

Host: We have time for one more topic and you gave me a lead in to it, Senator. This country has never elected an independent. No one has ever run successfully for office without a strong political party and hefty financial contributions. But no woman has ever been elected vice president either. If your other policies don't defeat you, certainly you can see that naming a woman, especially a young and inexperienced one such as Ms. MacMurray as your running mate, could turn into a major political blunder.

Conley: Hailey MacMurray is far from being a political blunder, Lyman. She is smart, capable, and a proven leader. You insult the good people of Virginia when you refer to her as a political blunder. They have elected her to the Congress. She is a widow and a good mother to her son, Adam. She graduated at the top of her Air Force Academy class, qualified as one of our best fighter pilots, and changed careers when her husband was killed in a crash. She worked as a Foreign Service Officer and is fluent in French, Russian and Chinese. She has advised our ambassadors on national security and serves as one of the few members of Congress recognized as a true expert in foreign affairs. You would do well to apologize quickly for that remark, Lyman, because you're not in the same league with Hailey MacMurray.

Pollsters reported the Conley-MacMurray share of the voters favor rose another ten points as a result of Senator Conley's interview on the Lyman Trevolt program.

The conference championship game was a breeze compared to the trench warfare the Redskins had waged against the Bears. Adam came to visit his friend, Mark, but without his mother, who was working on her travel itinerary with Katlyn, "the slave driver," her close friend's new nickname. Adam explained his mother's absence and swore Mark to secrecy about the campaign to win the White House. "But," the boy whispered in a desperate voice, "call her anyway. She likes you."

"Some matchmaker that boy is, Mark. Did I hear right?" Jason had eagle ears as well as excellent vision. "Hailey is running for Vice President?"

Mark studied the bolts holding his locker together as if his life was bound within their threads. "Yeah, you heard and it's a national secret." The big pass catcher had lost his enthusiasm and his best friend couldn't help notice.

"So what. Call her anyway. Let her know you're interested." Jason stopped short. "Hell, I feel like I'm talking to my high school wide receiver who wouldn't ask the homecoming queen to the prom."

"What happened? Did you decide to take her?"

Jason grinned and got a faraway look. "Never made it to the actual dance, you understand. And don't go thinking I'll call the lady myself. I saw her on the field last week. Adam is right. She likes you and I'm tired of seeing your hang dog face moping around here. Call her, and then clear it from your mind so we can concentrate on beating the Broncos in San Diego."

Thirteen

The invitation was a trap. Bill Conley felt it in his bones, along with the aches of arthritis that plagued him in winter months. He and Hailey had argued for the better part of the night about accepting the News Channel's invitation to appear on their *Celebrity Spotlight* show. Even his wife, Elizabeth, had turned traitor on him and joined forces with Hailey, who wanted to do the show herself. She was confident she could add to their gathering surge in the polls. Bill Conley wasn't so sure.

Matilda Pratterly was nothing more than a vicious gossip digging for filth and long-buried scandals. More than one aspiring politician had been ruined with her innuendoes about "possible" sexual liaisons, "rumored" financial shell games, and "exaggerated" stories of youthful folly. Bill was certain that Matty The Tattler—her tabloid nickname—was intent on making Hailey look bad.

He watched the two women sitting across from him in his family room as they hunched forward to present their case for his better judgment. The silver haired senator smiled back at two lovely people, both beautiful inside and out. The women's beauty, combined with their intelligence and strength, created an enormous force he found hard to resist. Thank God they were on his side; determined to get him elected president. He would let them argue a while longer, then acquiesce gracefully as was his habit in the face of overwhelming intellect.

Bill reminisced, thinking back to the time he and Elizabeth had sat in these same comfortable leather chairs only six months before to decide on his vice presidential running mate. Each described numerous characteristics and qualifications, some seemingly impossible for a single person to achieve, and both knew they were talking about the same person: Hailey.

"She has to be smart, Bill," Elizabeth had fired the first shot at their imaginary marker board. "I won't have people saying you've picked a pretty face, an airhead, or worse, someone who gives the slightest impression she may have slept her way to the top."

"And I want youth, Elizabeth. Folks are going to wonder how many years I have left. If they vote for me, they need to know there's energy surrounding me. And yes, a spotless reputation. A woman who made it on her own, a good mother as well as an achiever outside the home." His infectious humor brought a loving smile to her face.

That their choice would be a woman had been understood before his own public statement to run. They believed no party would chance losing an election by choosing a woman for either of the top positions. No candidate would allow his ego to be superseded by the presence of a smart or attractive woman. Elizabeth and Bill Conley adamantly rejected those power-hungry beliefs. It was time to refocus the political system and restore public confidence. It was time for a woman! And only a strong man, one not motivated by power and ego, could choose her.

"She must be battle-tested." Elizabeth returned to her serious side. "It would be nice to go outside the Beltway, but frankly, you need someone who has been to war in Washington." She paused and reached for his hand. "Sweetheart, I have spent many hours talking to your running mate. Her son always comes first. She knows the Hill and is effective in creating coalitions. She is the best person for the job, man or woman. Truth be told, there is only one person better at that and I sleep with him." Her accompanying smile was fulsome and Bill squeezed her hand.

Senator Bill Conley returned to the present and broke into the two-person dialogue battering him. "OK, ladies. Go for it. Hailey, call them back and say you'll do it, but under one condition. It has to be a live telecast. I don't want them to ask you a hundred questions so they can edit a tape to suit themselves. They'll make you look bad no matter what you've said."

"Did you call her?" Jason remained a pest even in the afterglow of beating the Broncos soundly in the Super Bowl. Both men relaxed on Mark's deck overlooking the valley and the little town of Crested Butte.

"I left a message. She called back in about a week and left a message wishing us luck. I called and talked to her campaign manager who emailed their schedule. She said I might be luckier if I just showed up at a stop along the way and took her to dinner."

"Sounds brassy. Why don't you go for it?"

"She's too busy, Jason. Plus I have to get ready for the summer camps."

Matilda Pratterly was an unhappy TV show host. Imagine some guest who didn't have a chance of winning the election demanding she, Matty, the queen of magazine television, run a live show! It was preposterous. Unheard of. But the ratings should go through the roof, so she acquiesced.

> Host: Welcome to our show, *Celebrity Spotlight*. I'm your host, Matilda Pratterly. My guest tonight is Miss Hailey MacMurray, a member of Congress from Virginia and vice presidential running mate to Senator Bill Conley, the independent candidate from Colorado. Welcome, Miss MacMurray, or may I call you Hailey?
>
> Hailey: Hailey will do, Matty, and I was married, so I prefer Ms. instead of Miss MacMurray, as pretty much the rest of the country recognizes.
>
> Host: Excuse me then. Not a good start, I suppose. Tell me, Hailey, why doesn't Senator Conley like to be interviewed on popular radio and TV? And by the way, just love that suit. For our folks in the audience, *Ms.* MacMurray is wearing a navy suit, skirt to her ankles, with off-white buttons down the front, and matching navy pumps.
>
> Hailey: Thanks, Matty. Senator Conley remembers too well your interviews with previous candidates and first families. He did ask me to let you know he sleeps with his wife and no one else since that seems to be the main focus of your in-depth interviews. *Audience bursts into raucous laughter.*
>
> Host: Oh my! Well, I'm sure my audience understands that I'm much more interested in other subjects as well. So, who do you sleep with, Hailey?
>
> Hailey: Thanks for proving my point. I came prepared to air all my dirty laundry tonight, Matty. For the past five years I have slept

with Chipper—(the attractive Virginian paused to let the gasps and murmurs of the studio audience die down)—a black, long-haired cat my son Adam rescued from the Dumb Friends League.

Host: How cute. But there must have been lovers in your past. Surely you haven't been without a man since your husband's tragic death twelve years ago?

Hailey: Yes.

Host: Yes to what, Hailey?

Hailey: Yes, there have been no lovers. Also, to straighten out some recent tabloid stories, I'm not gay either. I also haven't slept with any aliens. So sorry to disappoint.

Host: I find that hard to believe. Really? Not even a short relationship that could have blossomed into the real thing? Oh come on now.

Hailey: Just call me Ms. Spic and Span, Matty. Not much excitement for a single mom providing for her son and traveling from one diplomatic assignment after another. I home-schooled Adam when I wasn't at work. After he got old enough to stay up later, he became my escort. That helped keep the potential boyfriends away. Yet I can understand your skepticism. You must find it as humorous as I do that the tabloids report so much personal information. Just this morning I read one saying you're on husband number four now; that you never divorced number two; and, that you remain separated from the third fellow as well. Then there are those rumors about that Latin cameraman from last summer. Frankly, doesn't all that gossip drag you down? (Hailey had spoken lightly of the gossip news that was more truth than fiction in "Matty the Tattler's" case. But the TV host's expression turned sour.)

Host: We'll take a short break and be right back, ladies and gentlemen.

They were now off camera with the set temporarily darkened.

"I ask the questions, *Miss* MacMurray. This show is about your life not mine. I'll dig wherever I think my audience wants me to," Matilda sputtered, her exasperation at agreeing to a live telecast obvious.

Hailey smiled graciously at her host. She enjoyed interviews like this, whereas Bill Conley detested them. Her friend and mentor felt that his record was public and the voters could take it or leave it. She agreed with him, too.

But this was fun. It was her job to add some personality to their quest for the White House. She also understood that women voters wanted to identify with a candidate of their gender. And, she had nothing to hide. That couldn't be said for her host.

"Matty, try asking a few questions about our candidacy, about the contest for the presidency. I have some views on the major issues. Sure, others have reported on those views, but always in a serious setting. An informal airing on your show might be interesting to your viewers."

Consternation consumed Matilda Pratterly's face. Hailey understood immediately that the woman had not prepared for serious questions. And, following the old legal saw, she didn't dare ask a question if she didn't already know the answer. Of course she had been fishing when she wanted to know about Hailey's bed partners, but had struck out.

Matilda did not reply and Hailey understood friendly chit chat was over. A palpable tension descended onto the set as the lights came back up. Matilda motioned to a production assistant who scuttled off stage. He returned just before the commercial break was over with a sheaf of papers, presumably with some meaningful questions.

> Host: Welcome back. Ms. MacMurray, can you tell our audience why you favor aborting helpless babies?
>
> Hailey: I am pro-life, pro-family, and pro-choice, Miss Pratterly. My public record is clear on that. Senator Conley and I will enforce the laws of the country which allow abortions, but we do not want the government to interfere in the patient-doctor relationship. Friends advised me to abort my pregnancy. So did my husband. I was at the top of the heap of test pilots and enjoying the ride. Giving birth meant certain death to a promising career. I made the right choice for me. Yet I won't judge others who choose differently, and it certainly is not pro-life to kill medical professionals who assist women who choose abortion.
>
> Host: (Stumped for a reply, the host scanned her impromptu list for another question.) Why do you want to do away with all guns?
>
> Hailey: I don't. There are many hunters down in the Virginia Blue Ridge country who understand my position, Ms. Pratterly. Gun safety is the issue, not the right to bear arms. It is insane to leave a loaded gun in your home where a child can pick it up. It is also insane to preach about rights to own guns when the real issue

is the sale of automatic weapons at astronomical profits. There is
no rational excuse for the sale of high-tech weaponry to the public.
And let me be clear on a related matter. It is an insult to local
police, state police, the National Guard and every member of the
United States military for citizens to claim the right to bear arms
for protection against their own government. Militia compounds
out West are operating outside the laws of this country and our
administration plans to put them out of business.

Host: My sources tell me that Adam smokes pot regularly and
you condone it. How can you pretend to represent the women of
this country with such flagrant disregard for morality?

Hailey: Good Lord, Matty! What a tangled web of fabrications
someone has woven. Adam found rabbit tobacco in a field near
our home in Blue Ridge. I found out about it when he came home,
green to the gills. He and a friend had rolled their own smokes and
gotten sick. Neither boy will smoke again, I assure you. But that
happened when he was eight. A lifetime ago for an eleven-year-
old, wouldn't you say? I gave him a second chance, sort of like
those you've wished for, Matty. Is it three times you've been to the
Reynolds Clinic? Or four? Isn't it time for questions from your
audience, Matty?

Host: Of course, uh, I've just received a few from our producer
that I'll read out loud to you. Here's one. "Where do you stand on
women's rights? Don't you think you're just window dressing for
Senator Conley's campaign?" Whew, a toughie, Ms. MacMurray.
I'd like to know the answer myself.

Hailey: Both Senator Conley and I support the principles behind
the Equal Rights Amendment to the Constitution. We will continue
that support and encourage a new initiative to get that amendment
going again. As for my being window dressing, look at the polls,
Ms. Pratterly. It is now three weeks before the election and the
voters say they favor Conley and MacMurray by a good margin.
I've negotiated with the Russians and the Chinese. They didn't
think I was just a pretty face. I have flown fighter jets and favor a
strong military. The Pentagon likes my stance. So do veteran's
groups. That's not a toughie, Matty. Ask me how to provide health
care for an aging population when the Congress rejects all proposals
sent over by the White House as too expensive. There is no easy

answer to that one, but we'll tackle it head on.

Host: Ah, here's one I've just been handed. It's from a member of our audience. What would you do if you became President and got pregnant?

Hailey: I'd expect my husband to go through labor and delivery with me and I'd expect the Vice President to run the country according to the requirements in the Constitution until I left the hospital. Of course, I'm not married and I don't sleep around, so that is a very hypothetical question. Thinking more about it, I'd schedule cabinet meetings and press conferences around feeding times and my husband would watch our child during State of the Union speeches. Bottom line, I'd make adjustments the same as married couples everywhere make. And no, I wouldn't allow the press into the delivery room. But practically speaking, Bill Conley is a healthy man and a smart one. That scenario is not one I consider probable.

All probabilities got tossed in November. Conley-MacMurray beat the incumbent and the other party's challenger by a two-to-one margin. The fantasy had become reality, the surreal real. Political columnists wrote about the phenomenon for months leading up to the January 20th inauguration. Those supporting more conservative positions insisted the liberals had caused the entire mess. Liberal media accused the "Right" of a massive conspiracy. A few, like the *Post's* Dan Roberts, nailed the right answer with ease.

The Second American Revolution

Observing the political gridlock and outright money laundering inside the Beltway surrounding America's Capitol City, one could have predicted the crushing victory by Bill Conley and Hailey MacMurray. For too long Washington politics have been separated from the common folk, openly pandering to a steady flow of special interest lobbying, and to be truthful, gobs of campaign financing. For too long the American public has been fed a constant diet of popular politics wherein the "best" politicians are the top money collectors. Read any campaign news from previous elections and the opening paragraph will attest to the power of candidate X to bring in the bucks. Thus, it was always reasoned that said candidate was winning, never so much as for morality, ethics, or integrity, but rather for the sole ability to scrounge and beg for financial backing.

The voters are not stupid, as some elected officials appeared to have hoped. It turns out our system works; just slowly as the framers of the Constitution insisted. The people finally gathered themselves into one massive voice and threw out the rascals gambling in our nation's cradle of democracy, Washington, DC. Enough, the voters said. Power corrupts and buying power corrupts down to the bone. And so the political Bermuda Triangle became a reality. The forces required to sink corrupt influence peddling came together in the form of two independent candidates. Conley and MacMurray promised nothing but honesty and integrity and ethical management of the federal government. They promised to remain accountable only to the American people. With such a promise they gained the most powerful "sponsor" ever seen in our American system of government, the source of authority for the Constitution itself: the people.

Resumes flooded the President-elect's office and home. He ignored them all; didn't know them. Hailey kept a busy schedule and missed the entire football season. She was reconciled to a lengthy courtship if Mark ever got around to asking her out and she found time to go. Washington was electric by mid-January: Bill Conley was being inaugurated, and the Skins were returning to the Super Bowl.

Fourteen

Change was literally in the air on this Inauguration Day for the Conley-MacMurray administration, as a balmy wind drifted up the Potomac and warmed the usually winter-chilled canyons of federal buildings in Washington. Men eschewed overcoats in the early spring-like atmosphere. Women wore bright, spring-like colors. And politically, voters and elected public servants anticipated their newly-elected leaders to reveal changes.

The Chief Justice of the Supreme Court swore in Bill Conley and Hailey MacMurray. Then the President of the United States took charge.

"My fellow Americans, distinguished guests, members of Congress, and the Supreme Court, I accept the challenge of the Presidency of the United States humbly and with honor. I have lived here off and on as a Senator from Colorado for the past several years and feel I know how this place works. Or, as has been the case too many times, how it doesn't work. And I believe I know why.

"Since my election last November, I have avoided this town, our nation's capitol. I decided to travel the country and listen to the American people; ask them what they wanted me to do. I promised nothing during the campaign. Didn't want to build up a load of issues the Congress could stonewall and dicker with. I don't have a majority backing me in the Congress; however, I am grateful for the newly-elected independent members of both houses. The people sent fifty new, independent representatives to the House and elected ten new independent senators. This is the highest number of independent members of Congress ever in our history. I believe those folks will be a strong block of votes in the center in my support. I also firmly believe that the people are sending a message to us, to both the executive and legislative branches. That message is to get on with the nation's business. And that is what I will do.

"There are many changes I can make without Congressional approval, and I fully intend to make them. Most of my ideas for change and improvement have come from the people. It is important for me to emphasize today that I have heard the voices of the people, and I fully intend to heed their wishes and to continue listening.

"The most dramatic change I can make is by setting an example for future presidents. I intend to return the office of the presidency to the people. For we have gotten sidetracked, tied up in affairs that don't serve the people. I am the first independent candidate ever elected president, and the only person elected to the highest office without the backing of a political party. My vice president is the first woman to hold that office. Selecting Hailey MacMurray to be my vice president is perhaps the most significant and symbolic action I could have taken. The voters were wise in their ability to see her as a capable leader. They did not criticize her for being a woman, as one of my opponents dared to do. The other candidate mistakenly sent his vice presidential candidate out to debate her, while no one invited me to a single debate. And the people told me after the election that no other event during the campaign affected them as strongly.

"Your new Vice President is smart, eager, and determined to make a difference. She has extensive diplomatic experience. I also know her as a strong woman. Her strength is double-edged: Hailey was one of our top fighter test pilots, and had the courage and compassion to change her goals to provide her son with a secure future. I'm not still campaigning for election when I bring up Hailey MacMurray's qualifications. I will treat her like no Vice President in the history of our country. Her role in my administration will unfold in the coming months. She will carry dual responsibilities, not only as Vice President, but also as executive officer of my cabinet. As such, she will ensure my directives are carried out. And, in this role, I'm certain the American people will see as much of her as they do me, and they will be pleased with their choice.

"Well, here we are. Elected and sworn in as your president and vice president. Here is our promise to the American people. Here is what I will and won't do.

"I will serve one four-year term only. That's enough. You deserve someone with continuing vitality and energy and you will get the chance to choose another person in four years. It has long been my belief that a president should have one six-year term. Most presidents in the past have wasted their first two years in office appointing people to jobs as payment for either campaign contributions or for running their campaigns. If they are lucky enough to be reelected, they waste their last two years being labeled a lame duck. It's simple math to see that a president elected for eight years only gives you four. The rest of the time he meets with fund-raisers, makes political appointments, and sits frustrated on his lame duck nest at the other end of Pennsylvania Ave.

"Now, as I look around the crowd here, I see some faces frozen in horror and others grinning as they mentally begin to plan their campaigns for the presidency four years hence. But let me make clear why I will not run for reelection. Goodness, you're thinking, the guy just got here with a landslide victory of almost three to one versus each of the two main party candidates. Nothing like it in the history of the country. And he announces his retirement date before he serves a full day. But I will work for you for four years. I will not waste your time campaigning to raise money, either for myself or another person running for the next office. For me, there will be no next office. I will not appoint a single individual as payment for services rendered or for a sleepover in the Lincoln bedroom.

"Think about that. Past presidents have appointed political friends to their executive staffs and cabinet positions. And, in turn, those political appointees have inserted political friends further down in their organizations. That won't happen under my presidency. I promise you that. It is what I want, and more importantly, it is what the American people told me they wanted. Frankly, significant laws were passed back in the nineteenth century setting up a civil service system based on open competition for jobs. Today, the federal government has been politicized down to journeyman level. Today that ends. Traditionally, incoming presidents ask for the resignations of every political appointee and all scheduled employees who are readily identifiable as having gotten their jobs through political connections. To date most of those individuals have complied with my request. But there are others belonging in the category of hangers on. Many of these individuals have burrowed into the hide of the bureaucratic beast, seeking to wait out an incumbent administration and surface later when their side comes back into power.

"Vice President MacMurray will find these individuals and persuade them to seek employment elsewhere. You, the American people, may wonder how this will be done. I can tell you that I spent almost fifty years working in military intelligence. I promise you we will find these people. This is important, primarily because many of those jobs you have been paying for are a waste of money. There is no work being done by these individuals. A few may be found to contribute to the common good and if that proves out then they can stay. But hear me out on this issue. Cronies and political friends have no place in my administration. It is time to stop rewarding financial backers with public jobs.

"I will have no managers and executives under me campaigning either for me or for themselves during my term as President. My Cabinet appointees are anxious to be public servants. They will not be celebrities seeking office. They will work hard for me, and better still, for you, to make the government work better.

"Americans visiting Washington, DC will find it easier to park here. First and foremost, the slots circling my new home that are reserved for government officials will be opened to the public. And wherever I find excessive parking facilities for executives I will eliminate them. I know, I know, you're saying to yourselves, here's our new President giving his first and only inauguration speech and he's going on and on about parking. But remember: This is not our town; it is America's capitol city. We need to make it easy for folks to come and see how their government works. Further, as head of the executive branch of our government, I have about three million people working for me. Therefore, I intend to be their Chief Executive Officer. I will ask for their advice and make personal contact with each agency and department. It is time we stopped blaming government workers for political mistakes.

"In two weeks I will address the Congress and the American people. Then I will tell you specific goals I have set for my administration. In the meantime, there will be no spokesperson for this administration that will be legitimately quoted in the media as an anonymous source at the White House. Federal civil servants do not have the privilege to hide behind anonymity, and as their boss, I won't allow it. So, after the political analysts finish dissecting this speech to tell you what they think I really said and meant, ignore their remarks based on anonymous sources.

"In closing, I want to state the overriding vision I have as your president. The American people come first. I work for them and no one else. Thank you for the honor and privilege to serve."

Millions of viewers stayed tuned to television commentaries and analysis that filled the gap between the president's inauguration speech and the parade. One network was typical.

Moderator: Welcome to our continuing coverage of the inauguration of President Bill Conley. I'm your host, Charles Goodenhour of the News Channel. Joining me today are our two regular political analysts and commentators, Jocelyn Andrews and Mortimer Spurling. Jocelyn is Director of the Gross Manning Institute for Progressive Analysis, an independent conservative think tank. Mr. Spurling served four terms as a member of the House of Representatives from the fifth district of West Virginia and now runs his own consulting firm here in Washington.

Before I ask for their interpretation of the president's remarks, I want to point out to our audience that President Conley has not left the podium. He is acknowledging the standing ovation of the crowd that doesn't seem to want to lose sight of him. As I watched their reaction during his speech I caught sight of numerous people nodding in agreement; some had tears. I don't want to sound too mushy, since this was a challenging speech aimed at the old guard political structure, but I got the feeling President Conley was not speaking to anyone in the power elite class here in Washington. He spoke to the hearts of the people; perhaps becoming the voice of the people. Jocelyn, what's your take on this?

Andrews: Frankly, Charles I've never heard such a speech in my twenty-three years covering inaugural addresses. It was too short to suit me, and what's this business of saving the details for another time?

Spurling: That's exactly his point, Jocelyn. You always look for differences from the accepted protocol of Washington, DC. President Conley gave you none of that, and from my experience following his campaign, he never will. The man is just what he appears to be and nothing more; a trustworthy public servant who has captured the hearts of the American people. They know instinctively that he won't create scandals, and he won't have 'sleepovers,' as he quaintly put it. In short, he is his own man and declared himself today as their man.

Andrews: Oh, can it, Mortimer. We all know how enamored you get of any fresh face in town. But I can't see Conley surviving in the White House. He will have the shortest honeymoon of any president, if the Congress gives him one.

Goodenhour: Let me interject at this point, although we did take note that Ms. Andrews has already begun to address the President by his last name only, Bill Conley certainly looks presidential. Honestly, Jocelyn, isn't it possible to give the man one day in office before you start to disrespect him? Viewers can appreciate—if they missed his teleconferences—that our new president towers over a crowd at six and a half feet tall. He is an imposing figure. Intimidating, some have said. He's wearing a dark gray suit with blue pinstripes and a power tie that is a deep red. His hair is silver gray and worn in his usual crew cut. I must say, he seems physically fit. We're told—by an official press release and not any anonymous sources—he has maintained a svelte 220 pounds for most of his life. President Conley swims laps in the morning and never misses a walk with his lovely wife, Elizabeth, after dinner.

Spurling: Well, Charlie, now that you brought up our new First Lady, we have to comment on her role. President Conley openly describes her as his center. He gives her credit for keeping him fit, happy, and his own man. Just look at her standing beside him, beaming her admiration. Since no one else has described Mrs. Conley, I'll give it a go. Like her husband, Elizabeth Conley is tall and slender. We're told she turned down offers to become a model and chose instead to be the woman behind Bill Conley. I believe that is a wool sheath ensemble in royal blue that works beautifully with her coloring.

Andrews: Jeepers, Mortimer. You sound like an emcee at a fashion show. I'll cut to the chase on Elizabeth Conley as the woman behind the throne, Mort. Many think she is the brains in the family. The man doesn't make a move without checking with his old ball and chain first. I'm suspicious of a brainy First Lady. It's cause for me to wonder who will be in charge at 1600 Pennsylvania Avenue.

Spurling: Ridiculous! The American people know who they elected.

Goodenhour: OK, let's get back to the official presidential party on the stage. President Conley and Vice President MacMurray are working their way through the crowd of dignitaries and invited personal friends, receiving congratulations all around. Ms. MacMurray is, uh, quite frankly, a knockout. She is also tall at five ten, the maximum height allowed for a woman at the Air Force Academy, where she received her officer's commission. Today she is wearing a deep crimson-colored suit with a skirt to mid-calf. Frankly, I've never seen her in anything more revealing. To her credit, photographers have never captured the Vice President in skimpy or showy clothing. She dresses quite well, if you ask me, and the men in our viewing audience will appreciate the subtlety this very attractive woman conveys. There is a hint of a figure always smartly subdued by fashionable and professional-looking attire. Her beautiful chestnut-brown hair comes to her shoulders and glistens in this bright sunshiny day. Her eyes—

Andrews: Oh please, Charlie. We all know you're smitten. You sound like a character out of a sleazy romance novel. Next I expect you to say she appears cool as a cucumber but has unbridled passion inside just waiting for release when the right fellow comes along. Cripes! You men. I'd be asking why she never remarried or even dates eligible bachelors to give her son a good father. The religious right has wondered about this as well. Is she gay? A prude? A cold fish, maybe? And what really happened to her husband? Why didn't she take his last name? I could list a hundred questions that have been put forward by the media in their attempt to unravel the mysterious Ms. MacMurray. I, for one, am not so easily taken in by her credentials as dramatically recounted by Mr. Conley.

Spurling: Now, now, Jocelyn, draw in those female talons. A bit of envy is apparent in your cutting remarks on the subject. I offer Exhibit A for your perusal, her son Adam. The mothers in the electorate made clear their admiration of the Vice President's decision to devote her life to her son. And in case you have forgotten, Ms. MacMurray's husband was also a test pilot. When he died in a crash, she got out, realizing her son needed her more than she needed to succeed at such a dangerous occupation. Honestly, Jocelyn, what is there to gripe about? Look at that boy. He is his mother's shadow escort to everything. She is with him constantly and he is a good son. Straight A's in spite of traveling with her throughout the campaign. Good looking boy too. Rather gangly at this age approaching his early teens, but the girls are ga ga over him.

Andrews: Ga ga? Spare me the hyperbole, Mort. You sound as stricken about the boy as Charlie here is about the mother. Next you'll be telling me she bakes apple pies and loves baseball. How smaltzy can you get.

Goodenhour: Actually she does like baseball, although she is a big football fan and loves our Redskins. And, as you may have forgotten, Ms. MacMurray was an All-American in volleyball at the Academy. She was reputed to be their best spiker. Maybe a bit of foreshadow to her role at the Conley White House. But back to center stage. The President is breaking tradition again by advancing into the crowd of spectators at the base of the Capitol steps. The Vice President is not far behind, covering his flank as we might expect her to do when the real work begins. Adam and Mrs. Conley are doing likewise. Amazing. And yet, the people are not crowding around the man and his small entourage. As he did during the campaign, the man is in no hurry and people know he will greet almost everyone personally. The Secret Service agents must be going crazy.

Spurling: Wonderful. Just wonderful. Watch the people. They all catch his eye and return a look of respect, a characteristic sorely missed in recent times. It's as if they know he has changed things and they approve.

Andrews: Sure they do. Just wait until his programs get stalled in Congress. Wait until he goes on TV and rants about partisan politics, of which he is not a part. The people will then realize they have elected a lame duck from the get-go.

Fifteen

While TV commentators delved into the deeper political ramifications of the President's speech, the new First Family and Vice President joined Congressional leadership in the traditional luncheon before the parade. This event was also televised, and although hardly as popular as the parade, it symbolically represented a form of loyalty oath from the legislature to the new chief executive. Those attending needed to eat and that need temporarily overcame doubts as to how long the promises of cooperation made after lunch would last.

Senator Kent Kraft, Senate Majority Leader, was the first to speak. "Mr. President, Mrs. Conley, Madam Vice President, and distinguished guests. As Majority Leader of the Senate, it is my privilege to welcome you here for our traditional luncheon. Our purpose today is to offer you a pledge of our loyalty and commitment to work with your administration." The senate manipulator supreme, as identified by political analysts for years, was brief if not eloquent. No one doubted the man's loyalty to building power and influence inside the Beltway.

The Speaker of the House of Representatives, Congressman Cantwell "Ned" Nederthal, stood up next. "Likewise, Mr. President, as Speaker, I offer our loyalty and everlasting commitment to working hand in hand with you to meet the needs and desires of the people." Commentators noted the immense lack of stature, in all aspects of the term, by the Mississippi representative. Everyone knew the man had simply outlived the other representatives. "Now, Sir, may I invite you to join us in a toast to your success.

Here, here, to the President of the United States." All networks quickly surmised these to be the shortest welcoming speeches in history.

President Bill Conley chuckled as he rose to address the diners. "Be seated please and thank you, Ned, for that gracious toast. Thanks to both you and Kent for your commitment to work with us. Ladies and gentlemen, as I look around the room, I see familiar faces. Colleagues who showed me a thing or two when I came here as a reluctant senator. I say 'reluctant,' because Elizabeth can verify that I aspired to some time off playing a little golf after retiring from the Army. But a few things happened to preclude that, and they probably saved me from gaining too much weight from my wife's home cooking.

"And, here I am. I was one of you, and I know how hard you work trying to do right by your constituents. It is an awesome responsibility to consider that all of your constituents are mine collectively. It is your duty to represent the wishes and demands of 435 Congressional districts and fifty states. In doing so, I fully expect us to butt heads over some issues because I will be looking at the total picture. The executive and legislative branches have always argued and the creators of the Constitution must be gleeful as they watch their experiment come to fruition. Never have so many argued about the right thing to do. And of course, everyone is certain they are right.

"So let me make it clear that you will hear from me on the issues. However, I will ask that you bring your differences to me so we can work out effective compromises and do the people's business. I value your perspectives, for they cover the country in a myriad of opinions and needs. Equally, I expect you to hear my voice as I reflect what I interpret to be the national good.

"I promise to be an accessible president. Come straight to me with your concerns because you won't find an insulating layer of advisors and consultants blocking your way. If I'm out of town, talk to Hailey. She speaks for me. Ah, I see some heads turning on that point. Let me be clear. Vice President MacMurray runs my White House in my absence. I know this is another precedent breaker, but you see I have very little ego when it comes to taking credit or getting the blame. Past Vice Presidents have sat ensconced in a separate little corner waiting to be called to the big dance. In my administration, my vice president is the maitre 'd, the one person I go to first. There is so much to manage as it is, and Hailey MacMurray will be the manager I rely on the most. After all, she worked with many of you during her terms in the House representing southwestern Virginia. Most of you know her. And from my conversations with Hailey, she surely knows you. So come over to my house for a visit any time, whether I'm in town or out visiting. You'll find a place to park if the tourists don't get there first.

"Where will I be? I see a few of you murmuring to each other. Good question. I will be listening to the people. I will go to your districts to learn, and you're welcome to come along. In these last several months I have been refreshed by the voices of the people beyond the Potomac. It is invigorating to go out there and listen and I envy members of this branch of our government who do just that on a regular basis. Yes, come with me so we can hear those voices together, agree on what we hear, and return here to do our part. There's plenty of room on my plane.

"One final note of business and I'll go march in the parade. My home is considered the People's House by most Americans. I will make it open to visitors, well, as open as my guards let me. That policy starts today, right after the parade. You have heard there are to be no inaugural balls. I have replaced them with an open White House, where Elizabeth, myself and Vice President MacMurray will host a reception. We saved announcing it for security reasons, and since everyone is invited we skipped sending out invitations. But I'm sure news will spread quickly after this fine luncheon is done.

"Thanks for your hospitality. Now come, Elizabeth, Hailey. It's time to walk."

The three honored guests stood together and left the members of Congress to chew on the President's words. Silence descended upon the dining room as many left behind recognized a shift in the foundation of once-familiar ground.

Speaker Nederthal latched onto Senator Kraft's elbow. He was perplexed as usual and not aware of the shifting political winds and their effect on his domain. "What is this, Kent? Is he trying out some kind of experiment at the expense of his presidency? First he announces his resignation, taking effect in four years. That's a crazy move, but not as foolish as turning over the government to that woman. She's too smart for her own good if you ask me. Asks too many questions. And just like her new boss, she accepts no contributions. Hell, the woman won't even take lunch with a lobbyist, much less keep an appointment with them. Folks down in Virginia's Blue Ridge country consider her some kind of Joan of Arc for Christ sake."

"Easy now, Ned." Senator Kraft sighed as he took on his usual role of explaining the larger picture to his friend from Mississippi. "I expect the man to feel his oats for a month or so and then revert to custom. Give him his head for a short time. Take the bit in his teeth, so to speak. Let him kick over the traces like a stallion on the loose; win a few minor races. We can rein him in down the road."

"Do you really think that's possible, gentlemen?" Senator Burch Magnum offered his opinion to the two political bosses. "President Conley set more than a few precedents before today's stunning announcements. When was the last time a President won a majority of votes by such a wide margin? He beat our two parties combined. Simply unheard of, and we all thought we'd never see the day. I kind of like this independent move myself."

"Burch, I'm not surprised," Kent Kraft retorted. "Your California went wild over the man. Sort of feel the earth shifting under you, eh?"

"Might have to do a little shifting myself, Kent. What would that do to the Senate, do you wonder? Hmmm, if I kick over the traces, as you aptly put it, that deadlocks both parties in the Senate and the independents have to be courted by both sides on any issue it would seem. Sounds like a lot of fun."

The Speaker shook his head, disgusted at the whole turn of affairs. He left the senators to haggle over how to gather votes to control their chamber and joined an animated group of representatives near the exit.

James Buxton, Minority Leader in the House, sputtered to the group, his face resembling an enlarged radish with sprigs of white hair scatter-shot from its core. "I lost five more to the center independents right after that confounded speech, Mr. Speaker. Harry Jackson now has better than a couple dozen vote margin over my party."

"Make that closer to twenty, Jimmy," Harry Jackson, the Majority Whip drawled. "We had a few turncoats ourselves. And if those damned center folk band together they control everything. Next thing they'll be demanding their own committee chairs, more office staff, and better lockers in the gym. Hell, I don't know where this cow is going to pasture, but someone sure left the barn door open."

"You say we lost a few, Harry?" Cantwell Nederthal broke into the conversation, asserting his primacy over the group.

"There's three for sure and several others who are hinting mighty strongly, Ned." The drawling Texan replied.

"Look around the room, Ned," Jackson suggested. "Did you ever see so many little groups gathered in the corners after one of these lunches? Hell no. Crap! Most would have been out the door to fetch their wives or guests to get a plumb seat on the reviewing stand. Not a few would be heading home to catch a few Z's so they could make it through the godawful dancing, except there ain't no dancing cause there ain't no parties."

"I smell anarchy, fellows," Jimmy Buxton added. Nederthal and Jackson followed Buxton's glare to a larger group across the dining hall. Simultaneously, members of that bunch popped their heads up and returned their own glares in seeming defiance. Soon groups formed and melded around the room as new alliances were cemented in clandestine huddles.

Sixteen

The ancient black and white TV flickered in the bowels of the Archives building at Seventh and Pennsylvania Avenues. Norton Roscoe had seen his future. As the prophetic words of the new president echoed down the canyons of Washington's bureaucracy, the call to serve pummeled Norton into action. He had waited his whole career to hear just the right phrasing on inaugural day. And, in his opinion, President Bill Conley had sounded the trumpet as loudly as JFK had back in 1961.

Roscoe was an expert in records retention. He worked in the stacks, a labyrinth of curling steel shelving and dividers that formed barely usable offices surrounding the exhibit areas of the famous building. Many visitors came to pay homage to the Constitution and Declaration of Independence, located nineteen, seven-foot stack floors directly below Norton's perch. They never saw the retention expert who, in turn, had no use for them. He steadfastly served his country reading and grading old papers eight hours a day, setting their lifespan as either temporary or permanent. Truth be told, he knew his importance. Without his expertise, there would be no historical exhibits for the uneducated gawkers. He, Norton Roscoe, made the final determination on what documents were kept and what got tossed. At least he did that for the odd, misplaced presidential papers that sifted into his cubbyhole, rather than directly to the presidential library responsible. He sneered at the reality that some of the more popular documents landed in the presidential libraries, but Norton had the good stuff. He was certain of that.

He was a patient man, of slight frame and hairless from the neck up—a gift of heredity. He squinted through trifocals long out of date, but preferred the dim lighting the stacks afforded. Today he had reported to work, ignoring the national celebration outside. He might catch a glimpse of the parade later taking advantage of his bird's-eye view from a small window on the building's north side. VIPs and invited guests of Archives' top management would schmooze all afternoon eating fancy sandwiches and toasting their longevity down on "Mahogany Row." Norton never ventured to the main floor of offices, amazingly designed into the original structure. He wanted no part in their elitist deliberations.

Mahogany Row was named for the ceiling-high, thick, polished wooden doors separating National Archives management from staff. Above and below this floor were the mysterious crawl spaces known as the stacks—makeshift work areas designed by engineers, apparently while following rats in a maze. Hindsight was the strength of the historian-managers who dreamed up the Archives building back in the late 1930s. They saw little need for more than a huge exhibit hall and plush offices for themselves. Beyond that would be spare storage for the few historical papers deemed worthy of placement in this hallowed sarcophagus. Who knew World War II would generate so much valuable history that had been documented by millions of boxes of paper to be evaluated, screened, graded—by latter day experts like Roscoe—and stored. The molding stacks fermented in dark corners, nourished by the same underground river that continuously harassed the FBI across the street. Retention experts—Norton considered himself their prime member—crawled into the stacks and remained, like lichen under rocks. Some needed no other air to breathe.

However, Norton had heard the call today. He would be contacted soon to serve at the White House as he had always known would happen. They would need his expertise to set up their files and separate the wheat from the chaff. Otherwise, like many administrations before, a veritable flood of uncatalogued papers would cripple their work. It didn't matter how much computers had aided and simplified communications and record keeping. There still had to be a system to organize records in whatever form they took. Norton's gut burned to be the chosen expert to lead the team of records analysts into the People's House. He had time to gather his thoughts before his new president marched by him below. He would draft a memo to the Archivist, volunteering his time.

Then there was his squirrelly group of stack buddies to call off. Their Friday afternoon bomb scares had to cease for now. Once a month whoever drew short straw called in sick at lunch, then made another call to security claiming to have planted a bomb on one of the 22 stack floors in one of the two million archives boxes. The result was always the same. The building emptied and workers got sent home while dogs and police searched in vain for the nonexistent bomb. It was great fun and a lovely diversion to start the weekend. But now was a serious time. Norton had heard the call to serve.

On Mahogany Row, the offices of the Archivist of the United States were indeed jammed with high-ranking "Nartians," an insider euphemism for employees who kept the nation's history intact. Dr. Dalbert Forrester, current Archivist appointed two Presidents ago, mulled over his scotch. His inner circle of office chiefs clung to his intellectual girth like catfish ready to snarf up any crumbs of encouragement in a world gone mad.

"Gentlemen, I admit we didn't plan one earthly objective for what we believed to be an impossible outcome. I had detailed budget projections with hefty increases all around in case President Hathaway was re-elected. Of course, I reduced those optimistic projections for a potential defeat of Hathaway and resulting overthrow by Elbert's ascendancy. But never—"

"It's OK, Woody," Justin Cole, Chief of Retention Policy interjected. Once Woody digressed he could end up in another century, preferably several preceding the Industrial Revolution in which he appeared to be more comfortable. "None of us believed Conley could win. He wasn't on any of our appropriations or oversight committees when he was a senator either. The man probably knows less about our little independent agency than we know about him. Don't forget, the most recent President didn't think to challenge your ten-year appointment by his predecessor. Why should this character? Don't worry, we'll muddle through as always. Outlast the bastards as usual. Seems to work."

Nathan Alsbach, Archival Executive Officer, grimaced at this last comment. "Not this time, JC. I got a memo actually signed by our new Vice President, as head of Conley's transition team." Alsbach paused to acknowledge the disapproving grimaces of his colleagues. "It seems Ms. MacMurray wants a team of analysts to provide direction on a revamped White House records system. She even named who she wanted to lead the team." Alsbach paused again for effect, exchanging grins all around. It was understood that Woody detested these demands, but went along with them. He never sent over his best people, though.

"We can't spare a soul, Nat. Not a blasted soul. Tell her that. Put it in writing and I'll sign the damn thing myself." Woody fumed, verbally exhausting months of stress to no one who would disagree.

"Does that bitch think she can really pull strings?" JC was a known misogynist and he reserved his most putrid vitriol for uppity women. Especially repugnant to the archival boss for retention policy was any female who had gone higher on the ladder than JC himself. "That's right, Woody. Stonewall her. Let her come crawling to us for help. I bet she'd offer a nice prize in return."

The government's top paper shufflers chuckled over their drinks. They had lost interest in the grand parade. Experts at examining the past, planning for what was to come taxed them immensely. Their remorse over failing to plan for the impossible election result was an emotion repeated hundreds of times around the city that afternoon. The more advanced thinkers among bureaucratic politicians were furiously planning even at this late hour. Old line bosses ignored the clear warning Bill Conley had shot across their bow. This group also considered the vice president a nice bit of fluff they could bamboozle with their usual budget shell game.

Some laughed at the mild threat to purge the bureaucracy of political appointees. These operatives had friends and political cronies buried deeply in the short hairs of Uncle Sam's administrative hide. They would not be easily ferreted out. Most expected to last a good part of the third millennium.

Seventeen

The National Park Service horseback patrols reported the largest crowd in memory. Conservative estimates guessed a million citizens had bunched along Pennsylvania Avenue to welcome their new president. A hurricane of activity preceded such affairs. Stoplights were removed from the center of the street. Sewer covers were checked and sealed. Every structure was searched; most were secured with armed teams. Top-level bureaucrats and their guests crowded around windows, permanently sealed and bullet-proofed, looking down on the parade route up the avenue. All had been searched and cleared by the Secret Service.

Newcomers to the capitol gawked at the gigantic buildings that lined the main avenues leading west from Capitol Hill. Someone had once said the entire environment was designed to intimidate, humble, and inspire. The federal government was so big! How could a President, usually a man with an immense ego, attempt to rein it in and get something done? Most had barely nudged the monster a degree or so to left or right. Still others ignored the enormous administrative machinery and appointed their own layer of cronies to make sense of it. But the career civil servants always outlasted them. Temporarily, though, a president might feel he had some control over nearly three million workers who called him boss.

A myriad of forces had aligned perfectly at the precise moment to elect Bill Conley President and Hailey MacMurray Vice President. No one ever expected Congress to act in a timely manner. Yet, some action was expected and required. Single-issue congressmen, lobbyists, and a veritable flood of influence-pedaling money had gridlocked a once-proud capitol city. Political traffic had imploded. Nothing got done.

The people had voted for a man and a woman who promised only their hard work and honesty. Neither owed a dime to campaign financiers. For sure, money had come in by the buckets from ordinary voters tired of the political action committee "idea" commercials. But every penny had been put in a trust account and doled out for travel and a few ads. Leftover money either went back to contributors or to charities designated by a separate advisory group. The message to the people had been simple: the Conley campaign had made it to the top without sponsors who would come calling for a payoff. "Unheard of," many said. "About time," said the majority.

Conley and MacMurray had made no promises. As leaders of the executive branch of the federal government, they vowed to manage it effectively and that was promise enough.

The time for scoffing was over. The people had voted a solid mandate for the new White House team. Enough independent candidates had won seats in both chambers of Congress to control votes on any issue. Vitriol between the two major parties definitely prohibited any coalition on their part to thwart this popular president. Rats were scuttling sinking ships and converting to the independent religion minute by minute. Power was shifting. Old-line consultants and senior power brokers had worn the wrong shoes to the game. Their slippery-bottomed sneakers no longer dug into a grass-roots turf grown by the people. This was a special turf with automatic weed control aimed at political manipulators and small-sighted politicians making a career out of slurping at the public trough.

President Bill Conley and his wife Elizabeth, along with Vice President Hailey MacMurray and her son Adam, strolled down Pennsylvania Avenue to begin the longest walk ever on inauguration day. It beat Jimmy Carter's stroll in distance and time. The crowd applauded and cheered them on as heroes who had slain the toothless dragon of party politics. Both pairs remained as unconventional as the people had come to expect. All four had changed into running shoes for the long hike and kept the Secret Service agents busy as they crisscrossed the street waving and shaking hands. They were not in a hurry. This was their parade. Their time had come.

"Wow! Mom, check out that girl in the shocking pink micro skirt." Adam was off to meet a new friend before Hailey could grab his arm. Jennette caught up with him, snagging the boy before the precocious "teen vamp" with bare legs and pierced midriff could create a scene.

"Stop right there, Adam. You know my rules: no jumping into crowds unless I'm with you," she said.

Adam was instantly chastened and embarrassed. "Sorry, Jennette. Guess I wanted to make contact with the voters." He grinned, caught inches before his hand could accept the proffered note from the flirtatious young girl. Jennette took it for him and thanked the young lady courteously. Bystanders laughed at the exchange between the Vice President's famous son and her senior Secret Service agent.

Jennette could see that providing security for Hailey was going to require creativity and innovation. Adam was a young boy in a man's body. He was tall, lithe, muscular and athletic. Good looks didn't come close to describing him. He had his mother's chestnut brown hair and height, combined with his father's striking features: clear blue eyes, perfect nose, strong chin and a quick friendly smile that alone would get him elected if he ever chose to run for public office.

Adam and Jennette strolled along together now that she had contained his eagerness. Both sensed the eagle eyes of the Vice President without craning their necks a millimeter. The mother-son relationship was on national display today and the TV news minicams caught every wink, frown, and misstep.

Hailey had politely asked the media to let her son have a normal life in the Washington fishbowl. It was Jennette's job to add a protective cushion regardless of the promises her boss received from the major TV and publishing corporations. Both women knew all bets would be off if Adam slipped one degree.

Jennette unfolded the perfumed note and read an invitation to a party in Georgetown for tonight. It was signed "Melody," and sealed with a bright red lipstick kiss. The assertive young girl had added her phone number and address as well. Jennette sighed and slipped the note into her pocket with another dozen or so just like it. And they hadn't even gotten to the National Gallery of Art at Third and Pennsylvania! She viewed the parade route as a path filled with temptations. The voters longed for a "clean" administration not beholding to anyone. Jennette and Hailey silently hoped Adam could grow up and be whatever he wanted to be without someone leading him astray.

"Here's another one, Jennette." Adam returned to her side and brought her back to present time. He held a pink note between his thumb and index finger as if it contained pollutants. Jennette cursed to herself for thinking too much of what could happen and took the note. She was not thinking like an agent so much as a family friend and surrogate aunt to the boy.

Hailey watched her son and let inner joy take over her consciousness. Adam was a treasure she needn't worry about. He understood so much for a growing boy. Jennette was probably more uptight than she. The nation's first female Vice President returned her attention to the people along the street and went to shake some hands. She was flanked by two young agents who had collected notes along the way too. Men were overcome by a single woman holding a powerful political office. Many apparently thought this would be their best opportunity to get a date. The two agents, Nick and Charlie, were struggling to keep a straight face. They took turns reading the notes within earshot of Hailey and a few made her cheeks turn pink with their suggestions.

Was this another first, she wondered? Probably. All the other women who had marched in this particular parade had been married and somewhat older. Hailey contemplated the rumors about her social life. She had even listened to some of the chatty TV and radio shows. "Must have a secret guy hidden away in the Virginia mountains," some speculated. "A gorgeous babe like her must have her dance card filled for years to come," said others. *Phooey*, she thought. If the first female Vice President remained an enigma to most men, she'd enjoy the advantage.

"Ouch, that's a little too friendly, sir." Hailey grimaced as she retrieved her hand from an overly masculine fellow who had laced his morning coffee with too much testosterone. Nick and Charlie herded him back to the crowd gracefully and came quickly to her side.

"You OK, ma'am?" Nick looked worried and Charlie held her right hand as if it were a sack full of precious jewels.

"I'm fine, guys. Got caught daydreaming for a second and took the wrong hand. I said I'm OK, Charlie. Let go my hand." She laughed softly and Charlie went scarlet from ear to ear.

Hailey cleared her mind and continued walking. She followed President Conley's example and strolled; they were all enjoying this time and in no hurry. Yet, as usual, her thoughts went to the work she would begin, had already started—grab hold of the bureaucracy and use it. First she had to shake loose a century of patronage, political favors returned with jobs at every level. Thirst for power and control had pushed aside civil service reforms. Presidents had held bureaucrats at bay for decades, stiff-arming program managers and stifling lawfully enacted programs.

Regular folks outside Washington's Beltway had witnessed the DC two-step for too long. It was one step forward and the next back. Like a couple going through a nasty divorce, the two major parties opposed each other simply because that was what was expected. Neither could remember their positions, platforms, and promises to the people. Each voted against the other because it was—because it wasn't their idea? Who could remember? Or, it could be that the other party had stolen a perfectly good idea and bastardized it with amendments surely designed to sink it?

Hailey remembered Koestler's frightening novel, *Darkness at Noon*. Enough brainwashing and one might actually believe the title of the book had come true in the nation's capitol the way some members of Congress debated the issues. Problem was, a young generation had lost faith in the system. Hailey had been asked over and over during the campaign just who the people in Washington worked for. When she answered "they"—meaning the President and the Congress—were public servants employed by the people, one young woman in Idaho retorted vehemently, "No, Ma'am. That's not true and I'll never believe it. Those people work for corporations."

At another stop in California, a young college student worried her with his question on authority, misuse of a power, and ultimate responsibility in government. What's the source, he had asked? The students in the crowd had scoffed at her answer.

"You are the source. We the people set up this government. The ultimate authority comes from us," she had said proudly. But they hadn't bought it. One lad cried out that it was more likely those pointy-headed bureaucrats who don't answer to anybody and never got elected. "No," another shouted across the auditorium, "look at who contributed to the campaigns. Follow the money."

It was no wonder militia groups built stockades in the Rockies and refused to pay taxes. No wonder states had begun to sound like a confederation of hagglers. Local politicians were scrounging for national recognition with premature and incomplete claims of solutions to national issues. States' rights advocates crawled out of the woodwork, challenging the legal ability of the IRS to levy an income tax. If a lie was big enough, and repeated enough, some folks believed it. It was an American "darkness" occurring around the clock, a darkness sucking the political guts out of Washington.

The Secret Service had authorized one TV minicam crew to walk with President and Mrs. Conley up the avenue. Every network received the same live feed. But the narration by political analysts and commentators differed immensely. The Independent News Channel picked Lyman Trevolt to host its panel of experts.

Trevolt: Welcome back to our live coverage of the inaugural parade. From the looks of the President's progress, I'd say we're in for a long walk. Hopefully his programs won't take so long to make it back up to the Hill.

Joining me in our makeshift studio across from the reviewing stand in front of the White House are Jocelyn Andrews and Mortimer Spurling, who guided us through the ceremonies and speeches earlier from the steps of the Capitol Building.

Andrews: Lyman, our viewers can see President Conley just now approaching the Federal Trade Commission and that's a hot spot he'll have to extinguish early in his administration. The FTC was a moribund little country club in the early sixties until Nader's Raiders infiltrated it. Their expose caused a firestorm in Washington. Succeeding administrations either built up staff or attempted to dismantle the entire place. Conley will be fighting both parties on this one.

Spurling: At least we all know where the man stands on that issue, Jocelyn. He printed issue papers on at least a hundred topics and got them published free of charge across the country. Both President Conley and Vice President MacMurray personally signed each one-page statement. I'm reminded of John Anderson's campaign in 1980. Some said if there had been a test for the presidency, John Anderson would have passed it with high marks. The voters have told us they think President Conley would score even higher.

Trevolt: Folks you're looking at Nolan's Deli right across from the FTC. When you visit this town, be sure to get a Reuben sandwich there. Best in the world. Well worth the wait.

Andrews: Back to that Anderson statement by Mortimer, Lyman. I found John Anderson, a so-called perfect presidential candidate, appallingly dry and tediously dull. If I had to assign high marks for aridness to Mr. Conley, he'd surpass Congressman Anderson for sure. Nothing colorful or exciting about the man. I'm not sure what the American people bought on that score.

Spurling: Nobody bought anything, Jocelyn. That's his point. He offered his leadership and made no promises, only solid statements about his positions on everything from soup to nuts, the whole nine yards, kit and caboodle, and all the trite expressions imaginable.

Trevolt: So, I gather the two of you have a difference of opinion on our new president. Jocelyn, tell me, what president would you compare Mr. Conley to?

Andrews: Oh, for sure, Coolidge. The man doesn't say anything. He sends out his flunky vice presidential candidate to do all the dirty work of campaigning. His wife is rumored to be the smart one in the family. And he—

Trevolt: Sorry to interrupt you, Jocelyn but the presidential party is in front of the National Archives and higher management officials there are waving from their second floor windows.

Spurling: Some of them won't be waving very long, Lyman. President Conley is on record in writing that he'll appoint—wait, let me check my notes to get this quote right. Here it is, "I will put an actual manager over the Archivist. Historians are nice people; they just always seem to be looking backwards."

Andrews: Yet another battle, Mort. The historical associations will go ballistic if he tries to do that. But on this point I have to agree with Mr. Conley. For the important job they do, the Archives has a putrid reputation of recycled bad management.

Trevolt: There's the FBI headquarters. Another battle, Mortimer?

Spurling: Afraid so, Lyman. Director Kraft can't seem to decide if he's staffing a crime fighting organization or a network of spies. But he will be hard to unseat with the connections he has in the Congress. We all know Senator Kensington Kraft, his older brother, shoe-horned Ronald Kraft into his position.

Trevolt: Let's revisit a question I posed to Jocelyn earlier, Mortimer. What president would you compare Mr. Conley to?

Spurling: Washington, without a doubt. Lincoln next, and he might be the best combination of the two we could hope for.

Andrews: That's total malarkey, Mort. You're talking about national icons; men who framed the presidency and the nation.

They were great men and Conley hasn't served a day in office. Come on, man. Wake up.

Spurling: I knew that would get a rise out of you, Jocelyn. But think on this. The voters want a leader, not a politician. Conley is a proven military leader and a successful politician. He sets the example. He compromises so well the combatants can't figure out how they came to agree, they just do. I've read his statements, all of them. This man will grab control and manage the federal government and the Hill. He'll get results.

Trevolt: Speaking of results, there is the lovely Vice President and her doting son just passing the DC Government Building. Her addition to the Conley ticket sure brought in the male voters. What a treat she has turned out to be. Women admire and respect her while men just want to unravel her mystery. She's a hero in her own right.

Andrews: Don't make me barf, Lyman. She's a rookie thrown into the deep end of the pool. This town will eat her alive.

Eighteen

For the first time in recent memory there was a party at the White House and expensive limos were not lined up out front. There was no room for them. The celebration of the inauguration had continued onto President Conley's front yard, crowded with "regular" people invited through the open gates. Well wishers flowed around the Rose Garden in back, inundating the south lawn usually reserved for staged welcome-back crowds and helicopters. Floodlights created a soft glow at 1600 Pennsylvania Avenue, eliminating shadows wherever possible—one of the few concessions the new president had made to the Secret Service.

Bill, Elizabeth and Hailey had started a receiving line inside, and had been forced to move outside. They moved among the crowd and through warming tents that seemed to cover the entire White House grounds. Each tent contained a buffet line with hot food and tables set up for family-style eating. Heaters, set up to cut the predicted chill of this January night, easily kept the tents cozy due to the mysterious warm breezes continuing up the Potomac. Even so, most folks gobbled down their food and left for home or the nearest warm bar to continue celebrating.

Dutch McKinley had his hands full and yet he was having a good time along with everyone else. Being in charge of security for "Eagle," his code name for President Conley, was sure different.

"Let the people come to me, Dutch," Bill Conley had ordered. "Put your agents out in the crowd and do your metal scanning routines as quickly as possible. I intend to be the people's president and keep in contact with them.

That means personal contact." His new boss had grinned. He was an affable man and his orders were always succinct, spoken in such a way that no one felt hammered down. Yet there was no doubt the man was in charge. He meant what he said.

Dutch had served under Conley in the Army intelligence service in Berlin. He would give his life for the man. He knew instantly when he had first met Major General Conley that the man would do likewise. The general, now President, gave loyalty and received it fourfold. He was leadership in spades: decisive, intelligent, smart, morally incorruptible, empathetic, and tough.

It wasn't that President Conley was reckless in directing so much personal contact with an unknown crowd of people. Rather, Dutch understood that the people needed to connect with their leader as never before. Their new president understood this better than any of his predecessors.

Bill Conley had never rubbed shoulders with an elite social class and wouldn't start now. Dutch had seen the list of changes President Conley sent to the Office of Presidential Protocol. The State Department would have a fit when they learned that formal black tie state dinners were gone. In their place would be Friday night buffets where foreign dignitaries and more of those regular people would mingle with members of the executive and legislative branches. There would be private dinners and lunches with the First Family in their living quarters, but no sleepovers. The President had a large family and they would be his only guests overnight. "Besides," President-elect Conley had joked to Dutch weeks ago, "I don't want to hold back for fear some visitor will wonder why the president is whooping for joy, or Elizabeth, too, for that matter."

"Mr. President, congratulations on your inauguration." The chubby fellow in construction clothes shook Bill Conley's hand firmly. The parade watchers around the worker waited their turn; no one crowded, pushed or shoved. President Conley had an aura of charisma and power that demanded respect, yet his friendly smile encouraged those in his presence to come forward. It was a secret ingredient the big man could not explain. He had always looked presidential, a leader people followed without fully understanding why.

"Thanks, Sir," President Conley said. "How's the job going?" He listened to the man chatter and continued to shake hands with other folks. He noticed agents being as unobtrusive as possible circulating amongst the immediate crowd. He caught the man's name and logged it permanently.

"Mr. Jenkins, keep up the good work on that project. We need to improve the looks of that old building. Now see if you can locate the food for me, I'm starved." Jenkins went off on a mission like a shot. Alice nudged her boss's elbow from the side.

"Mr. President, there's a line near the east gate with everything you like to eat, Sir," she said. Alice had been with Bill Conley for all his years in the Senate. Her job tonight was to record what people asked President Conley and set up a tickler on each item. Tad Jenkins would be surprised in a few days with a personal note wishing him the best from his new friend in the White House.

President Conley searched over the heads of the crowd for Elizabeth and saw her waving him over to the buffet. He sauntered over to her, creating a human wave in his wake. As he approached the line he took his wife's hand and stood at the back waiting his turn. Alice smiled as the crowded line turned as one and motioned him to the front. He just shook his head and enjoyed the wait, greeting new friends while shuffling forward. It was a habit left over from his days in the Army, he had explained to her early on. A commander waited until the troops were fed and went last. It was just one of many little things Bill Conley did that endeared him to Alice and to a large majority of voters.

The man refused special "perks." He rode the Metro subway while in the Senate, often beating Alice to work. He did not have a limo or driver, and reluctantly would use the official presidential vehicle after today. President Conley had briefed his cabinet appointees extensively on his policy for ethics in public service. He would lead by example and expect them to do the same, or their tenure would be quite short.

Lobbyists and top CEOs from private industry had bugged Alice for weeks trying to get appointments for a private meeting with President-elect Conley. She had turned them all down until one intelligent woman inquired if a public meeting request was the key to getting in. Alice scheduled her immediately and word got around quickly to the rest. Bill Conley's lesson in government operations was simple: as long as he worked for the people there could be no such thing as a private meeting. What went on in the Oval Office was for public record and consumption. The only exception would be true national security issues.

Members of the communications media had a shock too. Under Bill Conley there would be no "anonymous sources," or "unidentified White House spokesmen or women." This meant that in one simple move Conley had abolished the practice of White House trial balloons. Media correspondents groaned at the prospect of their confidential sources drying up, until they realized whatever they heard was reportable and on the record. There would be no more witch hunts to find the culprit who leaked confidential information because there would be no private conversations.

And why should there be? thought Alice. If the public paid for ninety-nine percent of the work going on in Washington, they had a right to know about it. Such an easy principle had stumped several Presidents and more Vice Presidents who felt above the crowd, claiming executive privilege to camouflage special attention given to big contributors and party cronies.

Over in another buffet line Mark Daniel was starving. The all-pro tight end found himself at the end of the longest buffet line he'd ever seen. He should have eaten before coming here on a lark. But here he was, and unsure of his next move. On the football field Mark was sure-footed and never uncertain of his next move. He was in his thirteenth year as a Redskin starter. He knew football and playing jazz piano; politics was like another world. Why had he come? And tonight of all times?

The short answer was to congratulate the Vice President. OK, so that wasn't exactly the whole truth. He had to admit she was a mystery he couldn't avoid. Hailey MacMurray had come down on the playing field just that one time. They had played phone tag with busy schedules since. Jason ragged him daily to get assertive and just go see her.

Mark's teammates had razzed him after that encounter on the field. The whole team knew Hailey was his fantasy dream date, the one woman he ever considered calling, yet he never seemed to find the courage. And now she was out of reach. Had she ever been approachable? If he had been intimidated before when the gorgeous Virginian was a mere Congresswoman, he was totally flummoxed by her new status. Plus, he now had to wend his way through thousands of partygoers crowding around the President and Vice President, wishing them good luck. Then a guiding angel disguised as the Vice President's son found him.

"Hey, Mark. It's great to see you. Too bad we can't toss the ball around. Too many people." Adam MacMurray had slipped away from Jennette when he spotted his hero.

"Adam, hey yourself. Great to see you," Mark said. Relief smoothed his worried look. Then he noticed the buffet table drawing near as the line picked up speed. "Did you eat yet?"

"I was too excited to eat before. Now I'm starved. Lately I want to eat everything in sight."

The two friends collected a pile of food and found a spot beside one of the heaters in a corner of the tent. They said nothing for a solid ten minutes while they scarfed down the scrumptious White House cooking. Mark was first to come up for air.

"I wanted to congratulate your mom and say hello to President Conley, but my stomach got in the way."

Adam laughed. "Mine too, Mark. Lately I feel like I've lost my best friend, my mother. I know she's busy and important now to millions of people. So I've been telling myself to play it cool, and don't worry. But I just don't see her much. The two of them, Mom and Senator, uh, President Conley are always in a meeting. I have Jennette following me everywhere. She's a neat lady and all that, but she's not Mom."

He sympathized with the lonely boy. Mark wondered if he would ever get to see Hailey, while her son thought he might not see her again. They formed a brotherhood of guys-in-waiting, but for wildly different reasons. Mark was truly smitten, a condition millions of other American men dreamed about. Adam just wanted to retain the close relationship he and his mom had always had. And here they sat without a clue to reaching their goals. The two shared the moment staring into the crowd at everything, at nothing. Their reverie shattered quickly.

"Hello, fellows. How did you get stuck in a corner?" Hailey MacMurray stood looking down at her beautiful son and his friend who was looking especially handsome tonight. She had thought to glance at Mark and speak to her son about something else but stopped, caught in a mesmerizing gaze from the football player. Her eyes stayed locked on the tight end as if she were the quarterback getting ready to drill a pass over the middle. Adam came to her side and hugged her, and still, Hailey just stood silently, gazing, as Mark rose quickly to his feet and reached out a big paw to shake her hand.

"Madam Vice President, congratulations," he said while she puzzled over that soft right hand. Finally she retrieved her hand and found her voice.

"Thanks, Mark. But we consider you a family friend, and I'd really prefer that you call me Hailey." She was embarrassing him and didn't want to stop looking directly into his friendly eyes. Stumped for a reply, it was Mark's turn to lose his voice. Then she remembered her son and turned her attention to him.

"Hey, kiddo. Did you get plenty to eat? Wasn't that salty Virginia ham great? And the red eye gravy over grits. Mmmmm, yummy."

"Yuck, Mom. You know I hate that stuff. Me and Mark didn't touch any of it. Us men chomped down on some great burgers and fries. Real American food."

It was Hailey's turn to yuck. "Yeah, real healthy. Might as well drink a glass of grease. Maybe that's why your grammar lessons need to be beefed up. Try saying Mark and I, and we men."

"Yes, Madam Vice President," her precocious son fired back and saluted. He had her full attention now. Hailey grabbed her son, kissed him loudly on the cheek, and hugged him ferociously—a public display certain to embarrass any teen.

"You grow any taller and I'll be kissing your neck, buster."

"Not if you can't catch me. You'll be too busy anyway."

There. It was out and she knew why Adam's hug had been just as ferocious as her own. She had to fit him in somehow and that consternation bothered her more than the work awaiting her in the morning.

Mark sensed her troubled mood. "Uh, Hailey, Adam, I have a proposal for you. I know this is a very busy time and all, but, uh, I was wondering if maybe Adam might like to come to my football camp out in Crested Butte? It'll be after school is over and he can bunk with me in my cabin." Adam's eyes went wide and he looked up at his mom all excited.

"Wow, that's great, Mark. How about it, Mom? I'd love to go."

Hailey knew when it was time to bend and this situation called for it. Besides, she might be able to slip away from town a few days and connect with the big football player. They had promised to get together two seasons ago.

"It's a deal, honey. I'll even take you out there myself and come pick you up. How's that?" She received another big hug from her son and smiled at Mark. "That's a heck of a way to get a date. You're a very patient man, Mark Daniel. And I apologize for being so unavailable."

"I have this feeling the wait will be worth it, Hailey." This time he gazed into her eyes and Hailey felt the heat rise from inside. "I'm pretty sure I can get tickets to the Super Bowl if you can break away."

She shook her head and was thankful Adam had wandered back in line for dessert. "Oh my, thanks, Mark. But I'll be too busy. Tomorrow I start a special project I intend to do personally. A lot of folks in this town are going to be very unhappy with me over it. I can't justify going out of town and having fun after firing so many people, my main mission for several months. Thanks anyway and good luck next Sunday." She took his hand again but held it and pulled him to her. For a moment Hailey put aside the gossip and possible sleazy photographs that might ensue. She grinned up at the big man and kissed him lightly on the cheek. Hailey backed away then returned to hug him, and sighed when she felt those big arms returning the gesture.

"There is plenty of room at my place for you and all your guards, Hailey. I'd return the kiss now except that lots of people are staring this way. But thanks. I needed that."

"Me too, Mark. Please excuse me. I have to talk to some folks over in the corner from Blue Ridge." Her exit was not quick enough to preclude numerous flashes from nearby photographers. *Poor man*, she thought. *Tomorrow the NFL's Man of the Year for two straight years will be in the papers for reasons other than sports.*

The papers published a variety of stories to accompany their snapshots of that "innocent" kiss.

Mrs. Perfect Meets Mr. Clean
Guests at the White House Barbeque were pleasantly surprised last night when the Vice President placed an innocent kiss on her son's favorite football player. Our sources reveal the favorite son and star player have been friends for years. Can Mom be planning to get friendly with the Redskins' All-Pro receiver as well? *Washington Post*

Secret Affair No Longer Concealed
Inside tattlers report the spic-and-span Vice President has been meeting Mark Daniel for a sexual rendezvous weekly for years. Our intrepid cameraman caught up with the two love birds last night and captured this clench out in the open. Passion was quelled when the President broke up the display to lecture his errant female second-in-command on the proper etiquette at official political functions. *National Enquirer*

Vice Lady Bares All

"I can't keep my hands off him. He's just such a hunk." Pilfered clandestine government memorandums passed to this reporter show the Vice President definitely in heat over the star Washington football player, Mark Daniel. MacMurray was apparently unable to control herself even in face of extreme jealousy by her only son, Adam, who ran off in hysterics after witnessing this unabated and flagrantly assertive display unbecoming a Vice President. *Confessions Today*

Matilda Pratterly was ecstatic and devoted her entire show the following night to gossip and innuendo on what the press had labeled as "The Kiss."

"Audience, tonight we have a special guest who witnessed The Kiss up close and personal. Welcome Mrs. Evelyn Grosbil from Milwaukee." (Applause. Mrs. Grosbil walks on stage with dignity. She is dressed in a navy blue suit. Her hair is spun into a tight bun pinned to the nape of her neck. She wears no makeup and does not smile. One senses without hearing her speak that Mrs. Grosbil has had every one of her sensibilities affronted.)

"Good evening, Evelyn, may I call you that? and please call me Matty." (The host chats on without waiting for a response.) "Tell us the circumstances in which you witnessed this overt display of affection."

"Well, Royster and I, that's my husband, had just taken our seats after standing in line over an hour for that mediocre food served by what we thought was supposed to be prepared by the White House chef but turned out to be catered. Imagine. Anyway, we found seats together and saw this woman groping a man right out in the open. Then he groped her and we, both Royster and myself, thought it was just awful and right in front of people and on the very White House lawn."

"And did you realize who the people were who were doing this groping as you term it, Mrs. Grosbil?"

"Not at first but we couldn't help looking. Everybody was watching and this went on and on, it seemed for minutes. We were absolutely shocked when this man and woman separated, reluctantly I might add, and revealed their identities. Honestly. Just what have we elected? And right away Royster and I felt so sorry for that poor child left to witness such a brazen display and we think he must have run off because no one saw him afterwards. Poor, poor, dear, dear boy."

"Very interesting, Evelyn. And now we'll hear from another eye witness. Harold Warriner, please come on out here and tell us what you saw."

Harold Warriner was dressed in slacks and sweater and wore tennis shoes. Harold was infinitely less offended than Evelyn about the whole deal and his eyes said he had found The Kiss exciting, maybe even promising.

"I was right there finishing my barbecue sandwich and tossing down a brew. Pretty good food I thought. Then this gal, turns out to be our new Vice President and what a looker, shooeee, well she is talking to this big fellow and suddenly just out and out grabs him and jerks him to her. Then she plants one right on his kisser. 'Hoo boy,' I said to myself. This was a real show and them two stayed liplocked a long time. You could tell it wasn't the first time they ever done that. No sir."

"Thanks, Harold. Ladies and gentlemen, our next guest is Dr. Lavonne Griegos Sternman, a noted psychosocial analyst. Welcome, Dr. Sternman."

A gaily attired woman waddled onto the set. Sternman was beyond obesity and her Hawaiian muumuu seemed appropriate. Several in the audience stifled laughs unsuccessfully when they observed the fluid agitation of flesh roiling for escape beneath the immense garment. As the good doctor took her seat, the previously adequate guest chair sagged. With propriety, the camera switched quickly to the host capturing Matilda's eyes widening in shock at a pending disaster. Switching back to the recently arrived guest expert, the camera caught the exposure of fleshy legs as the woman fluffed her dress. Previously stifled laughs from the audience turned to groans.

"Good Dr. Sternman, can you interpret what this means, based on these eye witnesses?"

Dr. Lavonne, as she preferred, peered through half lenses perched on the tip of her bulbous nose and gave the air of a woman referencing an encyclopedic memory. She tilted her head back and spoke down to all viewers. "Yes, of course. My first analysis and gut reaction"—(this phrasing was picked up in the morning papers and termed appropriate for the speaker) "—is that this was an obvious sexually repressive dysfunctional episode, or SRDE as known psychosocially. Persons with this condition, in this case a single mother in a tense situation, have no control, and cannot predict such outbursts. It is an unfortunate circumstance, but treatable with lengthy professional counseling and medication."

"My, my, that's so sad, doctor." Matilda spoke with unbridled false sympathy. "And now we'll take questions from the audience." (Fade to black.)

Nineteen

Dr. Dalbert Forrester stoked his meerschaum pipe, a gift from the Jordanian Archivist, and stretched leisurely in his leather recliner. Untouchable was the key word that popped into his head. His domain was safe from the "angel of death," as Vice President MacMurray had been christened in these initial weeks of President Conley's administration.

MacMurray had cut a swath through the major departments in town that would generate headline news for months. Evidently her job was to personally clean out those political appointees who were trying to hide, or stay out of sight for the next four years. "Hellfire, woman," Woody chuckled. He'd been approved by both parties and was ensconced permanently. And of course he was a political appointee, wasn't everybody in the important positions in this town? The learned historian knew he was cocky and arrogant with his tenure assured. His sponsors in the historical associations would not tolerate a President who placed a "manager" over an archivist. It was blasphemy!

What could they get him on anyway? His desk was spotless; he delegated every action that drifted his way. Decisions? Never ever. Let the office heads lose theirs. No, Woody continued to research his next textbook on documentary evidence of archival records of the 1830s, a fascinating subject. Time passed quickly. This was a day greatly anticipated around town, the day of the new president's address to Congress. Who knew what folderol the man would dream up next? Regardless, Woody rested assured that the National Archives would be overlooked. It had always been so.

His only concession to the new administration had been to purchase a smoke filtering device that sat on his desk quietly sucking up the drifting haze from his beloved meerschaum pipe. Morganthau over in Treasury had been canned only yesterday when caught puffing on a Havanna Special cigar in his private restroom. Of course, everyone knew the man was hanging on by a thread not a hundred yards from the President's office. Never had been a more political animal in town. But, Dalbert reflected, he was a small fish in town. He was glad too, that he'd purchased the costly filter. When not smoking he could switch the controls to blow air across his desk to enhance the building's inferior air conditioning.

His intercom buzzed like a band saw interrupting a church service.

"Dr.Foresteryouhaveavisitor." Earlene blurted her rude announcement as one word and Woody jumped from his papers.

"I have no scheduled appointments, Ms. Jackson. I require more time to complete my inspect—"

His reply was shattered as the huge mahogany inner office door swung open, propelled by the angel of death herself.

Woody had the grace to stand and stutter, "Good mor-morning, Madam Vice President. What a lovely surprise." The archivist grimaced at her entourage of two other women: Caroline Jankowski, Woody's own top female management official, and another striking woman with glorious blonde hair who must have been a few inches over six feet. He would have appreciated a longer glance at the blonde, but even the backward looking historian realized this was no social call.

"Dr. Forrester, I've come to offer you another assignment." Hailey MacMurray began a short speech she had presented many times since taking office barely two weeks ago. However, in this particular case, her script was altered to suit a dire situation. "You may have heard that the President ordered political appointees to resign. You have not done so. Why not?" Hailey remained standing directly across the man's desk, keeping all in the room on their feet.

"I, I have served without disruption for the previous administration without complaint and assumed my services would be continued. There was nothing political about it, Madam Vice President."

"Your duties will be continued; just not in this position, Dr. Dalbert. In other offices around town I have found outright hangers on, political hacks hoping to continue to get paid for nothing. People whiling away the public's time and money for no good cause. Now, one might describe their actions as malfeasance, or misfeasance, more likely as plain illegal, since they do nothing for pay. Yet I know about your performance, or lack of one, for the past seven years. I studied your record when I worked on your budget. You do a credible job as an archivist, producing research papers and lecturing on American history. But when it comes to running the National Archives, I can only describe your work as non-feasance, meaning you don't run it."

Woody gripped his beloved meerschaum tightly until his thumb slipped into the bowl of lit tobacco. His shock at the vice president's words delayed the pain for mere seconds, then he yelped. "Aieyeee!" The pipe flipped into the air and flopped onto the sheaf of ancient papers. Wounded in all aspects of the definition, Dr. Forrester sucked his anguished digit and flapped at the smoldering sparks igniting the highly flammable and only copy of his research. He groped for the filter switch and managed to turn it on HIGH to suck up the smoke. Instead, he ended up pointing the device across his smoldering desk. This errant act succeeded in blowing fresh air into the flames, increasing them, and scattering smoking papers around the poor man's office.

Caroline and Jennette helped collect papers and extinguish remaining sparks. Vice President MacMurray stood fast in her spot facing the archivist, and contained a laugh at the sight. When she felt enough decorum had returned, Hailey tossed in her fait accompli. "You have also ignored my request for assistance in reorganizing the White House records system. Certainly a month's notice is sufficient. Where is the team of experts the Archives has graciously supplied to previous administrations?"

Jennette snorted behind her boss. Poor fellow. His was not the first scene of complete embarrassment Hailey had caused. The woman was relentless in carrying out her orders. She never made an appointment. Shock value was maximized. And funny thing, it only took one significant visit to the top appointee in each agency and the rest fell like feathers from a pillow fight. They scattered as if a leaf blower had attacked. Jennette and her co-workers at Secret Service scoffed at the "angel of death" moniker. Their boss' title would more appropriately be "*Vise* President."

"I was going to discuss the matter of that team of experts with Ms. Jankowski momentarily." Forrester struggled to collect his composure. "She is responsible for that project and I'm beginning to wonder at her inaction." He glared at Caroline Jankowski, beseeching her to sacrifice her reputation, fall on her sword, in the true samurai warrior tradition, and beg forgiveness for her oversight.

"I can only assume we would have that discussion when you told me about the request, Dr. Forrester." Caroline Jankowski returned her former superior's glare stoically. The man was toast.

Hailey slid an executive order across the desk to the fallen archivist. Woody delicately retrieved the edict with his remaining good hand and read his fate.

"You have an hour to pack up and catch the shuttle to the Suitland Records Center, Dr. Forrester. As you see by President Conley's orders, your new position will be at the center. Ms. Jankowski will take over here as Executive Director over all operations. Her first duty will be to implement the recommendations of the audit reports gone dormant the last several administrations and under your management." Hailey turned and left with Caroline and Jennette right behind her.

The three women said nothing until they had cleared the building on the Pennsylvania Avenue side.

"Thanks, Madam Vice President." Caroline said. "I owe you big time for this. You won't be sorry."

Hailey looked seriously at her good friend from the Women's Connection. "No, Caroline, you owe us nothing. And I don't have to tell you what public service means either. Your allegiance is to the people, as it always has been. If the other rats don't jump ship after today, email their names to my office. Do the same when the historical associations start carping. But after the President's State of the Union speech tonight, I don't think you'll be bothered by anybody." Hailey paused only a second. "And another thing, lady. When you and Jennette and I are out on the town like this, please call me Hailey."

Caroline beamed her appreciation and hugged Hailey in return. "You take good care of her, Jennette." The Vice President's two close friends hugged, and the "angel of death" walked to her next victim across the street at FBI. Ronald Kraft had bollixed up criminal investigations and domestic spying far too long. It would be his choice to retire or take a desk job in Nome, Alaska.

Twenty

"Mr. Speaker, the President of the United States." The Sergeant at Arms bellowed his announcement, one familiar to most Americans, and stepped aside for President Bill Conley to make his entrance. TV narrators lamented their lack of background information about his speech. No one had received advance copies, not even members of Congress. It was one more precedent-breaker. Certainly the chamber would be silent at every pause of the address. No one would be turning pages looking for mention of their favorite programs. How would anyone know when to applaud and smile knowingly in case the minicams turned to them?

Bill Conley walked down the center of the aisle like a true independent, favoring neither party on either side. He smiled and waved to several colleagues and set a record for the shortest time getting to the podium to speak.

The News Network's Lyman Trevolt broke the silence of the moment to analyze the promenade by America's new president.

"Ladies and gentlemen, the President appears most businesslike this evening and perhaps in a bit of a hurry. As you can see, he hasn't bothered to shake hands on the way to speak tonight, but seems cheerful. We have no information on the content of his speech or we would be telling you about it beforehand. There, the President has reached the speaker's platform and is shaking hands, first with the Speaker of the House, Cantwell Nederthal, and now with Vice President MacMurray. The applause is polite, if on the moderate side, since everyone has been kept in the dark about what the President will say."

Trevolt continued his narration, speaking over the traditional introduction of the president by the Speaker of the House.

"Vice President MacMurray has been the news generator since she and the President were sworn in barely two weeks ago. Ms. MacMurray has, in the words of many long-time Washington political pundits, cut a swath of destruction through the upper layers of political office holders in this town. Only this morning she is reported to have dumped FBI Director Ronald Kraft, younger brother of Senate Majority Leader Kensington Kraft. This move is a definite blunder and assured of gaining a powerful enemy in the Senate. Kent Kraft is reported to be furious that no one from the White—"

"Madam Vice President, Mr. Speaker, Members of Congress and distinguished guests. I asked for this time tonight to present a framework for my administration." The chamber was silent as the president paused. Bill Conley swept his gaze from left to right, gathering the attention of everyone there. Finally, he looked up to the reserved seating in the gallery where Elizabeth sat with their four sons and their wives, along with their daughter, Sara Wolf, and her husband, Joe. He smiled and waved and his ten grandchildren stood and clapped their own greeting to the delight of the gallery.

"First, I want to commend Vice President MacMurray for her diligent work these last fourteen days." A smattering of applause crept from the contingent of independent members. "There is more to be done to relieve the vast numbers of political appointees of their burdens. Yet, executives are now in place in every agency of my administration who will continue what the Vice President started."

Murmurs arose from the chamber from both sides of the aisle as understanding spread that no appointees had been named to replace those forcibly removed by the so-called "angel of death." The president paused again and let the words sink in fully.

"I promised there would be no political pay offs, and tonight I confirm that promise has been kept. And further, career senior executive service managers are now officially in charge of running their respective agencies and programs. The key word here is officially, because in reality these men and women have always done this, they just never got the publicity and never sought it.

"I have directed each of these managers to implement outstanding audit report recommendations for improvement. Too often oversight committees up here on the Hill have made recommendations that have been ignored. Investigations and inspections by the General Accounting Office, GAO, the Office of Management and Budget, OMB, and especially an endless procession of blue ribbon presidential committees have directed improvements that have been ignored. This ignorance derives from political expediency as well as pay backs to financial supporters. This practice stops tonight!" Bill Conley's voice thundered down on his audience and the gallery erupted in shouts and applause.

The national statesman allowed the interruption to last ten seconds and held up one hand. There was immediate silence.

"Each agency has thirty days to give me a list of their improvement goals and another year in which to implement them. Any exceptions, that is, past recommendations that cannot be implemented, require my personal approval." The president looked directly into the cameras, ignoring his immediate audience.

"My fellow Americans, you may wonder at this cornerstone to the framework I have promised. I can sense some of you in your homes saying, OK get on with it. Who cares about the bureaucracy anyway? Think of it this way. Let's say you are avid sports fans and have voted to increase local taxes to build a brand new stadium at a cost of a trillion dollars. You also want a winning team, so you raise those taxes again another trillion to buy the best players and coaches. You sit down to enjoy the *game,* one you have been taxed heavily for, and the referees stand on opposite sides of the field arguing about the rules. They don't meet in the middle to work out anything so the game can be played. They don't even flip a coin to see who kicks off. No, they just shout back and forth while their trillion-dollar team sits idling, waiting for orders to charge." Again the big man stopped his speech and looked around from face to face in the immediate audience. Heads nodded at his simple analogy, but there were many frowns as political capitalists calculated gains and losses.

"I consider myself the head referee and vow to stand in the middle of the field, calling all sides to gather round and play ball." Another tumult broke loose in the gallery. Members on the floor stood and joined in the celebration with mild applause. President Conley had not only thrown down the gauntlet, he had virtually stomped it into the ground.

The applause continued for a few moments more and Lyman Trevolt sought an opportunity to provide playback analysis. "There is much speculation on just what the president means with that last statement. One can only guess at—" Once more Trevolt's instant analysis was halted abruptly as the show's director cut back to the president.

"Vice President MacMurray will be my executive officer in charge of implementing recommendations. Cabinet secretaries will work closely with her and she will report to me. Some hesitant managers in this town have discovered miserably that Hailey MacMurray is certain of her mission and demands respect for the Office of the President. Those who choose to ignore her follow a foolish path.

"This first year could be called my own house cleaning. Or, getting my own house in order. It is a necessity before I can suggest anything new. Included in it are massive streamlining programs for the two main charges to the federal government explicit in the Constitution. First is to care for the health and welfare of the people. Second is to provide for the common defense.

"As a senator and before that an Army officer, I grew tired of the ping pong analysis aimed at our military. During election campaigns those out of office felt the military was in ruins and needed a massive infusion of money. Simultaneously, incumbents ran on a platform proclaiming ours the best military in the world. Who knew the truth?

"Likewise, the budget swung aggressively from large increases for the military and sharp decreases for health and human services, to just the opposite. Each side of the debate went through cycles of poverty and plenty every four to eight years. So, tonight I'm announcing an end to the cycle. There will be no more new money for any program or department until I judge them effective with what they already have."

Trevolt sought to take advantage of the tumultuous applause from the gallery. "This plainly won't wash. Conservative hawks are demanding a twenty percent military spending hike with a complimentary cut in health and human services. At the same time, senior citizen lobbyists are demanding government-sponsored, cradle-to-grave health care." But Lyman had an audience of one, as his director shut down his video and audio feed, then slid his right index finger across his throat signaling the verbose commentator to can it.

"It is no secret where I stand on the issue of strong military or providing for the health and welfare of the people. I have a strong military right this minute and intend to keep it that way. But the people come first and they always will.

"Tonight I'm announcing one single goal for this year. A strong democracy has an educated and participating citizenry. Virtually every President declares himself to be an education president and I'm no different. Developing a participating citizenry is another matter. I know I am a stronger patriot and believer in our system of values for having served in the Army. I am certain that mandatory national service creates participating citizens and will propose legislation to make it so." Conservatives on both sides of the political spectrum stood and cheered with the gallery.

"Understand me on this issue. Not everyone should have to serve in the military. There are many service opportunities out there. Literally thousands of non-profit organizations work without fanfare expanding our American culture, creating and supporting community development and continuity. Young people need to invest themselves in America by serving in some capacity. I believe they will care more deeply about the freedoms we too often take for granted. Older citizens need the opportunity to give back. We are wasting talents of people who have been downsized, retired early, or retired at any age. I will send you legislation to use that talent."

The audience rose and applauded courteously if moderately. Most understood national service only in terms of fighting men and women serving in the military.

"Let's go back to our mission of providing for the common defense. Since my election I have been swarmed over by defense contractors, retired military officers running consulting firms, and many old colleagues. I must say their theme is consistent: more money for defense." Ecstatic applause erupted from hawks who were standing and cheering while they clapped furiously.

"I have thought about no other responsibility more than providing for the common defense. Being a retired Army officer, many have thought I would automatically bump up defense spending and cut all domestic programs." Again the hawks flapped their wings. "I have no such desire." A loud groan escaped the military-industrial complex representatives, while cheers swelled from the breasts of liberal and environmental doves. "Neither do I plan to combine our forces as suggested by some of my more liberal friends." This time the groan emanated from the doves. "Were I to try to fit Army and Navy and Air Force personnel into one box, I'm certain the weakest country on Earth would be able to defeat us. We would be too busy squabbling to mount a counterattack.

"No, I will do something simpler. The biggest waste in military spending is not on personnel, it is on procurement. And that function will be consolidated under the direct management of the Secretary of Defense.

"Other specific defense-oriented management actions include these: a one hundred percent withdrawal of American forces from Europe—the European Union and NATO no longer need our immediate presence; a four-year base draw down that will affect all fifty states—my list of proposed base closings will be sent to you tomorrow; a modernized military education program that will fully pay for college or technical training for every member; and finally, my Secretary of Defense has been directed to look for duplication and eliminate it.

"Since I have mentioned procurement, I will toss out another idea on the subject. I propose a meeting with Congressional leadership to discuss a test program for one civilian agency. The test would allow the agency to ignore all current rules and regulations governing procurement." Turmoil erupted on the floor as members began arguing and some even shouted their disapproval of the idea. For a few minutes it sounded like the Prime Minister of Great Britain had exposed a personal scandal in the halls of Parliament and was being heckled by backbenchers.

"Yes, I know. It is a sensitive topic. But listen to my reasons. We waste time and money adhering to a labyrinthine conglomerate of stifling rules for buying things. There are many checks and cross-checks that conflict and confound honest workers. If this condition exists, buy from a woman-owned business. That condition requires an African-American purchase. Another purchase goes out for bid. Another doesn't unless certain other conditions come into play. We spend billions daily keeping track of the rules, and the goods are always late, always over-priced. Why? The vendors know the game and raise the ante three-fold. If they win the bid they won't get paid on time, because our rules require us to "age" their invoices. If they lose the bid they have wasted thousands researching extraordinarily stringent specifications. Only the big businesses can afford a permanent staff to do the research. The little guy loses."

Bill Conley paused to drink some water and peruse the angry crowd of politicians roiling below him. He turned his head and looked back over his left shoulder at the Speaker. Cantwell Nederthal's face was purple. He glanced over his right shoulder at Hailey and received a big grin in return. The President chuckled when she mouthed "Go for it."

"Now that I've riled up my *former* colleagues in this chamber, I'd like to speak directly to the American people. Elected officials in this town have used the incredible purchasing arm of your government to spend trillions. In doing so, they have made up thousands of rules to ensure that money was doled out fairly. I'm here tonight to tell you those rules have failed. Any savings dreamed up by government accountants are washed away by the billions I mentioned earlier that are spent making sure we stick by the rules.

My proposal is simple. Let one agency ignore the rules for one year, then compare the results.

"Let's cut to the chase and address our primary goal in this government, taking care of the people we work for. I look back on my years in the Senate and can remember days when that body seemed to have forgotten where the authority for our system of government comes from. This description also fits the House on occasion." Bill Conley stopped and stared, almost in defiance, at the elected elite below. Then he struck the podium hard with his fisted right hand bringing heads up, jarring his audience to rapt attention. "The people. The people elect us to do their business. The people grant us the authority to govern them responsibly. Power and authority in this country come from the people. And, last November the people sent a clear message to us: get with it, fix Social Security, and provide a workable healthcare system as a *right* for all, not just a privilege purchased at the going market rate only by those with money."

Pandemonium erupted. The President looked out at a foot-stomping, standing ovation. Everyone in the gallery and on the chamber floor was up. All applauded and cheered. He let it ride as he scanned the crowd left to right and center, then right to left. Bill Conley had spoken eloquently as the voice of the people. Political pundits recognized the moment even without having an advance copy of his speech. As the tumult rose from the guts of the Capitol Building, experts on politics chose the time to break in with instant analysis. They had wondered, they reported as if collectively, when a man, a President, would step to the plate and challenge the 9,000-pound gorilla perched on the pitcher's mound.

This independent man the people had elected, they reported, was challenging a century of politics as usual. He made it clear he had no use for a government that doled out pork in the form of military bases for every community, a weapons factory here, a warehouse there. He threatened millions of patronage ties that sewed up procurement so that good-ole-boy networks made off with the choicest cuts from the hog. And evidently he was not through.

"I have just one more matter to declare to the Congress and the American people. While a United States Senator, I met men and women in both houses of Congress who were dedicated, honest, and hardworking. These citizens tried to do what they thought was best for their constituents and the nation as a whole. But, I also ran into folks who had done little more than make a career out of public service. They abused privileges. They allocated money for pork projects in their districts willy-nilly, without regard for the general good. They traveled extensively on the tab of lobbyists and financial backers who expected favors in return. And even today, they win reelection consistently with money that has strings attached.

"Inside the Beltway, the phrase 'Show me the money' has come to mean contribute big bucks and get my vote in return. My own campaign showed that a candidate could run for office in this country without committing his soul to the devil. That said, I will send legislation to the Congress proposing all elections at the federal level be publicly funded and that all campaigning via radio and TV be restricted to National Public Radio and Public TV." This time only the gallery rose to applaud. Senate and House members sat in silence, fuming.

"An abrogation of the right to free speech will be the primary argument against this proposal. That farcical platitude has been paraded about by free market campaigners for decades. It doesn't wash with me or the American people. Now let's get to work."

Lyman Trevolt had regained his audio and visual feed from the director and searched for words to describe the scene in the House Chamber.

"Ladies and gentlemen, tonight the President left no ox un-gored, to use a trite expression. He poked and prodded every political sore spot existing in this town, and, dare I say, made a few new enemies. Not the least of these may be the powerful defense lobby. Or perhaps he'll get his biggest challenge from the American Medical Association. Then don't forget every minority group striving for an advantage at the public procurement trough. Certainly those senior members of Congress will object to his characterization of them as slurping at the trough behind a façade of public service. And that brings to mind the powerful media lobby that rakes in billions in profit from each election by jacking up rates for political advertising."

Viewers reported the News Channel picture faded to black immediately after this statement by Trevolt. When the lights came up, an anonymous voice introduced the rebuttal speeches by both major parties. However, ratings services noted a sharp drop in viewership during the blackout and that the drop had occurred on all other networks even absent a black screen. Doberman ratings reported fewer than ten percent had stayed tuned to hear the laments of the party leaders. Haverford Polling Systems, a noted independent consortium considered the top political think tank outside the Beltway, had the most astounding news.

The speech, reported Pat Verstraete, Haverford's chief socio-political analyst, was a national watershed event. It was akin to a landmark political achievement unheralded in American history. It was a milestone, a phenomenon, and a miracle combined. The people, Verstraete emphasized, had given their new president a 90 percent approval rating. It was more than clear that Bill Conley had spoken for them. He was their voice in Washington.

Elizabeth worried over her husband as she watched him deep in sleep. He was exhausted and she was the only one who knew what the past year had done to him. His checkups were excellent. He was, after all, a marvelous physical specimen. If there had been a medical problem, the public would know. They had a right to that information. Yet Elizabeth knew her man like no one else did. She understood completely that he had given the rest of his life to his country. She knew it in her heart. It had been their tacit agreement.

The strain was there for every President. All of them aged dramatically during their terms in office. Even the younger, more energetic fellows slowed down, grayed on top and gained what Bill called a "worry gut." It was said that Lincoln had stopped eating and sleeping and lived on huge doses of laudanum. Many close to him believed that he would not have lived long after the War concluded. Poor Abraham didn't have a choice.

Now it was Bill Conley's turn. She sighed aloud as her own sleep escaped her this night when his words had galvanized a nation thirsty for leadership. She had had fifty incredible years with this wonderful man. He had always put her first and loved her to distraction. Yes, they had a tacit agreement. His country was now first and he would be lucky to last his allotted four years. Elizabeth at once mourned her loss and rejoiced in her love and pride. Theirs had been a mating for life. Now the country and Bill's hand-picked successor would bear the fruits of his dedication.

Twenty-one

The revolution was not peaceful, although no guns were involved. The people were making themselves heard in their capitol. Noise reverberated over phone lines, through the internet, and into strident letters and cards. Make it so, they clamored. No more pussyfooting around. We want action posters flooded the halls of Congress. What President Bill Conley had envisioned was happening. Washington, DC had been turned upside down. Not a shot was fired, but it was the second biggest revolution in the country's history.

On every trip back home, members of Congress experienced the fury of a populace once scorned. All wanted to know how Senator So and So was voting to support the president? What was Representative Ambivalent doing to reform healthcare? The pressure was relentless. Even the news media had been caught up in the furor. Voting records now made front page news in a Conley versus Congress power struggle.

Aging senior politicos struggled to keep up with the whirlwind pace of change. The White House had become "Camp Conley," so nicknamed by the press for the continual rounds of meetings sometimes going through the night. Congressional leadership, program experts from agency offices, and both the President and Vice President attended these lengthy sessions. The White House kitchen went on a three-shift schedule to meet the demands of the hungry politicians involved.

Results began to show. Joint task forces formed with members from both houses of Congress and program experts. One person was chosen from each task force to inform the press; there were no conflicting reports resulting in liberal and conservative approaches. Compromise and results were the key words. All of these rules of engagement had come straight from Bill Conley. For the President and a growing number of task force members, political maneuvering, posturing, pandering for votes and the money to get them had become irrelevant.

Similar groups formed to solve other problems. One was headed by Norton Roscoe of the National Archives to simplify the ever-shifting records system in the White House. But Norton was not a pleased participant.

"What is it this time, Norton?" Caroline Jankowski covered the mouthpiece of her phone to hide an exasperated sigh. The man was a pain in the butt.

"This assignment is not what I expected, Ms. Jankowski. You sent me over here to work on presidential papers and I haven't even met the man. I'm to reform White House records and I don't even have access to the building. Instead, I'm stuck three levels below ground in a sub-basement, in a windowless cubicle with five boring records officers in the Old Executive Building indexing old file folders."

"Well, Norton, what did you expect? Do you want a say in reforming the Pentagon? Un uh, not your field. Streamlining procurement? Not a chance. Writing new legislation? No, sir. Mr. Roscoe, you are in that cubicle doing exactly what I directed you to do. If that isn't your cup of tea, you can return to the stacks."

"At least give me a chance to see where the records are created. Please?" Norton whined, obsequious, fawning.

"OK. I'll call you back with a contact. Will that be good enough?"

"Yes, Ma'am," replied the insincere bureaucrat.

Caroline hung up and buzzed her secretary's intercom.

"Janet, bring in the personnel folder for Norton Roscoe, would you?" *Guy gets the assignment of a lifetime and all he can think of is touring the White House. Cripes, what have I let loose over there?* She smiled her thanks as her secretary dropped the file on her desk.

She had handpicked the team for this assignment based on expertise. Roscoe had been named team leader, although his background held not one iota of experience as such and he did not have the reputation of a team player. Yet he was her best expert in the field. He had been the first to volunteer and had included several novel ideas in his request memo. Obviously the man knew his stuff. Why did he have to be such a griper? But his file showed her the answer. There she noted memo after memo complaining about "issues" from the grade of toilet paper to the color of the building to air conditioning in the 22nd stack floor. A few valid items out of dozens of petty ones. Still, the man's record revealed nothing harmful. At least there was nothing to deny him a simple tour and a friendly handshake from the President.

Elizabeth felt sorry for Adam. The boy was lost in the hubbub surrounding his mother. Now he stood in her office doorway, forlorn, asking permission to enter.

"Come in, sweetie. I've missed you." She stood and opened her arms wide to hug her special grandson. They had become best buddies during the campaign, often sharing seats side by side while Bill and Hailey consulted with voters and campaign staff.

Adam grinned and hugged the First Lady with an extra jolt of friendship. They were equal in height when she wore heels, as she did today. Yet Elizabeth sensed more to the hug than just a friendly greeting. An underlying desperation made the boy's gesture tenuous. She pulled back and gave him her truth-serum stare eye to eye.

"OK, mister, what's going on? You aren't too cheerful, that's plain enough to see."

"Aw, Gran, sometimes you act like Superman with x-ray vision. But yeah, you're right. I need a little advice and there is no way I can talk to guys at school. They all think I'm stuck up and spoiled. What could I complain about they'd say. I can't even get in to see Jennette; she's so busy guarding the Vice President." This last bit came out with a hint of sarcasm and the boy looked down in embarrassment.

Elizabeth led him to her comfortable arm chairs beside the office window and pushed him gently down into one. She took the one opposite and faced this special child smiling.

"OK, let's see if I can guess the problem for a spoiled rotten son of the first woman Vice President of the United States who has the world in the palm of his hand and doesn't know what to do with it." They both laughed and Adam relaxed slumping back into the soft cushions.

His surrogate grandmother continued. "Could it be girls? Or the lack thereof?" She pursed her lips, and Adam grinned. Both remembered the stories of the numerous invitations he had received during the parade. "No, didn't think so. The waiting list is so long for your dating services you're booked up to age 50, I believe." Adam laughed. Her spontaneous humor always closed any generation gap between them. It was like having a grandma and pal combined.

"Is it friends, I wonder? Nah, no way. Your soccer team is over here practically every weekend to practice on the south lawn, then scarf down pizza and watch the latest movies in my basement. Hmmmmm, couldn't be grades. You never make less than A's in everything; and if you did, your mother would whip the tar out of you." But this attempt at a joke caused Adam to lose his humorous expression. He now wore a downward frown and glanced out the window at nothing.

She knew then the problem. It was a beautiful sight even in the boy's miserable state. He missed his mother at a time when most young boys wanted nothing to do with parents who turned dumb as turnips during their adolescence. Such a bond Hailey and Adam had forged, and he looked like he had lost his best friend.

"You'd like that wouldn't you? Get your mother's attention long enough for her to whip the tar out of you. She's been so busy you feel left out, that the problem?" He nodded meekly and faced her squarely.

"Yes, that's a good part of it. There's more, though. And it's, uh, kind of personal." He searched her face for the green light to unload and got a signal to keep going. "The weekends used to belong to me. Mom and I would go hiking or see a movie or drive down to the Virginia mountains and just goof off. I knew that routine would change when she got elected, but I never figured it would just stop."

"Adam, sweetheart, my husband and your mother are making a big difference. They're working their buns off, to use an old Army expression. I miss Bill tremendously, but it's a sacrifice I saw coming." She paused and ruminated, turning to focus on the magnificent spire of the Washington Monument to the south. It was too big a sacrifice for a 12-year-old, though. The boy's face reflected her optimism and gained a slight smile. There's more to say was his message. His enthusiasm was at half throttle and Elizabeth spotted it.

"But there's more to it, right?" He grinned. "Tell me, Adam. Get it out so we can deal with it." His features grew serious and a deep breath followed.

"Mom needs a fellow. There, I said it and I've told no one else." He blurted this out and stopped to catch her reaction. When she nodded, urging him to continue, he unleashed a flood. "I know better than everybody that my mother gave up everything for me. She made me her fellow from the start and never changed. So yes, I am spoiled, or I was. But in the last few years I realized how lonely she actually was. Guys would call her and she always turned them down and I was the reason. She didn't have a sitter, or the two of us had plans, or whatever excuse she could dream up she used." Adam gulped in air and rushed on. "I felt important growing up. My mom took us all over the world. She spoke foreign languages and negotiated with leaders from important countries. She got elected to Congress. She was beautiful and I was her fellow. Always."

Elizabeth spared him further analysis. "But you understand better now, don't you?" He nodded. "You'll always be her son, but you can't be her fellow. Is that it?"

"I see her looking at couples. She has this little half-smile, part happy for the couple, part sad for what she and my dad lost. I just feel that she feels left out of something and won't date any guys because of me. She doesn't need to feel that way anymore and I can't seem to say that to her." His pleading look made Elizabeth choke on emotion. Such depth. Compassion. Unselfish compassion and empathy from a son to a mother. She was in awe at this young man, no longer a boy.

Adolescence was a self-centering time. Boys and girls grew selfish, detached, and unconcerned for their parents. But this boy was different. He had been raised under special circumstances at apparently high personal sacrifice. And he was asking for help from the only person he could talk to, the First Lady of the United States. God give her strength.

Twenty-two

Calder Murchison spoke softly into his cell phone, but his message exploded into Senator Kent Kraft's ear 1500 miles away.

"Find a way to sidetrack this circus, Kent, or I will, and you don't want that to happen."

"Cal, you saw the speech. You read the papers and watch national news every night. The country is backing him almost one hundred percent. There's never been anything like it. He's got both sides of the aisle working their balls off and cooperating for God's sake. I can't do anything about it. You can't just call in your markers in face of overwhelming odds like this. Wait it out. Let's see how long this goes and then we'll find a weak spot. He will screw up. They all do eventually." The Senate Majority Leader was frantic. His biggest sponsor demanded action for his financial backing. Taking no for an answer wasn't in his vocabulary.

"That your final answer, Kraft? Wait a while? Sorry, not good enough." Calder pushed the Talk button to make another call. "Joseph, send Thomas into my office now."

Thomas Crews was the newest management intern under Murchison's mammoth umbrella organization. He was identical to the CEO in philosophy, background, and every belief, especially political. He had been recruited as a sophomore at Kansas State University and given a full ride through his remaining two years in undergraduate school. Following that, Thomas had received his MBA, a company car and townhouse, all *gratis*, from his benefactor. He now rapped diligently on the man's office door, willing to do what it took to climb the ladder.

Calder eyed his personal prodigy wistfully. The man was a gorgeous specimen. Tall, fit, tanned and with blue eyes designed to lead any woman to his bed at first sight. Calder breathed deeply and directed the assignment that would take this incredible stud away for an indefinite time.

"Thomas, I want you to go to Washington and do a little project for me. Report to Senator Kraft's office tomorrow. He'll have further instructions. You do know the Vice President, don't you?"

"Sure, Cal. Who doesn't? A real looker, but cold as ice water they say." Thomas smiled at Calder with such warmth his mentor almost changed his mind.

"I'm asking it to matter just for a short time, Thomas. I want to nail this bitch. Generate a little negative press, you know? Instigate some rumors, sly sexual innuendos, perhaps with a handsome Midwestern hunk half her age. Take it as far as you can go. I'll compensate you highly. I promise."

Lucinda stood in the doorway and observed her boss, Senate Majority Leader Kensington Kraft, bent over the usual pile of paperwork. The shiny spot centered on his head had receded at a faster rate these last few months, matching the senator's receding influence on the Hill. She was no dummy. Lucinda had a network of friends in the other party and had started inviting staffers from the independents to her afternoon tea parties. She would find a comfortable spot to land when the boss went down in flames, as she knew he surely would.

The powerful secretary had 30 years service in the rarefied air of the legislative branch of this government. Many considered her to have more seniority than most junior senators and certainly more than those lesser beings over in the House. But she made no enemies and not a single ripple could be traced to her initiative. Yet, Lucinda Hatcher controlled every scrap of paper her boss read and signed, only if she said it was OK. If you wanted to measure power in this city, follow the paper trail.

"Senator Kraft, there's a young man out here to see you. Says you're expecting him. His name is Thomas Crews; 'management intern from Cal's office' is how he put it."

Kent Kraft sighed deeply and laid down his papers. He removed his reading glasses and wiped his sleeve across his face as if removing a bucket of sweat along with a few worries. He looked back at Lucinda standing calmly wearing her professional neutral expression of benevolence as always. She knew damn well he would see this fellow and had no choice. Lucinda managed his money spread out in numerous accounts. She and Cal's secretary, Eloise, were friends from ages ago. She could act calmly because it wasn't her short hairs being yanked out by the roots.

"Of course, Mrs. Hatcher, please show the gentleman in and bring us some coffee if you please." When the woman played her formal cards in front of strangers he could match her spade for spade.

Thomas Crews appeared in Kent's office as if arriving on a fluffy cloud. The man glided he was so smooth. Kent felt like puking.

"Welcome, Mr. Crews. How may I help you this fine morning?" But the senator's routine voter-from-back-home spiel fizzled with the sharp dresser from Cal's office.

"Morning, Senator." Kent shook Thomas's hand, more like a limp rag, and watched the arrogant youth settle in his best leather chair, putting down roots. "Thought I'd go with you to the meeting this afternoon over at the White House. Cal said you needed some extra *support* and I volunteered. Frankly, I'm anxious to meet Vice President MacMurray who's said to be a real looker up close and personal. Would you agree, Senator?"

"How old are you, Crews? Twenty-five, six, seven, somewhere along in there?"

"Something around those figures, Senator, but what relevance is that?"

"Vice President MacMurray is a decade older than you. She is a single mother who has the voters, men and women, in the palm of her hand. There is not and has never been a breath of scandal around her. Everyone has tried to smear her and failed. Now here you come toting your *GQ* wardrobe and runway-model face in my office, insulting me and the whole system of government with the harebrained scheme that you'll get to her. You'll find a weak spot that can be used as leverage to defame this woman." Kent Kraft stood, his face turning redder the more he sputtered. "Get out. Get out of my office and don't come back."

Crews didn't move. He retrieved his cell phone from a coat pocket and punched a pre-programmed button.

"Hello, it's me and you need to remind the senator of a few markers he owes you." Crews slid the innocuous instrument across the mammoth desk, reclined in the buttery soft cushions of his chair, and watched. Kent Kraft's replies to the mostly one-way conversation with Cal Murchison came in the form of grunts, a few "OKs" and several "Understands". At the end he uttered one word, "Fine," and tossed the phone back to Crews.

"My car leaves at 12:30 from the east side. Be there promptly. Now get out before I call security."

Crews had not been gone a minute before Lucinda entered the senator's office, slammed the door behind her and plopped down in a straight-backed chair centered across from him. Kent knew an angry woman when he saw one. Lucinda's breath drew in and out with a snarl.

"Senator Kraft, Kent, this is my notice. You take that piece of shit, adolescent jerk into the White House meeting and I am history. The boy model flitted by my desk whistling and humming something about getting a date with a doll over at 1600 Pennsylvania Avenue. While you and Cal had your little chat, Eloise called me from Kansas City. She's as pissed off as I am."

"Lucinda, let me—"

"Don't interrupt me, Kent. I have some information to impart. Information you've obviously ignored since the inauguration last January." Her brows rose an inch and closed the space between. The glare she shot at the Senate Majority Leader silenced him. "Your mail is running nine to one in favor of supporting this president and his goals. The entire office staff has done nothing for months but answer the phone from constituents wanting to know when you'll follow their leader. *Their* leader, Kent. And they weren't referring to your brother Ronny, or anybody else up here on the Hill. And what's more, I like him. I like Hailey MacMurray, too. They are the real deal. I ought to know, I've seen enough flakes and fakers pass through this town the last 30 years.

"When I was assigned to you, your freshman term, I thought here was a man going to the top. You had the desire to serve the public. Do some good. But as the years went by you became more interested in games and manipulating people and taxpayer money. You're not the only person around here to get that way, just the worst." Lucinda stood and Kent Kraft stood with her, surprising them both. She turned and left. Kent slumped into his chair and rolled it around to stare out the window.

Twenty-three

Hailey approached Elizabeth's sitting room with more than trepidation. She had to talk to someone about her feelings and the First Lady was her best hope.

"Quit standing outside my door fretting and get in here. I've been expecting you for weeks." Elizabeth sounded assertive as always. Hailey squared her shoulders, breathed deeply, and took the plunge.

"OK, Superwoman, can you read my mind?" The close friends laughed, clearing the air.

"No, but I don't have to. I can read the papers. They all think you're up to something with Mark. The poor guy can't even go to the bathroom without reading about this illicit affair you two are having and he hasn't even enjoyed the benefits."

"All this gossip and innuendo doesn't bother you? You're an amazing woman, Elizabeth. Not once have you asked me about my personal life and why I chose to remain single. Fact is, you gave one interview to the *LA Times* saying my status was to be admired. So how can you remain so calm now? I embarrassed the President and expected you to call me on it." Hailey's voice had risen as she stood and walked to the bay window that revealed the White House Rose Garden below. Her frustration was transparent.

Elizabeth came to her side and reached for her hand. "Hailey, I love you like a daughter and perhaps that's the reason. You know our daughter Sara; she was just as stubborn as you and wanted to be the best son her father could ever wish for. She excelled at everything masculine trying to get Bill's attention. She finally met the right fellow, her husband, Joe Wolf. He was exactly what she needed and vice versa. Joe accepted her as she was, especially her femininity. But why am I saying this to you? Well, sometimes we women struggle too hard against our natural inclinations. We feel unfairly judged as pretty pieces of fluff without a brain in our dainty little heads. So we sometimes decide to kick over the traces and deny that we are women, that we actually do like men and damnit some guys are just, ummm, what's the current slang for it, yes, some are *hot*." Hailey's eyes widened as Elizabeth paused, letting her lecture soak in.

"You hit several nerves, Elizabeth. Yes, I have built up quite a battle front. And it works mostly. Until I see how close you and the President are, and how much he relishes confiding in you, sharing just about everything, I'd imagine. When I see you two holding hands and exchanging a special smile, I sort of, well, I feel empty, like all this politicking might not be as good as what you have." Hailey faced the First Lady and perceived deep understanding and friendship.

"It isn't, Hailey. But I'm not saying you, especially, can't be a successful Vice President and even more and remain single. That stuff, work life, is just frosting when you compare it to, say, raising a child like Adam. You've achieved much. Received many accolades, and of course, provided wonderful service to this great country. Added to the list is your supreme example of what women can do. But I'm guessing that isn't enough."

Hailey looked back to the garden below and reflected. "You are a mind reader. Don't try to deny it. No, it isn't enough. And, I'm at a loss for what to do about it. I know Adam and Jennette sense it. All the excitement and thrill of streamlining the bureaucracy, meeting with foreign diplomats, negotiating with members of Congress, all of that vanishes in a heartbeat when I enter that empty mansion up on Massachusetts Avenue. There I live a solitary life out of the limelight as much as possible. It is lonely."

"Come sit by me and talk. Let's open this can of worms and see if we can latch onto some ideas. First though, tell me about your husband. Was he so marvelous you don't expect another man to come up to par?"

"No, not all. But he was quite a hunk, or hot, as you put it. Reckless would best describe him and that's what did him in. I was a country girl from the backwoods of Virginia's Blue Ridge Mountains and he completely overwhelmed me. We were both in the top levels of our class at the Air Force Academy. We went to separate flight schools for a few years, and then connected at test pilot school. We became lovers soon after." Hailey looked away from the older woman, almost too embarrassed to speak the next line. "He was the first and only man I was ever intimate with, and I was pretty naïve about sex. We must have been lucky at first and then I got pregnant. He married me to make it official, but it was obvious that the pregnancy took the spark out of our relationship." Hailey sighed and drew back into herself. Elizabeth said nothing, allowing her friend to gather herself and hopefully continue.

"Morning sickness kept me out of fighter jets and I got a desk job. My husband didn't slow down a whit, even with his added responsibilities of me and his baby. He got more and more daring and took on the toughest assignments. A prototype fighter jet virtually blew apart, taking him with it. The rest you know." The young woman forced a smile that never reached her eyes.

"What a gift he gave you, though, Hailey. Adam is a darling child, or really, a young man, who loves his mother very much. You have done a magnificent job raising him. But really, there were no other men? Forgive me, I'm prying and I don't care. You're my friend and I feel you need to talk to someone who won't go write a book about it."

"It's OK, Elizabeth. I agree it's time to deal with it. Really, there were none that mattered. I can put them in neat little categories. Some wanted a quick roll in the sack. I guess they figured I would be like a divorcee who was desperate for love or sex or something. Some didn't want a relationship with a woman who had a child. And some didn't want a woman who was determined to work, and who might just be a tad smarter. Those three types of fellows took up my years at the State Department. Oddly enough, the characteristics of the men didn't change when I got elected. Plus, I couldn't seem to be with my son enough. Time with Adam gave me the utmost pleasure and gratification. Until lately I thought I had it all."

Hailey's wise friend sat back against the sofa cushions and let the air out through her teeth in exasperation. "I have another category for you, my dear. Some men can't get up enough gumption to approach a beautiful woman, and that you are."

"Sounds like the voice of experience, Elizabeth."

"For a short time only. Yet it was frustrating. I'd make eye contact with a fellow and we'd exchange smiles. I'd think, yeah, maybe he'll say something. Then, nah. He'd skeeter off sort of like a puppy that's been swatted for peeing on the floor." Both ladies chuckled at this image. "Bill just walked up to me and said, 'Hello, beautiful,' and I was done in. He was the one who told me about the beautiful woman syndrome. Of course I acted like I wasn't in that category, except I felt he was right on. Later he'd point out guys looking that way, either at me surreptitiously, or at another gal. It was true. To date Bill has told me I'm beautiful so many times I accept it and don't let it bother me. What about you, Hailey?" The First Lady grinned as the Vice President frowned and shook her head.

"I guess that's not my concern where men are involved. I'd just like to have a good conversation and make a friend. But that seems impossible with this job. The press has me in bed with any man I look at. Poor Mark now has his name tossed around the media cesspool in connection with me and I just talked with him and held his hand. Speaking of that, did you ever shake his hand?" Elizabeth nodded and smiled. "How can such a tough football player have such soft, tender hands? I mean, he's really masculine and good looking in a rugged way, yet his hands are wonderfully soft."

"Adam really likes Mark, you know. He told me Mark was his best buddy. I have listened to your son describing such a tender love for his mother and wanting her to be happy. It was clear to him that you needed a fellow and that was perfectly fine with him for your sake." It was Hailey's turn to sink into the sofa's cushions and sigh.

"Looks like I'm outnumbered. But what can I do? I don't want to put any guy into the media spotlight. It just isn't fair. His whole life will become public knowledge. He'll have no privacy. All his past deeds will be blown out of proportion to make him look awful or a crook or worse."

"It won't matter to the right man, Hailey. And let me tell you one more thing, young lady. I'm proud to have you as a friend. You're doing a marvelous job for us. Bill tells me every night he couldn't do his job without you. And, Sweetie, there is no higher compliment than that. You're like a president-in-training, and when the time comes the people will embrace you."

"Hold on a minute. What do you mean *when* the time comes? The President isn't even six months into office. He'll have many years left after he retires. Bill Conley is the healthiest guy I know."

"Of course he is. I meant to say *if* the time comes. Then too, someone needs to take his job for the next four years. I see by the look on your face you haven't had time to consider that possibility, you've been so busy. But, think on it."

"Hi, Mom. Jennette said you wanted to talk about something." Adam knew he was in trouble. There was a look she gave him. A serious one meaning he'd crossed wires somehow and his mother was going to uncross them.

"Let's go for a walk, shall we?" Hailey's routine for dealing with her precocious child was to take a walk. Both understood her invitation to be the equivalent of a whipping out behind the barn if she ever deigned to do such. The walk also gave them complete privacy from the agents and military guards posted around the former Naval Observatory that had become the home of the Vice President.

The late afternoon sun raised the humidity level in Washington to that of the temperature, both hovering at the 90-degree mark. Miserable was the word for the nation's capitol city built on a swamp. Breathing was difficult for those with respiratory illnesses, with the air taking on the quality of molasses in its reluctance to move. But this factor never bothered mother and son, who relished the atmosphere and exercised in it daily. They neared their favorite bench in the shade of an ancient oak and sat.

"You've been a busy boy, haven't you, Adam?" Now Hailey's smile showed the warmth and love reserved only for him and Adam relaxed somewhat. He did recognize, however, that it was time to come forth with nothing but the truth. Prevarication never gained purchase between the two of them in this extraordinary relationship.

"Mom, I've always felt special having you all to myself. My school chums envy me because I get to be with you so much." Adam reddened and looked away.

"Keep going." His mother wouldn't let him off the hook that easy.

"They say it's neat to have such an important mom, who's, uh, so cool." He grinned his best, hoping to wiggle out of the gentle prodding from his mother.

"Really? They say I'm cool, huh?"

"Not exactly in those words. More like guy talk and I can't repeat their descriptions. They just admire you. As much as boys my age can."

"So it's a bonus for you to have a mom who is a cool chick?"

"It is and it isn't." He flinched at his mother's raised eyebrows and rushed on. "See, Mom, this is hard to come right out with, but they all figure you must have guys taking you out all the time and the guys dream about what that would be like. You know? Harmless stuff."

"But you know otherwise, don't you? You know I haven't gone out on a date in a long time. You know about my classification of the men I've dated. And, uh, you know what most of those guys dated me for and I won't go into it." Hailey had embarrassed herself and quickly examined the rough bark on the ancient oak.

"Yeah, I know. And for a while it was way OK with me, 'cause every time you had one of *those dates*," Adam pronounced this with a large dollop of sarcasm, "you always took me out to some great dinner and movie, or we went on a vacation and had a blast."

"And that's no longer OK with you?"

"No, I understand it's not enough."

"You want me to spend more money on you, and take you on even better vacations?" They laughed at her intentional misreading. Hailey faced him directly and took his hands in hers. "Come right out with it, sweetheart. Tell me what you want."

"I think you need a boyfriend so you won't be lonely." He had said it and his remaining breath left him in a tremendous sigh.

"And you plan for that person to be Mark because he's your best buddy, right?"

Caught. There was no wiggle room out of this one, and the boy nodded, daring to look directly into her eyes.

"I told Gran and she must have talked to Jennette. I said you looked lonely and I thought it was time you stopped giving me all your personal attention, and that I wouldn't mind at all if you found a boyfriend and Mark would be ideal." Adam hesitated a fraction as his mother folded her arms. Not a good sign.

"Maybe I don't want a fellow. Did you think about that? Maybe I'd like to pick the person out, that is, assuming I decided I wanted to go out with someone. Did you consider that?"

"I know you, Mom. I saw you watching the President and Gran and how affectionate they were together. I understand it's natural for adults to have adult relationships. It's not something I'm particularly interested in and I'm not sure what it's all about, but whatever Gran has is really special. I want that for you. I guess I'm telling you it's OK with me. I'm old enough and don't need you all to myself anymore. Besides, Gran says you need someone to talk to."

Hailey let the tears slide down her cheeks as she listened to the love her son was expressing. He was a gift, a unique young man without a jealous bone or thought. She gathered him close and held him tightly as his arms wound around her.

Adam leaned back and gained a sad expression. "Didn't mean to upset you, Mom."

"You make me very happy, Adam. These are tears of gratitude for having such a grown up son. And yes, I talked to your co-conspirator. But I have a personal request you must obey, OK?"

"Sure, Mom. What is it?"

"Let me think on it and make my own decisions. Any move I make will cause any person I see to be hounded by the press and they will insinuate more than will be the case. Poor Mark has already felt the consequences of our little greeting at the barbecue. The press camps outside his home just waiting for me to show up for a late night rendezvous."

Adam's shoulders slumped. "Does that mean we can't go see him this summer at his football camp?"

"No, we won't miss your camp. But we need to be careful. Watch what we say. Any extra words can and will be taken out of context and spread all over the papers in the morning."

"Does this mean you'll give Mark a shot at being your guy?"

Hailey laughed. "It means I'm going to visit a close family friend to make sure he takes care of you this summer. Sometimes being friends first is the best thing to do."

Twenty-four

Bill Conley looked around the huge conference table. His Energy Task Force was shaping up. Kent Kraft had arrived with a new fellow named Crews from the Murchison Corporation. A so-called volunteer who just wanted to do what he could to help. Of course he did. Cal Murchison *was* energy in the Midwest. If Cal had it his way, the only participants in this room would be CEOs of companies just like his. Bill was strongly moved to throw him out but decided to let Hailey deal with him. *A pretty boy*, Bill noted. He had taken the seat directly across from the Vice President and stared at her the whole meeting. Hailey, as usual, ignored any overtures by men in the vicinity. And this guy looked like a weasel.

Burch Magnum had offered some productive ideas today. Golly, what's come over the man? First he bolts his party and turns independent. Now he's actually compromising! Motivation? Haven't a clue on that, but California is so big every conceivable interest resides there.

And Kent Kraft had come up with some surprising ideas; a few that Bill knew would not set well with his prime sponsor, Cal Murchison. The Senate Majority Leader was acting like his own man these days, seeming to disavow old strings that had jerked him like Pinocchio in the past.

That left old Ned Nederthal and his new buddy Jimmy Buxton from the opposing party. What a pair. They hardly uttered a word during the meeting and their eyebrows had a healthy workout from all the expressions going on between them. Each is bursting to hold a press conference and neither knows what to say. A first for these two old Southern Democrats, now adrift on the far right without a paddle.

The environmentalists' friend, Harry Jackson, seemed speechless as well. None of these birds thought it would ever come to this: an energy policy taking the best parts of every view and actually formulated within six months, start to finish.

Bill Conley was pleased at what he saw taking place. It was all about options and choices and seeing the other fellow's point of view. *Where had the system gotten off track?* he wondered. We could use the old whipping post and blame Watergate, with its notion that the end justified the means, and some people, such as a president, are above the law. Perhaps the fault lay amongst the ruins of the pro-life, pro-choice debate. Or perhaps it was the residual anti-war sentiment still strong nearly a quarter century after Vietnam. Now there was this debate between the energy industry and the environmentalists where each side insists, or did until this task force, that their position is the only possible choice. And don't leave out guns. Lord no. Let's not take away the right to bear arms, another all or nothing argument.

Whatever the subject, the opposing sides denigrated the character and merit of their opposition, shouted them down, called them despicable names, spent millions campaigning against a choice other than theirs. And the message to voters was, "You're either for us or against us."

Then there was Social Security and health care, where everyone complained and no workable solutions seemed possible. Tomorrow that group would meet for its discussion of a first draft policy statement and the fur would fly.

Thomas Crews was mesmerized by the woman across from him. She was beautiful, yes, but she had such depth. She was obviously the *de facto* manager of this conglomeration of political top dogs. He heard little of the discussion, never taking his eyes from the smooth skin of her face and hands, her full lips. Women in college and in his expanding business world usually acknowledged his looking, and his looks. Peers considered him vain. Thomas allowed them their envy, ignoring it equally. He'd been gifted with physical beauty and a personality that had successfully charmed many into his bed. But this woman would take a special effort. If only she would look his way. There! She sees me. Someone is laughing at the other end of the table. Who? What was said?

"Mr. Crews, I said was there some input you had on the subject, or did you come here to sit and stare at me?" Hailey was determined to wrap up this two-hour session and exclude the senator's little pet from future discussions. Crews snapped to attention in his seat, quickly slipping his hands off the table. "Unless you have some ideas for this task force, and apparently, as your silence indicates, you don't, then this will be your last meeting." She crossed her arms, and waited. Snickers bubbled up from around the table as Crews reddened at her challenge.

"Yes, Crews, I'd also be interested in your position, especially regarding wind power out West." Burch Magnum enjoyed skewering Cal Murchison, albeit in the form of his gofer. "Your boss contributed big bucks to my opponent in the last election, indirectly of course, in the form of an issue ad strongly denouncing the feasibility of wind as an energy resource. It would seem you agree since you've said nothing and apparently have no resource of that nature yourself." Laughter arose from everyone seated at the table except for Thomas, who sputtered and moved his lips without issuing a word, proving Magnum's point.

The President interrupted everyone, jumping into the fray. "All right, that's enough. Let the poor lad alone." Kraft glared at Crews, who glanced at Hailey who sat stone faced, arms crossed.

Senator Kraft broke the impasse. "I apologize, Mr. President, Madam Vice President. I was told by a valuable aide that bringing Mr. Crews here would be a mistake, and it was."

Bill Conley had seen and heard enough. "Mr. Crews, you're excused from this meeting and all others in this building. You may leave now." Crews scurried out with obvious relief at his expulsion. The President spoke directly to the Senate Majority Leader in a low voice. "Kent, I appreciate your position, but if we let Crews stay in these meetings, then Harry will want somebody who can report back to the Environmental Coalition and the Sierra Club. And Burch will insist on representatives from the ninety-nine interest groups out in California." Everyone chuckled at this, including Hailey, who had visibly relaxed since Crews' departure.

"Fact is, we need you to represent the nation on this without folks like our dearly departed young man listening in. Here you can speak candidly, as Hailey certainly demonstrated." Now it was the Vice President's turn to be embarrassed. "I have given you my word that what is said here stays here until we agree; compromise if you will, on a public statement. My mail indicates the people want us to deal with this together. Do you all agree?"

214

Heads nodded around the table. Public sentiment had finally been aroused. Based on recent polls, bickering inside the Beltway would lose many incumbents their jobs unless results were forthcoming. The president held a winning hand and everyone in the room knew it. All there also knew he had kept his word. There had been no leaks from the White House, and no credit or discredit ascribed to any one member of the task force. Surprisingly, as with the other groups similarly established, the Energy Task Force had become a team effort, creating the conversational buzz around town.

Their business finished for the day, the president adjourned the meeting.

"Senator Kraft, wait a minute and let's talk." President Conley motioned for the still angry and embarrassed senator to remain while the others filed out of the conference room. The two political warriors sat at one end of the long cabinet room table facing each other.

"Mr. President, that won't happen again." Kraft foresaw the venture of Thomas Crews into the task force meeting as the issue.

"I'm not concerned about Crews, Kent. This is just between us, and I'm just plain Bill right now." His opponent in the upper chamber of Congress relaxed and let a partial smile crease his expression.

"OK, Bill. What's on your mind?"

"I thought you might have some words to say about how we dumped your brother. Didn't want that to remain stuck in your craw."

Kraft drummed his fingertips on the table and took in a deep breath, almost a sigh. "Well, you know what is said during these times of transition. Live by the sword, die by the sword. Ronnie got his position by some shrewd maneuvering on my part. I had high hopes for him; they just didn't pan out.

"Then I expected to hear a complaint from you. You know, challenging the White House by politicizing an important law enforcement position, one that was supposed to be off limits. Yet, you've kept pretty quiet about it. Guess I was looking for another shoe to drop somewhere along the line and bringing Crews into this meeting could have been that shoe. Was it?"

"No, Bill. It wasn't. Between us, Ronnie was not up to the job and I knew it. It was a silk purse, sow's ear conundrum. He had people around him who screwed up. You caught one of them when you stomped into FBI Headquarters some time back to support that whistle blower. I could have gone to the press and made a fuss about your Vice President running roughshod over good people, tossing them out of their jobs, messing up careers. But that's the game in town, for many years the only one. No, it was embarrassing to me and to Ronnie, but frankly, Bill, you needed to fire him."

The two political leaders took the measure of one another. The President smiled and nodded his approval and appreciation for the Senate Majority Leader's candor and honesty. The senator relaxed even more with the knowledge that what was being said would never surface outside this moment. Yet Kraft had more to say.

"I admire what you're trying to do, Mr. President. I know personally from past conversations you and I had back in the Senate that you only wanted to retire and had no aspirations for this job. So when the people spoke through their votes and elected you, I had to think about what had happened; figure how to react in the face of an overwhelming verdict. You didn't just win, you whaled the shit out of both parties and that told me something. Honestly, I asked myself, was I in town to be a public servant anymore, or had I lost sight of that, and just wanted to maneuver, grab power, manipulate people and programs. That had become my game and maybe you shook me up. No, not even maybe. You did shake me up."

"And you're cooperating on this task force, Senator, and contributing. I can see a change in attitude. So can Hailey, and we both appreciate it. Also, I don't for one minute intend to take you for granted as being on my side in every issue. I expect you to argue and disagree. You will, it's your nature. And that's good. I'm proud of you."

Kent couldn't remember when anyone had said those words to him. Maybe it was his mother when he graduated from law school. He knew it was never his father. The two men stood and exchanged a parting handshake. The President left the room pleased with a good man and worthy opponent, who could step out of the routine political morass and still grow. The senator left with the knowledge he'd been with a natural leader, one he respected. Now he had to rush back to his office and beg Lucinda to stay on as his secretary.

Hailey stood by Alice's desk outside the Oval Office shuffling through her notes on the task force meeting. The moment was pregnant with exasperation and Alice meant to bring it out in the open.

"Madam Vice President," the president's secretary spoke in the voice she reserved for pompous heads of state, "that handsome young man left a message for you." Alice gloated over the note she handed to an exasperated Hailey. "He took some time to compose it, Ma'am. He also offered his apologies to me for interrupting my busy work day and using the President's personal stationery. But, let me quote him as best as I can. He was, hmmmm, 'awestruck by you, never having been so close to such a beautiful, smart woman in such an important position.'" Alice finished off her soliloquy by batting her eyes demurely, as befit a Southern belle.

"Oh, so original, Alice. And cut out this 'Madam' and 'Ma'am' stuff, will you?" Hailey unfolded the innocuous piece of paper and read aloud.

"Dear Vice President MacMurray, please accept my heartfelt apologies for losing my composure today. Yes, I do work for Cal Murchison, but that association has nothing to do with the reason for this note. For sure Cal wanted some inside information and I was sent to try and collect it. But I forgot all about that when I saw your smile. I don't believe I heard a word of discussion and was thus shocked when asked to contribute to the meeting. I had nothing but you on my mind. Please allow me to make amends by escorting you to dinner tomorrow night. Just have your secretary contact me at the Washington Hilton and I'll make arrangements. Ever your admirer, Thomas Crews.

"Aw, how sweet. Alice, please call Mr. Crews and decline his marvelous invitation. You can copy our standard form letter we've sent all the others. Oh, and place this dear note in with the others."

"Of course, Hailey." Alice smirked at the phoniness of the message that was not unlike her file drawer full of similar ones. She turned clockwise and grabbed the bottom drawer of a four-drawer cabinet. She opened the drawer to reveal a hodgepodge of "notes" from the many admirers of the Vice President. There was no order to the mess and that's the way both Alice and Hailey wanted it. Caroline Jankowski over at the Archives had termed it a "drop file" and that it certainly was. For virtually every guy behind every note had been dropped from the Vice President's sight.

The dropped files were but a sampling of the flood of correspondence Hailey received from men and a few women around the country. Other more tasteless scribblings had been turned over to the Secret Service for follow-up.

"Have a seat and spare me a minute of your time, Hailey. You look worried. Something on your mind?"

Hailey collapsed in a plush chair designed for visiting dignitaries. "It's nothing much, Alice. Just that I had a conversation with the First Lady the other day and I can't seem to think my way through it. The discussion was like no other I've had with anyone else in my life." Hailey looked into Alice's eyes for some sign to continue and saw understanding. Alice was part of the

First Family and smiled knowingly. Her expression said "talk to me."

"In short, Elizabeth said I needed to find a man and get into a relationship for the good of the country, and for my own sake as well."

"She doesn't mince words, does she?"

"Ok, so I boiled it down. We had a heart to heart talk and it affected me in several ways, Alice. First I got worried that the President might be ill and no one knew it. Then I started re-evaluating my single status. No one ever said those things to me. Ever. Not like she did."

Alice reopened the bottom drawer and pulled out a random handful of notes. "OK, pick one and go for it." But the serious look on the Vice President's face made her toss the papers in the trash immediately. "I'm sorry, Hailey. I guess it's not funny. And no, the President is fit as a horse, so no worry there." Alice slid her chair closer and reached for Hailey's hands. "Elizabeth wants you to be happy and we both know you're in a lonely job. Who can you talk to? Turn to? Everybody needs somebody and even your son recognizes it."

Hailey withdrew from her friend. "Thanks, Alice."

"I don't think there's much anyone can do when the President himself tosses your man out of the White House, Cal." Senator Kraft used the office of the presidency to squirm his way from between a rock and a hard place.

But Murchison wasn't going down without a fight. "So that's it, you're thinking, eh, Kent? One puny attempt and you turn tail and skedaddle? I expect more, and by damn I sure paid for it. I don't care what Conley said, get that boy close enough to that woman and watch him go to work. That's your responsibility, Kraft."

The senator let the silence build before replying. "No, I don't think so. And if it means losing your support, then so be it, Murchison. We were all put on good behavior by the top man himself today and I'm going to stick with him on this. No, you want some flunky to play games with that woman, you figure out a way. I'm done with Crews."

"Then I'm done with you, Senator. Goodbye."

Kent set the phone back on its receiver and felt peace overtake his mind and body. He wheeled around from his credenza and saw Lucinda standing in front of his desk, smiling. He grinned back easily.

"I'm learning to take your advice. Yes, Crews went with me to the meeting.

He embarrassed himself and the President threw him out. But I disavowed any connection to the man and did not support him. Just now I severed ties with Cal. There will be a bunch of people in this building who will be mighty surprised with me. But you are right. I lost sight of what we're here for. From now on I want you to tell me off whenever you feel it's necessary. I need your advice and I want you to stay. Please."

Twenty-five

Tony Martin was ready. He had six months experience running the Veteran's Administration without adhering to federal procurement regulations and today was his turn to testify on Capitol Hill. That he would do, if he could slog his way through the phalanx of reporters and cameras that blocked his way.

The honeymoon afforded every new president by Congress was definitely over. Never had so much popular will been enacted—"rammed through" was the phrase used by the *Times* and *Post* just this morning. And Tony had been Bill Conley's handpicked lightning rod. Today he faced a Congressional panel anxious to reassert itself.

No one questioned Tony's qualifications. He was a career senior executive service hot shot. For the decade before becoming the VA's department head in the Conley administration, Tony Martin had been the agency's troubleshooter. Whenever a region or hospital went *sour*, Tony was ordered in to clean up the mess. The press compared him to a bowling ball that not only rolled a strike every time, but cleaned up both left and right gutters. Spares were not acceptable to Mr. Martin, the human bowling ball. And buying equipment, supplies, and whatever else his agency's offices needed, had been his number one priority.

Regional managers cringed to find Tony camped on their doorstep for a surprise inspection. He had carte blanche to go wherever he saw the need. And there certainly was a need for improved procurement. For example, the Denver office had blundered miserably in the previous administration. Local management had authorized millions to renovate a World War II building in the Federal Center with not one single entry being refitted for the handicapped. Veterans in wheelchairs had blocked all the entrances until access was enabled by temporary wooden ramps leading through the service entrance.

Worse yet was the innovative accommodation dreamed up by the political appointee in charge. The man, a realtor from Idaho who had contributed highly to the incumbent, ignored all regulations and procured temporary commercial office space across the street at five times the authorized government rate. The new facility was applauded initially by the wheeling vets, but VA management officials learned too late that, although access was easier via push-button doors, not a single stall in the restrooms was wide enough to fit wheelchairs. Further, bids to install automatic doors on the newly-renovated federal building came in at three times the going commercial rate. Vendors knew when they had a sure thing.

A short man, Tony was swallowed whole by the media whale greeting him on the east steps of the Capitol building. Microphones thrust in his face blurred his vision and caused him to forge a zigzag path toward his goal. He had come alone, fearless and welcoming the opportunity to report to the legislative branch. They could hammer away at him forever. He had testified many times before and had a hide like a buffalo. But suddenly the crowding media erupted as one thundering herd and stampeded away, abandoning Tony Martin.

Relieved and shocked, he turned to view their retreating backsides and smiled at his savior. Hailey MacMurray was stepping out of her car, cheerfully acknowledging the gaggling news media. How did she do it, he wondered? Where he had faced chaos and 120-decibel shouting, the Vice President had raised one hand and accepted one question at a time, calmly, taking her time as always, just like her boss. She strolled easily up the steps, joining Tony with a wink.

"Pleasure to see you here, Madam Vice President," he chirped, delighted for her reassuring presence.

"I know you can do this by yourself, Tony, but we wanted to show a little support. The President wanted me to be your escort today." She beamed at the administrator who looked up at her from his five-and-a-half foot stature. Hailey had spoken only to him, but loud enough for nearby reporters to catch her on tape. Tony realized this moment was the news of the day and not what would happen in the hearing about to unfold inside. Immediately after her casual remark, network researchers were frantically searching their files for a precedent. Had a Vice President ever escorted an agency head to a joint committee meeting? Not likely. Was it proper for the person who ran the Senate to appear before a congressional hearing in support of a member of the executive branch? Constitutional scholars were being called in by prime time newscasters to give their interpretations.

"Care to comment on the substance of your remarks to the committee, Mr. Martin?" Harlin McMasters of Network News punched in his question ahead of the pack.

Tony looked to his escort for a signal and got a nod of approval. "I'd rather tell the members of Congress first, then report to you afterwards. They'll accuse me of stealing their thunder." Hailey and the pack laughed hard at this comment. More than one witness under previous presidents had been skewered for leaking testimony. After six months in office, the whole country knew Bill Conley's rule number one: no leaks and no anonymous White House sources, the latter successfully precluding the former.

The Joint Committee on Government Procurement Practices consisted of prime political "beef." The key leadership positions of both chambers had appointed themselves as members. Kent Kraft and Cantwell Nederthal shared the committee chairmanship. Jimmy Buxton and Harry Jackson balanced both major parties from the House. Burch Magnum had bulled his way into the fray, claiming to represent independent voters and the most populous state, California. All had been given scripts written by their respective committee staffs and based on data provided by the Legislative Research Service of the Library of Congress and the Congressional Budget Office. These scripts were neutered screenplays, leaving innuendo and drama up to the actors. Conservatives and liberals could take identical lines of script and spin them off in opposite directions, depending on whose constituency was being either gored or favored.

The large hearing room was lined with minicams and photographers. A bank of cameras rested on the floor beneath the raised platform fronting the committee. Some were aimed at the empty witness table, while others were glued to positions along the platform's podium. The divided audience contained vendors both for and against the free-for-all system being run by Tony Martin.

The loud buzzing of anticipation in the room hushed when Hailey and Tony entered. Runners and stringers for the media were dispatched to phone in initial reports. Burch Magnum grinned and stood out of respect for the Vice President. He began the applause that soon grew to his fellow committee members, and finally to the audience as Hailey and Tony proceeded down the aisle and were recognized.

Jimmy Buxton and Harry Jackson were mortified, yet clapped profusely, realizing they were on live TV. Ned vainly tried to conceal his anger at this blatant display of showboating by the administration. Kent grinned at the audacity.

"Is there no respect for custom and protocol? This is our turf, godammit," Ned mumbled to Kent as the witnesses took their seats.

"She's got brass balls; I'll say that for her." Kent chuckled. "But the show must go on."

Ned rose to the bait. "Madam Vice President, it is an honor to have you with us today. May I inquire as to your purpose in attending this hearing?"

"Thank you, Mr. Speaker. The President and I have heard Mr. Martin's briefing and support it. I'm here to demonstrate that we stand firmly with the VA Administrator. And also, I kind of missed being up here and wanted to say hello to some old friends." She hesitated a beat eying each member individually, steadily. "That is, all of you on the committee, Mr. Speaker. Now, if you please, it really is Mr. Martin's show and I'd like him to tell you about his successful program."

Burch turned and whispered to Rose, who was seated behind him taking notes. "She is magnificent, isn't she? Took control away from both chambers of Congress in their own hearing. Introduced the administration's witness and avoided pontificating speeches by the chairmen in one fell swoop." He admired his secretary and her efficiency. Lately he had also noticed Rose had freshened her appearance and spruced up her wardrobe somewhat. She was an attractive woman and certainly ran his office effectively. Smiling, Burch turned his attention back to the witness table.

"Thank you Madam Vice President, Mr. Speaker, Majority Leader Kraft, Mr. Buxton, Mr. Jackson, and Senator Magnum." Tony and Burch exchanged nods of recognition. They had known each other for the senator's entire career in politics. Burch had tried unsuccessfully to lure the super executive away from the executive branch to run his committee staff. They shared a mutual respect rarely acknowledged on the Hill. Most of the time it was senior executives like Tony and top staff on the Hill who worked closely to write legislation. All done for the good of the country, and regardless of party affiliation.

"Nationwide, the Veterans Administration has reduced costs in procurement by thirty percent in our first six months of operation. That means we have saved the taxpayers about fifty-six million dollars so far." Tony paused as the committee turned pages of the handouts they had been given only moments before his arrival. Flashbulbs lit the room and buzzing arose from the audience. Those vendors in favor of the President's program clapped loudly and Senator Magnum joined them. The rest of the committee frantically leafed through several pages of handouts, and peered through trifocals looking for some detail to nitpick.

Tony continued his prepared statement, preempting interruption. "As predicted, we have increased purchases by small businesses, and gained lower bids from the large corporations. Our guiding principle has been to judge purchases both on quality and on cost. Further, we have shortened our schedule of payments to no more than two weeks from the time we receive an invoice to the day the check goes in the mail." This brought shouts from the supporting vendors and more applause. It was a fantasy come true. Unbelievable in government history. Recent legislation, specifically the Prompt Payment Act, required payment within 30 days but everyone knew many agencies had antiquated systems and were dragging their administrative feet getting them up to speed. Again the committee shuffled through Tony's briefing paper looking for some avenue of attack. Finding none, several tried to speak, only to be drowned out by the powerful conclusion of the administrator's statement.

"You'll see a number of attachments to your briefing papers. Those are letters from various organizations representing minority groups, women's rights groups, the American Small Purchasing Association, the National Association of Purchasing Officers, and others. All support our program. That concludes my statement and I'll be glad to take your questions." Tony sat back and wiped his forehead. Hailey leaned over and clapped him on the back.

"Good job. Now comes the fun part, Tony." Both turned to confront the unhappy faces staring down at them. Only one friend remained, Burch Magnum, and he gave them a thumbs up sign. Kent Kraft kept a neutral expression.

"Mr. Martin," Ned Nederthal, Speaker of the House, took charge. "I have numerous letters from good folks back in my home state complaining about your program. They assert unfair treatment and biased selection of vendors down there. One in particular says he had done business for over twenty years with the hospital in Biloxi and now seems to be shut out of the whole shooting match."

"Yes, Sir, that would be Hammond Medical Supplies, Mr. Speaker. I'd say that would be twenty years of shafting us with overpriced goods." The audience erupted again. This time supporters of some committee members led the chorus.

"I take grievous offense to that remark, Mr. Martin." Ned barked into his microphone and banged his gavel for order. Hailey covered her mouth to hide a smile. "What kind of proof do you have for such an audacious statement?"

"Plenty, Mr. Speaker. I let the hospital administrator down there make the decision. Local control and decision making is the key to the success of our program. Terri Benson went to several manufacturing facilities before she made her selection. She found superior quality and much lower costs at almost every other supplier. She picked the best deal and it surely was not Hammond. That single decision alone saved us over a hundred thousand dollars."

"But you eliminated a loyal supplier who had done considerable business down there, Mr. Martin. George Hammond runs a smooth operation and hires over two hundred fine Mississippians to manufacture those goods."

"Mr. Hammond also pays the lowest wages of all the companies Terri Benson surveyed. And charges about 25 percent more than the going market rate. Frankly, Mr. Speaker, we have asked the General Accounting Office to look into several companies, especially Hammond. Other than close political connections, I can see no justification for any VA procurements going to George Hammond in the past." Tony's strong retort created a smattering of applause that was quickly gaveled down by an irate co-chairman.

"Meeting adjourned," bellowed Nederthal.

Hailey and Tony Martin stood as four of the five committee members left the room. Only Burch Magnum stayed to congratulate his old friend. Rose went with him, glued to his side, and still taking notes.

"Incredible, Tony. Absolutely marvelous. I've never seen that old curmudgeon high tail it so fast. You've got a set of brass ones, my friend." The Independent senator from California sneaked an embarrassed look at the two women present. He and Tony would have to share a beer over this one in a place where they could let loose with some guy talk.

Rose and Hailey greeted each other with hugs. Rose had been one of those old friends Hailey had come to see. And now they stifled laughter at the senator's Mr. Clean act.

"Where're the women, Burch?" Hailey needled him. "When it comes to shopping, we're experts. Right, Rose?"

"Shucks, Madam Vice President, you know how hard it was for me to get on this panel. Ned and Kent weren't about to tolerate any women." Burch looked from one woman to the other and found no sympathy. Both stood with arms folded, feet tapping.

Hailey broke the impasse. "Rose you look splendid. Trimmed down. New makeover. Nice outfit. Hmmmm. Who's the fellow?" Hailey pursed her lips, knowing the answer to her own question. She grinned as Rose turned red.

"Oh well, you never can tell when a nice young staffer will get desperate. And what about you? I see the tabloid have you in bed with an entire pro football team. You must be exhausted."

"It is tiresome, Rose. I think I need a vacation. Might have to see what it's like in the Rocky Mountains this summer. I hear the ski resorts have some great bargain rates in the off season."

Rose motioned to her friend to step away from the two guys who were backslapping and jawing with friendly vendors from the audience.

"I think he's starting to notice, Hailey. Still, though, he won't take the hint to sever his arrangement with the estranged wife back in California. Frankly, I'm about ready to jump him but I don't want to end up as another Capitol Hill groupie." She turned thoughtful and reached for Hailey's hand. "Would this Colorado vacation be planned anywhere near Crested Butte?"

"You've been talking to the First Lady or Jennette or Adam, haven't you?" Hailey tilted her head back from her good friend and received an embarrassed grin in answer. "I won't play dumb with you, Rose. Adam is going out there after school lets out to be in Mark's football camp for a few weeks. I promised to take him out and come pick him up, planning on a few days rest each trip."

"I remember some sage advice from a close friend during the last campaign. It went something like, 'Get back in the fray and go for it.'" Hailey rolled her eyes being confronted with her own words. "Do we have some kind of double standard going here, Madam Vice President? Hmmmm?"

"Got me there, Rose. I just hate to bring all the attention on the poor guy when the media smells something brewing. Also, I seem to lack confidence when it comes to men. I got bitten the first time and can't afford another big mistake in my position."

"Got bitten? Another big mistake? What on earth are you talking about, Hailey? That was in another life. Your husband was killed in an accident, sure, but look what he gave you. Adam is a gift, an invaluable one. You were always telling the women up here in our Connection meetings to look for the positives and not dwell on the negatives of the past. Is that some more sage advice your throw out but ignore personally?" Rose pulled Hailey farther off to the side to avoid the ears of a few reporters nearby.

"I don't care if you are the Vice President, you're my friend, and that's more important to me. Do you like Mark, or is this just some maneuver to appease your immediate family and friends?"

Hailey expelled her breath, ruffling the hair on her forehead. She checked for more reporters and turned to look directly at Rose.

"I do like him. Very much. And maybe that's part of my problem. I've put on the brakes for so long I sometimes think I would do as you suggest and jump him. But there must be other women in his life. Why is he still single? He's so good on and off the football field. He seems perfect. Adam is nuts about him and is always telling people they are best buddies. Yet I'm so used to being overly cautious and wonder if he's too good to be true."

"You don't read the sports page do you, Hailey?" The Vice President shook her head in bewilderment. Rose continued, "Mark and his best friend, Jason Cramer, may appear as opposites but they share something in common. Both are on record, as least in interviews with *Sports Illustrated* and *ESPN*, saying they won't settle down until their playing days are over. They are dedicated professional football players and work hard to keep it that way, despite the public image Mark's friend Jason projects. I suspect most of his bravado is just marketing hype anyway. But Mark is straight as an arrow." Hailey raised her eyebrows at this out-of-date term and Rose chuckled. "OK, maybe he's not as celibate as a monk, but his fans respect his dedication, and there has never been a serious relationship, at least none the reporters got wind of." Rose held Hailey's arms softly at the elbow. "Listen well, dear. You have accomplished more than any other woman in the history of this country. You have shown the world women can be on top *and* have a family *and* be a good parent. Hear me now." Rose gently shook those elbows. "That is the cake, Hailey. Men are the icing. Just dessert, if you will. And it's about time you sat down to a full course dinner."

Twenty-six

Air Force One didn't have enough runway to land in Gunnison, the nearest airport to Crested Butte. So Hailey, Adam and their guards, Jennette, Nick, and Charlie, took a helicopter over from Peterson AFB in Colorado Springs. Their chopper landed on the ski resort's golf course near the ninth green that was encircled by reporters. There was such a crowd waiting, a mixture of tourists and townsfolk and media, that it was impossible to consider walking up Elm Street to Mark's restaurant.

Hailey mentally stepped back from the fracas forming around her and appreciated the eye-startling, clear blue sky Colorado was famous for. It promised to be hot at 9,000 feet altitude and no cloud cover. Then bone-chilling cold tonight when all the heat escaped. Gunnison, about 30 miles south of here, was known as one of the coldest places in the country and a hunter's paradise.

The valley was idyllic. Three rivers, the Slate, East, and Taylor, drained the ski slopes of Mount Crested Butte and surrounding peaks of the Gunnison National Forest on the west slope of the Continental Divide. These rivers fed into the Gunnison River flowing through its namesake town. Farther to the west the Gunnison carved the Black Canyon with its sheer 2,000-foot-deep crevices.

The sight lowered her blood pressure and stress level just standing here. She supposed one could four-wheel it over Keebler Pass to escape to the north, but why leave? It was beautiful and especially peaceful here. In some ways the mountains reminded her of home in southwestern Virginia.

Nick and Charlie drove up in four-seater golf carts to collect them. This unexpected mode of transportation left the hounds of the press stranded with none of their redundant questions answered. She kept one hand on Adam's right arm as a reminder to be on good behavior. Golly she loved this child. She hadn't asked for a knight protector but he had surely filled out the armor.

They glided up Elm going slowly and quietly, with the electric motors of the carts whisking them along as if on a cloud. There was Madge's Trinkets, a throwback to the 60's hippy fashions. Every few feet a raised wooden square box hosted mountain flowers that seemed to grow five feet high, as if making up for the short season. Colors ranged from blue columbines to pink zinnias to red, white, and lavender roses.

The Blue Goose Emporium appeared next, touting veggie sandwiches and herbal drinks guaranteed to heal all aches and pains. She might have to stop by and sample a gallon or two. The Hotel Tilford looked like it did when the Pony Express rode through. Newly remodeled, it advertised. She returned the friendly waves of townsfolk on both sides of the street. Hailey smiled as several women shouted encouragement, promising to hang tough with her.

This was America. Outside the hullabaloo of Washington, real people led real lives and were mostly friendly. In this part of the country there was little interest in the political maneuverings of lobbyists and game players. Hailey wondered what the press would think when they discovered her party was spending a few days at Mark's cabin halfway up Keebler Pass. He had warned her that it was kind of rustic but had plenty of room for everybody, including several shifts of Secret Service agents. But, he had added, he had removed all the phones. Clever of him to dream like that. Each agent had a radio and a cell phone. She could not be so disconnected, but the thought was nice.

And she had thought about Mark. A lot. They shared more than friendship; it just hadn't been quite defined. The man was like a best pal to her son. Of all the potential suitors she had considered, and she had to admit she had considered several despite what she said to friends and press alike, Mark was a tempting favorite. She was tentative, testing her feelings lain dormant for so long. She did have feelings. They were not totally in focus though. Still, Hailey knew herself well and vowed to trust her reactions, her gut feelings.

She spotted his restaurant about the time her stomach rumbled in complaint. There was a true gut reaction and she acted on it.

"There's Mark's place, Adam. Are you ready for something to eat?"

"Absolutely, Mom." He alighted from the cart and reached a hand back to her, bowing at the waist. It was an old game they played. She was a helpless damsel and he Sir Walter Raleigh back from the Colonies. "If you please, Madam." He took her hand and guided her to safety on the sidewalk. There had actually been an occasion when the silly boy had removed his windbreaker and draped it over a rain-filled gutter. They had laughed at first, then had to roll up the soaked jacket and toss it in the trunk of their car. Afterwards, Adam had gotten cold and Hailey had been the one to take her jacket and place it around his shoulders.

They were friends really. And because they were so close, she rarely thought of a life outside their sphere of togetherness. Yet he had been the one to suggest otherwise. She was overwhelmed with his desire to see her happy, connected with a soul mate. It was as if her son had taken the role of her father and dared to let her go for her happiness. But he was 12, and beyond his years in caring and thoughtfulness.

Hailey ignored the tumult surrounding her small group. The reporters had caught up and began lobbing loaded questions. Minicams turned on and she would become the regional, if not the national, news lead this evening.

Jennette took charge and gathered the news pundits to her side for a little chat. "Folks, give us a little cooperation if you will. The Vice President is tired and needs some time to rest and relax. I guarantee you'll get a daily briefing from me and possibly a news conference from Mrs. MacMurray, if she has anything to say. But for now, please give us some space." Jennette smiled at the crowd, but her body language spoke for her. She stood arms akimbo like Gary Cooper in *High Noon.*

Hailey perused the menu tacked to the front door. She chuckled to herself. Looked like trout was the perennial special of the day. It read April 15, almost two months ago. Must be some dependable fishermen around to keep Mark's chef supplied on a daily basis.

"Welcome to Crested Butte, Madam Vice President." Mark stood in the open doorway.

"Thanks, Mark. Let that be the last time you don't call me by my first name." He offered his hand. She ignored it and slid between his arms to hug him. Passersby smiled at them and a few cameras clicked for posterity, or the nightly news. Hailey backed away a little, looked directly into his broadening smile, then inched forward again and kissed him lightly on the mouth. From behind them came a sultry comment.

"You two going to grope out here in public or go inside so we can eat? I'm starved." Jennette came forward and hugged Mark, too.

Mark spoke. "OK, Jennette, I can take a hint. Inside, all of you, including those sneaky guys in brand new tennis shoes pretending to be examining the roof for snipers. You're on vacation. Relax." But he couldn't begin to. Hailey had knocked him off stride. No, it was way beyond that. She'd shot him into another galaxy. He only realized halfway to their booth that they were holding hands. It felt like they'd been this close a long time. If he'd had some strategy for courting her, it had been superseded by the lady in a heartbeat. After they were seated, he patted the cushioned back of the booth searching for something solid and familiar. His world had shifted like the tectonic plates shoving California into the Pacific.

Dinner was a watchful experience. Mark watched Adam tear into a thick steak—fish was not one of his favorites and the boy seemed to be inhaling his food. In between stuffing his mouth, Adam had a million questions. How many guys were in the football camp? How long did they practice? When did they eat? What did they do at night? And on and on. Mark gave short answers that satisfied the young boy's curiosity and encouraged him to relax and enjoy this time. It would be fun, and he'd get some good exercise.

Hailey dug into her trout special and kept a steady eye on both fellows across the table. Adam was doing a good job of cross examination for her and she enjoyed observing. Adam and Mark had become fast buddies from the start. Mark never took his concentration elsewhere. His attention stuck with her son and he listened to the boy. Hailey saw true affection and mutual respect. It was clear she could remove any prequalification about accepting her son first. This was a personal revelation for Hailey. Her struggles to compete for survival were history. Her son was beyond happy; she only needed to open herself to the possibilities. This would not be a struggle because she knew her feelings and they grew stronger by the minute for this athlete/artist/musician.

Jennette watched her friend watching the other two. Her sixth sense told her a decision was in the making. She had observed Hailey MacMurray many times before. Her friend seemed to wear a bemused expression, signaling that her mind was certain of its decision. Did all women decide things like this? Did they appraise a man and categorize him as to a No, a Maybe, or a Yes? Jennette had always chosen the latter option in her wild years after her husband had been killed. She didn't look for any qualities other than was the guy available to take to bed. Now her friend provided a much better approach. And Jennette seemed to understand without asking outright. The two women accepted their ESP-like relationship. What affected one affected the other.

Their empathic zones crisscrossed, forming an unspoken realization. In this particular case, Jennette recognized that Mark had been chosen, or, in the male vernacular, he was a "goner." Hailey had set her cap.

The deck on Mark's "rustic cabin" stretched around three sides of the 5,000-square-foot building. Guest bedrooms had walk-out patios in the back facing the forested slope of Keebler Pass. Mark had explained that these rooms were for other pro athletes who helped out at the football camps. The men apparently took turns sleeping in the bunkhouse next door which housed and fed the 25 boys per two-week camp. Back in Mark's cabin there were two master suites facing the valley, each with double doors leading to an adjoining second floor deck. There, Hailey finally drew in a relaxing breath seated in an aspen-framed lounger.

The cabin was settled in, and the only sounds came from an occasional crunch of an agent's booted foot patrolling the landscape. Jennette and her team, the day shift, and Adam, were asleep in the smaller guest rooms exhausted from a combination of jet lag, altitude and mountain air. But first, everyone in Hailey's vacation party had collectively gulped at what was termed a cabin. Resort hotel was more like it. Mark could easily convert the place into a bed and breakfast. The bottom floor boasted an indoor-outdoor heated pool, exercise room, game room, spa and sauna. These amenities answered Adam's questions about what to do at night.

The main floor consisted of a gigantic great room with stone fireplace large enough for eight-foot logs, kitchen, and hallway leading to the back rooms. Centered in the great room was Mark's Steinway, a prized possession he said didn't belong in a restaurant. He had promised to play for them after they had all gotten over the trip and time change. Mark, Hailey noted, had a separate and quite eclectic life apart from the glitzy sports world and public view. He cooked at home and at his restaurant, although Morgan Cutcher, his primary chef, had taken on another sous chef as relief so his boss could spend more time with his football camps.

Remarkably, Hailey observed, there were no signs of Mark's pro football career displayed anywhere. *Had they been taken down?* she wondered. *Or, did he have them stuffed in a Fibber McGee closet?* He seemed to have so many varied interests. His walls were covered in Navajo rugs, authentic ones. Discretely placed sculptures depicted a tired cowboy astride his bucking horse, a shaggy Rocky Mountain sheep, an Indian warrior searching the plains for buffalo, and a grizzled silver miner toting his gear and wearing a huge smile, no doubt at his latest strike. All of these sandstone creations possessed a miniscule "MD" initialed near the bottom. Hailey knew he was an artist, she just hadn't realized how accomplished he was. She also remembered those gentle hands of his.

"A penny," spoke a deep voice from the other master suite's double doors. Hailey turned to see her host propped against the frame, smiling in the luminescent, silvery shading of the full moon.

"For my thoughts?" Hailey stood as he approached slowly.

"None other. You've had some day and ought to be asleep. What's going on in that beautiful head of yours?" A man with self-esteem and confidence, one who managed now to be with Hailey MacMurray, and not the Vice President of the United States, came to her side. He leaned on the railing and searched his valley, giving her a profile that was calming, protective. Hailey felt secure from gossip, political intrigue, and fallacious slander in his presence.

"I'm nervous, to be honest. You're an amazing person, Mark. I didn't know what to expect when I got here." Hailey swallowed, even more nervous now. If she thought sleep would be just around the corner, her system had deemed otherwise as her pulse bumped up a level. She managed a throaty chuckle.

"I don't want to scare you away. I came out to talk, to get to know you and then after a while, tell you more about me in exchange. You know what I mean. Get beyond being good friends. Call it a personal goal that I've been very patient with. But it is something I'm serious about."

She had to touch his arm as a sort of grounding. She discovered she needed to feel part of him just like she needed an anchor. Certain of her footing, Hailey opened her heart. She revealed the story behind her marriage. Along with this, came her feelings of rejection from Adam's father—Mark noted she never used his name or referred to the man as her husband.

"I almost quit when he was killed. It was like losing all my dreams. You might say my heart and ego were shattered severely. He had rejected me and our baby. I asked for a leave of absence and scuttled back into the hills of Virginia to salve my wounds."

"But you obviously came out of hibernation. What made you do that, Hailey?"

"Marie. She let me sulk around the house for a week and then handed over my mother's diary with pages marked that had been written after my dad had died. My mother wrote about how her life had ended with my father's passing. Marie shocked me by saying that was pathetic bullshit. She said I had too much to offer to shrivel up and hide. I got defensive at first, shouting in protection of my mother's memory. Then I got mad at Marie who just took it without flinching. She let me rail on. I shut myself in my room and wouldn't come out, for, oh, maybe thirty minutes. It took that long for me to recognize what Marie had done. She'd broken the spell. I was back to being me and determined to live beyond the legacy my mother had left." Hailey glanced back to Mark and her voice softened. "I haven't stopped going since."

Mark pulled her into his chest, enfolding strong arms around her protectively. She let down sorrow, anguish, and a recurring fear at having almost given up. He accepted her tears, welcomed the silent shuddering of her body, taking on her pain like an empathic lover. He offered her trust and knew she accepted, felt it. Gradually, Hailey raised her face to his and kissed him. She began to relax against his body and molded herself into his muscular frame.

Mark accepted her affection and made no move to take the kiss further. He let her explore his face with kisses, test his lips with hers and open his mouth with her tongue. Every move would be her doing and he continued to be a steady rock, caressing her back and shoulders with his strong hands. He'd thought of this moment since the first time Hailey had stood on the field waiting for him to approach her. She was a strong woman, yet fragile. All her life, it was now clear to him, Hailey had stood up for herself without parents, without a husband, and lately, without a family other than close friends. Her kisses, her arms pressed around his, and her hands grasping the nape of his neck, pulling him forward for a deeper kiss, told him everything. She was giving him a gift and he would slow things down, not mess it up.

She pulled back and held him at arm's length. His smile was reassuring, loving, and she understood what he was about. Hailey led him to the lounge chairs to sit and talk. That she wanted to lead him back to her bed had been made clear from her needy kisses and both understood. Yet, this relationship had begun out on the field in the moment when he had approached her with her son. Now they needed to build trust to become intimate emotionally before tackling the physical part. She relished the time with Mark this night, without the confused feelings of sexual complications. It was like no other time in her life.

They stayed at Mark's two more nights. Each evening the Vice President and her man sat on the deck and talked. His parents had retired to Phoenix and came up occasionally in the summer to visit. Mark was an only child who loved children and had devoted his off-season to them. He'd gone to Western State College down in Gunnison on an academic scholarship, but had become a local hero playing football. And that was pretty much it as far as growing up. That and his commitment with his best pal, Jason Cramer, to find a mate after his playing days were over. Yes, he admitted and appreciated his gifts of music and sculpting. He used the proceeds from the sale of his pieces to fund a trust for young people. He didn't need that much money; the Redskins paid him enough.

Colorado was like other states, he explained. Everyone talked about putting education first, but when times got tough the first programs to be cut were sports and art. From Mark's disgust with the state and local governments to keep adequate money in school budgets, he'd set up the football camps and the art scholarships. He'd also built a network of athletes who felt the same way, and had established inner-city programs and open air activities like his camps. It was all without recognition except for the occasional award like his NFL Man of the Year trophies which Hailey found out in the boy's bunkhouse with the rest of his football memorabilia.

Their last night in Crested Butte was like a dream.

"Mark, I learned today that someone else will have to come out and pick up Adam. The President needs me on this last push for an energy policy. I-I'd hoped for more time now that we know each other."

"Don't worry about Adam. We'll take good care of him and Nick is staying here as an undercover waterboy, so there will be official security. But the boy is determined to be a regular guy and sleep in the bunkhouse and do the drills like the other boys." He leaned against the railing of the deck and spoke to the valley. "I'll be here another month, then take part in the early training camp back in Northern Virginia with the rookies and quarterbacks. Maybe we can see each other then."

She was falling, no, had fallen in love with him and a month was too long. "This is frustrating. I have such strong feelings and this job is getting in the way." Now she spoke to the valley and Mark turned her to face him.

"I love you, Hailey. Be patient. I won't go away. I love Adam too. When the time is right, when you're ready, we'll take it to another level."

Twenty-seven

Burch Magnum, newly announced independent senator from California, and head of the Energy Task Force, had lost 25 pounds and felt great. He had been working out every morning in the Senate Gym and dieting like a madman. Burch no longer used his office as a part time apartment. He had run up a ton of credit card debt renting a nearby townhouse and furnishing it magnificently. Today he was a free man after all. Burch read the final divorce papers from his estranged wife back in California. They had used each other. *Used and abused*, he thought ruefully. He had needed her family's financial backing and connections for his initial senatorial bid. She had thrived on his celebrity and power status in the elite debating club that was the upper chamber of the Congress. He couldn't remember the last time they'd slept together without faking it. Marcella was a man-eater. Her sex drive kept a horde of young studs panting. Burch's position in Washington lent some respectability to her reputation. But no longer.

He'd asked for nothing, even though California was an equal property state and he could have been due a pile of money. No. He wanted a clean break with no strings and she had granted him one. Burch grinned as he scanned the signed document. Yes, Marcella had met her match in a rising star, one Morgan Stelth, who was half her age and in possession of apparently unflagging abilities. His celebrity status—at 26 he earned $20 million per film—was enough to knock Burch off Marcella's podium.

She had even called Burch the minute she'd received his lawyer's divorce decree, or so she said. Breathless, Marcella had panted out her involvement with "The Stelth Man," as his fan club called him. Burch had finally asked his ex-wife to stop providing details of the man's athletic prowess in her bed. The images had been comedic at best.

Now what? he ruminated. It was time to see if his instincts were correct about a lady he'd admired for a long time.

Rose entered his office to shut off the lights and save the work on his PC. "Oh, excuse me, Senator. I thought you left hours ago. I just got back from the gym. Guess I assumed too much." Her face was flushed from exercise and the heat of Washington's lingering summer. Her hair, still wet from a quick dousing to cool off, hung in strings down her shoulders and over her back. Rose had obviously figured her boss would be gone because she still wore sweaty gym shorts and a workout tank top. Burch thought she was the sexiest woman he'd ever seen.

It hadn't slipped past his notice that she had gone on a diet and strict exercise regimen for the past six months. Her wardrobe had transitioned from dowdy secretarial to downright appealing. There was nothing specifically flirtatious about Rose and the clothes she now wore. He just seemed to be more attracted to her loose sheath dresses—following the popular style of the Vice President—the kind the press labeled bland but which left everything to a man's imagination. True, there was an occasional brightly colored blouse, always with an extra button undone, always catching his eye. And those skirts with the side slit part way up her thigh. It was just enough to keep him looking.

"Burch, is everything alright? You're sitting there like someone hit you over the head with a poleax. Say something. Please. Now you have me worried." Rose moved to the front of his desk and stopped. She was worried and her boss saw her not for the first time as a beautiful woman.

"I was looking over that information you dug up for me on Mark Daniel. Sort of checking out the competition, you know. Heck, I'm only 55, been on a diet, you know, and lost some weight. I sort of feel like I can compete with the young stallions lining up to court the Vice President. I was thinking a little romancing by the right man would do the trick. After all, the woman was married and has a child. She couldn't be a total iceberg. Perhaps I could be the one to do the thawing." He winked at Rose like she was another guy in a locker room conversation. He noted with satisfaction her demeanor turning sour and he continued laying it on.

"Shoot, my age shouldn't matter, and I have had almost daily contact with the "angel of death" as she's known inside the Beltway. Marcella doesn't count. She wouldn't leave California and pays my affairs here no mind. Yet time is not on my side if I read the latest gossip rags correctly."

Burch glanced over to a stack of newspapers on the corner of his desk. Their headlines blared the town gossip. "VP Caught Visiting Secret Lover" screamed the Monday headlines of the *Weekly Trumpet.* "Does MacMurray Fancy Daniel?" leveled the sports section banner of the *Washington Post,* in a side bar next to a telephoto close up of the innocent kiss at the inauguration barbecue.

"Then I thought, hell, Daniel is a younger man and not even in the political power circle, the elite group of the social hierarchy in DC that runs the town." Burch let his gaze drift to the ceiling at this false statement. Bill Conley had turned that show on its ear. He'd never recognized any elite political circle. "Eschewed it," was the proper term used by the *New York Times* report in Sunday's editorial.

"Thanks for this valuable information on Mark Daniel, Rose. I don't follow football much and thought I'd catch up on this fellow. See what he's like, you know?"

"Checking up on the competition? Senator Magnum, really." Rose shot him a seductive smile that froze before it reached her eyes. The expression on her boss's face revealed her comment had struck a nerve. Rose was furious.

"Really, Senator. The woman was in the House for years and nobody paid her any attention. Now that she's elected Vice President, guys are stumbling all over themselves figuring out angles to seduce her. I just wonder if the same would be true if she were a single man. Would all the women in the Congress go on diets and plan strategies of seduction?" Rose was steamed and didn't notice the faint smile forming on her boss's face. She foraged on, incensed at the silly games men played.

"Does any man really think all he has to do is dress up and go courting this woman and she'll swoon at his feet? She's the Vice President for cripes sake, and a mother, and damn good at both jobs. So you guys had better appeal to those two sides of her life or you're out of the game. Shoot, I doubt you'd make it onto the playing field." Rose turned and stomped back to her desk, slamming the door on her way out. She stormed around her paperwork island three times and walked back into the senator's office.

"I'm terribly sorry, Burch. I lost my cool. The thing is, women have invested a lot in Hailey MacMurray. We want to see her succeed and be accepted as a smart person, not just another pretty face whose life will be just fine if she can only find the right man. Anyway, I'm sorry."

Burch did his best to act deflated and chastened. "I guess you nailed me, Rose. Your description fits me exactly." His secretary turned to flee.

"Wait, Rose. Please come back and sit for a moment." She reversed her steps reluctantly and sat primly on the edge of a less comfortable wing back chair. Burch came from behind his executive desk and sat facing her, leaning forward earnestly.

"You're absolutely right. But I'm not upset about it. Yes, that's what guys are thinking. I thought of myself as one of them for maybe five seconds about, oh, maybe four years or so ago when Hailey first came to town." Rose squirmed in her seat, appearing not the least relaxed with this revelation.

"I didn't mean you, Senator. I just sort of blurted out my feelings without thinking. Please accept my apology. Let me get out of here before I revert to the standard feminine defense and start crying."

"No, no. Stay please, Rose. I'm not mad at you. In fact, I feel relieved in a way. I need to talk with someone I can trust." He smiled at her and Rose slumped back into the chair, letting her breath escape.

"Mercy, Senator. Give me a minute here." She sucked in several deep breaths and put both hands to her stomach. "OK, all systems cleared. But you do the talking and I'll listen for a change." Both laughed and their long friendship returned from hibernation.

"Well, I must confess to you that I have been dieting and exercising in hopes of beating the competition to the finish line with the ladies." Burch startled mid-sentence when Rose looked at him. He had never been appraised by a woman so boldly, and turned crimson.

"Senator Magnum, do you realize how attractive you are? The secretary's network ranks you at the top of its ladder of eligible men." Burch only got redder. "Honestly, they do. Yes, we all noticed that you trimmed down and stopped living in this dump. Buff is the word, Senator Magnum. The women on Capitol Hill agree you are the buffest guy over 50, and the best catch. So, since we're being candid here, why are you angling for the Vice President when she hasn't shown interest in a single guy up here, and she was a member of Congress for four years?"

"I'm afraid my answer will cause you to lose all credibility with me, Rose. As I sit here taking in the honest appraisal from a good friend, I'm embarrassed at my answer. Frankly I don't know why. Marcella only stayed in our marriage because she liked to tell people she was married to a United States Senator. I'm not personally interested in Hailey MacMurray. Not for over four years, as I said before. She is a nice woman, and I have the utmost respect for her. I consider it an honor to be her friend. Was I trying to get into the White House by courting her? Not at all. Do I want to be a father to her son? Not at all. I'm too busy, and too old for that. I couldn't keep up with her from what I hear. The woman runs five miles a day and swims laps too. I don't even walk much." Burch paused looking down at his feet after confessing. This was turning out to be the best performance of his career.

"Senator, Burch, how many men in this town are thinking like that, do you reckon? I'll bet you half the Congress has contemplated divorce, diet and exercise as a package deal. I know from the buzz among the secretaries. None are being very professional about it. Our Vice President has become the butt of locker room humor and insinuation. Not a soul seems to be taking her seriously, yet the voters do. And that should tell you something." Burch continued examining his shoes. After a long silence, he stared into the trusting eyes of his faithful secretary.

"You're right on all counts. It's really immature. I like Hailey. She is smart and a good mother and quite attractive all at once. It's more than most men can take in. I guess I fell for it, too. I should have known better. Now, what to do? Guess I'll drop back and punt." Rose stood to go but her boss stopped her with a questioning look.

"Top of the ladder, eh? Mind telling me a few names? Maybe it's time to formally separate, divorce my 'California Connection' and find sincere companionship."

It was Rose's turn to be embarrassed. She was itching to leave and began edging toward the door.

"Rose, dear, for someone who edits my letters and corrects my grammatical errors, you haven't paid any attention to what I've been saying just now. I'll repeat a few. I *was* interested in Hailey four years ago, and my ex-wife *used* to like to say she *was* married to a senator. Now, how long would it take you to get out of those clothes?"

"I beg your pardon?" She took two full steps back and folded her arms.

"Sorry, uh, let me rephrase that. Would you like to help me celebrate a major victory over dinner tonight? I'd pick you up after you change clothes." He smiled at his second attempt and Rose dropped her arms. She sidled over to the nearest leather arm chair and sank into it, flummoxed.

Burch followed the swaying motion of her breasts beneath the tank top. She was braless and her excitement was evident through the thin material. He was thankful to be seated. It was agonizing. He'd given thousands of political speeches and never had his mouth been this dry. His own pulse jumped up a notch and he swallowed to find his voice.

"I, uh, just read over the final divorce papers, Rose. Looks like I'm a free man. Marcella has agreed to my terms and has even set her wedding date with her new stud muffin out in Hollywood. I thought maybe we could go out to, to, hell, to start over. I mean, you and me. Not as boss and secretary. But, uh, sort of like, a date. There, what do you think?"

A different Rose stood up from her chair. Her smile was confident. "Give me thirty minutes to shower and change. I thought you'd never ask." She turned and fled before either could change their mind.

Twenty-eight

He accepted his Pulitzer with scorn for the established press. *It's about time you assholes recognized true class and reporting. I deserved this years ago but you always thought of the big boys at the* Times *or the* Post. *So here's what I think of your prize.* And there beside the prestigious podium of the National Press Club, Mallard Flyweather whipped out his nubby prick and thoroughly soaked the statue. In prime time. On all the networks. Making headlines for weeks. Winning endorsements and syndication in the very institutions he so despised. Even now his phone was ringing off the hook with yet another offer for his appearance or reprint of an article for syndication in over 500 newspapers across the land.

The sleaze master of the *Weekly Trumpet* thrashed about in his dream state, roiling both himself and the bedding, unwashed for a month, into a putrid entanglement. When he was rendered immobile by the tangled sheets he awoke. His phone continued to ring. His night sweats soaked him as completely as if he were that dream Pulitzer.

"Shit, damn, piss." Mallard freed one hand and jerked the offending instrument to his ear. "Who the fuck is this? It better be important."

"Shut up and listen carefully." A voice Mallard hadn't heard in months froze his anger and brought him to the side of the bed, feet planted on the cold linoleum, alert. His heart rate was astronomical and with pudgy fingers Mallard felt for his blood pressure pills on the night stand. His obesity was winning out over the crusade for recognition and riches as a gossip reporter. He was in a death spiral, writing more slanderous tripe daily in a race with a weakening heart grown stingy with pumping pressure to supply adequate oxygen. The intermittent dizziness gradually left him. The man every politician in town hated stood to walk around the room and calm his erratic arrhythmia.

"Take a little trip to southwestern Virginia. Visit a clerk named Hanson at the Blue Ridge Court House. He'll supply you with dirt on the pure and innocent Vice President to last the rest of your publishing career. You'll get my usual fee for each article published. Do the job right and the *Free States News* will distribute every word to its syndicated affiliates."

"I need something up front. Expenses. Transportation. Also an excuse for the leave of absence from the *Trumpet*."

"You'll find a cashier's check waiting at the Random Rental car agency at Dulles Airport. Your editor is clued in and hot for this series. Don't blow it and end up in a drunk tank like last time."

Mallard kissed the receiver and slammed it down. This was his chance and he was going to nail that smart-assed bitch pretending to be so righteous. Hell, everybody had a past and Mallard was getting a shot at bringing down the White House charade. His pulse had dropped to a steady 95 beats, not great, but he could get by on it.

"Mr. President, Caroline Jankowski over at the Archives asked me to introduce you to their expert in presidential records." Alice guided Norton Roscoe into the Oval Office for his brief appointment. Roscoe became animated, as if just winning an Academy Award, and strode to the President's desk. Bill Conley looked up from his security briefing papers in time to catch the man's hand shake thrust vigorously into his face.

"Norton Roscoe at your service, Mr. President. I've been waiting a long time for this." The President shot a curious glance at Alice, who shrugged at the strutting rooster practically jumping out of his skin as he pumped her boss's hand. Dutch McKinley left his station just inside the secure office to the president's left and came to stand beside Roscoe. Something was strange. Dutch had noticed the little man before, rummaging in the basement storage areas—he acted more like a mole able to stand on his hind feet. He had been pestering offices all over the grounds, searching their files, writing down notes, and mumbling to himself. So this was what an expert in presidential papers did? What a job. But if the guy didn't calm down, Dutch would remove him quickly.

Norton noticed the burly Secret Service agent. "Sir, I have a couple of items to discuss with *you*." Roscoe nodded toward the agent in an attempt to have him dismissed. Dutch ground his teeth and reached for the little man's arm.

"Have a seat, Mr. Roscoe." Bill Conley moved around his desk and headed for the facing sofas in the center of the room. "Had your morning coffee yet?" Roscoe brightened and skittered to the sofa across from the President. Dutch and Alice shook heads simultaneously. Both wished their leader wasn't so friendly and open, especially to an obvious goof ball like Roscoe.

"Thanks, Mr. President. I'd like a cup." Norton turned to glare at Alice, expecting her to fetch it. But she had left the office for Dutch to observe. Bill Conley filled a cup for Roscoe from the side table and refilled his own mug.

"What's on your mind, Sir?" The President ignored the idiosyncrasies of the records expert and sipped his coffee. "I already signed the Memorandum of Agreement to pay for your time, and another paper ensuring everything we create is officially catalogued and scheduled. If you have other issues, go talk to Alice."

"I'm concerned about management over at the Archives. Women have never been particularly suited at grasping the big picture, if you get my drift. Now, Ms. Jankowski is a nice lady, but I have some ideas and would like to give it a shot. With your authorization of course, Sir." Norton rattled out his master plan with supreme confidence, based on decades of preparation down in the stacks. This was his opportunity to show his stuff. He had received the call to serve.

Bill Conley and Dutch shared a look of exasperation. They recognized yet another loony with "Potomac fever," a condition that short-circuited common sense. It was usually diagnosed in career civil servants who never left the boundaries of the District of Columbia, but who nevertheless believed their country would perish without their service at the highest levels of government.

"Mr. Roscoe, I suggest you commit your ideas to paper and send them up your supervisory ladder to Mrs. Jankowski. She has my full support and is doing a great job. I know she'll listen to what you have to say."

"But, Sir, I—"

"Good day, Sir." The President rose and headed back to the work piled on his desk. Norton was slow to realize he had blown his chance for greatness and grabbed for Bill Conley's arm, pulling him back. Taken by surprise, the President jerked the little man's hand away and pushed him back. Dutch stepped in Roscoe's path and shoved him to the nearest exit. Like a mole,

Roscoe's eyes darted side to side in a frantic search for presidential favor. Seeing none, he snapped.

"No! You have to appoint me. I know what to do." His shouts brought Alice to the door. She reversed her steps and pushed the button on her desk calling for reinforcements.

"Calm down, fellow." Dutch wanted the man out of this office and gave one last try at a peaceful resolution. It failed. Roscoe lurched at the agent, grasping for his throat. Dutch jumped back from his reach then grabbed Roscoe's wrists in one hand and slapped him hard. Whether from faint or shock, the would-be presidential advisor and pretend Archivist dropped in his tracks as two agents rushed into the room.

Dutch gave orders. "Take him to George Washington Hospital. No, make that Saint Elizabeth's for psychiatric evaluation. Better use a straight jacket in case he wakes up." Dutch turned to his boss. "Everything's under control. You OK, Sir?"

"Fine, Dutch. Too bad. Good work, though." The President shuffled a few pages and concentrated on his briefing. To an infrequent visitor, he appeared serene in the face of an unnerving incident. Dutch knew different. The big man's hand shook as he reached for his mug. Something new going on here, thought the old friend and protector.

Twenty-nine

"Don't know why those big city fellers haven't nosed around here before. Never did like her. Uppity and acting out of place, you askin' me." Gordy Hanson had not stopped griping and whining since he'd met Mallard for supper at the Blue Bird Diner across the county line. He droned on and on, suffocating Mallard with his drawling toxic venom. The "big city" reporter kept looking over at the manila envelope under Hanson's elbow. He was itching to read the contents but had nevertheless decided to hear out this nutcase. The man had as much social life as Mallard, who recognized his own pathetic existence mirrored for introspection.

"Knew her old man 'fore she got famous. Mother too. Word 'round town was he died from mine fever and his woman went soon after from a broken heart." Hanson looked skyward with dubious sincerity.

"What on earth is mine fever?" Mallard knew nothing about Virginia's coal mining back country. But he might as well learn something so he could sound authentic when his articles were reprinted nationwide.

"Some sorta plague like them homos get, only from too much damp and coal dust. Gradually eats away at your guts. I hear. Turns up differ'nt in differ'nt fellers. Some get pneumonia, while others catch whatever sickness comes along. Turns out to be long and sufferin' for many a poor devil. They say MacMurray went slow and painful and it killed his old lady to sit by and watch."

"What does any of this have to do with our lady in question and the information you have for me in that envelope?"

"Well, hell, that's when the conspiracy started 'round here, dontcha know?" Mallard perked up now. A conspiracy was just what he needed to get his series going in the right direction. "Afore you know it, folks was taking up a collection for poor little Hailey. It was Hailey this and Hailey that. Give all you can to help out the stranded orphan. Bullshit! Stranded orphan my ass. That child was adopted by the whole dang town. She had it bettern the rest of us piled in a heap."

"How's that? Didn't relatives come to claim her?" Mallard slipped his notebook onto the table top and began outlining.

"Didn't have none. Parents run away from wherever it was they come from; cut all ties to family according to old folks around here. That's another bad thing, you askin' me. So then old Adam Knowles and his wife Marie just sort of took her in as their own." Mallard reflected on this. Hailey MacMurray's biography stated her son was named for Knowles, who had been dead over ten years. His wife was in a nursing home around here and she was on his list of people to interview.

"I got copies of the court papers saying all that was legal, but it sure looks fishy to me. Anyway, the girl turned out to be a whizbang student athlete. Got her a scholarship. Supposed to never have used the money all the folks contributed. Huh. Old man Knowles never took a dime either. Said he always wanted a kid and Hailey was very special to him." Hanson raised himself up in the booth and seemed to spit out his next utterance. "Ba-lo-ney. Nobody ever found the money the bank said had been in a trust fund. Seems mighty suspicious to me. Got the clippins' from the paper on that too, right here." Hanson slapped the bulging envelope and Mallard drooled at the possibilities.

"Sure do want to thank you, Mr. Hanson. This would appear to be sufficient evidence for my research—"

"Just you wait a darned minute, mister. I ain't nearly done here. Best stuff I got has to do with that young 'un."

"You mean the Vice President's early childhood?" Mallard was confused with the man's belligerence.

"Naw, suh. Talkin' 'bout the boy. The one named for old man Knowles. Her son."

Mallard was incredulous. No one could touch the golden child of Washington. He was off limits, even by Mallard's own gossip rag. "Sorry, Hanson, but I can't use that information. I'd get tarred and feathered for it."

"You gotta at least hear it. The paper is in the envelope anyway. It's about when she got hitched and all to that pilot feller." Mallard perked up, realizing his target may be Hailey MacMurray after all.

"OK, spill it. What do you have for me?"

"She was knocked up." Gordy Hanson delivered his pronouncement proud as a peacock. He strummed his fingers annoyingly on the table, eyes darting over Mallard's face like ants spotting a dead bug.

"Knocked up? How do you know that? Everyone knows she got married legitimately and had a child soon after. What information do you have?" Mallard's pulse spurted now and the inside of his head beat like a drum. His system had overloaded. He needed his medication. His senses had alerted his body before his mind could comprehend what the hillbilly hick was alluding to.

Hanson grinned widely, displaying a large gap where an important upper tooth had gone missing. He did not respond to Mallard's question and reached into the damning envelope to scratch amongst its ruins for his quarry.

"Found it. Hah! Mildred got mad when she saw me copy this. Supposed to be locked up, she said. Bullshit, I says. Everybody's in cahoots tryin' to keep a secret." He spread the document open and turned it for the inquisitive reporter to read. Gordy let Mallard scan the marriage license only half a minute though. "Boy was born in March the following year." He let another hideous grin escape and waited for Mallard's reaction.

"And this is dated around Thanksgiving of the preceding year." Mallard said. Awareness filled his mind and his heart sped up another notch. Maybe the dream wasn't so far off after all.

"Word around the court house says the feller wasn't all that juiced to be getting hitched either. Seemed anxious, put up to it, if you get my drift. Hear they went straight to Judge Anderson's chambers and did the deed, uh, got married. The feller left his wife here with Mr. and Mrs. Knowles. Emaline remembered it. She's clerkin' down at Hobson's dry goods now. Lost her job at the courthouse a ways back. Said she typed it up and all, then witnessed them sign in front of the judge. 'Cordin' to Emaline, gal's belly was already showing alright." Hanson eyes glistened with a sinister leer and his head waggled to and fro like a bobble doll. Mallard lurched for his pills, gulping two to quell the pistoning muscle threatening to explode in his chest.

Emaline Traup was a mammoth. *Hefty was a polite way to describe her*, Mallard thought. He listened to her rant about life's unfairness and the luck some people, especially that vamp, Hailey MacMurray, fell into. Mallard was caught between Emaline's bulk blocking the dry goods aisle on one end and barrels of ten penny nails guarding the other—Floyd Hobson never lost a dime to kleptos, Emaline had reported.

"I says to Myrtle, over at the Cut and Curl, Myrtle, I says, all that luck don't help none if'n a feller goes in bareback. We laughed, gawdamighty, did we laugh. Too bad. Woman has all the luck, free ride to college, and still ain't smart enough to use a rubber. Me, hell, I tell every man I meet down at Jack's Twofers Friday nights, I says, 'Honey, no glove no love.'" Emaline guffawed and affectionately clubbed Mallard on the shoulder, numbing his writing hand.

"No wonder he went off and got hisself kilt. No wonder a' tall." Mallard waited, his hand incapacitated momentarily, and grew wary of the toothsome leer his behemoth informant shot at him. It was a look that contracted his scrotum.

"Honey, whatchu doing later on? I get off in a couple hours. What say we down a few at Jack's? Huh?"

Trapped. Mallard's heart thudded like a jackhammer run amok. The woman weighed a far distance past 300, easy, and that was guessing at the girth bulging beneath the tent she wore. Her three-decker beehive do, elegantly styled at the Cut and Curl, was bigger than her head and that was twice as large as Mallard's.

"Good idea, Miss Traup. I have one more interview to conduct, and then I'll meet you there." He sidled past her, turning his back to protect vital parts. But his escape was not complete as Emaline grabbed a handful of his butt and squeezed.

"Sure thing, Honey. Later, you heah."

Mallard squelched his need to cry and ran to safety outside. Lord that was close. These mountain women were a vicious and randy bunch. He decided to check out of his room and leave town right after interviewing old Mrs. Knowles. Emaline Traup would hunt him down for standing her up tonight.

Mallard pulled into a visitor's space at The Willows nursing home. He left the car and took in the restful setting amongst a park filled with oak, maple and long leaf pines. Several gazebos invited residents and guests to "come inside and set a spell." Concrete walkways lazed through the park, enabling wheelchairs and aluminum walkers to pass by easily. His heart slowed markedly for the first time since arriving in this backwoods hick town. *Truly, some architectural engineers had outdone themselves with this place,* Mallard thought. He could live here as an old man if he ever got that far. But his second thought had him wondering where the money had come from to build such a place. Surely not from the kind of people he'd been talking to.

The building was friendly and welcoming. Its one-story, white frame construction belied the fact that the occupants had come here to die. He cringed at the image of wrinkled old people wasting away inside, drool covering their protective bibs, the smell of urine wafting up from their adult-size Pampers.

Mallard squared his shoulders and walked to the screened porch to ring the bell. Immediately, several residents left their seats and came over to check him out. Each in turn tried to turn the handle of the door. Was it to let him in or themselves out, he wondered? But the door was firmly secured.

Frightful seconds passed as Mallard waited for his salvation. His silent hosts shook their heads. They hovered inches from him, anticipating his entry, their hands caressing the screen that blessedly separated them from Mallard.

"Hello there." Thank God an orderly or nurse of some sort was approaching. "Don't get too many visitors this time of day. Almost dinner time, but come on in and we'll set another plate for you." He watched her punch a sequence of buttons on a panel attached to the door frame, then open the door. Before he could step inside, the curious and silent residents pushed forward.

"Now Bess, Everett, Rosie, you all let this gentleman alone." She smiled with sincere affection at the three seniors, speaking in a soft, gentle voice that surprised Mallard. "Go wash your hands and get ready for supper." The mention of something to eat easily distracted them and they shuffled away, allowing Mallard entry.

"Thanks for letting me in and rescuing me, uh…" he strained to read her nametag, "Ms. Johnson. I stopped by to visit Mrs. Knowles. I'm a distant cousin and some of her folks in Tennessee asked me to check on her. Crandall, Miles Crandall is my name." He offered his hand and received a healthy grasp in return.

"Sure thing, Mr. Crandall. Marie will be delighted to see you I'm sure. Come right this way." Mallard followed her along the brightly lighted hall and noted the décor matching the early 20th century. Spurring from either side of the hall were themed rooms: an old country general store, a post office, a library, an ice cream parlor, and a bakery. The latter establishment infused the hallway with the aroma of freshly baked cookies. Farther down the way, a nurse's aide pushed a cart offering cookies to the residents she encountered. Another room held an array of exercise equipment. Mallard spied a punching bag, a treadmill, and numerous gadgets used to stretch and work aging muscles. An elderly gentleman lay on a bench, hoisting dumbbells alternately with his weather-beaten arms.

Ms. Johnson noted Mallard's interest and commented. "That's Mr. Sam Ashley," she said. "Keeps in shape in case they call him back to the mine, dontcha know? He works out every day. Tough old bird. Healthiest person in here, at least physically. His mind doesn't work all that good anymore. Sort of like Mrs. Knowles."

The nurse turned to continue down the hall and stopped short. "Well, Lord almighty. Here she is. Looky, Miss Marie, I brought you a visitor." Mallard faced a bright-eyed woman less than five feet in height who could not have weighed more than 75 pounds. He forgot the script he'd conjured up for the occasion. He stood mesmerized by her inspecting gaze from behind the aluminum frame of her walker.

Marie Knowles' eyes watered, her jaw slackened, and her mouth opened part way anticipating speech. None came. A piece of cookie slipped from the corner of her mouth and joined a cluster of crumbs on the floor. Marie fixed Mallard with an anxious expression, and her lips began to quiver. The gossip reporter, used to dealing with important celebrities, politicians, and business executives, was done under and as speechless as his quarry.

"Daddy?" Marie choked out her query. "Daddy, is that you?"

"No, Ma'am." Mallard shook his head violently in denial.

"Oh, Adam, you've come back. How wonderful!"

"No. No, Mrs. Knowles." Again Mallard shook his head, panicking.

"No, I can see you clearly now, Edward." Marie chattered on, determined to place Mallard's face and identity with a past decade.

"Marie, this is Mr. Crandall from Tennessee. He's some relation to your folks down there and came to visit." Nurse Johnson spoke to Mallard as if instructing a child to ride a bike. "Just take it easy, sir. She'll be glad to talk with you; only you can expect her to call you every name but your own." Nurse Johnson glanced down the hall, catching sight of several residents arguing over the rights to a wheelchair neither needed. "Excuse me, sir. I have to play Henry Kissinger over there. Be right back."

"Tennessee?" Marie boomed in a voice loud enough for some residents to reach for the controls on their hearing aids. "I don't have any folks down in Tennessee. Whoever heard such a thing?" She paralyzed Mallard with a disgusted look and turned her walker for the dining room. His visit was over.

"May I help you, sir?" A fresh administrative voice came from behind him. Mallard turned to face a young woman dressed in a business suit who had stepped from her office. "I'm Wendy Tucker, Mr. Crandall. Come on in my office. I'll be glad to fill you in on Mrs. Knowles." Mallard followed her in as if gaining the safety of an American embassy in a foreign land. "Please have a seat, sir. What information can I help you with?" Ms. Tucker projected a professional, yet neutral smile and Mallard relaxed.

"Well, Ma'am, I was passing through and felt it my duty to see how Mrs. Knowles was doing. Folks down home were wondering about her financial situation, if you know what I mean."

"May I ask, sir, what relation you are to Mrs. Knowles?" Wendy Tucker's expression hardened a notch and Mallard flinched. This was unexpected.

"My father was Adam Knowles' brother's nephew on their mother's side. We're from Crosley, about 90 miles west of Knoxville." The office professional's face relaxed and Mallard smiled. He was through the password phase of his investigation.

She turned to a shelf of notebooks and retrieved one labeled "Marie Knowles." Wendy Tucker leafed through the pages until she found what she was looking for.

"Diet is good. Eats well and loves our homemade cookies. Nurses have to keep a box of Trix cereal at their station to give her something to nibble on between meals. Marie loves her sweets. Let's see. Gets around fairly well using her walker despite two broken hips. Oh, she positively loves her orthopedic surgeon. Keeps asking Dr. Masters to take her to a movie." Wendy Tucker flipped through another section of reports. And Mallard tried to cut through more boring details.

"How's the money holding up? Are her finances in order, Ms. Tucker? I can only assume she's on Medicaid. Is that correct?"

Something indefinable about Wendy Tucker's demeanor shifted, and Mallard sensed his game was over.

"You're a reporter, aren't you, sir?" She stood and walked to her office door pointing to the hall. "You don't give two hoots about Marie Knowles. But to answer your last question, No, Marie's bills are not paid by Medicaid, and any further information about her or her personal finances is none of your business." She turned abruptly and headed for the screen door. She punched the security code buttons furiously, and then popped the door open ushering Mallard back outside.

He strode past her arrogantly. He had enough to write columns for months. The roar of disapproval he'd generate would give him more than enough material to trash the Vice President. He'd found personal misconduct of an officer who got knocked up and had forced a shotgun wedding. He'd found her enemies, jealous and itching to voice their dislike all these years, suspecting a conspiracy. And he'd found the missing trust fund, he figured, providing Marie Knowles a plush retirement in a backwoods nursing home. Now he had to get out of town before Emaline came looking for him.

Thirty

It was just the three of them, up in the Maryland countryside, walking through spring-filled hardwood forests. Dogwoods and rhododendrons permeated the pastoral setting with a mix of pink and white and flush red blooms. Jennette, Elizabeth and Adam reveled in the solitude after the turmoil back in town. The attractive agent had readily agreed to provide security for the First Lady and her special grandchild. She just hadn't bothered to tell her two friends about the bevy of agents spread out through the woods and undercover in camouflage gear. Maybe the president's wife wouldn't notice the extra food the cook was preparing or the lights over in the bunkhouse quarters used by her fellow agents.

Jennette knew Adam was down in spirits. It was not like him to want to be away from his mother for an entire weekend. Yet, the boy and the First Lady had chatted away two days so far and neither seemed empty of conversation. They looked like two co-conspirators hatching a plot to overthrow the government—a very unlikely scenario since their closest relatives ran it. Or, perhaps they were trying to figure out how to get Hailey to take more time to build a relationship with Mark Daniel.

This was something Jennette had thought about since returning from Crested Butte earlier in the summer. Hailey was lonely and was not hiding it well. Jennette could sympathize. Although the pressures of being Vice President were beyond Jennette, she easily recognized the symptoms of loneliness: deep sighs at passing couples holding hands during their morning jogs and a kind of wistfulness only another widow could spot.

The two women had become close friends through the Women's Connection meetings at Elizabeth's Capitol Hill house. They had attended a conference of military wives struggling to survive the loss of their husbands. Hailey had been a guest speaker encouraging those women by recounting her own story of tragedy. Both knew it wasn't easy, only Hailey worked through it in a positive way while Jennette's path hadn't been. They had become fast friends even if their paths had been contrary to each other's. Jennette had no children and recovered from her shock using a string of lovers in the early years. When she woke up one morning not recognizing her bed partner, she swore off that practice. Jennette took her version of a cold shower by joining the Secret Service. Hailey became the golden girl of the State Department, her drive always centered on providing for her son, Adam.

The Secret Service was under orders to make Jennette available to the Vice President as security and as a best pal. That role had easily evolved into personal confidant and advisor. Jennette still carried a weapon and the communications gear required of an agent. She just had access to the personal life of her friend no other agent ever had.

"Jennette, we need your opinion. Jennette! Earth to Jennette, this is Adam calling, over."

"Huh, oops, sorry folks, must have been daydreaming. What did you want, Adam?" She was chagrined being caught off guard. Some security agent she was today.

"I was commenting to Gran that it's a good thing you got a bunch of friends hiding in the bushes to protect us, 'cause you're in la la land." Adam giggled, standing with his hands tucked under his arms. The First Lady snorted, then laughed at her own sound as they all gave in to the moment.

Elizabeth took the lead from the Vice President's precocious son. "Jennette, don't worry. We think of you as a friend and want you here for that. Adam's right though. Those guys in the woods don't blend in very well, yet we feel perfectly safe." She touched Jennette's arm affectionately, and beamed one of her sincere smiles that had won many votes for her husband.

"OK, repeat the question, Adam. You want my opinion on what?" She mimicked his stance and added a tapping foot to show some adult exasperation.

"Well, er, let me put it this way. You're a girl, right? I mean, of course you are, but what I'm trying to say is, what does a girl want? No, that's not it. I'll start over. What kind of guy appeals to you?" Adam saw a strange expression cloud his protector's face and decided to get to the point. Elizabeth just grinned and didn't offer any support as the boy dug his hole deeper. "I'll be straight with you, alright? What kind of guy would go for Mom?"

Jennette's mouth dropped open and she looked from Elizabeth to Adam and back again. "Is this the Conley-MacMurray Dating Service, convening in the Maryland woods? You got to be kidding. Most of the men in this country, and many more around the world, would go for your mom. She's attractive, smart, intelligent, talented, and the best mom in the world to you. And I forgot to add she's also the Vice President and doing a bang up job of it." Jennette cocked her head to the side with a quizzical expression. "Are you a mind reader, Adam? I was just thinking about your mother, my friend. But as a woman, I can tell you that your mother has made a decision on the type of man she wants."

Her walking companions stopped in their tracks and waited for an explanation. When Jennette only smiled like a canary-eating cat, Elizabeth grew impatient. "OK, woman, out with it. Don't keep us in suspense."

The shapely agent spoke to Adam. "Who would you think? Who would be the perfect fellow for your mother?"

His eyes opened and excitement brightened his face. "Mark! It's got to be Mark. Please say it is."

"I trust you're certain of your answer, Jennette." The First Lady was being subtle about protecting the boy's feelings.

"She kissed him and he kissed her back. How's that for proof? She doesn't even look at other men as we jog by them in the mornings. More proof. They talked every night out on the deck out in Crested Butte, just the two of them. OK? Plus, I know her. She wouldn't open up to someone who didn't include her son in the equation." Elizabeth and Adam gaped at this revelation and Jennette pushed her chin up in triumph with her scoop of the news. But there was more to be said.

"My only wish would be to kind of do something to hurry things along. I know this will sound strange coming from someone who has publicly sworn off men, but, oh my, how to say this. Hailey MacMurray doesn't need any man to be successful. She's proved that beyond doubt. It's just that companionship and having a sympathetic shoulder to lean on that we all need, men and women. You know, Elizabeth, pillow talk with a fellow who's always in your corner."

Adam added his own two cents to the equation. "There's also the making love part." He'd blurted out the memory of his mother explaining procreation as if it were a natural thing to say and the reaction of his older women companions told him he'd overstepped a boundary.

"Young man," Elizabeth said, "that topic is off limits for someone your age. I don't care how candid your mother has been explaining things to you." The First Lady tried to maintain a stern look. Fortunately, Adam hung his head before her mirth became apparent. Jennette had to turn away and cough to hide her laugh.

Elizabeth decided to call a summit meeting. "This requires a strategy session back at the house, with perhaps a small glass of wine as an appetizer." She noted Adam's look of anticipation and gave him her strongest frown. "For me and Jennette, young man. Your mother would flail us if we gave you a drop."

She hadn't been a military wife for fifty years for nothing. Elizabeth knew battlefield tactics and strategies, especially when it came to young boys. She had talked one of Jennette's compatriots into tying up Adam in a video game while the two women put their heads together. The young agent was instructed to suggest a game of Horse, shooting hoops against the garage basket if the game became tedious. The women had big plans to make and wanted no interference, even if it was the most tender and thoughtful attempt at matchmaking she'd ever witnessed.

Elizabeth and Jennette settled in the cozy family room with their wine and got down to serious girl talk.

"I understand this is not an easy topic for you, Jennette. I know you are a widow too. It must get lonely with the work you do."

"It does, Ma'am, but I went about being a widow completely cockeyed at first and finally chose to ignore the urge to take on another mate. Hailey took the high road. She put her energy into Adam and doesn't seem to have ever considered men as potential partners. Guys are just co-workers and friends to her."

"How did you two become such good friends?"

Jennette told her about the discussions she and Hailey had during and after the Women's Connection meetings. "It was a case of mutual respect, I guess. We got to talking over a glass of wine at a conference. Neither of us was interested in dating. Hailey rarely accepted any offers, and I just used them and dropped them right away. It's not a time of my life I'm proud of, frankly. But Hailey saw past all that mess and kept encouraging me to succeed regardless, single or attached. She is the definition of a loyal friend."

The First Lady became pensive and both women settled into a

companionable silence. Elizabeth spoke after a long sigh. "It takes a special guy for such a special lady, one who will be our next President. And those brave enough to ask her out always get turned down because she has built up this guilt cushion of excuses involving her son."

"You sound pretty certain Hailey will be the next President, Ma'am. I'd love to see that, but what makes you so certain?"

The First Lady turned to face her confidant and spoke from her heart. "She's the right person at the right time. More than qualified. And," Elizabeth finally had to say out loud what she felt inside, "I don't think my husband will live out his term." Jennette sat back on the sofa, her hand to her heart, gasping. Elizabeth closed the short distance between them and held the Secret Service agent's shoulders with both hands gently shaking her.

"I'm sorry, Jennette. I knew saying that would upset you, but I had to say it. I watch Bill sleeping at night and get the strongest premonition. I visualize my husband tiring, giving all he has, and even with his superior health I know, just know, there will be nothing left after he serves as president. It's like seeing a giant sacrifice in the making and I can do nothing to stop it. Bill can't go higher than this and I know him. He will work himself hard to make good his word. It will take his life."

Jennette slumped into the plush cushions and let the tears fall. She believed this great woman. She understood what Elizabeth was saying. The pressure was over the top. Expectations were off the scale. The whole country looked to Bill Conley to right the ship of state, and by his sheer will it was happening. Hailey and senior executives in the administration were working hard on the details of each task force, writing legislation, abolishing aberrant rules and administrivia at an inconceivable rate. But, the President held the mandate and used it every minute of every day. He attended meetings and strategy sessions at all hours, pressing forward, cajoling, bullying when necessary, calling in markers from his days in the Senate, and most importantly, traveling the country to conduct town meetings and feel the pulse of the people. Federal agencies fell in line immediately, following his leadership, thirsty for action, rejuvenated. And all the President had done was to trust them and give them praise.

The press no longer compared him to great presidents of the past. Now they reported "The Man" was unique, his kind never seen before, and above all, he was an honest man who kept his word.

Jennette tried to compose herself and used Elizabeth's handkerchief to wipe her face. "How can you bear it?"

Her answer came in a deep sigh choked with emotion. "I realized I gave him up when he got elected. He was no longer mine. His country owned his soul and Bill embraced it wholly. He was the most marvelous partner, and lover to me, and father to our children for all those years and it was time. Like Lincoln has been described, Bill Conley belongs to the ages."

The agent put her arms around the First Lady, hugged her tight and felt her deep sobs shudder through their bodies. When they finally pulled back, both took time to gain steady breath, get composed. Then they were smiling.

"Thanks, Jennette. I had to tell someone and it can't be Hailey. It would break her heart to think such a thing. She loves the President. He has become a surrogate grandfather to Adam, and assuredly a father to her. But let's get back to the reason for this little camping trip to the mountains. Our goal is to finagle our good friend, the Vice President, into a solid relationship with this gorgeous football player."

"Hold on, please. I can't just jump from a discussion of something so serious to such a trivial matter. Sorry, but my insides are jumbled up at the moment."

"How long were you married, Jennette?"

"That's so far in the past it seems irrelevant. Less than two years. Closer to 18 months, and my husband was in combat for half that time. Why?"

"Just checking your pulse, and taking your temperature on the subject of marriage. I'm sorry you didn't have more time together, or you might be able to understand why I don't consider nudging Hailey into a lifetime partnership a trivial matter. And don't tell a soul that I am saying this. Some women's groups would hang me in effigy. Do I think Hailey would make a great President as a single woman and a single mom? Absolutely. I have no doubt that she would. But that's on the public and political side of things. I want our first woman President to have it all. I mean the contentment that comes from a permanent companion. Having the confidence created by emotional intimacy from someone she can trust with all her thoughts. Sharing pillow talk as you said. I want her to have someone in her corner forever, always supporting her, even when the political nasties insult her, and the gossip rags bombard her with vicious lies and innuendoes. She has to have someone she can let down in front of because, believe me, the public is not ready for a woman president who cries."

"Something I've never seen her do," Jennette said. "She's tough and wants to hide her femininity. She has told me that. No wonder some gossip columnists have tried to paint the two of us as lesbian lovers." Both women rolled their eyes at this absurdity.

"There's another reason I want her to have a strong relationship, and not just a relationship for appearance sake. Adam wants his mother to have a boyfriend." Elizabeth chuckled as Jennette's mouth dropped. "Really. You should have heard him talking about it. That's the main reason I brought him up here. Her son recognizes she is a lonely person, and it's not something he can fix. He needs to share her because he realizes she needs more than him. Can you imagine another adolescent boy saying that?"

"No, but I can believe Adam would. He's a golden child. Unselfish to the bone. I wish there were two of him so I could adopt one."

Early summer workouts were mainly for rookies trying to make the team, players returning from injuries, and for veterans who simply wanted to see their future competition first hand. Mark Daniel just loved working out in the cool mornings without pads. He had come in early this year from Crested Butte. His football camps were finished and all his assistant coaches were reporting to their own summer practices.

Mark was always in great shape and wanted to keep it that way. Even with his future secure from a long-term contract with the 'Skins, he still wanted to perform at his best and that meant showing the rookies he could walk the walk on the field. His skills hadn't diminished much since college thanks to great genes and a workout regimen that drove other NFL tight ends mad when they came to his private camp during the off season. Twice a day Mark jogged up the hill behind his home and left a trail of huffing, panting peers in his wake. The hill was used simultaneously by tourists as they rode the lifts to the top of the ski slopes of Mt. Crested Butte over two miles above sea level.

Endorsements had made him a wealthy man. What better image than the NFL's Man of the Year two years running to sell your product? Mark supported charities in person, year round, not like some of his cohorts around the league who showed up for a photo session and disappeared afterwards. He was nicknamed "Mr. Clean" by his friends, who wondered if the right woman could ever hog tie him. But he had insisted to his buddies he was merely waiting until he could focus on it. After all, he said, it would be unfair to start a family and then desert them over half the year while he played football. He'd never see his kids play sports after school, or go to parent-teacher conferences. And, if he couldn't be a full time husband and father, well then, by golly, he just wouldn't be one. Period.

Eldon Rampert was this year's Butkus Award winner as the nation's top linebacker, and he was out to impress the coaches. Eldon was the Skins' top draft choice. He'd signed a contract, else he wouldn't be allowed on the practice field. However, he figured to use this workut to up the ante for his signing bonus, a small-print incentive clause he'd insisted on. He was shaped like a giant V, with granite shoulders starting right below his ears. Eldon had no neck, but he made up for this oversight with a chest rivaling a bull's and *guns*, arms in football language, the size of a twenty-year-old white oak, and just as hard.

This phenomenal physical specimen had speed to burn and was covering the receivers in pass drills like the proverbial blanket. All but one. Mark Daniel blew by Eldon on every route, infuriating the young stud muffin. Even worse, the old geezer always said "Nice try" after each play, as if Eldon could add half a second to his 40-yard dash speed so he could catch the bastard. Daniel never seemed to tire in the Virginia humidity and always ran back at full speed to the huddle, while Eldon walked leisurely to the sideline to wait for his next repetition. *I'll get him next time*, the young bull thought.

The offensive linemen jumped at the snap of the ball and ballet-danced on toes in their pass-blocking set. Eldon keyed on Daniel, who seemed to be strolling downfield this time, heading straight for him. *Must be some kind of delayed route*, Eldon thought. *OK, I'll play along with this shit*. Daniel added another gear to his speed and bumped the linebacker up to full throttle. They went head to head ten yards, twenty, and Eldon grew confident. He was doing it! This time the old bastard couldn't shake him. But Daniel had another gear left and broke hard right at the same time Eldon stutter-stepped, then spun around, got his feet tangled up and landed flat on his bony ass. Mark Daniel, all-pro tight end, caught the post-route pass over his shoulder another twenty yards behind the flattened rookie.

Hoots and laughter welled up from the remaining players as Eldon jumped up. Mark trotted by him with his usual "nice try" comment and tossed him the ball. Son of a bitch. Eldon knew what he had to do now. Nobody, not even Mr. Nice Guy, was going to show him up again. Eldon trudged to the sidelines and waited until the all-pro took his spot for another pass play. Eldon lined up ten yards deep and waited for the snap. Daniel flew off the line this time and Eldon could see embarrassment starting. Worse, his incentive bonus was taking a major hit. He turned and fled to the rear as the speedy tight end gathered steam. Lord the man was a machine!

It was a straight fly pattern and Mark was letting out all the stops. He paid no attention to the rookie linebacker. He had tested the man's speed and knew he could be taken. Oddly, the rookie turned and ran away from him five yards before Mark approached him. Dumb move. If this weren't a simple drill to go straight down the field, Mark would have stopped or turned right or left and the idiot would be all by himself, guarding the air. But Mark kept to the pattern, giving the rookie quarterback the chance to show off his million-dollar arm. He went by the linebacker and saw out of the corner of his eye that the fellow seemed to be falling down. Probably tripped on his feet like last time.

It happened in a split second. Mark felt a tremendous blow to his right knee. Excruciating pain enveloped his right leg, and the turf crashed into his face, knocking him out.

"Gran, Jennette, come quick! You gotta see this. Hurry, it's ESPN's Sportscenter." Adam burst into the room and ran back out just as fast.

The women rushed to discover the reason for Adam's excitement and found him scant inches from the giant screen, frozen in his tracks. Unseen narrators guided viewers through replays of a gruesome sports accident at the Redskins' training camp.

"There's Daniel as he flashes by the rookie on a fly pattern. Now watch closely as Rampert obviously fakes tripping and slams into the star tight end's right knee. Here's a slow motion close-up of the impact, and remember, this was a light workout without helmets and pads. There was supposed to be no physical contact, only drills and repetitions for receivers, quarterbacks and defenders. If you're a bit squeamish, you might not want to watch this, folks."

Adam and his companions stood silently and watched. They saw Eldon Rampert trip, the horrendous impact, then bone shattering through Mark Daniel's flesh as the telephoto lens zeroed in. It was appalling. Worse, the TV producers reversed and replayed the malicious scene over and over. Each time they warned viewers not to watch.

"Bastard," Adam muttered. His fists were clenched as he cursed his good friend's attacker. "Dumb rookie out for glory and now he's ruined Mark's leg and maybe his career." The boy began to shake uncontrollably and Elizabeth walked to his side and encircled him in a firm embrace.

"I'm so sorry, Adam. When did this happen?"

"Yesterday afternoon, they said. Mark went into surgery this morning at Fairfax Hospital in northern Virginia." He turned tearful eyes to the First Lady and begged. "Gran, please let's go see him."

"By all means. Go pack your stuff and we're out of here." She motioned to Jennette to follow her back into the family room. "Call Hailey and tell her we'll be picking her up on the way down." Elizabeth's wink at the Secret Service agent held more meaning than usual. Jennette smiled, nodding her understanding.

Adam was ecstatic when he saw the helicopter land outside. This meant they would get to the hospital in minutes from Camp David. The trip to DC was swift, but instead of bypassing the political hub of the nation, the chopper drove straight for the center of town, a destination the boy knew would take them over the White House.

"Gran, Jennette, what's up? Are we driving from downtown? That'll take an hour in Washington traffic."

"Well, young man, in order to get permission to use this whirly bird we had to add an official passenger; someone actually authorized to divert this aircraft from its original destination." The First Lady wondered if the boy would swallow her pack of lies.

Adam looked from Jennette to Elizabeth and back again. He pondered what had been said. Studied his hands. Checked the view once more, then stealthily brought the two women back into perspective. A big grin creased his face.

"The President is lucky to have you as his First Lady, Gran. You make a good advisor and great strategist." Elizabeth grinned back in reply. He turned to Jennette with his Superman-like reasoning. "How did you convince Mom to give up her Sunday off?"

"It was actually easier than I had bargained for, Mr. Smarty Pants. And any more details of the conversation I had with the Vice President are classified top secret. Got that, Buster?"

"Just remember, you two. No smiles and cute remarks. Mark is seriously hurt, and might not feel like visitors so early after his operation." Elizabeth pinned them with her official glare.

"But, Gran, Mark is just like Mom, a loner. He has no family and lives by himself in a townhouse. He'll be all by himself and feeling sad 'cause no one has come to visit. Just wait and see."

Adam had guessed correctly at the identification of their official passenger and greeted Hailey with a big bear hug. But he was totally wrong about no one visiting Mark Daniel. Fortunately, the chopper could land near the emergency room door close to the building. The front parking lot was crammed with Sunday visitors and a host of TV vans transmitting the latest on the NFL super star's medical status.

Jennette was on the phone to the hospital administrator's office immediately. Her cohorts had arrived near the landing pad and provided some aid in maneuvering through the haranguing crowd of reporters who had spotted the First Helicopter. Once inside, their group was shunted off to a staff-only elevator and whisked to the floor on which Mark's private room was located. But there the special treatment collapsed, as the hall was crowded with more sports reporters who turned as one on the arrival of Vice President MacMurray and the First Lady.

Hailey walked confidently straight toward the questioners and stopped in their midst.

"Ladies, gentlemen, we're here to visit a close family friend and my son's favorite football player. Adam will answer your questions. Please make it brief, we don't want to waste our visiting time with a full fledged press conference." She brought Adam forth and stood behind him as questions filled the air. Jennette and Elizabeth shared secret smiles watching from the back of the crowd as Hailey held her son's arms firmly, keeping him from scooting off. But Adam responded beyond anyone's anticipation.

"Mark is my best buddy. I saw the tape on ESPN and had to come over to see him. These other people were in the chopper at the time and agreed to accompany me. That's all I have to say. Thank you." He turned to enter Mark's room and was hit with a volley of questions from the rear.

"Is Mark Daniel a close friend of your mom's?"

"How long have Vice President MacMurray and Mark Daniel been seeing each other secretly?"

"When did they have their first date?"

"Are they sleeping together?"

This last blast of insanity came from Mallard Flyweather form the *Weekly Trumpet*. His impertinence and the other questions were ignored as Hailey, Elizabeth, and Jennette filed into the room with Adam and shut the door.

Jennette scanned the darkened room. Mark Daniel was propped up reading a book with a small light attached to the cover. This was the only source of illumination since the curtains were fully closed and the main ceiling light was turned off. Soft snoring reached her ears from the corner where Jason Cramer slouched in an arm chair. He had obviously been in Mark's room overnight and looked it. His blonde hair was tousled in all directions. His clothes were bunched and wrinkled. His shoes lay haphazard in the middle of the floor. Still, Jennette sighed to herself. Lord what a hunk. The darling of the sports media and jetsetter—rumored to be recently connected to the latest European supermodel—was totally gorgeous even in complete disarray.

Hailey and Adam were now on opposite sides of Mark's bed talking in low voices, at his request, so they wouldn't wake up Jason. Jennette moved to stand beside Elizabeth at the foot of the bed and both watched for reactions from either Hailey or Mark. Adam was already signing the cast that stretched from Mark's waist to his toes on his right leg. His name fit neatly among what looked like a hundred others.

"What a wonderful surprise. Thanks for coming," Mark said. "I heard the mob outside. Jason has been my press liaison all night, keeping them at bay. I don't know how you put up with their baloney." He had lost himself in Hailey's brown eyes and received a warm smile in return.

"I just follow the President's example and say nothing until I hear a question worth answering. But more importantly, how do you feel and can you play again?" With composure, Hailey grasped Mark's hand in both of hers and slid onto the side of his bed. The two women at the end of the bed smiled and moved back into the shadows near the window, closer to the still-snoring quarterback. Adam was too busy reading famous autographs to notice.

Mark visibly swallowed. "Lousy and no," he said. "Surgery was successful for a regular person who doesn't have to run, block and tackle for a living. I have enough painkillers in me to put an army to sleep, but that doesn't erase the fact that I have an artificial knee and steel rods hip to knee and knee to ankle supporting bones that are fractured in a bunch of places." He smiled sardonically. "You remember the Six Million Dollar Man?" Hailey nodded. "Well, I'm the Ten Dollar Tight End. Walking will take months, and running, oh, maybe never again. But another shot like the one at practice and I'll be in a wheel chair for good."

"Mark, that's terrible. I'm so sorry." She squeezed his hand in reassurance. "What can I do to help?"

Adam was now zoned in on their semi-private conversation and offered his opinion. "Mom, we have lots of room in that big old house. Mark can stay with us," the boy had advanced his hopes beyond reason and got a laugh from everyone in the room, including the slumbering quarterback, now arisen.

"Some dream I had. There was this bevy of gorgeous women surrounding me and I wake up to find it's true." Elizabeth and Jennette looked back over their shoulders, catching the jetsetter appraising their backsides.

"Take a pill, Cramer. Have a little respect for the most important women in the country." Mark had turned crimson at his best friend's bar room remarks and strained to sit up and right the situation. But he was overreacting. Hailey chuckled, and, realizing her position on the bed, quickly stood and brought her hands to her sides. Elizabeth laughed at Hailey's predicament, then fixed the haughty fellow with a steely glare. Jennette turned to face the football player, hands on her hips. She was ready to do battle with the irreverent scamp.

"Pardon me, Mrs. Conley, Madam Vice President," Jason apologized with a hint of smugness, his toothy smile brightening the mood. He was used to performing before an audience of billions in Super Bowls and his poise filled the room. Adam stood bug-eyed in total admiration. Hailey nodded her acceptance of the apology. Elizabeth relaxed. But Jennette remained stone still and angry. She stepped towards the recalcitrant fellow.

Jason feigned shock and trepidation, raising his hands to ward off an imaginary attack. "Now hold on, sugar. Don't go all ballistic on me. I sincerely meant what I said, and you are one fabulous creature. Dinner tonight? I'll throw on some fresh duds and clean up a bit. Pick you up at eight? What's your address? Phone number?"

Jennette heard the sniggers behind her and turned to see Garfield grins from Mark to Adam to his mom and the First Lady. She discovered she was the only person in the room lacking a sense of humor. Inside she was discombobulated. Here she was guarding the Vice President after spending a weekend with the First Lady planning strategies to get Hailey out on a date, and she gets asked out instead.

"You don't even know me and you hit on me here in poor Mark's hospital room. Is this how you make a pick up for your one-night stands those reporters out in the hall love to write about?"

Jason didn't miss a beat. "Of course I know you. You're Jennette Marshall. Single, widowed, and I'm very sorry for that. Hailey MacMurray's best friend and personal Secret Service agent and confidant. I'd say you're about six feet tall, beautiful blonde hair with some random streaks of red that sort of glows brilliantly when the light is behind you. High cheek bones that could have given you a model's career and full luscious lips. Ummm. Eyes a light green, still shooting sparks even with your lessening anger and confusion. And your body is to die for. Is eight too early?"

Jennette's mouth dropped at the man's blatant arrogance and flattery. She was stunned and appalled all together. She could find no words.

"Perhaps we should all leave the room," Mark said. "I apologize for my former friend and press agent. But you all can plainly see why he is the first quarterback ever to rush for more yards than the other members of his backfield combined."

Hailey approached Jason and held out her hand. They shook with equal respect and exchanged a private moment of understanding.

"Jennette is off duty tonight, Jason. But the decision is hers. I think your timing, although awkward, may be excellent."

"Hailey, er, Madam Vice President, I, oh damn—" Jennette had found her voice and decided to escape the scrutiny of a room filling with more embarrassment by the second. She stepped quickly to the door and jerked it open, only to shut it firmly in face of an expectant crowd of reporters. "What am I doing? I'm on duty guarding the Vice President who *was* my best friend." She turned to Elizabeth with a frantic plea. "Help."

Elizabeth crossed to the frenzied agent and whispered softly. "Just say yes, Jennette. You might have a good time and the fellow seems to like you, truth be told." Before she could appeal to Hailey for backup, Jennette noticed her friend slipping a piece of paper to Jason.

"I suggest you give the lady a call to confirm things, Mr. Cramer." Hailey winked at the big man who now had all the information he had requested with his proposal for a dinner date. She was unaware of her son giving similar information to Mark Daniel on another slip of paper. The permanently injured football star now had a direct line to Adam's mother. Mark and Adam shook hands vigorously. They couldn't contain their secrecy and laughed heartily.

"I suggest you confirm things, Mr. Daniel," Adam said, parodying his famous mother.

Mark Daniel's VIP visitors stayed another hour discussing his condition and plans now that his football career was ended. Jennette stood by the door wearing a confused expression. To her chagrin, Jason stayed busy on the phone canceling other plans for the evening with someone who wouldn't take no for an answer.

"Did you ladies have a good time up in the Maryland woods?" Bill Conley was exhausted and had missed his bedmate this past weekend. He had worked long hours battling the task force on energy policy and had run out of the stuff himself.

Elizabeth lay on her side, watching his deep breathing as her lifemate drifted into sleep. She knew there were a few precious moments yet before he was lost for the night.

"I think it was marvelous, sweetie. Next time come with us and you'll see. An idea has been building in the back of my mind ever since we got back."

"Ummm. OK, go for it, as long as we can make this place work better." He was drifting away, struggling to keep contact.

"We need another task force on fitness and exercise, don't you think?" She paused, then gently touched his arm to get a response.

"Sure, it's been done before. Usually led by some Hollywood star. Got anybody in mind?"

"A couple of fellows, I believe. Now rest, dear. I love you." Elizabeth received no reply as usual. Her husband was down for the night and she wondered how any human could withstand his job.

Thirty-one

"You paged me, Ma'am?" Jennette was slightly out of breath having run up from the sub-basement where she had been analyzing messages in the White House Communication Center.

"Had lunch, yet, Jennette?" Hailey wore a tempting smile.

"Skipped it today, too much going on. Why, did you order one of Chan's special subs?" She looked hopefully at her friend, who pursed her lips in a slow smile of affirmation.

"Two, plus iced tea. Lemon for me, none for you. How 'bout it?" Hailey grinned as the svelte agent licked her lips in anticipation. If anyone in Washington needed to diet it was not Jennette. "And, if you behave, I also happen to have your favorite dessert, carrot cake."

"Need to talk, Hailey?" Their friendship went back through some tough times, and this was how their best conversations got started, over food. Hailey nodded and passed a huge sub sandwich to Jennette.

"First we eat." And eating was fast as always, a race to get to the good part, talking.

"OK, give. What's on the mind of the Vice President of the United States that can only be shared with her top advisor?"

"How was your dinner date last week?" Jennette blanched and looked away. "Backed out did you?"

"He's a playboy! For God's sake, Hailey. I knew about him. I read the papers. There's always a gorgeous dame on his arm at cocktail parties, or taking a trip to some exotic place in his private jet, or going to a movie premier.

He uses them and tosses them aside. If you looked up noncommittal in the dictionary, Jason Cramer's picture would be there." Jennette stopped pacing around Hailey's chair and slapped both hands on her hips. "You wouldn't give him the time of day if the shoe was on your foot. So what's this all about? And another thing. When was the last time you went out with a guy?"

"You're pushing me to get involved with Mark, so I thought I'd pry into your personal life, too. How's it feel coming back at you?" Hailey fired back. This was an old topic, always with the same conclusion: nothing came of it.

"Dear Hailey, you're like a sister and a best friend wrapped in one package. I am closer to you than anyone. You *are* lonely. You *do* need to find happiness just for you. Adam told Elizabeth that and she talked to me. So, yeah, we ganged up on you and tried playing matchmakers with our little trip to see Mark."

"And you got asked out by that gorgeous quarterback instead and didn't go. What kind of example is that?"

"Well pardon me, vice leader of the free world. I didn't know you needed someone to break the ice for you."

Hailey was up and circling her own chair and Jennette. Her breath came in short puffs of anger. Then she turned on her friend. "Lady, I don't know what to do. I really like Mark, maybe fallen for him. He told me he loved me and it felt marvelous until I got back to this town. I have too much to do and now he's seriously hurt. I have to sneak around to visit and act like we are only good family friends when I might just want to crawl into bed right there in the hospital and there's no way to do it. The poor man can't even get out of his hospital bed and the press is dragging him through the political gutter and the gossip rags have him sleeping with me and it goes on and on. Damn!" her voice exploded, bringing Nick and Charlie into the office on the run.

"Something up, Ma'am?" Nick queried the Vice President, as both agents searched the angry faces of two women squared off in the center of the room ready to duke it out.

"Butt out," Jennette said, and the two men backed away cautiously, both recognizing a situation not covered in the agency's manual.

Embarrassed, both women exchanged looks of repentance and took their seats. Jennette slid her chair closer and reached for Hailey's hands. "I'm sorry, Hailey. Elizabeth was so convincing. I love Adam like a son, and Mark is his best friend, so I just went with my gut feeling. I won't try to do any more matchmaking. Honest. I know it must be hard on you being the first female Vice President and having everyone trying to get you to do something you don't want to do."

"Who says I don't want to?" Hailey said.

Jennette sat up, eyes wide.

"Don't flake out on me. I confessed to liking Mark and wanting to go farther, and now it's like a big fishbowl in this town. Hell, the whole country. What kind of normal relationship would be possible for me?"

"For me either, although in a different way. So here's the Vice President's personal guard flitting about with a jet-set hunk living the high life off duty. Tell me that wouldn't draw down your standing in the polls."

Hailey let out her breath in exasperation. "Let's get Adam and go visit Mark. He's a guy and easy to talk to. Maybe we'll get some ideas. This conversation is getting us nowhere."

"Do you mind if we stop by my place? It's on the way, sort of, and I got a strange message from the condo manager I need to check out."

"Sure, go ahead. What did he say that was so strange?"

"Something about removing the mess from his foyer so the other tenants could come and go. Honestly, I didn't leave a mess this morning when I came to work. The trash goes into the compactor, so I don't have a clue."

Jennette drove, with Hailey riding shot gun. Nick and Charlie followed in the "tank," the SUV equipped for any emergency. They rode up Connecticut Avenue to pick up Adam before making the trek to see Mark. Jennette swung off the main drag onto her side street and pulled up to the remodeled three-storied structure dating back to the Second War. Apartments had been gutted and upgraded into plush condominium units. Both women walked to the door. Jennette slid her key into the door and hesitated.

"What's that smell? Ummmm, fragrant, like fresh flowers, only more like a garden full of them." Before she could open the door the manager pushed it outward and they were overwhelmed by the delightful fragrance of bouquets of flowers covering the foyer.

"Glad you could stop by, Ms. Marshall. Oh, geez, Madam Vice President. An honor to see you, Ma'am. Uh, your friend has some admirer, don't she?"

Hailey laughed. Jennette simply stood with her mouth dropped open, gazing at a hallway full of flowers. There was every kind a smart floral shop would carry, although it appeared this delivery would empty any moderately-sized one. Roses, all colors, simple daisies, daffodils, mums, and on and on into the back of the hall and fully blocking Jennette's doorway on the first floor. The foyer looked like a commercial for spring time deodorant.

Hailey retrieved one large card prominently attached to a gorgeous bouquet of roses. "Well, well, well. It says, 'Please say yes,' signed #6. Now who do we know that goes by the name #6?" Hailey turned to catch her friend's expression but the tall blonde had vanished down the hall and was frantically unlocking her door.

"Help me, Hailey. Before those two jokers look in here and start wisecracking." But it was too late, as Nick and Charlie, curious about the intermittent stop and apparent delay inside, peeked around the corner of the front entrance. Hailey passed them the card for their edification.

Nick made the connection first. "Number six! That's Cramer's number. Hey, Jennette, what'd you do to impress him?"

"Yeah, Jen," Charlie jumped into the fray. "You slip out on us or what?"

"OK, guys, lend a hand with this stuff." Hailey's command caused both men to button their lips and gather up the portable greenhouse.

Back in their car, Hailey turned to her friend, who drove seriously, hands tightly gripping the wheel, unsmiling. "Thought you turned him down for that dinner date?"

"I did. He calls every night. Started sending flowers a few days ago. Now this. If you weren't such a fan I'd break his arm."

"Maybe the guy really is smitten. I hear it actually happens. Two star-crossed lovers see each other for the first time and whammo, lightning strikes, sparks fly, and bones melt. They run through a field of, pardon the pun, flowers, and jump into each other's arms, together for eternity." Hailey sighed deeply and batted her eyes.

"With all due respect, Madam Vice President, can it! I told you, the guy plays around. This is not funny. Ralph, the guy managing the condos, the one I forgot to introduce you to, will spread this all over town. He now knows my real job and you can bet this will get to the papers. So, yeah, I'll call Mr. All-American Quarterback and tell him what he can do with his damn flowers."

Hailey smothered her laughter the rest of the way to her house. But when they arrived, the gate guard smiled and handed her a red rose with a note attached.

"Oh no, must be a plague." She opened the note. "Arrrggghhh. It's Murchison's flunky and he desperately seeks my presence for dinner."

"He was some kind of stud. Can I have him when you're through breaking his heart?" Jennette mimicked her boss' expression down to the eye-batting and smirked.

"Not a word to anyone or I'll start a rumor about you and number 6, lady."

"It's not like you don't get flowers and invitations every day, Hailey. Why does this one bother you?"

"It's hard to say. There's something fishy about him. I think the guy is on a mission and just wants to say he counted coups, and then run to the media about it."

"Counted coups?"

"Yeah, like the Indians. It was an honor for them to touch an enemy in battle and not kill him. So think about it. Murchison sends this character to town and his first day on the job he wangles his way into a presidential task force meeting and sits and stares at the lady vice president for two solid hours. He has enough ammunition already. Old Cal is back in Kansas City counting coups."

Hailey finished explaining to her son that future visits to the hospital would have to be discreet. Adam's shoulders slumped. "Does that mean we can't go see him tonight?"

"No, that's Jennette's problem to unravel. She'll come up with a plan and we'll go. But we need to be careful. Watch what we say. Any extra words can and will be taken out of context and spread all over the papers in the morning."

"Does this mean you'll give Mark a shot at being your guy?"

Hailey laughed. "It means I'm going to visit a close family friend to wish him well. Sometimes being friends first is the best thing to do."

"This is way cool, Jennette. How did you manage to come up with this plan?" Adam was adrift in a pretend spy scenario as he and his mother accompanied Jennette, Nick, and Charlie through the labyrinth of corridors in the basement of Fairfax hospital.

"Shhhh, keep quiet or you'll blow our cover. This leads to a service elevator that'll take us to Mark's floor. We should skip all the reporters in the main lobby. The hospital administrator promised to keep them away from Mark for the time being." Jennette crossed her fingers. That had better be the case or

Hailey would fire her in the morning. Maybe sooner. She had found an old blonde wig and a lab coat for the Vice President to wear. Nick and Charlie were chortling to themselves. They didn't think her scheme of disguises and use of secret passages would work. They had a point. Both she and Hailey stood out as above average in everything: size and looks. Neither felt comfortable in lab coats and hoped no one ordered them to the emergency room, stat!

They took the elevator to Mark's floor. Nick got off and looked left and right, then gave the all clear. Hailey's covert group hurried down the hall. At the door, a nurse exited the room and smiled at them, recognizing Hailey immediately.

"Go ahead on in; he's expecting you Mrs. MacMurray. It's an honor to see you, Ma'am." She shook Hailey's hand and moved on to her next patient.

Hailey caught the look from Charlie that said they would be lucky to get out as easily as they got in. Wincing, she nodded her agreement. Jennette took in the silent messages and rolled her eyes.

Adam went right to Mark's bed and began questioning him. The big tight end closed his laptop and greeted the boy with enthusiasm.

"Glad you could make it, champ. I see you brought your usual entourage." Mark acknowledged the adults standing behind Adam and gave Hailey a warm smile. She had grown timid, he thought and puzzled at how quickly she looked away and found solace in a corner chair.

Mark patted the side of his bed, motioning Adam to perch there and give him the latest news from the world of sports. The boy started talking at once and nodded at the sly wink from his friend, who had reopened the laptop.

"Found this neat game, Adam. Check it out." Adam went bug-eyed as Mark sent an instant message to "#6" telling him the *package* had arrived.

"But who's—"

Mark shushed the curious boy before he spoiled the game. "Some program, eh? But enough of that. It's great to see all of you."

"Uh, Ma'am," Charlie took his cue from Jennette, who was motioning toward the door. "We'll just be outside if you need us. Looks pretty secure in here and all. Come on, Nick, Jennette. Let's check out the perimeter."

Mark said, "Uh, Jennette, could you stay a minute longer? I want to tell you something." The blonde shrugged and shut the door behind her co-workers. She shot a puzzled look over to Hailey and received a shrug in return. Mark closed the laptop and turned his attention to the Secret Service agent. "You've been pretty hard for Jason to catch up to. Is something the matter?"

Jennette looked trapped and found no help from either Adam or Hailey. "OK, Mark, I'll be straight with you. The guy is smooth as silk and everyone knows he has a dame in every town, all of them as gorgeous as Hollywood starlets. So, yeah. I've ignored his calls and all the flowers. Why should I think he's sincere, with the reputation he has?"

"I thought that might be the case. And, I wanted to let you in on his little secret before he arrives and you give him another cold shoulder."

"What? You mean he's coming here? Tonight?" Again she glanced at Adam and caught a grin. "You knew about this didn't you?"

"Not until he got here, Jennette. I arranged this," Mark said. "Jason and I have been best friends since my rookie season. It turned out he ignored my small college background and picked me to be the main target for his pinpoint passes. The more I caught, the more we both gained success. I helped Jason escape the limelight initially, hiding him out in the Rocky Mountains during the off-season, and he helped me market myself to sponsors. The guy is a marketing genius, Jennette. All the jet set images are his ideas. All the women are hired models. He has his own company arrange all his events, all of course, picturing him with a beautiful dame on his arm. In the thirteen years I've known him, Jason has never had a serious relationship. He and I have that in common. We haven't felt we could devote enough time to it. I guess we can only concentrate on our careers. That is, until the right lady comes along." Mark sneaked a look over to Hailey and felt her steady gaze waiting for more details.

"You're kidding me, right? Sexy number six goes to the premiere of Heather MacArthur's latest top-grossing flick with Heather on his arm, and they go their separate ways when the crowd disperses?" Jennette was angry but her stance had relaxed somewhat, indicating a slight thaw was possible.

"Yep. That gig sold a bunch of movie tickets and a ton of Jason's after shave lotion. It was a straight trade with Heather. She produced the movie. Jason got his product on screen right before the big roll in the hay she enjoyed with her real life lover, and Jason escorted her, tripling the audience with his popular mug recognized the world over."

"But, the tabloids have been reporting on their affair for months." Jennette was flustered, but managed not to stutter in her confusion. "I saw those grainy photos of the lovely couple prancing about on the French Riviera, Heather topless and our number six without a stitch on." Adam giggled along with his mother, and Jennette raised both hands to her cheeks vainly trying to cover her embarrassment.

"Planted," Mark said. "That's an idea Jason stole from Heather's publicist. The article and photos were done by a freelance writer hired by 'QB6,' Jason's company. Of course both people, Jason and Heather, have hired lawyers to file gigantic suits and all the while the movie keeps selling tickets and Jason can't distill enough after shave to fill the backorders. The two people cavorting on the beach were hired lookalikes."

Jennette sat down hard on the nearest straight back chair. "Huh. You mean all those articles I read about wine women and jet setting are all fake?" Mark nodded. "Damn. Why go to so much trouble?"

"Image, Jennette. Jason is the highest paid player in the NFL, and a Rhodes Scholar from a top Ivy League school, but those two factors bring in a fraction that the jet set image earns him. Like someone else we know." He shot another glance at Hailey. "Jason has worked hard, gaining an image that constrains and boosts him up simultaneously. But, honestly, Jennette, the guy likes you and sincerely wants a chance. Go to dinner with him and see for yourself. You won't be disappointed. I told him I'd pave the way if he would cut the bull and be himself instead of 'Mr. Golden Arm.'"

Jennette jumped up as the door opened and the CEO of QB6 entered. The other people in the room faded into the wallpaper as the two stared at each other. Both breathed steadily. Steadily, but deeply, in anticipation of what, neither knew. The atmosphere could have been likened to the moment before a Super Bowl kickoff, tense, electric—close to Ted Williams walking to the plate and digging in.

"Go." Hailey broke the impasse and smiled at Jennette, who was finding it hard to move. Finally she found her legs and cautiously edged around the bed, never taking her eyes from the man she had fantasized over since their last visit.

Jason opened the door and checked with his pass-catching buddy for some positive signal.

"Your serve," Mark replied with a wink.

Outside Mark's room, Nick and Charlie witnessed the standoff between Jennette and Jason. After what seemed an impossibly long time the two agents took the hint.

"Uh, Jen, we'll just check out the nurse's station. You know, see if there're any urgent messages. Stuff like that." Charlie raised his eyebrows, questioning her for approval. His supervisor shot him a fleeting look of anxiety, and that was all Charlie needed for his answer. He pulled Nick away quickly before they got any more embarrassed at the explosion of emotions emanating from the two people staring at each other.

Jennette and Jason laughed as both drew in deep breaths. Jason was the first to regain his voice. "I want to apologize for being so pushy since we met. Looks like I owe Mark for smoothing the path." He paused, looked up and down the spic-and-span corridor, then brushed his palms against his hips. "Golly, I wasn't this nervous before starting my last Super Bowl." He held up his hands as proof, his fingers slightly jittery.

Jennette mirrored his motions with her own hands and they shared another chuckle. "What is going on here, Jason?"

"Honestly, I'm attracted to you and I think the feeling is mutual." He gazed into her eyes and found his answer. "Please believe me when I say I want to take you to dinner and get to know you. This isn't some quick pickup line the public would assume I'd be making. Don't think of me as some big name jet setter trying to put the make on you. I'm just a regular guy here, asking a very lovely woman for a date." Jason couldn't have been more humble if he had gotten on his knee right there on the hard linoleum.

"Yes. I'd love to go on a date with you, but it'll be difficult to treat you like some regular guy. It's a good thing Nick and Charlie are here for backup. If I had to draw my pistol I'm not sure I could pull the trigger. And since you have been honest with me, I'll just say the feeling is mutual." The super star's shoulders sagged in relief. "But, you have to give me some breathing room here. It's been a while. I swore off men for life. You have to know that." Jennette felt energized by the constancy of his gaze and added a significant footnote to her revelation. "I'm making an exception in your case. I'm off duty at six tomorrow night. You know the address. Come casual. I make a mean pasta salad. Oh, and I love Chardonnay."

Hailey discovered her pulse had quickened. She understood, as did Mark apparently, that their two friends were wildly attracted to each other. Also, it was a good thing Nick and Charlie were outside. Jennette's hand had been shaking too much to shoot straight. Yet not all the electricity had subsided when her best friend and the quarterback left the room. The Vice President subconsciously willed her system to relax. She stayed in her corner, content to observe her son. After their nights in Crested Butte she definitely thought of Mark as more than a family friend. She remembered his hands and their gentleness, and those strong arms securing her to him. He'd said he loved her and her son. She had said nothing. Now she had to smile at her son's ease with the man. They were really like two boys talking about their favorite pastime. Still, there was mutual admiration there. Mark treated Adam as an equal and listened when the 12-year-old spoke. He had managed to divert the boy away from discussing his injury and onto more pleasant topics. Soon they were into baseball and the plight of the hapless Orioles since Cal Ripkin's retirement. Next, it was Adam's turn to maneuver the conversation around to an invitation to spend a weekend at Camp David, and that sent Mark's attention to Hailey, who couldn't help looking surprised.

"OK, Buddy, I'll think it over and talk to your mom about it. Give us a minute will you?"

"Sure, Mark, I'll be right back." He scurried from the room, avoiding his mother's glare, and shut the door quietly.

Hailey took her cue to approach the bed. She didn't have a clue what to say. Yet it seemed the once-timid athlete had grown bolder since his injury.

"Alone at last. Thought it would never happen again." Hailey's eyes darted everywhere, seeking escape, and Mark laughed. "Sorry, didn't mean to sound like a pickup artist. That comment came out like something Cramer would say." He received a smile and ventured on. "When did you dye your hair? I really liked it brown and down to your shoulders."

"Jennette's idea. She figures to disguise me so the press will leave us alone, uh, me alone, well, you as well. Oh hell, I'm making a mess of this."

Understanding came to Mark and his grin widened. "Someone is trying to play Cupid, is that it?"

Hailey laughed in relief. "Someone? Everyone from the First Lady down to my son and all my guards, especially the tall blonde. But it would seem her mission reversed itself. Wow, that was some meeting you arranged."

"And you're like a fish out of water trying to keep everybody happy and forgetting about Hailey MacMurray as usual, aren't you?"

"You're very intuitive, Mark. Yes, I've been told to get a life and I thought I had a very busy one. But it would seem my close friends want more for me. I have been showered with concern, and, uh, let's call it encouragement, to get out there in the adult world and find a soul mate." Hailey stopped abruptly, marveling at her last sentence. "Are you in on this caper? Did they contact you?" She pinned him with a truth-demanding glare.

"They? Caper? I don't know about any *they* or a *caper*. All I know is the most beautiful woman in the world is standing by my bed. You think someone is trying to get us to be more than friends?"

"Exactly." She crossed her arms and turned to the window, as if her script for this conversation would scroll down and rescue her.

"Hailey, please turn around. I want you to see my face so you'll believe me when I say this."

She met his eyes and experienced his tranquility. Mark met her gaze with steadiness and confidence. He appeared neither bold nor arrogant. His affection for her was inscribed in his features as if he had borne it for ages.

"I have wanted you ever since the first time you and Adam came onto the field. I was a fool to wait to ask you for a date. I suppose intimidated is a good word here. We had something special out in Colorado and I spoke my true feelings that last night. Now things have changed. I feel inadequate, less of a man suitable for you. I'm not making this up. Adam may have sensed my feelings. It's hard to tell about him sometimes. He is one smart young man."

"Mark, don't—"

"Let me finish. This is harder than I ever imagined. You see, I know a lot about you. You have given Adam all your affection. So now maybe he's giving both of us big hints to get together and I can see you're at a loss. Me, I'm just a cripple who may not walk again. The injury has changed my life completely. I was secure in a very physical way. And now it's like I've had my legs swiped out from under me, literally and figuratively. You're here and obviously flustered, out of your element. I lie here and see a lost opportunity. I dedicated my life to playing football first, then finding the right woman to settle down with. I feel there is nothing I can offer you."

Hailey came to his side and took one of his gentle hands in hers. "Don't say that. I've begun to feel you have everything to offer. At the same time my close friends, including the First Lady, have started pressuring me to get serious about you. I like that idea, but not the pressure. And I certainly don't want to pressure you, not when you need to heal. You are down physically and spiritually now, but from what I know about my son's favorite football player, you'll come out of this. You will walk again, and with me beside you." Hailey leaned over the bed and kissed him, sealing her vow. "I'm so sorry, Mark. Sorry for your injury and for the end of your career. Sorrier still for being so slow to be with you. It may sound like a trite and corny line from an old fifties movie, but I'll be waiting for you."

"Hailey, don't."

"Don't try to wiggle out of it. It's taken me a lot of years to feel good about a man. Once I do, I hold on for good. Now rest and get better." She raised his hand to her lips and kissed it.

Thirty-two

Were there too many candles? She didn't want to appear excessively romantic here. Jennette surveyed her living room and the dining table she'd moved from the eat-in area of the kitchen. She quickly counted a couple dozen candles of all colors, shapes, and aromas. There was enough light to conduct a full-scale crime scene investigation and take photos without flashbulbs. What to do?

She had changed clothes every five minutes since leaving her bubble bath. When was the last time she had taken a bath? It had been fast showers for years, she reckoned. A luxurious soaking bath was for pampered females out on the hunt for "Mr. Right." Was she hunting? Her bedroom closet was askew and practically empty. Her rejects, from cocktail dresses to jeans and sweaters, were strewn across her bed. She settled for a neck-to-ankle sheath a la Hailey's everyday wear. It was a deep blue, matching her eyes and setting off her blonde hair.

Back to those candles. Yes, there were too many and she began snuffing out a few, then jumped when the doorbell chimed. Cripes! He's early. No, not at all. A fast check of the mantle clock showed Jason was precisely on time. Jennette had lost herself in inner dialogue and candle snuffing. But what was going on here? The man was younger, wasn't he? She had checked out his web site earlier. Thirty-six. Might be having a birthday this fall. Great, that would make her only five years older. He was a big star. She was a little security guard really, albeit for an important person, but she wasn't in Jason Cramer's league. Her bubble burst.

Jason punched the button again. Third time's a charm, they say. Had she stood him up? He was getting some strange looks from passersby. Soon somebody would recognize him and he'd have to sneak around back before a crowd gathered. There! He caught a glimpse of her eye checking him out through the peep hole. OK, this is good. She was unlocking the deadbolt. Next came the chain. Another deadbolt? Geez, this lady was a stickler for security.

The door opened a crack and Jennette peered around the corner as if checking for assault weapons. Finally the door swung open and he could see all of her. Jason sucked in air. She truly was a knockout and obviously extremely nervous tonight, clutching the side of the door as if she were walking the edge of a cliff. Her dress left everything to his imagination, with just the right swells and curves to render him into an embarrassing state as he stood in the bright light of her entranceway.

"Hi, Jennette. Brought you some replacements." He pushed the bouquet of cut flowers at her, diverting attention from his growing arousal. No woman had ever done this to him and it happened every time he saw her. Women might say their stomachs fluttered or whatever. Hell, he just flat got stiff at the sight of her.

Her mouth opened halfway and closed and opened several times before words escaped. "Come in, sorry, I, uh, lost track of time. These are lovely. Thanks." She grabbed the flowers and hurried into her kitchen to fetch a vase and water. "Give me a minute. I'll just take care of these first."

He heard drawers opening and slamming. Then a lower cabinet got burgled, its pots and pans rattling as she hunted down the proper container. Jason stood by the kitchen door and observed the super efficient Secret Service agent lose her cool in her own kitchen. The humorous sight at least relieved his own tension.

"I feel exactly the same way, Jennette." She jumped at his voice and turned to face him, holding the flowers in both hands as if warding off some witch's spell.

"Huh? Oh, damn, who knows where the vase is. You feel the same what?" Before he could reply her eyes widened. "Shit, I forgot to cook the pasta. How did that happen?" She blew out a stream of air to remove the strand of hair that had crept over her right eye.

Jason chuckled and moved a step closer. "I couldn't eat it if you had remembered."

"Me either. I mean, my stomach has been all fluttery the whole damn day, and, what do you mean you couldn't eat it? Did Nick and Charlie tell you I was a lousy cook?" He took another tentative step. "Stop! Just stay right there. I can see and hear you fine where you're standing.

"Do you have that Chardonnay you promised? I could use a glass to settle my nerves." She dropped the flowers in the sink and opened the fridge. "Glasses are in the right cabinet behind you. I think it'll take more than one drink to calm me down." She rummaged through her catchall drawer and miraculously found the cork screw. Her hands appeared to have regained their composure as they deftly sank the instrument into the cork and drew it out with a satisfying pop.

"Sounds like a good year." Jason had retrieved two wine glasses and held them for filling.

"Nothing but the best, and all of a year old. Says right here." She filled their glasses and noted that her hands had a grip. Her nerves had steadied and she knew what had to be said. "Come and sit down and let's discuss this, er, whatever is going on."

But he didn't listen to directions and stepped closer, blocking her avenue of escape. "Not so fast, lady. I want to offer a toast, first to our friends Mark and Hailey. May they be so lucky as us." He smiled and clinked her glass, then sipped from his. Jennette was frozen in place, holding her glass halfway to her lips.

"Lucky as us? I don't understand."

"Take a sip first. It's impolite to withhold that much when you have been asked to toast someone." She obeyed cautiously and he chuckled as her one sip turned into several.

He led her by the arm to her sofa and sat in an arm chair facing her. "Tell me about this serious discussion we need to have. No, wait, let me guess what it's about. You don't believe Mark when he says I'm not really a jet setter and don't have a string of women all over the world. Right?" Her eyebrows shot up. "My best friend doesn't lie, OK?"

"Yes, but—"

He interrupted her easily. "Also, I'm too young for you, right?" Again she uttered no words, but her slumping shoulders gave him a resounding answer.

Jennette struggled for the right way to say her piece. "I think this is a bad idea. I have a serious job and a serious commitment to my career, to Hailey. She's my best friend and if anything happened to her I'd die." She looked away as if her script in this fiasco had ended for the evening.

"Liar," he spoke with affection, and smiled as anger flared on her face. "You're chicken, Jennette. You swore off men years ago, or so I'm told. You're just as scared as your best friend to break over the traces and go for it. You've built a fort around your emotions and are frightened to see what would happen if you let them loose."

She stood and walked briskly into the kitchen to fetch the wine. This time the bottle returned with her and she refilled their glasses. Perhaps there was a bit of courage in the bottle. But she still felt giddy. She sat and tucked her legs underneath, smoothing the sheath and catching Jason's steady appraisal of her legs. She blushed when he fixed his eyes to hers.

His arousal was coming back with a vengeance. He had to do something to keep from charging the frightened woman. He crossed his legs and held one knee with both hands.

"I want to apologize again for acting so stupid that first night in Mark's hospital room."

"You embarrassed the First Lady and the Vice President. Both had to look away at your audacity. I felt bad for them." She leveled him with a humbling stare.

"I know. I called them and apologized, explaining my own circumstances." This surprised her as those unforgiving eyebrows raised again. "But tell me something," Jason continued. "I can imagine how bad you felt for your friends, yet I want to know how you felt for Jennette."

"Uh, I'm not sure what you're getting at here—"

"Oh, I think you understand perfectly. I never took my eyes off you. Couldn't then and can't now when I'm in a room with you. So tell me, honestly, how did what I said make you feel?"

Jennette took a large sip from her glass and felt relaxed, first mentally, then physically, sinking into the soft cushions of the sofa. She glanced to the ceiling and couldn't suppress a smile that grew wider as her eyes met Jason's across the room.

"Thrilled. I was thrilled, then embarrassed for my friends and also for me." She grew confident and knew it wasn't the wine speaking now. "I don't understand how you got here in my living room, but frankly I'm still thrilled, and scared to death because I haven't a clue how to go about this. Whatever *this* is." Her breath left in a rush and they laughed together.

"My jet setter handbook doesn't cover this either, Jennette. All I know is I'm strongly attracted to you. And yes, I've had plenty of models and gorgeous actresses to escort, and some to actually date, but none of them caused the electric charge you do."

Her thrill of excitement was expressed with one long growl of her stomach that produced a tortuous rumble audible as far away as the White House. She hugged a pillow to her middle and bent double laughing. Jason roared with laughter and stood up.

"That settles it, Jennette; I'll make the salad, while you handle the pasta. Did you remember to buy a loaf of French bread? Bread goes good with this stuff." He reached for her hand to haul her to her feet as if this were a regular routine on pasta night at their house. Just as easily, Jennette grabbed on for support and rose to stand beside him, closer than she had dared until now.

"Yes, I bought bread. Ummm, you smell delicious." They stood face to face, belly to belly, and stared into each other's eyes. Jennette closed the distance, fitting her body against his, and slid her arms around his neck. She couldn't ignore his excited state and gave in to her own passion. She kissed him lightly and moved her head back to check on his reaction. But as Jason moved forward to return her kiss, Jennette's stomach took control again, growling loud enough to become the dominant being in the room. And there they stood, heads resting together, arms circling, casually caressing, massaging. But the erotic moment had been shattered, and quickly their shoulders began to shake with laughter.

Preparing dinner lent insight to both. Jason rummaged for salad fixings as if he grazed in her fridge daily. She was impressed with his familiarity chopping and arranging the tomatoes, lettuce, cucumber, green peas and a wide assortment of items she'd never thought to put in a salad. Jason appreciated the speed with which she had the water boiling and sauce fresh from the bottle heating gently for the main course. Their conversation was anchored safely on their work: hers on the routine and oftentimes boring aspects of being a female Secret Service agent, even in the rarefied atmosphere surrounding the Vice President; his on the drills and practices in the summer heat all football players dreaded. They ate in a companionable silence acknowledging their need for sustenance.

Jennette finished the last of her wine and noted the empty bottle and equally drained glass by Jason's hand. She stood, never more certain of anything in her life. He stood as well and began to gather plates to help clear the table.

"They can wait. I can't." She came round the table and took his hand in hers. She laid her head on his shoulder and guided him to her bedroom across the hall. They reached the foot of the bed and stood in shadows and moonlight. There they continued the embrace that had been interrupted by another kind of hunger.

Jason's world buzzed. Before he thought to focus on the scene and his incredible good luck, Jennette was kissing him dizzy. The all-pro athlete caved in as she let loose her emotions, deepening the kiss, gently pushing her tongue inside, alternately grazing her tongue along his lips, then nipping at the edges with her teeth. He felt the subtle swells of her body; firm breasts moving across his chest, thighs boldly adjoining his, urging, trembling.

He found the zipper to the back of her dress and lowered it, as she unbuttoned his shirt and unfastened his belt. Their shoes had magically disappeared, as if some love god dispensed with such details at a time like this. Her silky dress slid to the floor with his shirt and slacks.

Naked, they rolled onto the bed, lips sealing the connection, unyielding to separation. Their bodies were matched well: slender, lithe, firm, and muscled proportionately. They were two people who exercised effortlessly, acknowledging and sustaining the gift of superior genes.

"It's been some time for me, Jason. Don't know how good I can keep a beat." Her breath came in raspy huffs, quickening his hands where a slower pace was needed. "Easy. Let me catch up. Ummm." Her hand closed around him. "You feel beautiful."

His hand stilled at her touch and his stomach clenched, holding back the pressure building from weeks of wanting her.

"I'm, uh—can't wait."

"Do it now," she urged, her voice frantic. Jason moved onto her welcoming body. She opened, yet tensed when his length covered hers head to toe. They shared another kiss to restore her confidence, then their bodies took over. He found the will to let her guide him again and eased his weight onto elbows. She touched him, held gently and guided urgently, pulling him forward, arching to complete their connection, digging her heels into the backs of his thighs.

He felt her jolt as the first shaking wave swept through. He had stilled, waiting for her to adjust, and that was enough to spark her initial tremors. Jennette's body reacted with thrusts that signaled Jason to begin his own. And she was not quiet about it. He felt her hands raking him from shoulders to thighs, urging, legs wrapping him, pulling him deeper. Each thrust brought more tremors and her cries. Jennette hummed between gasps and urgings, her appetite growing at each exclamation.

Jason lost control. She was writhing beneath him, raking his back, kissing any part of him she could reach and continuing to beg him to love her. He got his hands underneath and raised them both, surging fast and hard, mindless, gasping for air. He answered her cries at the end as their bodies collapsed. They felt glued together in contentment, sealed in a permanent union.

He drifted without feeling; somewhere there was a gentle breeze and no one to bother with his nakedness. Serene calm enveloped his soul. He could remain in this place forever.

Jennette drifted to the surface smiling. She faced her lover, joyful in the weight of his body, a weight that was secure, possessive—hers.

Thirty-three

Craig Hospital had a national reputation for re-habbing seriously injured patients like Mark Daniel. From his wheelchair, he stared at the browning foothills west of Denver. The all-pro tight end knew he couldn't make it back to the Redskins now. He had spent the latter days of summer in mental and physical agony watching his athletic career being sucked down the drain. And today he would learn from the battery of specialists tending him just what his prognosis was.

"Good morning, Mark." Dr. Ted Albers approached from the entrance to the fifth floor solarium. Albers was a short man with the build of a bowling ball. He wore his usual cheery expression, but the smile stopped below his eyes, a sign Mark didn't miss. "This is Dr. Majors from our counseling department, Mark. I brought her along to talk to you as well." The orthopedic surgeon stepped aside and allowed the petite psychiatrist to come forward and shake Mark's hand. The woman seemed absorbed in sympathy, with crow's feet deepening beside sad eyes that contorted into an unseemly squint.

His spirits sank another notch as he observed the excruciating facial contortions of the lady counselor. He had put his body through rehab, but little of his soul. He was fooling no one, especially himself. Now this professional mental therapist wanted to take over where surgery and physical therapy had run into a solid wall. A plateau was the term his physical therapist had used. His recovery had *plateaued*. Stopped Titanic-dead in the water and inexorably sinking was his personal diagnosis.

"Mark, I won't pull any punches with you. If we were just dealing with

288

muscle and ligament damage I'd give you a year, maybe 18 months, to rehab back to civilian walking status. Even then I wouldn't predict continuing your career in football." Albers sighed and gripped Mark's arm—they had become friends during his prolonged stay. "But the broken bones present another scenario that extremely complicates your recovery. Frankly, you'd be better off if I could insert a whole new set of leg bones. I'm sorry to have to tell you this, but," the doctor exhaled another pathetic sigh, "it looks like your career is finished, and, truthfully, merely walking again will be terribly painful, a difficult journey, my friend."

He searched their faces, switching from Albers to Majors and back again. He saw pity etched where stoic professionalism should have prevailed. And that cut it. He wouldn't argue with their diagnosis: permanent crippling trauma to his hip and leg, moderate depression requiring medication to level his mental state, prevent the deep troughs of despair and thoughts of demise. But damn if he'd become a whining wimp and waste away here in this place either.

"Ted, thanks for your candor. You knew I didn't want a sugar-coated pep talk. I know you did your best. There was too much damage, even for your skilled hands." He fixed the lady shrink with a steady gaze. "Dr. Majors, it is nice to make your acquaintance, but your services are not required." Her mouth dropped in protest and Mark cut her off abruptly. "I'm going home to get some fresh air. Home to Crested Butte to be precise. This time of the summer mountain flowers grow five feet high along the sidewalks and in front yards on Elk Avenue. Even Mount Crested Butte has lost the last bit of snow pack. The aspens are still green and won't turn golden for another month. Ed Chalmers has a handicapped accessible gondola at the base of the ski lifts that'll take me to the top. Cindy Cloud Walker runs a shop next to my place where I'll be able to get a relaxing massage whenever the leg acts up." He hesitated, thoughts of his beautiful valley filling his senses, and both doctors interrupted his tranquility.

"Mark, I'll need to recheck your leg periodically." Ted seemed to be begging him for another chance not to fail. Doctors, bless them; some day their training would help them deal with failure.

"You'll need the advice of a certified professional to monitor your medication, Mr. Daniel." Majors intoned axiomatically, taking responsibility as if Dr. Albers had released the patient to her custody.

Mark broke his reverie. His head tilted a bit to focus on the assertive lady shrink.

"I won't be taking medication other than painkillers, doctor. I did say no to your offer of assistance, didn't I?" He was regaining strength even with the medical odds piled against him. "And Ted, you may know Harry Flagler. He's retired, but usually on call for the skiers who break bones coming down the mountain. Harry will do the checking on my leg. His advice will suffice for a person who needs to be able to pull up to a piano and pound out jazz from time to time." Mark gave his surgeon a confident smile and received an acknowledging nod in return.

All football players, even the veterans, dreaded The Turk. Many lost sleep as the time approached for each team to reduce squad levels to the NFL limit for that segment of training camp. The Turk came before dawn, usually in the guise of an assistant coach who demanded the play book, and waited while the rejected player packed up and left. Former teammates discovered The Turk's work at breakfast when yesterday's buddy didn't show up to eat— nobody missed a meal during training camp.

Walter Madlock, legendary head coach of the Skins, was surprised to find his number one draft choice standing before him this morning. Eldon had been a big disappointment this summer, Madlock reckoned. Now the young recruit angrily slammed his play book onto Walter's desk, sending dust motes scurrying.

"You got a problem, Rampert?" Madlock's gravely voice rumbled from his gut.

"Yeah, I do, coach, and you know what it is, too. I quit this shitty team and you can stuff this book up your ass." Eldon was beyond cocky and arrogant. Those words failed to encompass his attitude.

Walter felt like ripping him a new asshole. "You got a chance, Rampert, and you failed miserably. Can't tackle, can't defend against the pass unless you tackle the receiver coming downfield." Madlock stood and breathed fire at the blatant son of a bitch. He had allowed the veterans to stick it to the rookie. Hell, nobody deserved it more after the cocky shitass had ruined one of the league's best players. Money had done it, really. Redskins management had wasted millions on a signing bonus that wasn't tied to the linebacker's actually making the team. Madlock knew about the missing pages from Rampert's play book and the shunning on and off the field. During drills, two plays were always called by the defensive captain: one for Rampert and another, the real one, for the rest of the defense. The kid always went the wrong way and was often clipped from behind by a behemoth offensive lineman enraged by Mark Daniel's fate. Well, good riddance. Maybe now Walter could glue together some kind of team spirit so they could at least break even this season. They sure as hell wouldn't have their top notch passing game, what with their tight end gone to the mountains to heal and Jason Cramer mooning over some woman who was a friend of the Vice President.

"Tell me again how you talked old Walter into a leave of absence from training camp?" Mark rode comfortably in the stretch limo hired by his quarterback friend for the ride from Denver to Crested Butte. His busted leg was slung atop a mountain of pillows on the luxurious bench seat across the back side of the ostentatious vehicle. He grinned at his friend who hadn't stopped holding Jennette's hand all the way down Highway 285 to Buena Vista. They were giddy teenagers who couldn't help themselves. Both were eons beyond smitten with each other and neither cared if the world knew.

"Said I had to go see a friend. He knew what I was up to. Hell, Mark, training camp is a disaster without you. We got rid of that bastard Rampert well enough, but it's like somebody popped our balloon and we can't patch the hole." Jason grinned. "Plus, there is the matter of this lady here and the fact that I sneak out of camp every night to see her."

Jennette flushed and melted against the big quarterback until Mark thought they would become one physical body. The sight blinded him with conflicting emotions: immense pain for his loss, and joy at his friend's good fortune. He looked away from them before he sank into a blue funk for which there were no pills.

He watched the blister-dry landscape with its dusty side roads leading to national forest access, blocked to humans. Fires were ravaging the state again and the economy was tanking. Campers either stayed home or went to Wyoming or Montana, states miraculously skipped by the burning infernos of this fire season.

Loggers and environmentalists blamed each other for the catastrophe as usual. Litigious wrangling tied the hands of fire managers who wanted to cut roads in the back country, and clear downed timber that enabled fire to spread more rapidly. Trophy log homes burned daily, mostly because owners added kindling in the form of cedar shake roofing or failed to remove brush from around their homes. There had always been fires here, but now a burgeoning population had begun filling the forests and cried for their government to do something.

Mark shook his head as their expensive chariot climbed Monarch Pass. Evergreens looked gray in their dryness. Fallen trees covered the open space between them. The ski lift swayed empty from high, hot winds at the summit. Traffic was light, especially after the governor had said the entire state was ablaze. The well-meaning politician might lose the election as a result, but Mark could see his point. One spark in these woods and there would be one hellatious fire. It might be better to warn people off so there were fewer humans to foul the environment. He turned his attention back to Jennette.

"Your boss give you some vacation?"

"Sort of, Mark. The Vice President is concerned about the fires and wanted me to do some checking. She's also interested in a nice secluded place for a vacation herself." Jennette's eyebrows rose, sending a subtle message back at him.

"From the looks of Colorado out my window, I'd say she ought to pick another state." That was unfair and he regretted it. He fixed his most confident expression and caught her eye. "Of course she's welcome to come out. I'd like to say I'd be happy to see her, but I wouldn't be much company. In the vernacular of the shrinks, I have a case of anhedonia." He paused and waited for a pitying expression to mold her face but was rewarded instead with sincere interest. "It means I don't have the ability to experience pleasure. Of any kind. Sure, I remember craving Hailey from the first time we met. I'd give anything to be in a room with her, just to watch her. But today that memory is painful, or rather it's nothing, and that's even sadder."

Jason cursed. Jennette shuddered and let her tears go silently, not moving to stop their course or dry her face.

"Wouldn't a visit cheer you up?" Her hopes reflected an eternal optimist's enthusiasm.

Mark forced a smile and shook his head. "It is a problem I have to work through, Jennette. She's too busy and troubled with running the government to worry about me. Anyway, we sort of called a truce on that." His smile never wavered, proving the condition.

Jennette left her seat, knelt close and hugged him. Mark comforted her and looked across to his friend with stoicism. Jason grew worry lines, and turned to stare at the dying forests.

Thirty-four

August in Washington was like Paris. Anyone who could left town and searched for a cool spot to vacation. The Parisians camped out along the Riviera, while mid-level civil service workers trekked to the Blue Ridge Mountains or south to East Coast beaches. Members of Congress flew to all parts of the globe on "fact-finding" trips, supposedly to further foreign relations. Higher ranking leadership from all three branches of the federal government left town for rest and relaxation.

This time of the year was commonly known as the dog days of summer. Humidity dripped and temperatures soared. There was little rain and only a few showers lasting scant minutes, raising the humidity to a stultifying level. It was the least one could expect with the nation's capitol sitting on top of swamp land and underground rivers.

Yet an unusual phenomenon occurred during August that rarely reached the eyes and ears of the populace beyond the District of Columbia: the government ran smooth as glass and there was no news.

In a typical administration, layers of political appointees would review and edit, review and edit. All pieces of paper, important or not, were scrutinized for adherence to the President's policies. Correct spin was spun around each notion, be it a simple letter to a citizen or promulgation of a testy regulation necessary for the implementation of law. And, as word always leaked of the latest implementation plans from the White House, news was made by members of Congress who called press conferences. Since everyone had left town, there were no press conferences.

But this August was extraordinarily different. There had been no political appointees in the Conley-MacMurray administration. Further, the Vice President had set a limit of two reviews for routine correspondence. This limit was a far cry from the norm of 12 to 24 levels in the major departments. In simple terms, the government's letter writer had her missive checked by her secretary and her supervisor. But beyond this phenomenal change, supervisors now made a few pen and ink changes, then returned the letter to the writer for signature, incredibly on the marked up original for mailing. In one instance, response time was cut from six months to two weeks, creating an efficiency tsunami. Most regional offices of Washington headquarters agencies handled their programs without the usual oversight and double-checking.

Relieved of the burden to micromanage mundane actions, senior executives and managers found time to do what their pay called for: manage. None could campaign for office or a political cause since the President had removed himself and each of his three million employees from such activity. Literally, thousands of offices, divisions, and branches—drawers in the federal bureaus—became inactive and were eliminated, their workers retired early, or transferred to understaffed programs.

Attempts by previous administrations to "get government off the backs of business" had led to a labyrinth of hoops entangling regulations in a mindless loop of delays. Vice President MacMurray ordered the decentralization of regulations management to the responsible agencies. She streamlined the Office of Management and Budget into a single White House adjunct for budget preparation and eliminated the elaborate management and oversight functions built up over decades of political interference. This single act emptied two entire rented office buildings across Lafayette Park from the White House and opened 350 parking spaces for tourists.

Newly appointed Archivist Caroline Jankowski abolished the Office of the Federal Register, the National Archives' bureau formerly responsible for setting policies for the issuance of regulations. With strong backing from the President, Mrs. Jankowski ordered each agency to store all temporary records on CD-Rom technology. This act led to the abolishment of the Office of Federal Records Centers and contracting out of storage to commercial centers which had operated much more efficiently for decades.

In a rare televised interview broadcast by a network consortium, President Conley explained the explosion of effectiveness and simplification his administration had created in such a short time.

Interviewer: Mr. President, you certainly have shaken up this town. Our polls show the public is overwhelmingly behind the moves you have taken to simplify the bureaucracy. Can you tell our viewers the secret behind this unprecedented success?

President Conley: I passed the buck to the Vice President. Simple as that. (Conley smiled and waited for his interviewer to stop laughing.) I learned early on to let people do their jobs. My job, as a manager, Army officer or President, was to remove barriers so the people who knew what needed to be done could come to work each day and actually do their jobs. Hailey MacMurray had to personally explain this to several agencies, but she was successful.

Interviewer: Can you give us some examples of these barriers you speak of, sir?

President Conley: Of course. Let's pretend you own a hardware store in Olathe, Colorado and you want to expand your business to sell irrigation equipment to farmers in the area. You decide that you'd like to know what the market would be for such an expansion. So you write to your Congressman for some help dredging data from the Commerce Department's Agricultural Census files. Your letter is covered by the congressman's formal letter to the Secretary of Commerce, who in turn sends it to the Census Bureau. At that establishment an assignment is made to their Agricultural Census Division and further down to an expert in those files. This person knows what information can be released and prepares a response letter and attaches your prized market analysis. Are you with me so far?

Interviewer: Yes, sir, but it sounds complicated. It must take weeks for a response.

President Conley: It took six months in one case, with twenty-seven levels of review between the knowledge expert and the Secretary of Commerce before your answer came back.

Interviewer: How much time does it take now, Mr. President?

President Conley: Two weeks max. Or, ten minutes if you go to the internet. Your letter would be signed by the person who wrote it and a phone number directly to the writer would make future contact easy.

Interviewer: But you skipped all those reviews. What happened to the reviewers?

President Conley: Gone. Unless they had legitimate work to do otherwise. Even more curious is the fact that a courtesy copy of your letter is sent to your Congressman. The public has told us they are getting responses from their representatives months after the letter from the civil servant.

Interviewer: Wouldn't the Secretary of Commerce want to control correspondence from his agency to members of Congress?

President Conley: That can be done after the fact and online. From time to time our top managers review a sampling of work done by their employees and pass on advice. Good work is rewarded in quarterly performance reviews, not at the end of the year. Suggestions are implemented within a week. The next level of management can reward by special Treasury check on the spot. (The President leaned forward, resting his forearms on his knees.) Understand what is at work here. I trust the people under me to do their jobs. In turn they demonstrate their trust on down the line. Trust is the key word. It's the difference between leading and controlling.

Interviewer: Is this some new kind of management philosophy like, oh, I don't know, theory X or something?

President Conley: The example I gave you came from an audit report over thirty years old. It was a recommendation just lying around waiting for some innovative manager to get up the courage to try it. Gumption is a good word for it. And if you remember, I warned everyone we would be implementing outstanding audit report recommendations.

Interviewer: Why did it take thirty years for such a marvelous idea to be used?

President Conley: (Grinning broadly.) Politics, pure and simple. Some political appointee in a succeeding administration ignored this recommendation and thousands like it. Basically these ideas are ignored because they're generated during another party's administration. There probably was fear that credit might go to the other party, and that just wouldn't do. Mind you, getting work done has been secondary to assigning credit. That was "BC." (Bill Conley waits for understanding to register and smiles benevolently when none develops on his interviewer's face.) That's "Before Conley."

He was exhausted, and couldn't hide it if he wanted to. Elizabeth had been giving him overly caring glances all morning. Her perennial smile had disappeared completely when he'd canceled his tee time at the Broadmoor Resort. He felt like a slug. First time in his life, he calculated. Energy sapped. Emotions drained. This job was wearing him down fast. How did Ike and the rest handle it, he wondered? He wasn't that old, but the constant pressure and ever-hounding press coverage had proven debilitating.

He sat alone on his deck and sipped at the iced tea Elizabeth had fixed just this morning. If he was lucky, they would stay here in Colorado Springs several weeks and enjoy some dry cool August evenings away from the White House. Hailey had the city under her thumb. Boy, did she.

The public loved her. The bureaucrats loved her. Even a growing number of Congressmen were praising her consistently now. Senator Burch Magnum had become her best ally on the Hill. Even Kent Kraft, who remained the loyal opposition officially, gathered votes needed for compromise legislation and that was brand new. In Bill Conley's view, Hailey had already earned the right to his job when his term ended in a few years. *Today*, he thought, *only a dwindling minority would disagree.*

The military respected her and showed no qualms being led by a woman. Hailey's two previous occupations before being elected to Congress were highly popular. Enrollment of women at the military academies had doubled. Female applications for Foreign Service Officer had tripled. Next year's midterm elections already touted the highest number of women candidates running for their party's primaries. Many were running without party affiliation. The system was turning over.

New coalitions were forming, destroying the old way of doing business. Even aging members of Congress were learning how to compromise and deal with representatives they wouldn't have spoken to just a year ago. There was a ground swell gaining steam for a constitutional amendment aimed at term limits.

"Bill. Are you asleep?" He jerked his head around and grimaced at Elizabeth's frown. "I called to you several times. Where were you?"

"Right here, sweetheart. Just reflecting on what a great choice we made picking Hailey. At the moment I'm not so sure running for President was good for us, though."

She sat beside him and reached for his hand. "We need to get away more,

Bill. This is the first time off for you since last summer. No wonder you're so tired." She patted his hand as if paying a visit to a senile resident of the local nursing home. And deep in his bones he felt like one.

"I'm bushed, Elizabeth. Feel like I've served four years already."

"Frankly, Bill, you've done more in nine months than most presidents do in eight years. You've laid a new foundation. Now let others carry the ball for you." She drew back to focus on his deeply creased forehead. "Are you well? Is there something you need to tell me?"

"I wish I knew, honey. I have less energy every morning. It's like I'm wading through cement that's drying quicker than I can move to escape. Doc Willingham says I check out OK, just need a vacation." He couldn't stifle a yawn and lurched to his feet turning toward the kitchen door. "Think I'll just catch a quick nap." He held her close and seemed to want to stay within her arms forever. After a moment he walked away for his nap. It was mid-morning.

The whoosh whoosh whoosh of the Presidential helicopter stirred the curtains in their kitchen early one morning a few days later. Bill Conley looked outside puzzled. "We going somewhere today, Elizabeth? I don't remember what was on tap."

The First Lady fixed her husband with a take-charge look. "Crested Butte. We thought the fresh air would put a little spring in your step."

His mind worked around this. His body might be tired, but he still had a steel trap memory.

"Part of your plan isn't it, dear." Both chuckled. She had pitched the idea of bringing Mark Daniel into their circle earlier in the summer when he was first injured. "Trying to play match maker, are you?"

She checked to see where the nearest agent was stationed before replying. "Somebody has to. Hailey works too hard to consider a social life. Heck, any life outside her official duties. Mark is pretty low these days according to Jennette." She paused and seemed to consider adding more. "Also, I think of it as insurance." She faced her husband of fifty years. They had always shared everything and now was not the time to keep secrets.

The President sat down heavily. He pondered his half eaten breakfast, then pushed it aside. *Yes*, he thought. *She would need a helpmate.* The job couldn't be done alone; Elizabeth proved that every minute of every day.

James Buchanan had been the country's only bachelor and frankly that was the only thing he was remembered for. He'd laughed heartily when one of his aides, Betsy Schuler, remarked that James never got much done because he didn't have a wife.

"I'm sorry, Bill. That was a crass way to put it." She pulled her chair to his side and stroked his neck and shoulder muscles, releasing the tension she felt there.

"They'll come at her from all angles; that's for sure. She'll need to unload on someone after her day is done. Just like I used to do before I started falling asleep so early. But then you figured that out already, didn't you?"

She nodded, and tears slipped out of the corners of her eyes, as if grieving for her loss had already begun. "You're the finest human being on the face of the earth, Bill Conley. You've made my life heaven on earth, too. But I wouldn't change where we've come to, even if it means a supreme sacrifice. You've given so much."

They embraced with trembling arms, letting down private emotions.

The chopper landed near the ninth hole of the Crested Butte Golf Course, just east of the Slate River. Elizabeth had arranged a tee time for her husband in case he caught a spurt of energy from the fresh mountain air. His clubs were hidden in another compartment.

The town of Crested Butte was almost within walking distance across the river to the west. Bill surprised his wife and Dutch's security detail as well when he decided to do just that. Elizabeth swelled with pride and hope. This trip was perfect for him, whether or not he could talk Mark Daniel out of his hibernation. But poor Dutch was frantically calling ahead to town police and the mayor's office. No one thought the President would merrily stroll right down Elk Avenue and greet local citizenry as he was doing now.

She was huffing, her breath coming in a bit ragged trying to keep up with a man suddenly rejuvenated by an elevation of just over 8,900 feet. Fortunately, it was a week day and tourists were scarce because of the fires and the governor's dire warning. Still, folks emptied the stores and cafes along the street. And began applauding. Hands were offered. He shook each one and learned names to go with faces. How he did it she had never understood. Too bad Alice wasn't handy to take notes and send these folks a greeting from the White House. Yet these people seemed satisfied just having their leader and spokesman strolling along Elk Avenue as if he did it every day.

"How does it happen, Mrs. Conley?" Dutch had finished his phone calls and dropped back to keep her company. "He plunges into a crowd and people show their respect by not crowding around and making it hard for my men. They understand he'll shake their hand and give them time."

"I marvel at it, Dutch. But that's how it should be, don't you think?" He nodded his agreement. "Look at him go. Such energy, and only yesterday he was ready for a nap at this time of day." She glanced at her husband's good friend and security coordinator. He was giving his reply some thought, lips sealed for the time being.

"Speak your mind, Dutch. You're like part of the family. You know that."

"I was thinking we need to do this more often, Ma'am. He's been slowing down considerably this summer. Oh, oh, looks like we've reached Daniel's place."

Bill Conley stared at the marquee of the one-story adobe building named "Just Jazz." A plaque beside the main entrance touted the establishment as being the first smokeless jazz bar and restaurant in Colorado. The billboard perched on the sidewalk advertised fresh rainbow trout for dinner and free entertainment nightly. The double doors were held open by metal clasps and soft piano jazz wafted from inside.

He walked in like any other hungry customer and noted it was close to lunch time. For the first time in months he felt invigorated. He'd had no nap and didn't think he would need one in this beautiful setting. Meeting folks along the street had boosted his spirits and reminded him why he had taken on the burdensome job of President.

The music stopped and Bill realized the famous proprietor, former football player, and jazz pianist was on his way to greet him. He found the ambience like a kiss of mountain flower fragrance. This was not a typical bar. Patrons went out back to smoke and the place remained clean as a result. Curtains and carpets were clean, unstained, and there was no putrid smell of cigarettes and spilt beer.

The décor was aspen wood and deep burgundy brick. Thick Aubusson carpets soaked up enough sound while allowing wide ponderosa pine planking to shine through. Velvety soft forest green wall coverings absorbed more sound. A man could stomp his boots across the wide planking and not upset the fussiest customers. Yet the acoustics had been extraordinary, allowing the soft jazz to meander all the way to the sidewalk.

The bar was a richly dark mahogany and appeared hand carved. It stretched the length of the room and shined from daily polishing. A tall blonde smiled back at him. She tended bar dressed in buckskin, looking like she'd just finished a photo shoot for *Hunter's* magazine.

"Welcome to my place, Mr. President." Mark shuffled forward favoring his right leg, using a cane to steady his balance. The president struggled to suppress his shock at what had become of the star athlete. Mark looked haggard, depleted. He must have dropped his weight to under 200 and his face looked ancient, pained.

"Mark, it's great to see you." He shook hands and noted the solid grip. *Not all has diminished*, he thought. Another glance at the injured man's face and Bill noted determination in his eyes. Plus, there was something else. Yes, there was anxiety, worry, and a severely damaged self-esteem. Well, no wonder. In a matter of seconds the man had lost his occupation, one that paid him well. Background information revealed that most of his endorsements had dwindled away, virtually overnight. There had been other, different offers, but all had been rejected by a man intent on vanishing into the Rocky Mountain ski country to nurse his wounds. Mark Daniel would not join the horde of ex-athletes rambling on in broadcast booths and comparing every play on the field to their heroic exploits in days gone by.

Elizabeth joined them and simply wrapped her arms around Mark, letting her embrace greet and heal. Mark stepped back, grinning, and motioned to a large booth.

"You folks hungry? We have a great fish special today."

"Thought you'd never ask," Bill said. He grabbed Elizabeth's hand and followed Mark.

The buckskin blonde sauntered over from the bar. "Howdy, Sir, Ma'am. What kin I getcha to drank?" She batted enormous lashes, flirting with the President. Elizabeth had to turn her head to keep from laughing out loud.

"Oklahoma," Bill said proudly as he squeezed his wife's hand beneath the table.

"You kiddin' me? Thas rite, Sir. Raised in Norman and a big Sooner fan."

"We'll both have iced tea, young lady." Elizabeth broke into the conversation. At this pace they'd be here until sundown before they ate.

Mark took charge. "Tell Mario to bring out the trout, Angela. I think the President and First Lady are hungry. I know I am. And talk to that huge fellow standing by the door to take his order." He motioned toward Dutch. The tall cowgirl from Oklahoma eyed her next victim and sauntered off.

Elizabeth slapped her husband's hand to draw his attention from the rear view. He feigned embarrassment and exchanged a grin with Mark.

"Angela's a cheerleader with the Redskins. She tends bar on the side and works for me in the off season."

"Is that all she does on the side?" The President spoke and simultaneously held out his hand for the customary slap. But this time he received a sharp elbow in the side.

"Where's the owner. I want another table, please." Elizabeth pinned both men with a sobering glare. Then her husband got straight to business.

"I know you're probably wondering how we just happened to drop by today, so I'll get to it." He noted the worry lines deepening on Mark's forehead in anticipation. "I want you to work for me, Mark. Turns out I never got around to appointing a celebrity to head up the President's Physical Fitness Campaign and I want you to do it."

He was speechless and shocked, all color draining from his worried face. Bill and Elizabeth reached for an arm simultaneously to comfort and encourage.

"Sir, I can't do that. Look at me. I can hardly walk anymore. Football is forgotten. Well heck, physical fitness is my worst trait after the accident. I'll be this way for the rest of my life." Mark shook his head, rejecting the offer.

Bill had his arguments ready. "I need you, Mark. I need you as a friend and as your president." His ice blue eyes held the injured man like a vise. "Before your injury your workout regimen put most other athletes to shame. Many of your opponents came to your training camp here in this beautiful valley to get in shape. Many also came to rehab; get over serious injuries. I know. I've seen the training videos you made. Everything you said was true." Mark smiled as if tasting these words of encouragement from the President.

Elizabeth stepped in with a softer touch. "It's no wonder you were NFL Man of the Year, Mark." She squeezed his arm as if to jog his memory. "We know that you sponsored your training facility out of your own pocket and invited kids from Front Range cities to come here at no expense. Mark, you helped hundreds of kids come out of their shells and many others to overcome serious injuries." Her tone firmed. "Look at me and tell me why you've abandoned your own advice. Why have you let everything slide? Why aren't you rehabbing yourself?"

He shrugged, helpless in debate with such a persuasive force. Angela rescued him with hot plates of steaming trout, rice, and vegetables. The President and First Lady sat back and let up their pressure. The meal passed in silence but for their compliments for excellent food. At the end, Bill and Elizabeth set their forks down and waited for an answer.

"You two are hard to say no to." Mark smiled and his acquiescence relaxed the three dinner companions. "You're right, Mrs. Conley. I didn't take my own advice. There was a time, right after the third operation I believe, when I didn't want to live anymore." Now it was his guests' turn to be shocked. But he quickly mollified them. "That was another lifetime, though. I came out here to think things through, and lately I just didn't have the ambition to push myself further. Frankly, I turned down some nice options because I didn't see myself having anything to offer." He met the President's gaze squarely and grinned. "Sir, I accept the challenge. But under a few conditions."

"What's this? Who dares put conditions on the President of the United States?" Bill puffed out his chest in mock indignation and they shared a laugh.

"Don't worry, sir. I think you'll find my conditions acceptable. First, I need to work here. I don't have any desire to sit in an office in Washington and push paper. I need this atmosphere and the support of the people in Crested Butte. We can video tape promos right here and send them all over the country. There's no need for me to travel, and until my condition improves, I just can't do that anyway."

"That's OK with me, Mark. We can send out support personnel, therapists, doctors, paper pushers—whatever you ask for. And somebody in this administration must know how to operate a video camera. Consider that done and approved."

Mark's face grew back those worry lines. "Actually, Mr. President, I don't want the government kicking in that kind of support. I don't want paperwork and paper pushers. If therapists and doctors want to volunteer, they're welcome. But I want to do this on my nickel, sir. No government money allowed. That avoids messy Congressional hearings and wrangling over allotments and obligations."

"Mark, that can get expensive." Elizabeth had a case of worry lines now. "Celebrities in the past have been paid and given this kind of support. Why not you?"

He leaned forward and clasped his hands together on the table. He looked from face to face of the two most powerful people in the country as if he held four aces in a game of poker.

"I could say I have personal reasons, because I know you two came to me partly for personal reasons." He smiled at their exchange of expressions. "But there's more to it than that. The press would eat this up: 'Washed up Friend of the President Gets Special Job,' the headlines would blare. Or, how about: 'Conley Breaks Promise of No Political Favoritism; Appoints Close

303

Friend to High-paying Job.'" It was the President's turn to develop creases on his forehead. Mark was right, and they all understood it. No matter what the honorable goal, the press would gleefully point out this break with Bill Conley's main campaign theme: No political appointees; no favoritism.

"I don't want a salary and don't need one. I have money and know where there's more that can be contributed. I'll work directly for you, sir, and only need your official stamp authorizing me to do this job."

"No. That's not how it'll work." Bill smiled at his host and new employee, who had gained a look of consternation. "No, Elizabeth and I went to the trouble to recruit our man. I think I'll delegate management and oversight of this program to the Vice President."

Thirty-five

The dream scene repeated itself every time Hailey had ice cream with Adam after a late supper. She knew it was only a dream, but some impending disaster was hidden in the background of her nightmare. It seemed to be lurking, waiting for the right opportunity.

The extraordinary commission consisted of men over the age of 75, all members of Congress, and all had opposed her in some way in the past. She was the only witness and the room was filled with TV crews and photographers. She wore maternity clothes. She was seven months pregnant. Their questions were frank, explicit, and even lurid. She had to answer them or forfeit her dreams, dreams to be a good mother, be a good example for other women. Yet they had no right. It was unfair. But then everything was in this dream.

"Where is your husband? Did he love you, or was this just some one night stand? Why did he leave? Where is the baby's father? Who is the father? How many times did you have sex with this man before you tricked him into getting you pregnant?"

Her answers came out feeble, muted, frail. She was interrupted before she could finish. And the questions grew highly personal.

"How many lovers did you have? Did you stay over night in motels to hide your affairs? Do you prefer men? Women?

"Mom, wake up. It's time to go." Adam shook her, rescuing her from more cross-examination. Hailey was drenched in sweat and tangled in the bedding. She brushed hair from her eyes and tried to smile at her puzzled son standing by the bed.

"Are you OK, Mom? You look really pale. I heard you mumbling and thought Jennette was in here talking to you."

She had screamed at her interrogators in frustration, frantic to overcome their audacity. She had nothing to hide, yet weariness and stress brought on paranoia for even the most innocent. And Hailey had a terrible case of it. The President had given her September off. Agencies were attending to routine bookkeeping, ending another fiscal year. Miraculously, the budget for the coming fiscal year starting October 1, had been shoved, mashed, pushed, and cajoled though the Congress. Members slowly drifted back to town and talked business on the cocktail circuit. October signaled the start of a new season of debates on the Hill.

"Mom? I lost you there. Are you OK?" Adam came closer and peered at her eyes.

"It's OK, honey. Just had a little bad dream. What time is it?"

"Time to go, Mom. I had breakfast already. I'm anxious to fly out to Colorado and see Mark again. Gramps says he's doing much better in his rehab."

"I need a shower and coffee, then I'll perk up. Go get your stuff together. I won't be long." She worked a smile on her face and must have been more convincing this time around. Adam left and she stumbled from her bed to wash away her demons.

Hailey let the hot water sluice over her body. It relaxed and massaged deeply. She had scrubbed every inch, as if eradicating the harmful questions put to her in the nightmare. She needed a break from this hectic circus.

She relaxed on her sun porch wrapped in a terry cloth robe and scanned the stack of newspapers. Not much new going on. Fires still raging out west. Drought was causing some ranchers to sit by their irrigation head gates to ward off water district ditch riders ordered to lock them up. There was another suicide bombing in Jerusalem, and the accompanying retaliation by the Israelis. The Yankees were in first place in the East. Some things never changed.

Huge banner headlines caught her eye as she neared the bottom of the pile. What paper was this? It was unfamiliar; more like a grocery store gossip sheet. But her stomach clenched as she read the blaring headline:

MACMURRAY FORCED SHOTGUN WEDDING
Despondent Husband Kills Self as Result
SECRET LIFE HIDDEN FROM VIRGINIA VOTERS
Exclusive report by Mallard Flyweather

How did this garbage get on her breakfast table, she wondered? These papers had her secretly having affairs with aliens, Elvis, and the crown prince of Saudi Arabia. They printed blatant lies, and now this. But when she scanned the lead paragraph, her heart stopped. Someone hated her down in Blue Ridge.

> First hand witnesses have told this reporter about a night of misery for the Vice President's deceased husband. Several recall MacMurray's forcefulness in pushing the hapless man through a quickie wedding in a favorable local judge's chambers barely weeks before her child was born. "I never seen a man so shook up," said one anonymous bystander, who was pressed into service as a witness against her better judgment by an angered MacMurray. "That woman ramrodded the whole affair just like she's bossing everybody around now. Shucks, the judge must have been paid something 'cause he shore let her have her way about it."

Hailey felt like laughing, crying, and slugging somebody simultaneously. She pounded the table and sloshed coffee from both cup and saucer.

"That's the reaction I'd hoped for." Jennette stood in the doorway, nostrils flaring. She looked ready to shoot anything that moved. "Did you get to the end yet?" Hailey shook her head. "Jerk says he's starting a 10-part series. The stupid ass claims to have eye witnesses who saw it all, and will tell all, about the 'not-so-spotless' personal life of our nation's first female Vice President. Son of a bitch!"

Hailey scanned the rest of the manipulated tripe serving as journalism and read about tomorrow's headline: "Mystery of the Missing Donations Solved," it promised. *What donations*, she wondered?

"Well, what are we going to tell them? Do you want me to call a press conference?" Lately, Jennette had transitioned from Secret Service agent to personal coordinator for her friend. The White House tacitly approved this subtle switch since everyone knew she was deeply involved with Jason Cramer. Other agents picked up the slack so protection increased. Jennette still wore her weapon and acted like an agent most of the time. It was those daily interruptions by her romantic life that necessitated sharper focus by another agent.

"Nothing," she replied. "I'm going on vacation. This bum can write all the garbage he wants. Nobody pays attention to Flyweather in this town. Plus, I can't panic every time some enterprising reporter creates a past fault."

Jennette looked astonished. "No response? You got to, Hailey. This idiot is making stuff up. It's all lies and you know it."

"Actually there is some truth to it, Jennette. Adam's father reluctantly met me in Blue Ridge and was visibly upset about getting married. Anyone there could have seen that. Also, we did technically get married 'mere weeks' before my baby was born." She sighed heavily and drew in breath. "Sixteen to be exact. But saying 'weeks before' makes it sound quite desperate, doesn't it?"

"What'll you say to Adam?" Jennette sat down and poured coffee for herself, refilling Hailey's spilled cup. She reached a hand to touch her friend's arm and offer support.

Hailey laughed. "We covered that five years ago when we talked about the inimitable 'facts of life.' I remember telling him the date I got married and the date he was born, one right after the other. Must have been some subconscious desire on my part to bring it out in the open. Anyway, first thing he does is count the intervening months on his fingers. When he didn't come up with nine, the number of months I'd just told him were required to grow a baby, he asked me why and I told him."

"What was his reaction?"

"He wanted to know how that was possible and I said his father and I had been lovers before he was conceived. I added that it was best to get married first, but that since we did afterwards everything was OK and he accepted that. Since then we have talked about the relationship I had with his father and Adam understands how it changed when I got pregnant."

"Why did you get married, Hailey? Women have had children as single mothers for some time now without being scorned like back in the fifties. Probably a good thing too, since the guys seem to stick less often when a baby is on the way."

"We had been in love up to that point, Jennette. Enough, I thought, to get married. Seemed like the obvious next step. But that's only what *I* thought, apparently, and we could lay some blame on hormones gone berserk during the first months of pregnancy. Don't forget, too, we were both military officers and could have faced some form of disciplinary action. At the time it seemed the practical thing to do, but then everything changed. He moved out of our apartment and went a little crazy. Partied and drank more than before. Autopsy reports said his blood alcohol level was over the line when he was killed."

Their intimate conversation was interrupted by Katlyn Arnold's appearance. Hailey saw less of her one-time campaign manager since the redhead now served as press secretary for the White House, doubling for Hailey and the President. Katlyn looked disheveled, exhausted, and ready to cave in. She slid into a chair between Hailey and Jennette and poured a cup of coffee. After several unladylike slurps, she got down to business.

"Sorry, ladies, but I have been through the wringer since before dawn." She looked Hailey squarely in the eye and let out both breath and exasperation. "The dog days of summer have bared their teeth, Madam Vice President, and they want your hide."

"Tell me, Katlyn." Hailey squared her shoulders and pulled her bathrobe together with both hands as a symbolic shield.

"All the biggies are following up on the Flyweather article. I have had two phones glued to my ears all morning. Reporters, both friendly and unkind, want the straight scoop. In a nutshell, they want you to come forward and tell them what happened." Katlyn slapped her pen down on a pad of paper in disgust, causing her large, bottle-thick glasses to slide down her nose. "Damnit, Hailey. This truly pisses me off. But I gotta tell 'em something. Help me out here. What do you want to do? I know the personal details. Just what do I tell them?" She bobbed her head, setting loose the fiery curls of her red hair like miniature pogo sticks. Jennette gave her a puzzled look that spoke miles. Until this morning, Hailey had confided more in Katlyn than in her best friend.

"No comment, Katlyn. You know it's sort of true. I was just telling Jennette about it. So what? A shotgun wedding? An outdated phrase, really. Fifty years ago that would have been news for a high school prom queen. But it's not any big deal now."

Clarisse, Hailey's housekeeper, appeared holding a cell phone by the antenna as if it were some vile-smelling vermin. "It's that Mr. Dan Roberts from the *Post*, Ma'am. He says you gave him your direct line if he ever had an emergency. Fellow claims this is an emergency."

"Thanks, Clarisse." Hailey stood, cleared her throat and took the phone. "Hello, Dan. What can I do for you today?" Jennette and Katlyn caught bits of her responses as she paced the patio. "No. I'm leaving for Colorado today, Dan. I have no comment whatsoever. Yes, I was five months pregnant at the time. And yes, my husband was not overly enthusiastic. But there was no shotgun involved. Ummmmm, I see. Interesting. Going there to see for yourself, eh? Nice little town. Stay at the Busy Bee Bed and Breakfast. Talk to Amelia over at the courthouse. She'll point you in the right direction. I've no idea about secret donations being found. No idea at all. Thanks, Dan. See you in a few weeks. Oh yeah. Call Katlyn if you need me out in Colorado."

Hailey turned to Katlyn and smiled. "The *Washington Post* will run its own investigation and my friend Dan Roberts will go to Blue Ridge today to start it. You heard what I said to him. That's what you tell the press."

She couldn't wait another second. Air Force One was 35,000 feet over Kansas and Hailey felt the pressure bearing down on her. Reporters would hound them at Colorado Springs where they'd switch to the helicopter, and again in Crested Butte. Security would shield them, but eventually she had to talk to her son. There were some parts she'd left out when he was ten.

"Adam, honey, let's go have a talk in the study. We'll be there in another hour and I need your ears, good buddy."

She admired her child as he stretched his lanky frame up from his window seat. Smart, handsome, a joy. Those were the first thoughts that hit her. Protect and secure came next. The reporters would not let up if they smelled blood. She led him to the rear of the giant plane and closed the door as Jennette took her station in the adjacent hallway.

"This sounds kind of serious, Mom. Really, Mark is doing much better. Just wait and see." He curled into a large recliner and rocked it gently.

"This isn't about Mark, honey. There's another matter I need to talk about."

"It's not about Gramps, is it? Gee, he sure looks tired lately. But he said his vacation in Colorado really perked him up." Adam looked hopefully at her. They both knew the words "another matter" meant serious business and worry lines creased his smooth face.

She held up a hand to stop his interruptions and guessing. "This is about me and your dad, Adam." Adam sat forward and stopped rocking. Hailey had his attention and felt saddened that his childhood was ending this way. Parents shouldn't have to say such things to their children. Children shouldn't have to hear such things, either. Their life was now officially open to the public and she would have him know the truth before her name was smeared beyond recognition.

"You know that your dad and I lived together before we got married. We were in love, and we were lovers. You know what that means." Hers was a statement, not a question, but Adam nodded his understanding regardless. "I got pregnant with you and it was a happy moment for me. Not so for your dad." Adam frowned at this new information and she rushed on. "You father was a true free spirit, Adam. The thought of starting a family so early was more than he wanted at the time. His main goal was to fly the fastest and highest of anyone. He wanted to be an astronaut." The boy's eyes widened in pride, then just as quickly, drew back to sadness at the lost future. His face sank and Hailey crossed to him and hugged his head to her middle. She leaned over and kissed the top of his head and sat beside him on the sofa.

"You never said any of this before, Mom. Why now?"

"A reporter has started a series of articles about my pregnancy, my marriage to your father, and about other things that happened in the past. He is making some hideous insinuations and some people will believe him. I want you to know the whole truth from me before you read it in the paper or see it on TV."

"There's more, huh?" He smiled bravely and reached for her hand. He was her first and best supporter, and worked to keep that job even now as his world was turning over.

"Your father didn't want to get married, at least not at first. He said he still loved me, but he wasn't really ready to make a lifetime commitment."

"He wanted you to get an abortion, didn't he?" Adam puffed up his chest in defiance of a long past threat.

"He suggested it in a fit of anger, but didn't really mean it, Adam. He didn't. He just wasn't too thrilled. You see movies and read books about the father's role in all this. The wife and mother-to-be needs tons of emotional support. The husband is supposed to be there for her, whatever that means in any particular relationship, and your father just couldn't get past his career goals to do that. He was upset, and, I have to admit, self-centered. He was dedicated to his job. A jet pilot has to have a huge ego; think he's top gun. Most of them know family takes concentration away from the ultimate goal to be the best flight jockey. When I discovered I had you inside me, all those career goals disappeared for me. I focused solely on you. Not so your father. He bounced to the other end of the spectrum."

Adam moved closer and slid his arm around her shoulders.

"He agreed to marry me, Adam. He did go that far. It was something I wanted and I felt we needed to do. Yet he was not comfortable with the whole situation." Hailey held his hands and turned to face him. "You'll see reports in the news that imply that I forced him to marry me. They aren't true." Adam angered immediately and turned red. "Not true, but enough will be implied that some people will think it true just because they see it on TV."

Hailey smiled in fond remembrance. "Remember when I told you about men and women and how babies were made?"

Adam blushed a different red this time and nodded. "And I counted fingers trying to figure out how I could have been born only four months after you were married. Geez, Mom, everybody ignores that stuff. Who cares anyway?"

"Nobody should, but this reporter has riled some folks. His report also says your father killed himself as a result." She sat back to wait for his reaction. His brain worked its way around this dilemma and Hailey never looked away from the anger she anticipated. His response made her proud.

"That's totally stupid, Mom. Is there more to this joke?"

"Afraid so. In fact, your father left me before you were born. He didn't want the responsibility of a wife and child and just moved out one day." She snapped her fingers. "Just like that." Adam's eyes went wide in amazement.

"Gramps says that's not the way to do it, Mom. He says the guy has to be strong for the wife and bond with his kids. That's what he did. He says it's the best thing he ever did, too." The boy's chin stuck out in defiance of his father's perceived cowardice.

"The President is an amazing man, Adam. He's right. But I was young and so was your father. He made mistakes, and some might have cost him his life. He returned to his carefree bachelor days, and began to go to bars the night before a test flight. Some said he took reckless chances in flight. Regardless, he had an accident and was killed." If Hailey thought her son would show any remorse for a lost parent, she was greatly mistaken.

"He left you? You had me inside you and he left us? Asshole! Sorry, Mom." Tears slipped down her cheeks and over her curving lips. Adam was her loyal protector and infinite defender. The child's father might have run, but he had given her such a gift in this boy. Mother and son hugged tightly and let down their emotions. They stayed that way until the intercom interrupted with instructions to fasten seatbelts for their landing in Colorado Springs.

Matilda was beyond her element tonight. She had Mallard Flyweather as her special guest and fresh footage from Colorado Springs of the arrival of the Vice President starting her vacation.

Matilda: So, Mr. Flyweather, I read your report today. Excellent work, I might add. (Mallard leered at the camera with a false smile and her stomach turned over. Illness oozed from his presence. He smelled like overcooked onions. His clothes were wrinkled, shoes unshined. The man was unsightly. She subtly tried to slide her chair farther away during close-up shots of him.)

Mallard: Thanks, Matty. It is amazing no one discovered this out until I started my own in-depth investigation. Took lots of leg work and digging, but I sure got the goods on Miss Perfect.

Matilda: Glorious digging, too, Mr. Flyweather. I always thought the woman a bit too good to be true. Can you give us a little preview of tomorrow's headline?

Mallard: Really can't say too much, Matty. (She ground her teeth at his familiarity.) Contractual obligations, you know. I can tell you this much, though. Some money has gone missing down in the Virginia coal mining country... (his leering smirk revealed yellowed teeth. Matilda was certain he would drool any minute) ...and I found it. (The sleazy reporter grinned broadly as the camera closed in. Excruciating detail of his dingy dentures led to a quick cut back to the host.)

Matilda: My, my, Mallard. We'll all—

Mallard: (Interrupting loudly.) Today's article will be reprinted in over five hundred papers coast to coast and more are signing on for the full series as we speak. (His voice reached a falsetto crescendo and his eyes bulged with self-promotion.)

Matilda: (Barely containing her anger, smoothed her skirt and plastered a half smile to her face.) Yes, of course, we'll all be anxious to see it and read it. Thank you, Mr. Flyweather, for visiting with us tonight.

Mallard: But I had some more comments—

Matilda: (Expertly cut off her guest and signaled her sound man to unplug his mike.) Ladies and gentlemen we have some exclusive footage rushed to our studios in Denver. Roll it, Jerry. (Videotape plays showing Air Force One landing in Colorado Springs. The

Vice President's entourage disembarks. Hailey MacMurray and her son, Adam, are shown walking past a phalanx of reporters and minicam crews. The studio audience hears shouting as reporters toss questions through the air.)

Reporter: Is the article true, Mrs. MacMurray? Did your husband kill himself over your marriage? (The audience groans at the tasteless question and some begin muttering in disgust as the camera zooms in for a close-up of the Vice President.)

Hailey: I won't comment on the article. It is false. That's all I have to say. (A majority in the audience applauds her answer. But anguish rumbles from the depths of the live participants as the camera zooms over for a reaction from Adam MacMurray. The applause grows louder and people stand to join in as the tape clearly shows the golden child of Washington flashing his middle finger at the boisterous muddle of reporters. Next, the close-up plainly shows the boy mouthing the word **asshole** at the offending reporter. Hailey turns and gently folds her son's hand down to his side, then shields him from view with her body. Seconds before the end of the tape, the television world glimpses her angry glare at the cameras.)

Matilda: (Chuckles as the camera returns to her spotlight alone on the stage.) Wow, such a reaction. Just what we want in our top government leaders.

Audience member: She's a mother, you bitch. Shut up! (The cameraman cuts too quickly to Matilda's close-up to find her signaling frantically for a commercial break. Her eyes stare widely as people remain standing and booing.)

Thirty-six

Adam couldn't understand why the crowd in the helicopter kept slapping him on the shoulder. Jennette was calling him all sorts of heroic names like Superguy and Toughman. Heck, the reporter had *attacked* his mother and he didn't care if she was Vice President. He simply wouldn't stand by and do nothing just because he was only 12. Still, Mom had kept him close by her side since his demonstration at the Colorado Springs airport. She had given him one of her semi-stern lectures that said don't do it again, but he knew she was proud of him.

He was excited to be going to Crested Butte. And they were still going. His mom had gotten a call from Gramps telling her not to change her plans. He wanted her to check on Mark's progress setting up the rehab site. Adam knew the unspoken message was for her to see if Mark was rehabbing himself, too. The President was the real super guy, though. He stood by Adam's mom like glue, never wavering.

Adam knew he shouldn't think of the President as his Grandpa. He might slip in public and say the wrong thing. He didn't care though. Mom had passed the phone to him when she was finished talking to the President and Adam rose three feet off his seat from the praise. "I'm mighty proud of you, young man," had been his words. "You named him correctly, Adam. He's an asshole, plain and simple." Then the two of them had shared a laugh.

Only one thing could be better, and that was for his mom to fall in love with Mark. Shoot, everybody was gunning for it and working on it except his mom and Mark it seemed. He'd just have to try a little harder. Maybe find some guys to hang out with and get out of her hair long enough for the two of them to have some time together.

Their chopper landed on the golf course near the ninth green as before. This time there were more reporters. Questions were lobbed onto the green like chip shots hoping for a hole in one. Hailey did her best to ignore the ruckus and felt her stress melting away. She compared it mentally to Huck Finn and Jim escaping to the Mississippi River for peace from the prejudice along the river bank cities. Crested Butte was her river. She felt at home.

Nick and Charlie drove up in four-seater golf carts to pick them up. She kept one hand on Adam's right arm as a reminder to be on good behavior. Hailey kept a neutral expression, yet her pride in Adam overflowed.

They glided up Elm as if in slow motion, quietly with the electric motors of the carts whisking them along as if on a cloud. The townsfolk were just as friendly as her last visit and she returned their waves and shouts of encouragement. Several women gave her the thumbs up sign and yelled for her to hang tough. No wonder the President had returned from his vacation invigorated and ready to do battle.

Hailey wondered how the press would report on her extended stay at Mark's cabin this time. Mark needed her and vice versa. That thought hit her and brought a secret smile to her lips. But what would he be like now? Their last conversation in his hospital room had been depressing. He was an injured man in every way: emotionally, psychologically, and physically. She had not wanted to pressure him; he needed time to heal. But his tentative dismissal of any future together had only strengthened her feelings for him. Hailey was not in the habit of taking no for an answer, and this time wouldn't be an exception.

Jennette took charge and huddled the news pundits around her. "It's a free country, so you can mill around town and do your journalism, ask questions, interview people, do whatever. Just leave the Vice President alone for a few days. Those are my words, not hers. Mrs. MacMurray has said she won't comment further on the false article by Flyweather. But I will, off the record, breaking the President's mandate." Jennette searched the faces of the reporters one by one then continued. "So they can fire me if they want to. But the article was a smear and false. It was total bullshit, but it gave some extreme groups fodder to hurt the Vice President and I won't keep silent about it. We asked you to leave Adam MacMurray alone and allow him to grow up without fanfare and most of you have done that. Now the false reporting has hurt both Adam and his mother, so I'd appreciate it if you would remember to keep the boy out of the glare of publicity. Listen to his mother. Hailey MacMurray is a sincere and honest person and you should believe what she says. I guarantee you'll get a daily briefing from me, and possibly a news conference from Mrs. MacMurray, if she has anything to say."

For a scant few seconds the media buzzing grew silent. Then one longtime member of the White House press corps who often served as pool reporter stepped forward. Jerry Spalding had known Jennette for years and counted her a friend. Now he was speaking for the group of reporters and everyone there understood that.

"Ms. Marshall, Jennette, Allen has asked me to apologize for his bumbling question back in Colorado Springs." The group stepped away from Allen, pointed and booed lustily. Jennette cracked up laughing and the chilly atmosphere melted.

"Thanks, Jerry, and you too, Allen," she said.

Jerry chuckled and began his rehearsed spiel, developed on the trip over the Continental Divide from Colorado Springs. "You may find this hard to believe, Jennette, but we're in an awkward position as journalists." He looked back at his colleagues and received their nods of approval before continuing. "See, we're on your side regarding this morning's headline story by Mallard Flyweather. There's not a reporter here who hasn't gotten called from their paper or station saying the public is incensed and behind Vice President MacMurray. If someone thought to defame her, it sure has backfired. Mrs. MacMurray is very popular and it'll take more than Flyweather's bullshit to hurt her."

Jennette grinned, then smiled broadly.

Jerry hurried on. "We would like an informal chat with the Vice President. Just me, actually. One reporter and one minicam to feed the hungry flock standing behind me. We want to give her a shot at squelching Flyweather's innuendoes."

"I have an idea, Jerry. I'll speak with her. Tell her what you're proposing. Right at this moment, she has no comment and she's said that once. It doesn't need repeating six different ways like you guys always do. Maybe she'll feel better about talking to you after a few days rest. Maybe not. I don't know. But I can tell you that Allen's technique was hurtful." She glared directly at the offending reporter. "Think next time. Her husband died in an awful accident.

She raised her son alone. You pick on one, you pick on both of them. Understand?" Jennette paused to let this sink in. "Let me tell you another thing."

Jerry interrupted. "As if you needed our permission, huh?" Laughter erupted all around, but ceased when Hailey's best friend didn't smile.

Gradually her face smoothed out and she sighed. "OK, I'll get off the soap box. It's just that I've known this woman for years and she is a good person through and through. You all know that. Flyweather is a slimeball and a dunce. I'm sure he could visit any one of our home towns and dredge up at least one person who didn't like us and write some dirt. Folks down in Virginia's mountains don't like strangers poking around their business. And I'm betting that if you really want some feedback, you ought to talk to people in Blue Ridge. Ask them who they voted for, and who contributes her own time and money for community causes. Without publicity either, mind you. Ask them. It'll knock your socks off." She turned and walked to stand behind Hailey and Adam, who were deciding on what to eat once they went inside. No one missed seeing the hand Hailey reached back to grasp her friend's in a silent thank you.

Several reporters took Jennette's advice literally and wandered away seeking the locals for main street opinions. The rest spread apart and backed up to give everyone room to breathe. Hailey stayed rooted in front of the outside menu looking at the familiar entrées, yet not seeing them. Her thoughts were on Mark. Now he was the president's advisor on physical fitness like no other had ever been. His first project was the advisor himself. She knew TV spots were already circulating among the networks, and especially on ESPN, showing Mark's own struggle at rehabilitation. Other top name athletes representing the major sports appeared in public commercials, many contributed by the networks gratis. The government paid nothing. All efforts to impose red tape had been spurned by the President's advisor. Such courage the man possessed. Not in pushing away public money for a public cause, but in allowing his personal struggle, one that involved physical, emotional and mental stress, to be opened to the nation. How could anyone not like the man?

On cue, the front door opened and Mark stood smiling a warm welcome. Like her first visit down to the playing field, Hailey stood in place. The two stared for a moment. Mark had added weight since the president's visit not quite a month ago. He was tanned and the worry lines were erased. He leaned against a cane leisurely, then moved to her. One step away, he shook Adam's hand and gave him the cane to hold. He stepped with confidence and open arms to the boy's mother, and Hailey embraced him. The pair ignored cameras clicking and the whir of video cameras. Adam grinned at Jennette.

Hailey clung to Mark and raised her face up to his for a greeting. Sidewalk observers, friends and reporters were treated to a long deep kiss. Some photographers rushed to transmit this initial scene, while others waited and were rewarded with a front-page quality shot. The emotional scene was heightened when Mark pulled back from Hailey and brought Adam to their side, where both adults enfolded the boy into their embrace. The tenderness was not lost on the best of the press corps. Most understood the Vice President and her son had always been a package deal and Mark Daniel had committed to that in one simple moment.

This time Jennette did not interrupt to urge them inside to eat and get out of public viewing. So what if she wore a side arm; the tears rolled down her cheeks regardless of her tough exterior and official duty. She knew it was an incongruous vision, but the tall Secret Service agent didn't really care. She watched the new family enter the restaurant and stayed behind to give them privacy. Jennette sniffed back her emotions and turned to keep others from entering. Jerry stepped forward and gave her a handkerchief.

"Wow!" he said.

They toured the rehab and training facility that afternoon and then enjoyed a private dinner prepared by Mark in his kitchen up in the cabin. Adam yawned and headed for his bedroom early. Jennette and the other agents kept to the outlying woods and the nearby bunkhouse. Hailey and Mark retired to their separate rooms and met on the upper deck as they'd done on her first visit.

Hailey said, "You look incredible. Strong and fit. So different from the last time I saw you."

"Your boss has a way of motivating people, and I realized I'd be an idiot to let you get away. Bill Conley may have given me a boost to break out of my doldrums, but you were my true inspiration. You and Adam."

They wrapped their arms around each other and gazed at the valley below, soaking in the beauty and solemnity. From concern for Mark's injured leg, Hailey led them to their favorite lounge chairs and they sat to talk. She revealed the story behind the malicious article in the morning's paper; confided everything as best she could.

"He must have a sponsor backing him, don't you think?"

"I have a pretty good idea who would do that, but Flyweather isn't worth any attention I would give him. So I won't respond directly to his articles. But Jennette has a good idea and I will follow up on it."

"What does Jason's future mate want to do?"

"They are a permanent couple, aren't they?"

"Absolutely. I'm surprised he's not out here with your group. He would be if the regular season hadn't started. But what does Jennette want to do?"

"One of the reporters asked for a one-on-one interview with me to set the record straight. Jerry is one of the better journalists and I'd like to invite him up here in a day or so. What do you think?"

"Excellent idea. In fact, why not invite the whole bunch and we'll have a cookout. Give them a lot more to write about."

Hailey saw his lips curl in a conniving grin. "Just how much more would you like to have them report, Mr. Daniel?"

"Oh, I think we'll have a good idea in a few days." He stood and kept good balance using the cane. He'd told her he had reached another plateau in rehabbing and the cane would be around for some time to come. He'd made it clear the rest of his body was in good working order and now offered his hand to her. Hailey took it and walked with Mark to his room.

Silvery moonlight cascaded through sheer curtains to provide faint illumination. They had waited a long time and had talked enough. Words weren't needed for the next phase of their relationship, yet Mark wanted to reassure the woman he loved. He pulled her down on the bed and they lay fully clothed and touched with hands anxious to comfort and pleasure. His soft hands grazed her cheeks so gently she sensed his caring down to her toes.

"I am certain of this, Hailey. I love you. And I love Adam. I knew the day I met Adam that he had a special mom. I just didn't realize you would turn out to be such a treasure."

Hailey framed his rugged face in her hands and kissed him quiet. Her hands smoothed over his strong arms, something she had wished for, longed for. The strength and security she knew would be there from this man were coupled with deep affection and love. "I love you, Mark."

They took it slow and enjoyed the journey, cherishing with soft touches and smooth caresses, pleasuring. They took turns discovering, initiating. Their bodies pressed and molded, memorizing each other. Silky hair. Muscled chest. Gentle hands. Hailey kissed the many scars lacing Mark's injured right leg. Mark nuzzled her breasts and pressed a hand between her legs. Hailey shuddered, surrendered to his claiming, and tumbled over the edge gloriously. There were tentative, intimate kisses, to taste and explore, to build trust. Their ecstasy derived from knowing love given and received. They joined and made themselves one.

Jennette took Adam on long hikes and trips to discover Crested Butte as she and her agent team left the couple to their privacy. Jerry Spalding knew he and his troop of reporters would have a scoop in a day or so. "For now," Jennette said, "let it brew and you won't be disappointed."

Mallard Flyweather's second article flashed across communications media nationwide. In an unbelievable stretch of the ridiculous, the gossip writer incurred the wrath of the Blue Ridge community first, and the nation second.

MacMurray Cops Trust Fund Charity Donations to Erase Campaign Debt
Confidential sources told this reporter that money contributed for Hailey MacMurray's upbringing by the small Virginia community mysteriously disappeared and the paper trail leads to the bankrupt campaign coffers of the current Vice President.

Jennette knew the real story and counted to ten thousand before deciding to keep the paper from the lovers another day. Katlyn Arnold received a call from Dan Roberts that he wanted another day or so to wrap up his investigation but that she would be pleased at the results. Matilda Pratterly continued to allow Flyweather on her show, ignoring her drop in the ratings. Hailey and Mark camped out in his kitchen and bedroom. They ate on the deck and talked of their future.

The third, and what proved to be final, installment of the Mallard Flyweather articles on Hailey MacMurray stirred up international disclaimers from Russia and China and got the Senate Majority Leader involved.

MacMurray Used Sex to Wrangle Deal with Russians and Chinese

Sources close to the situation have informed this reporter that the nation's vice president slept with the entire negotiating entourage from both countries to secure release of the Russian fighter jet that attacked civilian targets in China.

Charles Morgan had been called back into service as Bill Conley's Secretary of State and turned purple when he read the lead paragraph of Flyweather's attempt at immortality. He called Fang Shau and Anotoly Tushenko and had them issue a joint press release praising Hailey's work. Senator Kent Kraft called Calder Murchison with a warning.

"This looks like your work, Calder, and it looks pretty stupid. No one believes a word of it and you're endangering any influence you once had over energy policy. Call off Flyweather before the money is traced back to Kansas City or you'll be toast in this town."

Bill Conley did and said nothing. He refused to fight this battle. He saw it as just more free publicity for his successor if she chose to run when his term expired. Personal attacks were bound to come up some time in one form or another, without any basis in fact. He trusted Hailey to deal with it and chortled at Elizabeth's colorful language describing the intrepid gossip journalist.

They awoke on the third day of their sabbatical knowing a decision was made, had been in the making since Adam's first visit to Mark's locker room and their first sighting down on the field. Their lives were knitted and interwoven these last few days into permanency. But she would not take the lead this time. The man would have to do the honors.

Aspen leaves glittered golden on their deck and the breeze tossed them around their breakfast table. It was a sign of changing seasons and changing lives. Hailey glanced away to the valley and was content. When she looked back to the table she spied the small velvet box in place of her cereal bowl.

"Please marry me, Hailey. I don't want us apart ever again."

"Yes, absolutely." She slipped on the ring and came around the table to hug and kiss this man who had made her complete with his love and the acceptance of hers.

Thirty-seven

Townsfolk along Elm Street in Crested Butte knew something was different. By noon most recognized there were no reporters and cameramen stalking them for interviews as they had done for a solid and tiresome three straight days. Regular folks relaxed in the absence of any media buzz. For simple mountain people they had become jaded by all the national publicity, yet hoped for an increase in skier days when the winter snow flew.

Excitement and media buzz had all transferred to the huge deck surrounding Mark's rustic cabin. Reporters and their accompanying cameramen had finished a tour of the plush home of the ex-NFL football player and now gathered around a very happy couple facing them. Adam MacMurray was ensconced between his mother and his best pal and couldn't stop grinning. Mark left the talking to his fiancée.

Hailey simply held up her left hand to display the diamond on her ring finger. Questions deluged the trio: When was the wedding? No date had been set, but it would be soon. Where would it be? Hailey's hometown, Blue Ridge. Where would they live? Here, and back in Washington, and on and on the reporters queried until Jerry Spalding changed topics.

"What would you like to tell us in response to the articles of the past week?"

Mark took over the interview. He stood up tall and projected a demeanor he hoped the papers and TV would capture as a subtle warning. But his words were more important. "Thanks for asking, Jerry. We won't comment on the articles because nothing in them is true. It's all made up and everyone involved, from Hailey's home town to over in China, can verify what is true. So we will leave it up to you to print the truth as you find it. We refuse to engage in a tit for tat commentary. But, if a local loudmouth had said those things about my girlfriend, who wasn't the Vice President, I might call him outside and do more than talk about it. Hailey has advised me that politicians live by the sword and die by the sword. Thus, it may come to be that the author of these fallacious articles might die by the pen, the one we always hear is mightier than the sword."

Allen, the over-curious reporter who had offended the nation with his insensitive question at the Colorado Springs Airport, ventured onto thin ice. "Madam Vice President, don't you think the public will criticize this as a quickie, whirlwind romance? After all, you've only been here a few days."

"Allen, I discovered long ago that the American public is free to criticize anything anytime and we'll expect no exceptions." Hailey waited for the laughter to die down. "But if you judge relationships by the length of a courtship, then we didn't do so badly. I knew Mark loved my son years ago. Adam has been an instigator, along with certain others I won't name publicly." She glanced at her best friend and Jennette studied her shoes. "We have admired each other from a distance for some time and only lacked opportunity to get together. Yet, for a whirlwind romance, I think I caught the best fellow in the world. I love him dearly." Hailey turned to the big man beside her and planted a juicy smooch on his mouth, gaining applause and the continuous clicking of cameras.

"Adam, what do you have to say about all this? Aren't you just a tad jealous now that your mother has another man in her life?" Jerry asked his question with gentle probing. He knew the answer; just wanted to let the boy go on record to a captive audience.

Hailey and Mark pushed the boy out front and stepped back to let him speak. Adam glanced back over his shoulder at them and winked.

"This is the best deal in the world for me and my mom. Mark is a super guy and I couldn't ask for a better fellow for a dad. But am I jealous? Heck no. I've been trying to get them to date for it seems like forever." Adam paused and thought for a moment. Then just before a reporter could toss in another personal question his face broke out in a devious grin and he spoke again.

"I just want to say that when Mark takes that jerk outside, I want to be there so I can kick him where the sun doesn't shine." Hailey clasped a hand around his mouth and pulled him back into her grasp. But the young boy wasn't done. He wriggled away and blew apart two of the three accusations made by Mallard Flyweather in one sentence. "I was at the town meeting in Blue Ridge when Mom asked everybody if her trust fund could be used to fix up the nursing home and they all said yes. None of that money went for her campaign." Hailey tried to reach for her son and Mark used his long arms to hold her back. "And another thing, over in China, Mom and I shared this tiny little room and we were together all the time." The boy was huffing his breath in and out, upset and mad together. Loving hands from his mother and her fiancé reached for him and gathered him in an embrace.

Adam's proclamation broke up the official part of the press conference. Informal groups formed: some to chat about the engagement; some to compliment the lucky couple; others to eat the delicious spread Morgan Cutcher had prepared. Still others drifted to discreet corners of the deck and filed initial reports via laptops.

Dan Roberts scooped them all. His reporting ignored the Flyweather article concerning Hailey's pregnancy and its timing *vis a vis* her marriage date. His tone set the bar for following articles by most of the major papers. The photograph of The Willows nursing home, alongside a collection of towns folk he would quote concerning the vote to spend the trust fund, carried water with many Americans. Long term care of seniors was an issue in every community, and the vice president had always offered legislation in its support. Her hometown supporters were unanimous in saying Hailey talked the talk and walked the walk.

Yet, on the most recent insinuation that Hailey had traded sex for a diplomatic coup, Dan had to look no further than his own files. He collected updated quotes from Anatoly and Fang that set precedents in international support.

Dan Robert's Sunday edition commentary would gain him national prominence and early mention as a Pulitzer candidate.

About Time for a Pretty Face

The Vice President of the United States, Hailey MacMurray, has faced every challenge thrown at her. Accused of being just another pretty face, Mrs. MacMurray runs the federal bureaucracy on a day-by-day basis, which she began by firing political appointees

325

in her wake. No wilting daisy this pretty lady. Efficiency is at a record high and effectiveness even higher. Who to blame for this sudden anomaly? The President credits his second-in-command for all of it. Sit in on a cabinet meeting and you'll find the lovely lady with just a pretty face in charge of all aspects, on top of details no chief of staff ever corralled. And she's a mother. Who takes care of her son? In seemingly blind ignorance, others fault her for working too much and ignoring her child. Don't say that to the boy who accompanied her on a diplomatic mission because she couldn't get a sitter at the last minute. Still others whine that women don't like war and anything to do with the military. Foreign adversaries will take advantage of us with a woman in the White House. Oh really? If that's your argument, I'll take a dozen like Hailey MacMurray, who graduated at the top of her Air Force Academy class and piloted the nation's best fighter jets. And how many politicians of either sex claim no ties to any special interest; owe no political capital to anyone save the voters? It is time to recognize our good fortune. It's about time we had a pretty face around here like Mrs. MacMurray's.

Mallard kept dialing the TV station's central number and getting nowhere. Matilda, Matty he had once known her by, refused to return his calls and no longer scheduled him after his incinerating columns about that lusty woman acting like a Vice President. Reprint requests had dropped as well. He was certain there was a liberal media conspiracy out to wreck his career. Mallard's investigative reports were relegated to space deep within the gossip rags after the latest reports of aliens stealing Elvis's body. He'd even been abandoned by the late night talk shows. Leno and Letterman made a joke of his excellent research and writing skills. It just wasn't fair. Lately though, even Jay and Dave had wandered to other topics.

The reporter who had once dreamed of a Pulitzer slammed the phone down and it rang immediately. His pulse jumped to over a hundred beats per minute. Mallard downed another pill with a slug of bourbon before picking up. He sat down hard when he recognized the voice.

"Stop writing your bullshit. I won't pay another dime. You screwed up an air-tight prize." WHAM! Mallard was disconnected with a force that had his

326

ears ringing. It wasn't supposed to work this way. He wrote whatever he wanted to write, scandalous and inflammatory and insulting. True or false, libelous, it didn't matter. At least it didn't use to. Celebrities would joke about his articles. Some wrote letters to his paper commending his creativity. Hell, all he did was add a little punch to the drab political atmosphere around here.

Rats, the ticker started up again. Mallard downed a couple of pills—that was three day's worth just this afternoon. He refilled his glass with booze and chugged it. He needed sleep and stretched atop the gray sheets, unwashed since his trip to Blue Ridge. Everything slowed down and his breathing deepened at first, then grew shallow. He wasn't getting enough air and began panting like a little puppy; working to take in air with exaggeration. Still less filled his lungs and he began to exhale lengthy puffs of carbon dioxide until, finally, he expelled his last breath. He could make no effort to inhale, nor, he understood, did he want to. Death was that simple. His unfeeling heart slogged to a halt with only a beat or two more; then not at all. It felt…no, nothing felt. In limbo, he observed his wretched used up body still, then stiffen.

Thirty-eight

Jennette, Katlyn and Grandma Elizabeth had shushed Adam out of his mother's bedroom for the day. He ambled downstairs to visit with Gramps and Mark and Jason. He guessed it was time to join the men and leave the ladies alone. But his guy pals were gone. In their places were Mary Jo Tyler and Sara Wolf, who told him to just keep going outside where they had sent the men. They were busy decorating the living room for the small ceremony for family and close friends only.

Adam went outside and came face to face with a crush of folks setting up a backyard barbecue that spilled over into the neighbor's yards on either side. *Geez*, he thought, when his mother said they'd get married soon, she meant it. It had been barely a couple of weeks since they had come back from Colorado after getting engaged, and the wedding was today! Adam realized he was completely delighted with life. He sat to observe and enjoy the hustle and bustle of the army of ants in the form of his friends and neighbors. He would never forget his mother's happy news after Mark gave her that ring. "Adam, Mark and I are getting married, and right away." They had hugged and danced and jumped up and down. Then she had added, "I don't care if folks think we rushed it. You know we didn't. Plus, when you get older you'll understand better that when you find the person you love and want to live with the rest of your life, you want to start doing that now, not next year or at a convenient time."

He was content to sit and let the crowd of friends do all the work. Adam had showered and dressed up early to avoid all the women helping his mother.

Funny, she had dressed herself all her life except today. But his introspection on the mysteries of the female sex was interrupted by a friendly hand tousling his hair.

The President of the United States sat beside him and looked serious. "Hey there, young man. We wondered where you'd gone off to. We went for a ride to get some air away from all these women and thought you might like to go, but we couldn't find you."

"Hi, Gramps. I got stuck in limbo upstairs and came looking for you guys, but must have just missed you." The two quieted and sat in companionable silence while a whirlwind swirled around them. There was no press back here to lob questions at the important leader of the free world. Adam felt like they were in the eye of a hurricane though, and soon waves and high wind would intercede in the form of reporters and TV cameras. Just now, it was great to sit here with his honorary grandpa and watch.

"This must be exciting for you, Adam. Tell me what's on your mind. It's not every boy who can attend his mother's wedding."

This was what Adam loved about his grandfather. He talked like he was speaking to a grown man and he listened to what Adam said. Oh, he had lots to say and a ton of feelings. It was special to have this great man listen. Adam turned away and studied the fall colors to gather his thoughts. Blue Ridge was the most beautiful place in the world this time of the year. Brilliant oranges, reds and yellows had burst onto the trees. His feelings were just as colorful, bright with hope.

"I've looked at my mom's marriage from a bunch of angles. I tried to put myself in the shoes of different people, not just me." President Conley chuckled at the boy's serious and analytical mien. "I figure the voters will go crazy over it. I mean, this is a first again, right? There never has been a female Vice President, and now she's marrying a football hero. It's the American dream; a great match." Bill Conley roared with laughter and slapped Adam on the back. Both were laughing now and it took several minutes before Adam could get back to his analysis.

"If she wants to run for President when you leave office, who could beat her?" The current President smiled his acknowledgement of this profound but simple conclusion. "I mean, check out the image of all this. Beautiful lady marries handsome football star. Yet, she's smarter than anybody else except you. So she'd win the debates hands down."

"Good point, Adam. But she's really smarter than I am. I don't have the energy to keep up with her." It was the President's turn to study the fall colors, and another silence arose. "You haven't talked about the impact on you. You and your mother have been so close all your life and now there's Mark to add to the mix. I know the voters like what they see. I get mail every day praising her, some using your term of 'a good match.' Right now I'm interested in the Vice President's son and his feelings."

"Relief is the first word that pops into my head, sir. Relief that she has found a really genuine guy to love and who loves her just as much. And I thought Mark was the best person for her the first time I shook his hand. Just knew it. But golly, grownups are hard to figure. I thought they'd never get it together."

"You sound like the father of the bride, not the son." The boy grinned at this.

"Mom and I talk a lot. I have to watch what I say around the guys at school because she shares a bunch of stuff with me." The president's eyes widened in mirth. "Well, you know, most of the time she'd come home from a date, slam the door, and stomp back to the kitchen to fix a cup of tea. That was my signal to get out of bed and listen to her. She told me about guys and warned me not to be like that, you know, after a quick roll in the hay."

"Your mother told you stuff like that?"

"Not the specifics, OK. Just that she wasn't interested in those guys. But she was interested in guys, you know. Except the press and the rumor mills around town made up a bunch of garbage and now they can't do that anymore. She explained what it meant to set a double standard and I watched it happen to her so often. Lots of that is gone after today."

"You're a grownup today, Adam. Your mother would be proud."

"Well, thanks but I haven't gotten to the best part." The boy stared directly into the friendly eyes of his grandfather. "After today I'll have a dad for the first time. I decided out in Colorado when Mom told me the good news. After they get married, I'm going to call Mark—Dad."

The president gave the bride away. Jason Cramer served as Mark's best man. Jennette was maid of honor and wore her own engagement ring. Her future husband would plan a rather large extravaganza to publicize he was no longer available to jet set models. Judge Bradford Anderson married the couple with their son standing beside them.

Thirty-nine

Dan Roberts arrived at the White House gate for his one-on-one interview with the President. He had documented the roller coaster ride of this revolutionary administration for almost two years. Now it was winter, nearing the third year of Bill Conley's presidency. Dan had tried to remain objective about the Conley-MacMurray, now Daniel, administration. It had been fun to record the dynamic changes the independent president and his indomitable vice president had wrought. Tonight promised another break for his career as a journalist. He and the President would share a meal and as much conversation as either could tolerate. It was yet another first. Dan had asked for an interview and the old man had invited him to dinner.

The reporter was deep into research on a book about Bill Conley. His follow-up would be on the man's successor; a woman, he hoped. And why not hope? He was a voter too, and these two people had turned the government around. The people were beginning to get their money's worth. The president's popularity ratings remained high enough for him to beat any opponent or groups of them by a whopping two to one, the same as his victory margin two years ago. Unprecedented. But he would not run again. He'd said it and he meant it. Independents had devastated the field in the mid-term elections back in November, splitting both chambers of the Congress into thirds. At the same time, a Constitutional amendment to limit terms marched forward, gathering momentum as voters turned out more incumbents and discovered the system worked just as well. There was a good chance the next President would be in office for six years, and members of Congress would enjoy much less than the lifetime tenure of the past.

Roberts marveled at other changes while he waited in the lobby for his host to send for him. These were changes many pundits had labeled a fantasy. Now they were reality. Procurement, perhaps the biggest pork boondoggle, was now free and clear of rules and regulations. Tony Martin had won the day on that issue when he'd documented an almost one-third savings for his agency's test year. Energy policy required self-sufficiency for the country within a decade, and promoted alternative sources such as wind and solar power generation. Common sense had emerged from the shadow of Middle Eastern oil despots. The Vice President had forced health care and social security onto front burners during an election year. She dared those running for office to avoid the topics and fresh debate was the result. Still, these were thorny problems with no quick solutions. The populace had a solid guarantee that the Conley administration would fund health care.

The military, once thought to be the greatest beneficiary of an ex-general in the White House, thrived on a steady and sufficient budget, while a national draw-down of bases continued. The overwhelming bureaucracy, once thought to be beyond control, rolled along in harmony with the administration and grew smaller as programs were eliminated, budgets reduced. Parking in town got easier as the President had promised in his first and last inaugural address. Some agencies mandated use of the ultra modern and expensive Metro, and ridership jumped.

It seemed that a spirit of cooperation was born as the lowest civil servant recognized a common work ethic with the top man and woman in town: duty and loyalty to the people. Bureaucrats reported high job satisfaction now that they could anticipate coming to work and actually getting work done. Before Conley, or "BC" as popularly termed, multiple layers of political editing and control skewered good ideas, stymied administration and bloated information flow with party line flotsam and special interest lobbying. What would be next? Dan Roberts wondered.

"There's an oxymoron if I ever saw one: a Washington reporter deep in thought. Evening, Dan. Welcome to the People's House." Bill Conley shook hands, standing a head taller than the stocky reporter. He looked refreshed this evening. Probably coming from a swim, his afternoon custom of late.

"Good evening, Mr. President. Thanks for inviting me." The men had a mutual respect unlike most presidents and reporters. Dan Roberts had treated President Conley's administration with fair objectivity and had been criticized by some peers for being soft on the Vice President. The President led Dan upstairs to his private study where they could share a drink before dinner.

Bill Conley opened the refrigerator and looked back at his guest. "What'll it be, Dan? I just drink beer anymore, but there's a bunch of stuff in here: wine, vodka, bourbon."

"A beer sounds good, Mr. President. Reporters don't have fancy tastes, you know."

The President handed Dan a bottle of beer and both men settled into comfortable easy chairs. "Let's get one thing straight, Dan. Tonight you must call me Bill. Please. I'd be much more comfortable with that. When you write about problems with the government you can call me whatever bad names you wish."

Dan smiled. "Yes, Sir."

"Fine then," Bill said. "I'd like to offer a toast. Congratulations on that Pulitzer. Well deserved."

"Thanks, Bill." They sipped beers and a comfortable silence filled the room. "What did you want to talk about tonight? Usually I'm the one asking for an interview, and there is never a meal attached."

"I understand you're writing a book. Thought I'd offer my records to you before the Archives snatches them up for some library they're planning." He laughed as the reporter sat forward and choked on his beer.

"You're kidding me, right? You'd include documents on that spy network in Berlin, your days in the Senate, the FBI fiasco, selecting Hailey Daniel to run for office. All of that?"

Conley nodded. "Alice and Elizabeth know about it. Hailey welcomed it, thought somebody should write it who knew how to write; that was how she put it." The President paused to quaff more beer and fixed his reporter friend with a steady look. "We should eat first, but I thought we'd better talk before my mind goes soft and I can't think straight."

Dan Roberts saw a tired man drinking beer across from him. Others had guessed the man was slowing down from the awful grind of Washington. He wasn't traveling as much anymore, leaving most of the ceremonial appearances to Hailey Daniel. He still looked impervious, like a rock. Dan shivered inside. He sensed he was witnessing a scoop that could not be reported.

Dinner was basic guy food: steak and potatoes with a salad on the side. Bill Conley stuck to beer and the two men retired to the study for serious talk.

"You can print what you want when you want, Dan. Some topics you'll recognize as future items only you will know. It'll be up to you to write it up for the paper, or for your book. No one here will be looking over your shoulder and editing what you write. Most of my life was a secret, and in many cases, I'm the only person to know about it. Except for a few cases, everybody else is dead."

Dan let the big man talk, delving into subjects the Washington press would salivate to chew on. Underlying his description of tales from his military and political past though, was a message, a very subtle one that became clearer to Dan Roberts the longer the President talked: he was dying. This so-called chat was to tell his vision, his hope for the country. Realization hit Dan like a glass of ice water to his face. He stood mid-sentence during the president's recall of the FBI fiasco. His palms were sweaty, ears ringing.

"Easy, Dan. Sit back down and take deep breaths. Have another beer. You just turned pale there. Feeling sick?"

"Are you sick, Sir?"

"No. I'd have to let the public know about that. No, I'm winding down and I feel it coming on. My wife knows, although we never talk about it." Both men understood the definition of *it*. "Hailey suspects nothing. She's too busy running the place for me, letting me sit here and look presidential."

After a pause Dan continued their conversation. "How did you find Hailey Daniel, sir? Tell me about her."

"I got to read her dispatches from Paris and Moscow. Unofficially, of course, and you can write about that. Friends kept me informed after I left military service. Elizabeth balked at the big safe I put in the basement to store the classified documents that wafted to my home. Some Hailey wrote. I read her stuff and thought, here's a person who wades right into the thick of it, gets to the nub of an issue, and convinces people to solve problems. I didn't pay attention to her status as a mother. Hell, she outperformed men and women, single and married, with and without children. And that's all she wanted, to be rated on her work, not anything else.

"Then my daughter, Sara, calls from Virginia and says there's this woman running for Congress and how should she, my daughter, manage her campaign. Well, that was a hoot. Sara has her head in the clouds most of the time writing syrupy romance novels, and she's still goofy over her husband, Joe, after twenty-some years. I didn't think this was the best job for her. But she said this lady had to win, would win. Who was she, I asked? And Hailey's name popped up again. She did win and came to my home first thing."

Bill Conley paused and leaned toward Dan, man to man. "I had the same reaction to her most men do. Wow! Was she good looking and on top of being smart and all the things you know already. Whew, some combination. She and I had run identical campaigns and we stood for the same things. She was the future I thought; still do. So one night Elizabeth and I talked over our cocktails. We had decided to run. What the hell. Nothing got done anymore and you know all that. But I was already old; still healthy, but old. And I wanted youth and energy with me. Hailey was the best possible choice; the best person, not just the best woman. Every job I ever held I worked hard to train my successor and I treated this position the same. I put her in the hot seat. Threw everything at her. Let her solve problems, never second-guessed her. It's a fact no other Vice President was ever given a training program for the next position like I gave Hailey." Bill paused and smiled. "Fact is, some Vice Presidents were out and out dumb asses."

"What's your secret, Bill? You've gotten so much done in two years. How?"

"I trust people, Dan. Hire good people and let them do their jobs. It's pretty simple. Your government pays top dollar to federal workers. The party spoils system put them on a shelf. Frustrated the hell out of them. Hailey got the appointees out; kicked their butts beyond the Beltway. It took her most of the first year, but she did it. The workers left behind were free to work and the big majority didn't work for a party anyway. They owed their allegiance to the people. Hailey and I came into office with the same view and they welcomed us."

Dan saw the big man stifle a yawn and limited their talk to a final question. "I'm getting tired, sir, but I wanted to know what rabbit you might pull out of the hat this year?"

Bill didn't hesitate. "No more aid and comfort to dictators. Period. That'll throw some people for a loop. We will no longer support in any way a political leader who is not elected to office democratically. No aid, no weapons, no nothing. The average people in the street say we're hypocrites espousing democracy, then selling guns to Middle Eastern countries that harbor terrorists. Well, we are. But no more. But if you report that before my State of the Union Speech, everyone will say you're crazier than I am."

Dan left the White House in a daze. He had an open invitation to return, to interview anyone and to see any paper Alice or Elizabeth held. He'd called the President by his first name and now counted him a friend. Still, unease surrounded him. This next year would be significant, maybe dangerous.

Forty

Mr. and Mrs. Daniel had developed an accommodating routine. Neither wished to leave the marriage bed in the early morning hours to jog with Jennette and Adam. It was too much like starting a day that went downhill fast with meetings and conferences and ceremonial appearances. Hailey had a security briefing with the president early every day and a host of task force meetings and the occasional cabinet meeting to chair.

The newlyweds treasured their mutual discovery that each was a voracious lover. Each had forestalled love and lovemaking too long to start a day without its experience. Each had a strong, well-exercised body and craved the extraordinary release and expression of their committed relationship through uninhibited sex. Their routine involved separation of their intimate personal life from the official duties demanding Hailey's total concentration during the day. To this end, lovemaking came before the Vice President took charge of the nation's governmental affairs, and after the lights went out every night. The nation's first female Vice President enjoyed her ability to transition from wife and lover, to mother and friend, to elected leader.

Noted linguistics experts claim all languages have similar characteristics that can be described as levels of communication. Because Hailey was somewhat of an expert in languages, she discovered that adjusting to these different levels was easy and personally refreshing. At the top of formal communications was the category of official business language. Hailey used this level for international relations and working as President Conley's executive officer to run the federal bureaucracy. This was the language she and Bill

Conley spoke in public speeches, the language of laws, rules and regulations.

The next level for the President and Vice President was strikingly more casual. No other top leaders of the United States had operated more informally. Both insisted on being called by their first names by close friends and by many others as conversation drifted from the official to the casual. Above all, Bill and Hailey considered themselves public servants and regular people, although most voters considered them far above the usual cacophony of Washington politics. So it was that personal conversations with friends, relatives, and children would have been classified as casual by the linguistics experts.

Intimate communications was the last level in this hierarchy of languages described by the experts. Or, in the Vice President's case, it had evolved into the first and last level. Hailey's day began with an intimate "conversation" with Mark, moved to the casual level with Adam, Jennette and other friends, and leveled out at the formal or official level during the typical work day. Transitions were fuzzy, yet Hailey's casual and official communicants recognized her extraordinary buoyancy and indefatigable enthusiasm. Officials marveled at her boundless energy that never wavered. Close friends winked and credited Mark.

Hailey's day was serious, business-like and important, yet done with a *glow,* as Jennette called it, from an early morning romp in the sack. The Vice President took the lead more often now as Bill Conley stepped back and allowed a form of symbolic aura to envelop the Office of the President. He reckoned they had caused a political tsunami to crest at the two year mark and he would only monitor and advise his last two years. He had drawn the blueprint and now consciously let others take the spotlight. He often said that micromanaging and an outlandish ego had caused most Presidents to lose sight of the nation's business.

Charles Morgan was like a man reborn, traveling the world's capitols and shocking most everyone with the President's new foreign policy: No more support for dictators and despots, period. In worst cases, ambassadors were called back and embassies shut down. Tony Martin spread the revised gospel of procurement across remaining agencies, saving billions. Caroline Jankowski took on the entire federal bureaucracy with projects to eliminate archaic regulations and proposals for sunset laws.

Burch Magnum married Rose and began introducing legislation that implemented hours of task force compromises on health care and Social Security. Getting things done inside the Beltway was the new "Potomac fever."

Mark's day was low key. His rehab was over and the right leg as good as it was going to get. He could run, just not as fast or as far. Hailey trimmed her five-mile runs to three-mile jogs, leaving more time for other earlier "activities." After his wife left for work, Mark spent time with Adam and relished being called dad by the boy. Some days he volunteered at Adam's school as an aide. Other days he helped coach a sports team. He did this work because it brought him closer to Adam, but his example carried to athletes around the country. He was the husband of the Vice President and his time out in public was tracked and documented daily by the press.

The public understood that Washington was a different place. There was also a general agreement that the Vice Presidential couple was happy, content and very much in love.

Hailey's life was balanced for the first time as she and Mark loved each other more every day. Loving Mark was only half of the equation; he loved her equally in return. They slept naked and cuddled front to back just after the first snooze alarm sounded. Mark spooned her silky smooth body and reached around to caress and awaken her gradually. Hailey dozed in pleasure and knew it was only the beginning. Two could pleasure, she reckoned, and reached back, smoothing, caressing, holding. She traced the lines and indentations of those horrid scars on his leg, willing them gone.

Her personal secret was to begin each day with this intimate conversation, and Mark's roaming fingers on her front ensured that would happen. His fingers swept over her, claimed her in sensual massage. His fingers teased, building anticipation that might be fulfilled that morning or be put on hold until the evening. Other mornings Hailey became the masseuse. This contemporary "spooning" ritual lasted scant minutes until the second snooze alarm gave them accompanying music, soft jazz from their favorite station.

Most mornings they came face to face and silently agreed to meet urgent needs. They sought variety. He left the script to her creativity; let her take the lead. They gave freely, abandoning sensible thought. Their love and trust built to overflowing, to the level that a glance or slight touch during the day rekindled thoughts of their shared passion, their enduring link.

When the lights went out at night, Hailey and Mark continued their intimate conversation. Yet her transition was of necessity gradual to shed the official language of her day managing the government. Mark's first gift in the evenings was to be a strong shoulder and empathetic lover on the next pillow. He listened to the troubles of the world whispered in a tone of caring and perplexity. But he only listened. Hailey just needed to empty her mind of the day's turmoil and he knew she would charge forth the next day renewed in spirit, a renewal in which he took an active role. This night was typical.

"OK, that's enough about terrorism and the Middle East. I agree with you. Those people need their own revolution. Clear your mind of dictators and sheiks and despots. Relax and just let me help you feel better."

Hailey was talked out for one day and felt her period of transition was complete. "I don't suppose you have any special treatment in mind to ease my troubled mind, do you? Perhaps a therapy that would relax the rest of me too? Huh?" She purred in anticipation, becoming his lover, leaving her job and duties as a mother behind.

"Hmmm, yes, there is something that comes to mind. Now roll over." He slipped off the sheet and nudged her on her stomach. Mark straddled her bottom, and splashed massage oil from her shoulders to the small of her back. He heard the soft groans of anticipation coming from his mate and began working the wonder oil into tense muscles. Hands that formed beautiful sculpting out of stone spread relaxation into her neck and shoulders, arms and hands, hips and legs. He never hurried this phase of the therapy. This was his wife's reward for venturing forth to toil for the public's welfare. He considered this ministration his contribution as the nation's first male spouse in the Vice Presidential home. Of course there were side benefits for the provider.

He got to see her full shape from above, to pause, to marvel at the female body, his wife's beautiful body. Hailey was strong, yet extraordinarily feminine and affectionate. He was envied by many and deservedly so. No one else could strip her mind of its cares and then her body as well. His thoughts always took him back to the one and only time Adam had barged into their bedroom without knocking. Mark and the boy's mother were in this exact pose, wearing not a stitch and he was massaging her derriere. Mother and dad smiled back at the bewildered boy who turned red and hopped back into the hall after slamming the door. Thereafter they were assured of no interruptions.

Back in the present, Mark slid down to the end of the bed and oiled her feet. He took each leg and propped it on his shoulder for support before massaging her calf and upper thigh. The foot came last and always drew more soft murmurs as he worked his magic fingers in between toes and along the sole. This ritual was repeated for the other leg and Mark was rewarded with a sexy wiggle of her hips when he set that limb down. In the soft light of the built-in reading lamp overhead, Hailey's body glistened with an erotic sheen. This sight drew his breath up short every time.

She tingled all over. Each toe and finger possessed an electric charge. When she wiggled them the oil suffused the weight of her official worries. Hailey floated and went limber as Mark rolled her on her back. He used the oil liberally over breasts, around and around her stomach, and along the tops of her thighs and shins. It was heaven on earth. She let her arms flop to the side knowing her husband desired her acquiescence. She gave him complete entrée. Her first tremors of release were always a surprise built over the entire massage, her body charged by loving hands, shudders racing through her belly. How nice it was to be tended to, loved to the bones as her husband relished her intimately. She hugged him to her body and went over again. Enough. Perfect.

A different, but familiar scene of anticipation unfolded earlier that evening at 1600 Pennsylvania Avenue. Elizabeth closed her novel for a spell and glanced to the sleeping form of her husband. Her smile was wistful as she imagined the beauty in the union between Hailey and Mark. She shared a knowing look every day with Hailey when the newlywed Vice President floated into the downstairs offices, and sighed with satisfaction and contentment, but more than ever ready to fulfill her official duties. Bill kept back a little bit more each day and the staff understood he was handing off to Hailey.

Elizabeth lost sleep in her nightly vigil. Her lounge chair was near the window so she could see the Washington Monument across the Ellipse. She read words on a page and remembered nothing as she reflected on a lifetime of service, concerned for Bill's health. His work day shortened. Trips came less and less, and only out and back in the same day. Hailey traveled to foreign countries and maintained relationships with important leaders. She interrupted stalled labor-management negotiations and brokered compromises. And always with her husband by her side, and Adam, when school was out.

It was right and it was time. Elizabeth and Bill had agreed their team had to have youth, and the country would benefit long after the Conleys left the White House.

Anticipation was rife in another part of the world. Two former freedom fighters met in the Mideast palace constructed with profits from the sale of their country's black gold. One man was a frequent guest and maintained his base camp in the distant valley of the peasant land he had helped overrun twenty years ago. The other man called himself a king, but was no more than a terrorist, a term that fit each man better than freedom fighter or king. This self-titled king lived in luxury and rained terror on his own people to keep order and financial profits. His visitor this night preferred the flexibility of anonymity, a standing better suited for carrying out missions from his old friend.

"Saleem, what is your bidding on this matter?" The king allowed his friend this familiarity and approved his deference.

"Strike when they are weakest. Be patient. Wait for a signal. The man is reported to be declining markedly and the woman is a mere woman. When she is called upon to act, she will fail. It is the nature of their sex. Then we will strike. My friend, you must hold yourself back. The time will come."

Forty-one

Jason was taking Jennette for his bride this spring day at the White House. The President had offered it free. No other location guaranteed as much publicity for the retired quarterback to show the world and his admirers he was joining the married life. He had told most everyone that football without his buddy, old number 27, was not as much fun. Truth was, Jennette threatened to shoot him if he got one more hint of a concussion from being sacked. The way she put it, sacking him was her personal business now. She had resigned from the Secret Service and gladly turned in her gun.

The Vice President sat up gradually on the side of the bed and paused to will her dizziness away. She wanted this to be a day of pure joy for Jennette. Her friend had sworn off men, then overwhelmed an NFL quarterback to break her oath. But a sour taste rose in Hailey's mouth this morning, just like it had the past few days. It was time to take the test she'd asked Clarisse, her housekeeper, to sneak out and buy last night. She stood, woozy with the knowledge of her condition, even though this feeling had only happened once almost sixteen years ago. Golly, what could a girl expect? Those little eggs floated down every month and she and Mark ignored them by loving morning and night, in equal regularity.

This would be a child of love, no doubt of that. She had wished for a big strong man to love and she had him. Mark said he was a lucky man. Hailey joked that he certainly was, and depending on their circumstance at the time, both eventually "got lucky" wrestling over her snide remark. In a moment the test proved another kind of luck. Good thing Mark had taken his pal, Jason, out for a mild bachelor's party last night. Neither man wanted to face the wrath of his woman if he came home hungover today. Right now, Hailey wanted the test's secret for herself. She also needed to throw up.

Later that morning, on the ride down to the White House from the Vice President's mansion, Hailey fooled no one about her condition, especially her two men. Mark and Adam studied her face with serious looks. Her son had already asked if she were ill. Mark kept quiet with a concerned stare, as if he were using a microscope to examine ever pore of her face. Hailey tried looking away as their car cruised down Massachusetts Avenue but Mark kept at it, his eyes peering with Superman x-ray vision. Then she couldn't hide the smile forming at the corners of her mouth. Mark nodded with a grin. He knew. Poor Adam still thought his mother was ill and came to sit beside her and raise a gentle hand to her forehead, checking her temperature. Hailey reached for his hand and brought it to her lips for a kiss.

"You guys are merciless. Quit picking at me like I have spinach stuck in my teeth." She rolled her eyes and recognized the truth was her only defense. She kept Adam's hand in hers and held her other one out to Mark. Then, drawing a deep breath, she spoke. "I'm pregnant. It was to be my secret for today and you'd find out tomorrow, but heck. Come here, honey." Mark jumped beside her and kissed her with joy. The threesome hugged and laughed all the way to the ceremony.

It wasn't to be a Daniel family secret for long. One look from Elizabeth and she gave her husband's vice president the thumb's up sign. Jennette accepted Hailey's hug for good luck, then stood back and examined her friend.

"You devil. You did it!" Jennette whooped and danced holding her friend's hands, twirling in a circle. All the women assisting Jennette rushed over and the celebration began. Finally, Hailey held up a hand to ask for a moment of quiet.

"Ladies, this is Jennette's day. Do not say a word to anyone."

Her admonition forestalled nothing. Wives whispered to husbands, friends overheard, press caught wind easily and even the President learned Hailey's secret, albeit fifth hand. He glanced over to her and judged this was pretty new. She had the rest of the year to be pregnant and part of the beginning of the next even. It was another first for the Conley-Daniel administration. He would let a month go by for Hailey to get comfortable with running the country while growing a life inside. Then they would have to talk about her future. She had to be prepared.

Nick stayed close to Hailey's son during the wedding reception. Since his days at Adam's first football camp out in Crested Butte, he had drifted into being the primary guardian for the boy. Mother and dad were in love and into themselves and probably hadn't noticed the changes. Nick surely had. He checked the agency's manual for procedures on watching a famous son, especially one who had gained a sudden interest in the opposite sex. How close did he get when the boy went out on a date? Adam wanted to drive his own car and pick up a girl without a chaperone hanging over his shoulder. How should Nick handle that? Should he speak to Mark to make sure Adam knew about taking precautions? Man alive, this was getting to be a tough assignment.

Hoo boy, there she was. Robin Crane was the girl of the month, and had come to the reception with her parents. She was tall, very pretty and wearing a dress that Nick would forbid his own daughter to put on. Kids these days. Adam saw her and left his mother to greet her family. Nick sidled in that direction, hoping Robin's mom and dad would keep their little vamp with them, and reject the boy's offer of a tour for their daughter. According to the manual, it had happened before. First Family kids used all kinds of excuses to get their current flames upstairs where they could, well, they could do whatever. Nick felt the sweat sticking to his sides as it rolled down. No no. There they went, heading for the stairs. The devoted agent searched the crowd for either Mark or Hailey to call a halt to this potential "national security" incident, but nobody was paying attention. "God help me," he prayed, and followed the adventurous couple upstairs.

Forty-two

Her morning sickness gone and the public highly in favor of a Vice President being pregnant, Hailey sailed down the hall towards the Oval Office. The President had canceled everything this morning. The town was quiet, and apparently so was the rest of the world. Most cabinet officers and the entire Congress were on summer vacation during the dreaded dog days of August. Bill and Elizabeth promised to fly out to Colorado Springs for their annual vacation right after this meeting.

Alice beamed at her and came from behind her desk for a greeting. "You look wonderful, Ma'am. Rosy cheeks and a glow only pregnant ladies seem to get, especially those wildly in love. And there must be some regulation that prohibits a woman from wearing the same clothes even when she's four months along."

"Oh, Alice. Thank you. We still jog most mornings, and walk evenings after supper. But next month I'll have to break down and go up a size, or several. With Adam I gained very little extra weight and only took a few months after his birth to get back in shape. I call it a gift of genes from my mother."

"Well, I won't delay you any longer. They're waiting for you."

"Who's they?"

"Mr. and Mrs. Conley are double-teaming you today." Alice expressed one of her confidential secretarial smiles. "Lots of luck. I'd love to be a fly on the wall."

Elizabeth came to the door and escorted Hailey to the comfortable sofa facing her husband across a coffee table. The women sat together and the First Lady kept Hailey's hand comfortably in hers. Bill Conley gave her a warm smile.

"You look great, Hailey. How do you feel?"

"Super, Mr. President. Never better. Now what have you two schemed up for me today? The last time we three met like this you offered me a chance to be the Vice President. So what is it now?"

"My job, Hailey." He hadn't known what kind of reaction to expect, but Hailey froze and her forehead grew worry lines. The president laughed. "No, I'm not quitting today and I'll do my best to last out the entire four years. I meant to say— Oh hell. Elizabeth, you do the talking."

"Ah, you men always leave the tough job to the women." Elizabeth turned to her good friend, one to whom she had been a surrogate mother. "What the eloquent leader of the free world is trying to say, Hailey, is the major parties are already campaigning for the presidency this year. They are collecting money and so far there are ten fellows running: the usual seven Democrats to three Republicans. Alas, there are no women among them, despite your stellar example. These political animals have been waiting too long for this opportunity and they still aren't ready to chance losing with a woman on the ticket."

Hailey looked from Elizabeth to Bill Conley. She received neutral, but friendly stares. They would not pressure her to seek the presidency, it was something once described as requiring a "fire in the belly," and right now her belly was filling with new life. This was not an easy decision for her. She fixed her president with her own steely glare.

"You're sure you're not running again? You'd win another landslide, and it wouldn't be the first time a politician backed out of a commitment to limit his time in public office." Elizabeth squeezed her hand hard and Bill shook his head. She was getting two answers, both negative, but the First Lady's was perplexing.

"I'm out of gas, Hailey. When we decided to ask you to run with us I insisted first off the Vice President had to be young. It takes lots of energy to do this job and we both know I gave you the work of ten men, or," he laughed, his eyes dancing from his wife to his hoped-for successor, "five women."

Elizabeth took charge again. "Dear, you and I know what it is like to carry a child. Even though you didn't factor in politics in the creation of your baby, your timing is great. Your due date is sometime in January and you can wait until spring to announce if you'll run. Say anything now, and your potential opponents will claim it's your hormones speaking."

Hailey said nothing, and for the first time since the Conleys met her she had no response for them. Her silence was understandable to Bill and Elizabeth. She'd had her head down working and never looked up the road, especially with a baby on the way.

Bill spoke. "When we return, take your family out to Crested Butte and relax on that fabulous deck. Ask your mate what he thinks. Mark is a good man and his support is necessary. More than that, we can see you two have discovered our secret. You're a team. And when you talk to him, bring up the fact that once you decide to run both parties will ask you to switch from independent to them. Also tell him you'll need to choose the next President for your running mate. About that issue I, we, are dead serious. We believe the person chosen to run for Vice President should be thought of as the next President, not somebody who will balance the ticket and hold down the fort during August. Ask Mark about living in the People's House and raising an infant. No man has ever done that for a lady President. Personally, I know he'd do a wonderful job of it, but he needs to give you his feelings." Figuring the conversation had gone long enough, the President stood as the First Helicopter landed right on time. "There's our ride, honey. Hailey, take care of yourself and don't stir up any trouble."

He came around the table and hugged her, something he didn't do in public. But this woman was a close family friend. He loved her and his wife understood. Hailey and Elizabeth hugged and she felt a little more than friendship in the First Lady's tight grasp, as if she were imparting another silent message.

Hailey waved them gone out the back door. The President looked in need of a rest. He must be in his early eighties now. Yes, it was time for him to seek that much deserved retirement to Colorado Springs. She hadn't been attuned to his health. He was just always there, backing her up, usually getting people to do things his way, especially these days, by entering the room and projecting an immense aura of commanding authority. Still, she sensed there was more and headed for Alice. But the First Secretary was candid. No, the President wasn't ill. No, she held no secrets on order from either Bill or Elizabeth Conley. Alice held a bright smile, and for the first time, Hailey felt a difference. Yes, there was something and she would worry it to death; figure it out herself. She understood one certainty: the President was passing the mantle of leadership to her and expected her to take it.

September had become the Vice President's vacation month. Hailey had her feet resting on the swing lounge and her head in Mark's lap. His left hand lay on her tummy protecting their legacy, as if anything could pass by the agents sweeping the hills and forests around Crested Butte. Adam was in town escorting Robin in and out of the shops with Nick close behind. At least Hailey hoped Nick was close. Her son had become enamored of the girl overnight it felt. Nick had talked to Mark about, well, about father-son stuff. Mark had given his adopted son a candid lecture and wouldn't let her in the room for it. Brother, she hoped Adam listened. That would be a first, to have the Vice President and her son expecting simultaneously. No, erase that thought. Her mind sought any kind of worry to scratch at other than the big decision she must make.

"Who is it?" Mark broke the reverie 9,000 feet above sea level.

"What who? What are you talking about, honey?"

"You're avoiding the issue. Who is your choice for a vice presidential running mate? We've been here a week and you keep slipping into these solemn moods. If you were thinking about a name for our son, you'd be more cheerful."

"You're so sure your studly Y chromosomes will determine the outcome, eh, Macho Man? She might just be a little girl. How about that? Someone you could have an afternoon tea with out on the lawn." Mark waited for her to circle back to the original question. "You also sound pretty sure I want the job. Why?"

"I felt that was a foregone conclusion, sweetheart. You're the best person for it. The people love you. You deserve it. The country needs you and the job you and the President set out to do isn't completed. Plus, you're the loveliest pregnant Vice President this country ever had. Who could resist voting for us?"

"Us? Does that mean you want to be Vice President?" She cackled as he found her spot alongside her hip. He knew to poke just enough to tickle her pink.

"No. I wouldn't have that picayune office. It's a throwaway position for over-the-hill politicians with no power. No, I want to be top dog."

Hailey pushed up to face her husband turned comedian. "I see now. You married me to put yourself in the White House. Is that it?" Mark sealed his lips with a finger and grinned.

Hailey spoke. "Burch Magnum. Because he introduced Adam to you and Adam introduced you to me. Easy as pie. But what about me, or us, as you put it?"

"Don't aspiring presidential candidates these days talk to their spouses first before they go traipsing off the high board? It's time for you to announce that you'll run. I always expected you to. Want you to. And you need to." Mark held her shoulders with care, turning Hailey square with his body. "This is not about being the first female president. Bill Conley would admit it wasn't about being the first woman vice president. You are the best person for the job. You two started a revolution, one many characterized as a political fantasy. You worked for what people wanted in reality, but hadn't been attainable politically. You blew away the extremes that wouldn't compromise and brought the people back into the equation. You're not done. We need your leadership." Then he kissed her. They were sealed, mouth to mouth and heart to heart. The kiss lingered until Hailey stood and took his hand.

They stretched out on the big king size bed and kissed some more. They were like bears that found the mother load of honey without bees. They drank their fill only to discover an unquenchable thirst.

Hailey whispered intimately, "Adam came home from his first visit to your locker room and talked all night about how you had stood up and led the team out of its depression. He said his Uncle Burch claimed the country needed leaders like you. That if we had more like you all our problems would be solved. I truly believe that after listening to you. I love you so much, honey. I wouldn't try to be a president without you, couldn't be. I simply can't be anything without you now, and don't want it any other way."

"I can't wait for it to happen. But there are a few other things I have in mind first." His talented hands had smoothly undone buttons and bra during her impassioned words of love. Now his sculptor's hands molded her exposed breasts.

Hailey sucked in breath as Mark unfastened her shorts. Thoughts of running for office and choosing a running mate vanished. This was their escape from reality and it always worked. She had to remember to call Burch tonight and see if he and Rose could come out and spend a few days. But later. Damn these button fly jeans. Why couldn't the man have a Velcro fly?

Forty-three

Most agreed the federal government should shut down from mid-December to mid-January. Nothing got done. Older workers were forced to take their vacation time before the end of the year, or lose it permanently. Traffic was at a standstill most of the day, since more workers drove into town separately to shop and go home early. Gridlock was common east to west, from Capitol Hill to the Lincoln Memorial, and south to north, from Independence to Pennsylvania Avenue, and even on up to K Street. Visitors observed that the best time to attack Washington would be during a snowstorm New Year's Eve.

Elizabeth read her novel and glanced over occasionally to the sleeping form of her husband. They had retired earlier than usual this New Year's Eve after a quiet evening with friends. Bill had dozed off intermittently during the evening, and that was her signal to call an end to the gathering. She had that premonition again, only stronger this time, stronger than ever before.

She lived in two worlds. Bill worked through his official duties during the day and often napped mid-afternoon. Elizabeth went another direction and chaired several charities, held meetings, called family members this time of the year. That was the daytime. At night they often dined alone and conversation was limited to reflections on their history together.

Where had time gone? Bill was eighty last month. She was three years younger. It had been a good decision to serve one term. Voters shouldn't be asked to choose someone without the energy to fight for them. Yet the country had needed its ship set on the proper course and that had taken a statesman, a military leader without ego. They had been married almost sixty years and had served this country for most of their marriage. They had made a difference.

Elizabeth had thought about this moment for over a year. There was a different feel emanating from the silent shape next to her. She switched on the bedside lamp and moved to her husband's side, searching his face for some sign. His skin was smooth now, unwrinkled, worry free. His mouth was relaxed, a gentle upsweep of a grin hinted at is corners. He was at peace. Elizabeth kissed his forehead and smoothed her hands down his cheeks, still warm, but holding less heat than her hands now. She rested her cheek on his chest and cried. This would be her private time before the nation took him to its breast for mourning.

She sat up on the bed facing her wonderful lover and soul mate. Holding his hands, Elizabeth allowed her mind to clear of the tough times, and her face easily slipped into a smile of gladness, of celebration for such a fabulous life they had made together. That would be her request to the people. It was time for Bill Conley to let go. The people should be upbeat, not depressed. Yes, she wanted a subdued celebration, not a saddening, bleak breaking of spirit.

Hailey would indeed become President and carry their dreams forward. First though, she would call the White House physician and ask him to come. Her next call would be to the new President.

Hailey had slept poorly. Her child roamed around her insides like a customer in a curio shop, touching everything, feeling its heft, stretching and testing out a leg on her kidney, then the liver. Oh, it was like having a physical exam from the wrong perspective. And her husband. Ugh, Mark slept like a baby recently nursed, changed and put to bed. It wasn't fair to women. And this thought had to come from her hormones, just the same, guys had no idea what they started. Grumpy. She was grumpy, that was all, and left the bed to fix a cup of hot tea. That would calm the baby and her grouchiness. It was four in the morning and her day would drag on after this episode.

The phone rang when Hailey was halfway to the kitchenette off their master bedroom. She would think later that her first guess had been a terrorist attack. It would be perfect timing. There was a foot of snow on the streets and maneuvering anywhere in the District of Columbia would be treacherous. Her second thought was of the White House. Her tears flowed at the news from Elizabeth. The two women had lost their champion and sobbed over the phone together in sadness and grief. Each had been "married" to Bill Conley in different ways: Elizabeth as wife and lover, Hailey as devoted disciple. Mark was awake now and held her, comforting her shaking body.

In the limo riding down to see the First Lady, Hailey wondered at the moment. Mark and Adam sat on either side, each holding one of her hands, showing their steadfast support. They said nothing, in tacit understanding of her need to grieve and begin to think ahead. Her entourage looked like a roving diamond, with Secret Service SUVs to the front and back and on both sides. With Jennette resigned, Hailey had only men protecting her, yet at the moment when the ultimate authority passed from the President to her, only two women, Elizabeth and Hailey, had been there. The official act would come at noon when a Supreme Court Justice swore her in. But technically, Elizabeth had already done it.

This was the missing element she had wondered about last summer when the President asked if she'd run for his job. He knew it was more than running out of gas, and so did his wife. So, too, maybe did Alice. She remembered Elizabeth's request that Hailey direct a national celebration. She agreed. This couple had given much, shared tremendously, and succeeded in initiating a quiet, but firm, revolution. Before the Conleys, the country had been divided, fractious was a better term. Money had been the denomination behind power, the controlling influence. New ideas and the ability to mold compromises were not considered, not really possible. She knew that the great man who would lie in state in the People's House tomorrow had set this stage. Bill and Elizabeth Conley had sought this transfer to her from the start. Her continuing sad thought remained that her mentor would not be around to see her win the election and be inaugurated next January.

Elizabeth met Hailey at the front door and the two women hugged for a long time, experiencing a shared grief as their bodies shook with emotion. Then the First Lady backed away and held Hailey's arms in hers.

"This is your house now, Madam President, Hailey. Please come with me upstairs so we can talk a bit." Mark and Adam trailed behind the women and entered the bedroom to pay their respects to the president.

"I'll allow the public tomorrow to view his body, Hailey. They can come through the White House. But let me tell you that Bill and I had some specific requests if one of us were to die." She led the Daniel family to an adjoining room and they sat to hear her instructions. "First, we didn't want a viewing at all and our children didn't expect one. Yet, the people will want one, and Bill was theirs more than mine while he was President. Next, he wanted any ceremony to be here, in the White House, and only two speakers, you and me. His body will be cremated and the ashes given back to me. You can put up a marker in Arlington National Cemetery if you wish. Also he wouldn't want any procession down Pennsylvania Avenue with marching soldiers and a caisson with boots of the fallen leader reversed. Above all, I want this to be a celebration of his life, not a depressing event."

President Daniel responded. "So it will be, Elizabeth."

Not everyone agreed, especially Cantwell Nederthal, who proved a headache from the start. The Constitution clearly provides for the Vice President to succeed the president under the twenty-fifth amendment. The new President would then nominate a Vice President to be confirmed by both houses of the Congress. Until confirmed, the Speaker of the House was technically next in line to the President. In the days following the death of Bill Conley, Cantwell was determined to bestow his influence on the nation.

Cantwell's first act was to call a hasty press conference on the front steps of the White House and announce his proposed details for the national period of mourning. All of his details ran counter to the First Lady's. Protocol demanded, he postured, that the President lie in state in the Rotunda of the Capitol Building. There was to be a week of viewing, then a procession down Pennsylvania Avenue for interment in Arlington National Cemetery. Religious services would be at the National Cathedral, where leadership of both houses of Congress would eulogize their fallen leader.

Not two hours later, Hailey MacMurray Daniel was sworn in by Justice Margaret White as the President of the United States. Her first job as chief executive was to undo Mr. Nederthal's nifty plan. She held her first press conference immediately after the ceremony.

Hailey stood with Elizabeth by her side. The White House press corps was silent.

"President Conley died at three AM today and will lie in state here, in the White House, tomorrow. His family has requested a short viewing and would prefer no procession or military march in his honor. There will be a short memorial service, also in the White House, tomorrow evening for family and close friends only. Thereafter, the body will be cremated. I have directed a marker to be erected in Arlington National Cemetery in President Bill Conley's honor." Hailey paused and turned to Elizabeth Conley.

The First Lady spoke with a firm voice. "My husband was a man of the people. He was also a happy and content man. My tears are ones of joy and appreciation for having him almost sixty years. We talked about just such a circumstance as this and I want to pass on his wishes, my wishes. We do not want a period of national mourning. Rather, treat my husband's passing as a commemoration, a time of hope and anticipation for more good things to come. He and I wanted a revolution in thought and spirit to invade the American political system. I think we got it. So, it is a time to be thankful for what has happened during the Conley administration and to look forward to a positive future with President Daniel." She turned away from the bank of microphones, pressed a tissue to her eyes, and then came back. "Thank you for allowing us this time together. It has been a great ride."

Elizabeth and Hailey left the press room and rejoined their families. The First Lady was surrounded by children and grandchildren. She reassured some of the younger kids and gave them consoling hugs. Hailey spotted the Speaker of the House and moved to defuse a potential conflict.

"Mr. Speaker, thank you for coming here today. We appreciate your continuing support."

Cantwell was embarrassed at his gaffe and could only sputter a reply of little sense. "Er, Vice Pres, uh, Madame, no, no, Mrs. President sounds odd, doesn't it? At any rate, I only thought to relieve you ladies of a burdensome task."

"There, there, Cantwell," Hailey soothed the man like a hurt child, "the details are being handled. It would be appropriate for you to check with someone here before your next press conference. Mrs. Conley spoke her true desires just now."

"Good evening ladies and gentlemen. This is Charles Goodenhour of the News Channel and I'll be talking you through the memorial ceremony for the late President Bill Conley. My guest this hour is Dan Roberts of the *Washington Post*, who has become a friend of both presidential families, the Conleys and the Daniels. Welcome to our presentation, Dan. I admire your work and it's good to have you here."

"Thanks, Charles. It's an honor to get this opportunity to visit with you and your viewers, although I'll have to say it's not good to be here for this particular event."

"We can all certainly understand that sentiment, Dan. And I'd like to hear your view on this great president's time in office. But first let me tell our audience that the First Lady—President Daniel still calls her that to no one's objection—Elizabeth Conley, set her foot down and got what she and the late President's family wanted: a private ceremony and no lengthy period of national mourning. TV viewers around the world will be able to see and hear President Daniel speak, then Mrs. Conley, and finally the concluding memorial service conducted by General Arthur Richey, US Army Chaplain, Retired. Dan what can you tell us about General Richey?"

"He's an old Army friend of Bill Conley's, and you couldn't find a more non-denominational clergy in or out of the military. I interviewed him for my book on Bill Conley and learned he came to the White House often to hold private services. Those services and this private one are examples of the subtle way in which President Conley kept church and state separate. There was almost no press coverage of his religious views and that was exactly how he wanted it. Let there be no doubt that he was a deeply spiritual man with high moral character. He lived his spirituality every day and never pressed his particular brand of religion upon a single person."

"Certainly no one knows more about the private lives of Bill and Elizabeth Conley than you, Dan. What can you share with us? Oh, and tell me what you think about all these so-called breaks with protocol surrounding this event tonight."

"Charles, answering your two simple questions would fill up several books. But I'll start by saying Bill Conley was an independent maverick from the very beginning. He rose through officer ranks faster than just about anyone, especially faster for someone who ignored military protocol. He was a combat veteran and awarded numerous medals for valor. He achieved his greatest success both in the military and in politics by outthinking all those around him. In one of our final talks, he laughingly said he'd run into only two people he never tried to outsmart, one was his wife and the other was his successor, President Daniel."

"Dan, we have just a minute before the start of this service. Why is it private, limiting attendance here regardless of the national exposure of our cameras? Why did Elizabeth Conley reject a national mourning period?"

"Charles, Bill and Elizabeth kept their family life private and this service is for the most private kind of family circumstance. We are too used to putting a microscope over the intimate details of our public figures. Elizabeth Conley threw out that scope today. Also, Bill Conley instigated a real revolution in American politics and it continues with Hailey Daniel. Mrs. Conley is smart, Charles. Yes, she's grieving the loss of her husband of nearly sixty years, but she counts the joy of their union higher. She wants the nation to appreciate the positives. It's as simple as that."

"Just one more item before we cut to the service. Doesn't protocol reserve the right for the President of the United States to be the last speaker?"

"Always, Charles. You're seeing grace at its best. Hailey Daniel has no desire to draw attention from the serious matter of this proceeding. She told me the First Lady asked her to speak; else she would be just another spectator."

Mark and Adam Daniel escorted their new president to the podium. They were there to show their sympathy for the Conley family and to assist Hailey. Each held an arm to steady her. The baby was due in two weeks and she had stood all yesterday afternoon in the customary receiving line to accept the condolences of foreign heads of state.

"Elizabeth, members of the Conley family, please accept my personal sympathy and that of a grateful nation for your loss." Hailey looked into Elizabeth Conley's face and into the faces of each of the First Lady's five children, and ten grandchildren. "Bill Conley was the greatest man I ever met. He had no ego and said he owed whatever success he enjoyed to his wife. When the voters elected him they got a real team to run the country. Not President Conley and his Vice President, but a man and wife so intertwined in hope and dreams for the American spirit, nothing could separate them." Hailey squeezed her husband's hand and wiped tears.

"That vital spirit is here in this room and all across the country. It is a renewed spirit of hope that Bill and Elizabeth set out to create when they decided to run for the office of the President. Today, I thank both of them for letting me tag along." Some in the audience chuckled at this and Hailey paused to sip some water. "Bill Conley never blew his own horn; he didn't have to. He stirred up so many waves the publicity came free. He was so good at this we shared a press secretary and let the media carry the water for us." More laughter as secrets of the Conley-Daniel administration were revealed with subtlety.

"He trusted people to do the right thing. He trusted me to break the mold for women and to work hard on our policies, without ever calling me on the carpet to change what I was trying to do. It was a remarkable characteristic, a presidential expression of free will. He understood there were many ways to do a job and he allowed people the flexibility to do it. He told me once that even with his special memory he could never keep up with everything going on, and, another secret of ours, he didn't try. President Conley motivated everyone under him to do their best. Most did.

"President Bill Conley, more than any other person, was the voice of the people, their leading voice. In his honor, I'm designating tomorrow a national day of remembrance. I encourage the American people to celebrate what is good about our country in President Conley's memory. Thank you, Mr. President." Hailey stepped away from the podium and went to the Conley family where she hugged each one. Mark and Adam kept close to her, as if protecting their wife and mother. Elizabeth rose and walked to the podium.

"Bill wanted to retire and play golf. He was lousy at it. Friends kept sending him notes, letters, and packages of stuff teasing him back from the golf course. For that I'm thankful." Laughter came from the small gathering. "He had so much paper at one time we had to buy a safe to keep it secured. But the more he read about issues and problems that just were not getting solved, the more interest he took in politics. When the governor asked him to be an interim senator, I knew we'd end up here. I don't mean here in Washington serving in the Congress, but here in the People's House as President and First Lady.

"I knew this because I knew my husband. If something was out of whack he'd get on top of it and fix it, and by golly, look what he started! We have task forces made up of people who have been bickering at each other for years, who are now compromising. That's a lot to be joyful about. We have a growing independent movement. We have the cutting of ties to moneyed and special interests. Something else to jump for joy about. We have broken through the barrier separating political fantasy from what the people need and want. Today, we believe we can solve problems once again, and that is my husband's legacy: Hope for the future."

The First Lady surveyed her family, and then focused on Hailey. "Bill always said he wanted to work his way out of whatever job he had. He meant he wanted to leave the situation better than he had found it; ideally, he wanted to personally mentor his successor. His greatest success is President

Hailey Daniel. We sat down one evening four years ago and discussed who would run with us. Bill and I made a long list of characteristics because we saw it as choosing the next president, not a stand-in for ceremonial duties. We demanded someone smart, who could build coalitions, who was an independent thinker, who had youth and energy to outlast us, continue our goals long after we were gone. Hailey surpassed our wildest dreams. Some will say we chose her because she's a woman and a very attractive one, undoubtedly the loveliest person to grace the White House. That's not the reason. We chose Hailey because she is the best person, male or female."

Elizabeth looked down and drew breath from a deep sigh. "Some will wonder why I speak so much of Hailey at my husband's funeral service. Those close to Bill understand, though. He wanted to emphasize the positives about America, and Hailey represents everything that's good and positive. True, we have a large and growing family, with a couple of great grandkids on the way. But they understand that their father and grandfather gave his life in service to his country. They know his dreams will continue with our beautiful and quite expectant new President."

General Richey led the remainder of the service and Charles Goodenhour returned with his guest, Dan Roberts.

"Dan, what's your understanding of the words these two women said?"

"Neither minces words, Charles. Both loved Bill Conley, one as his wife, the other as his prime student. He became a surrogate father to President Daniel and grandfather to her son. It's like a family when you have the Conleys and Daniels together. Foreign countries might try to characterize them as a royal family, but nothing could be further from the truth."

"But there's no period of mourning, Dan. I'm not sure I understand that part."

"The President's message is to make it a day for remembering what her president did. She won't tell us what to do. Like her president, she trusts us to use tomorrow wisely. You can be sure, with such short notice, there won't be any grand Presidents' Day sales either."

"OK, let's go back to yesterday's reception for foreign dignitaries. President Daniel is obviously quite close to the Western Europeans, the Russians, and the Chinese. Being fluent in several languages doesn't hurt there. But there was flagrant disrespect shown by the Middle Eastern countries and other, shall we say, less democratic countries from Africa, and from Burma in particular. No representative came from those countries. Tell us what's happening behind the scenes, Dan."

"I'll answer the last part of your question first, Charles. Behind the scenes those countries are reluctant to recognize Hailey Daniel as a strong leader because she's a woman."

"But that's incredibly stupid. The whole world knows her background. She doesn't need to personally fight hand-to-hand combat when she can order the best damn military in the world to fight for her, us."

"Good point, Charles, but I'll bet you some small country will test her mettle. Call her out, so to speak, regardless of her constitutional role as Commander in Chief. And my guess, if I had to pick a country that would try, I'd say it would be a dictatorship that got the rug pulled from under it by Bill Conley's policy to stop supporting dictators. Meanwhile, consider what has happened in the Middle East. Those dictatorships are under massive pressure to democratize, to share their oil wealth with the people of their countries. We are no longer their biggest buyer, and our bases have been shut down, troops pulled out. Our own energy self-sufficiency grows, and our relations with Mexico, Russia, Venezuela, and other energy-producing and democratizing nations are better than ever."

Forty-four

Hailey waited a week after the day of remembrance to speak to a joint session of Congress. With luck, she'd speak and get back home before her water broke. Her reception was tumultuous when she entered the massive chamber and helped reassure the nation the chain of executive power was intact, as these symbolic gatherings always seemed to do.

"Mr. Speaker, President Pro Tem Garcia, members of Congress, ladies and gentlemen. Thank you for your greeting and affirmation. I asked to be here tonight because if I spoke here any farther along, you'd all be potential midwives." Laughter and applause erupted, signifying her audience's acceptance of a pregnant President who was young and healthy. No longer was a woman's pregnancy seen as a delicate condition to be treated like an illness. Hailey had jogged into her seventh month. The White House physician declared her in the best shape of any pregnant woman he'd ever examined. A maternity room had been set up in her White House living quarters. She would deliver this child naturally, surrounded by family.

"Elizabeth Conley asked me to thank all of you here in this chamber and out in the television audience for your remembrances. She says she'll take some time to rest and then get to work answering the thousands of letters and cards she received. I have asked Elizabeth to remain in her quarters in the White House and to continue to serve as our nation's First Lady. She has graciously accepted." Applause, clapping and whistles resounded in the chamber. Elizabeth Conley was a very popular First Lady. Losing both her and Bill Conley would have been too much at one time.

"It has been the standard for a Vice President who assumes the presidency after the death of the president to promise to continue his programs and policies. Tonight I come before you and make that pledge. I will remain an independent and continue to speak for the people. I will use my executive powers to bring folks together to solve problems. I will travel and listen to you as President Conley did, only give me a few weeks first." There was more laughter. Television cameras caught the President's hand as it pressed to her belly and she winced in plain sight. "Pardon me, got a little kick there." More laughter.

"Bill Conley's main goal in what would have been his last years in the White House was to stop pandering to dictatorships. That's enough work for one year and I will not add to it. I'll only say that we will emphasize more than ever a reduction of arms sales to those particular countries. We can do this through various economic incentives to American businesses. Specific ideas are in the works."

"About my condition. Usually folks don't pressure a pregnant woman about what she'll do after the baby comes. However, many wonder if she'll go back to work or stay at home with the baby. My loving husband, Mark, asked me to let you know he will be providing extraordinary child care for our baby. He will also follow President Conley's example and coach me through labor and delivery. About that, the women in the audience understand what goes on. So for the men, and after I say this you'll understand why I'm going into detail, I offer these words. I did not use any drugs when I delivered Adam. But there was a moment, well, maybe several, when some out-of-control yelling took place." Her audience broke up laughing. A few leaned forward and waited for her further detailed description.

"I assure you there will be times during my labor when you will not want me to make command decisions. For just such times, the Vice President takes over. I'll get to that in a minute. But let me say that when it comes to giving birth, my first time out I proved to be a pretty tough broad. I was never unconscious and don't plan to be this time. My labor was short for a first-timer and should be shorter this go round. I left the hospital within forty-eight hours and returned to duty the next week, albeit not flying jets." There was more laughter and murmurs from Congressional leaders around the chamber as an understanding of this section of their president's speech became clear.

"So to make it amply clear to the American people, I will be out of circulation as your President for a very short time, perhaps less than a few hours. My husband understands his personal span of time out of circulation will be longer."

Hoots and whistles filled the air and more laughter flowed. Hailey sipped water and pressed her hand to another kick while the chamber quieted.

"Amendment 25 to the Constitution requires me to nominate a person to take my place as Vice President. Bill Conley and Elizabeth advised me to make this decision last summer when I agreed that I would run for the presidency this coming fall." Now a standing ovation brought her audience to its feet and Hailey smiled at the reception she was getting. "Elizabeth also told me to announce my choice after my baby was born. She said some male chauvinists would accuse me of making a decision while under the influence of a hormonal imbalance." She stared at her captured audience somberly and waited. She had them. She was confident and it was easy to see. "Circumstances require me to take a chance on that. I looked for a good man because there are some out there and we ought to give them a chance once in a while." This got everyone on their feet clapping and laughing.

"I chose a man who is highly respected in this chamber. He is an independent thinker. He is energetic and a coalition builder. He speaks for the people and severed all ties to special interests and lobbyists years ago. He is my good friend, Senator Burch Magnum of California." The full chamber stood and applauded this popular choice and Hailey motioned Burch to come and stand with her. He left his chair on the chamber floor and joined her at the podium. She continued when the tumult receded. "Personally, you should know that the underlying reason I chose Burch is because he introduced Adam to Mark, and Adam introduced Mark to me. Thank you and good night." Hailey turned to the two men standing behind her, Speaker of the House, Cantwell Nederthal, and Senator Garcia, the President Pro Tem of the Senate.

"Gentlemen, I'd appreciate it if you'd confirm him tomorrow. We have a lot to do and this baby is coming early."

Expert media consultants and reporters had much to analyze that evening and in the following days regarding their new President's address to Congress and her choice of a Vice President. In one swipe Hailey had chosen a person both major parties had considered wooing for the second spot on their tickets. The ever more populated senior segment of voters approved of Burch Magnum. He had become their spokesman for access to better healthcare and a revamping of Social Security. Her choice was also a runaway favorite in

California, the most populous state in the nation. Those political pundits who watched such things proclaimed the ticket of Daniel and Magnum to be well-balanced: one woman, one man, an easterner/southerner and a westerner, both independents.

Dan Roberts became an overnight national media celebrity after his narration during the commemoration service on the News Channel. Pre-publication publicity for his book guaranteed him an outrageous advance and syndication in hundreds of newspapers across the country. He had a difficult time writing his twice weekly columns while being a frequent guest on TV talk shows. One guest spot brought the pro-administration reporter face-to-face with an early antagonist of the Conley-Daniel administration.

Good evening, folks. I'm Lyman Trevolt and this is my show, *Challenge to the Newsmakers.* Tonight my guests are the infamous pro-White House reporter, Dan Roberts, and a frequent critic of the current administration, Jocelyn Andrews, a political analyst and Director of the Gross Manning Institute for Progressive Analysis, an independent conservative think tank. Welcome to you both." (General audience applause and commercial break)

Trevolt: Mr. Roberts, let's start with you. Some would say we have an inexperienced woman who has ascended to the presidency. Further, she is about to be burdened additionally with a newborn and has chosen a personal pal to help her out. How can you defend that?

Roberts: That description doesn't fit anyone I know, Trevolt. We have an intelligent President who happens to be a mother and is expecting another child momentarily. She successfully raised one child and says her son, Adam, was always a joy, never a burden. Her choice of Senator Burch Magnum is an excellent one. The man has an extraordinary record, in addition to being a personal friend.

Trevolt: Jocelyn, any response to that analysis?

Andrews: Sounds like another media hound who is enamored of the good looking chick acting like a President to me. The current occupant of the White House is no leader. What did she ever do?

She gets elected from some dirt-poor picayune Congressional district somewhere in the South that nobody ever heard of. She pals around with Bill Conley's daughter. Gets up close and personal with the man's family and hitches a ride to the top. (Some hisses and boos emanate from the audience.)

Trevolt: Jarring analysis, Jocelyn. Roberts, any follow-up to that?

Roberts: (Seems at ease, like he's been through hostile interviews like this many times.) Ms. Andrews is on record bearing a considerable dislike for President Daniel ever since she narrated the inaugural address and parade. Looks like facts and reality don't come into play in her analysis, and her personal opinions carry no water with the American public.

Trevolt: I disagree with that statement. Many people question the president's qualifications. I agree with Jocelyn that the jury is out.

Roberts: Your jury must be out to lunch, Trevolt. (Audience laughs.) Just like it was when President Conley appeared on this show. The people's jury disagrees with you. President Daniel has an approval rating going through the roof. About eighty percent are in favor of her and of her choice for Vice President. And let me add this. These shows always describe me as pro this or that. Yes, I like the President and I liked her predecessor because they made it easy to report the news. There was never bullshit one day that was overruled the next after a trial balloon got shot down. Katlyn Arnold, White House Press Secretary, just lays it out there and tells us what happened. The major, major difference with Presidents Conley and Daniel in office is that they aren't seeking another term. They both worked hard to manage the government. President Daniel has an extraordinary record and she never talks about it.

Andrews: No, she doesn't have to because you do it for her.

Trevolt: Thanks for that rebuttal, Jocelyn. Now for a few messages from our sponsors.

There was another, more private, conversation in one particular Middle Eastern country. The king and his freedom fighter friend met several times after President Conley's death and came to a fateful decision.

"The timing is perfect, your majesty. Their country is wounded. Deeply so. The woman is full of child and cannot possibly handle the position. Our brothers, as you, refused to recognize her ascendancy to the puppet throne of the Western neo-colonialists."

"I agree, my friend. There is no second-in-command now. Only a technicality keeps this pretender in supposed power. She will deliver her baby and we will strike. I like your proposal. It will send a lightning bolt throughout the Arab world to unite."

On Capitol Hill, Cantwell Nederthal balked and held up confirmation hearings indefinitely. A different sort of "Potomac fever" had crawled into his gut and the idea of reverting back to being only the Speaker didn't appeal to the aging representative. No force on earth could budge him and Hailey went into labor a week after her nomination of Burch Magnum without his confirmation as Vice President. Instead, she faced a belligerent old fogey whose desires to lead the country had been awakened.

Forty-five

Mark reflected it was fortunate he'd kept his hands in shape playing piano and tossing the football around with Adam. He had massaged his laboring wife for only four hours and, frankly, he was tired. He wouldn't complain though. What Hailey was going through was absolutely amazing. He knew now why Bill Conley had practically ordered him to do this. He would always remember this scene as a beautiful celebration of love and life.

Just thirty minutes ago, Hailey had signed a statement to Congress relinquishing executive control to the Speaker of the House. That had been the point at which her contractions were just a minute apart and sweat began to pop out along her forehead. Katlyn had another statement ready for her to sign immediately after the birth of their child. So much for the official business of the country. Executive affairs now rested with a man who had puzzled everyone with his recalcitrance in holding up Burch Magnum's nomination. What damage could Cantwell do in the span of less than an hour?

But Mark's thoughts returned to his wife as she struggled through another painful contraction. His feelings returned quicker because she was squeezing both of his hands so hard and transferring her pain to him. Lord, she was strong! And magnificent. What a marvelous creation was this woman, his wife. All women were, in Mark's eyes today. They went through a nine-month siege on their bodies. They suffered constant indigestion and could take no medication for illness. No smoking or drinking either. Their feet swelled, backs ached, clothes didn't fit and the maternity outfits they wore were like carnival tents. Had they too much vanity, this was not an exercise to be undertaken. Vanity! He laughed out loud. This room was no place for it.

A crowd of medical personnel and Mark's assistant coaches surrounded Hailey's bed. Adam had already left for school before her water broke and the White House had gone into Operation Deliverance. Hailey had assigned this military sounding tag to the event because she said every woman considered it the most exhilarating, yet freeing physical experience possible. Exhilarating because a real live little person was issued from her body. Freeing because the nine-month assault of that same little life was finally over, internally at least.

Mark had allowed the doctor and nurses to take over and stood back to cheer along with his assistants. Elizabeth Conley wiped Hailey's brow with a damp cloth and purred endearments into her ear. She, like everyone else but Hailey, was garbed in surgical gown, mask, and head covering. All had scrubbed their hands furiously before passing the head nurse's inspection. Katlyn stood guard at the foot of the bed and occasionally rubbed one of Hailey's feet. Alice, who had stayed on as Elizabeth's assistant, was in charge of ice chips and delicately dispersed them as required. Meredith, now the President's White House secretary, kept a comforting hand on the bulging mound that was Hailey's baby, yet unborn. Clarisse had come to just stand in a corner and cheer; there was no more room bedside. Rose Magnum held her hand and kept her company. Sara Wolf and Mary Jo Tyler were on their way from Blue Ridge via chartered plane.

Women, it seemed to the lone man in the room, came together when childbirth was involved. Only Jennette was absent. She and Jason were on a Caribbean island basking in the sun.

Dr. Janice Browning stood between Hailey's bent knees and examined her pelvic area. The doctor's hands gently felt and probed, and then massaged the shiny crown that Mark could see just a smidgeon of. It wouldn't be long now, and Hailey continued to pant as her doctor instructed. He had learned that she would tell Hailey to push when the appropriate moment arrived. Meanwhile, the room was chaos as cheers and shouts of encouragement rose from Hailey's supporting cast. It reminded Mark of a football game. Hailey's stretches of panting and struggling to overcome the waves of pain were greeted by optimistic yells and clapping.

Two more gowned figures rushed into the room and Mary Jo Tyler let out a whoop. "OK, Hailey. I'm here. Time to deliver this child." Mark's eyes welled with tears. Mary Jo had been Hailey's original set up teammate in high school and wasn't going to miss this. Sara came over and gave him a whopping hug.

"See what you guys cause? How would you like to be all swelled up and helpless and have a bunch of people staring at your private parts like that?"

"If it's all that awful, Sara, why are women so attractive? Why do you entice us to get you into this dreadful condition in the first place?" But his smile said this line of conversation was all in jest.

"It's a god-awful mystery," she said. "One I hope we never solve."

Dr. Janice had been warned about the enthusiastic duo from her patient's hometown and looked up to catch Mary Jo's eye. Her expert hands felt Hailey's stomach begin to tighten and she simply nodded to the former all-state setter who had gone through this procedure four times.

"Push, Hailey. Push hard," Mary Joe yelled and the rest of the coaches joined in. She looked back at the doctor for confirmation and received another nod. "Keep it up. Good girl. Push, push, push."

Mark went to his wife's side and gathered her around the shoulders with his long arms. He felt her entire body succumb to the birthing of this baby. All her being, every muscle in her strong, once lithe body, worked in unison to get the child out. He watched the reflection in the overhead mirror and saw Janice holding a tiny head in her hands, reaching to turn shoulders. At that instant he and the doctor stared at each other, smiles creasing their eyes. This time no one had to coach Hailey and she grunted aloud with her effort to complete the miracle of birth. Her hands squeezed her husband's enough to break fingers on a normal guy, and it was done. The mirror showed a tiny body, entirely within the grasp of Dr. Janice Browning's capable hands.

Dr. Browning held the child aloft for all to see. "Congratulations, Hailey and Mark. You have a beautiful little girl." Jubilation erupted in the temporary White House maternity room. Assistant coaches danced and jumped and hugged. Mark was showered with kisses and embraces from all angles. Elizabeth Marie Daniel had been born after four hours and forty minutes of labor. It wasn't a record but it was an extraordinary deed, one unmatched in White House history.

Doctor and nurses went to work tending to mother and child. The baby was laid on its mother's chest and began searching for lunch. Hailey kissed her daughter and handed her up to the care of the medical staff. She kissed her husband soundly and cried tears of joy. Then she searched the room for her press secretary. Katlyn stepped forward, held out a clipboard and placed a pen in the president's hand. Hailey signed the statement signifying she was back in control and Katlyn rushed off to fax the document to Cantwell Nederthal.

Nick had just finished his patrol of the high school perimeter and found it sound. He shook his head at Adam's insistence about not having extra security around him now that his mother was the President. What the boy didn't know could save his life. Maria Hernandez attended all his classes and at twenty-five looked like a teen. Ted Washington was another secret from Adam and had become his best buddy on the school soccer and track teams, the First Son's favorite sports. Somehow Mark had convinced the boy to avoid football. An unmarked and hopefully inconspicuous SUV stayed parked across the street and was home to several agents with enough firepower to dissuade a small army. All agents assigned to protect Adam Daniel were in contact via radio. Maria and Ted wore special devices which vibrated instead of sounding off. All in all, Nick was satisfied his team could adequately protect the boy.

He had gotten the news of the President's successful delivery and knew the rest of the world would not be informed until Adam left school and heard it first hand. Telling him would be Nick's job in a few minutes. He checked his watch and scanned the neighborhood. A few cars drove through the slow zone now as the flashing lights warned them of children at school. Probably a few parents picking up kids for after school activities and doctor's appointments. Nick was tuned in to the routine. Most of the kids carpooled with other kids. Things sure had changed since he had been in high school. Those days he could count on both hands the number of kids with cars.

The bell rang and within seconds the front doors burst open and the stampede began. Nick started walking toward the building. Adam was never in the first few waves of kids. He would wait for Robin, whose last class was farthest from the front of the exit doors. They would saunter out holding hands and wait until Nick could spot them before kissing. Such spring fever, he sighed. The two teens were smitten with young love. What would it be like to feel that for the first time again? There they were, heading his way amongst a pack of friends, both popular students.

Nick heard the squeal of tires when Adam and Robin embraced, still a hundred feet from him. He glanced over his shoulder back at the street and saw a huge Range Rover careen around a corner and speed up, ignoring the flashing lights to drive slowly. He turned and ran for Adam just as the huge vehicle slid to a stop and a side panel swung open. GUN!

"Down, down, everybody get down," Nick shouted. But the kids froze and stood like deer in headlights, eyes wide in fright. Where was the backup in the SUV? Shots blasted through the calm suburban neighborhood and Nick ran, placing his body between Adam and the gun in the terrorist SUV. *Had to be terrorists*, he thought.

Kids screamed. Some ran. Some fell to the ground, shot. Windows burst inward and concrete splintered from errant bullets showered everywhere. More kids fell and Nick jerked to a halt as he got hit once in the leg. He went to one knee and looked up for Adam. His Adam, had to get to him, loved him like a son. But the boy was down protecting Robin. He covered the girl, who lay bleeding. Another shot caught Nick in his upper back as he stood. Ignoring pain, he staggered forward like a drunk man. He fell on top of the President's son, spent, dying. His body shook and jumped as several rounds from the assassins struck.

Ted jumped in front of the pile of bleeding bodies and took even more bullets. Maria crouched near the flag pole and fired at the SUV, emptying two full clips before the big gun was silenced. That was the moment she realized another SUV had laid an attack on the Secret Service SUV across the street. Her compatriots had wasted their attackers, but now staggered from their vehicle, wounded but determined to finish the bastards. She sprinted to the main car containing the gun that had downed so many kids and jerked open the driver's door. One man was alive and groaning from a wound in his chest. The rest were riddled with gunshots, dead.

On Capitol Hill, Cantwell ignored the fax from the White House and sprang into action when the Secret Service clamored into his office with the traumatic news of the massacre at Adam's school. They surrounded him, taking extreme precautions. He directed orders everywhere. Call the FBI, the CIA, and the Pentagon he demanded. Call a Congressional Leadership Council meeting, in his office, NOW!

Within minutes Senator Kent Kraft was there, along with other leaders of both parties. Kent wondered what the old guy would do now. He was no longer technically in charge. Kent had seen the fax from Katlyn Arnold since she had sent copies, along with a birth announcement, to all the leadership. He'd even wished Burch good luck as the next Vice President ran down the hall past his office. Senator Kraft didn't have to wait long for an answer to the Speaker's intentions.

"Gentlemen, by now you are all aware of the dastardly act perpetrated at the school. I called you here to discuss our options and to hear a preliminary report from Agent Miller." Cantwell stepped aside and relinquished the floor to Special Agent Charles Miller.

"Gentlemen, I'm sorry to report that apparent terrorists shot and killed six students, one teacher, and three of our agents at Adam Daniel's school late this afternoon. All of the gunmen were killed by Secret Service Agents on the scene. That's all the information I have at the present time." Agent Miller turned and left the room without offering to answer questions. Apparently, when the man said that was all the information he had, he was telling the truth.

Kent Kraft turned his glare back to the Speaker, who was fidgeting with a paperclip that had become mangled beyond use. That was the moment the Senate Majority Leader decided that Congress must act to get Burch Magnum installed as Vice President that day, if at all possible. He grimaced at Nederthal's next utterance.

Spoke the erstwhile temporary President/Speaker of the House, "Anybody got any suggestions?" Kent stood and left for the White House. There were leaders and there were people who were mere representatives. This latter group included Cantwell Nederthal, who could gather ideas, huddle them into neutral, meaningless laws and continue to get reelected. The man had no concept of executive decision-making.

Hailey slept two hours before Mark shook her awake. Before dozing off she had nursed her daughter and played with the minuscule toes that would remain round until the child walked in her first shoes. She gazed at her husband and saw sadness in place of the joy of before. He sat on the side of the bed and told her the complete story of the school shootings, an event the press had termed a massacre.

"Adam is OK, honey. He caught a stray bullet in the foot but that's all. He's at GW Hospital and anxious to come back here as soon as he's released." This bittersweet news did not smooth Mark's worry lines though.

"Tell me about the others. What happened to the other kids, honey?" Hailey sat up and motioned for him to put Elizabeth Marie in her arms. The infant appeared asleep at first, but immediately nuzzled onto her mother's left breast when her father placed her in the vicinity. It was one of the most beautiful sights and yet the sadness of the attack threatened to keep Hailey's milk from letting down. She took a breath and relaxed and the child fed hungrily.

"Robin was killed first as she and Adam hugged each other. If they had turned the other way the first shot would have gotten our son. Adam lay on top of her and Nick jumped on top of him. Ted Washington came along and helped. Both Nick and Ted are dead. They were shot a combined nine times with bullets that would have killed Adam, if not for their sacrifice." Mark stopped his ghastly narrative. Hailey continued to take deep breaths and relaxed her body so she could feed her child. Tears slid down her cheeks, but her face was set in a determined expression. At that moment, Hailey Daniel was a mother, a woman grieving for the loss of innocent lives, and an angry President of the United States.

Hair stood up on the back of Mark's neck. An electric tingling coursed through his body. He felt like an observer to a barroom fight after a drunken bully had insulted the town marshal. Anyone seeing his wife now would know the bully was going to be taken out back and have the shit kicked out of him. His respect and awe for his wife doubled at that moment and he realized anew why she was the President. Bill and Elizabeth Conley had seen the characteristics before anyone else. They had known what she could do, and all the days she'd spent running the government would now come to fruition.

He motioned for Katlyn to enter the room and he left. This was no longer a place for a husband. Little Elizabeth Marie's nursery was to become a temporary conference room for the most powerful person on the planet. He waited in the hall and Katlyn brought him the baby to hold and rock to sleep. His day care duties began early.

President Hailey Daniel met with her national security advisors within thirty minutes downstairs in the Oval Office. She was dressed, freshly made up, and her hair pulled back into a neat pony tail. The men and women seated around her desk had briefed her and awaited her orders. The FBI and CIA had worked together to interrogate the surviving gunman, a detail hidden from the media. They hadn't had to press the assassin for an explanation. He gladly confessed to an attempt on the First Son's life as a "gift" to the oppressed Arabian people from his supreme Majesty King Fassud Kalim. This act of jihad would send a message throughout the Arab world to rise up and kill Americans everywhere. The so-called "Arab Street" would rejoice with the deaths of the president's child and those radical students with him.

Senator Kent Kraft sat with other Congressional leaders and observed. He noted the marked difference between Cantwell Nederthal's "brainstorming get-together" and President Daniel's executive session. The air was electric with the current emanating from President Daniel. Kraft sensed what she would do and personally thanked Bill Conley for picking her.

"I want to recap what you have told me, General Trent. Make sure I have the facts straight before we go ahead." General George Trent, Chairman of the Joint Chiefs of Staff, nodded understanding to his commander in chief.

"The man bragged of his killings and his orders came directly from King Fassud Kalim. Correct?"

"Yes, Ma'am, he did," said the four-star general of the Air Force.

"We know where the King is and have him under observation around the clock. Correct?"

"Yes," answered General Trent.

"He lives in a palace. His harem and their guards, eunuchs you say, are kept in a separate building nearby. His guards, plus several top advisors, are with him tonight celebrating their victory over the American neo-colonialists as we meet. Some of those with him are known terrorist leaders, masterminds of Islamic Jihad, Hamas, and Hezbollah. Correct?"

"Yes, Madam President," General Trent said. Muscles twitched beneath his eyes as the general gained assurance of his coming orders.

"As I recall, one Tomahawk Cruise Missile can deliver a one-thousand-pound payload launched from a distance of around 690 miles, and a single missile is big enough to wipe out the King's palace. And you have close observers who can verify the hit. Correct?"

"Yes, Ma'am."

Hailey measured the advisors surrounding her and glanced over to the Congressional contingent raising her eyebrows in a questioning nod. "Comments?" All in the room knew by her resolute tone that her decision had been made. No one spoke.

"General Trent, fire two Tomahawks directly on the king's palace. Try not to hit the out building where the women and eunuchs live. As soon as your observers verify the hits, let me know and I will broadcast an announcement to the American people."

The general stood and saluted along with the other military brass. "President Daniel, congratulations on the birth of your daughter. How is she? And how is your son?"

Hailey broke into a broad smile. "Elizabeth Marie is beautiful and hungry,

General." Her smile faded as she spoke of Adam. "My son has a broken foot and a broken heart. His girlfriend died taking the shot aimed to kill him. He should be back here with us soon. Thanks for your concern. Please excuse me, ladies and gentlemen." All stood and a strong President, not four hours past giving birth, walked with conviction from the room.

Adam waited with Mark upstairs in the family sitting room. He rested his foot on an ottoman. A pair of crutches stood against the triple sofa where father and son watched over Elizabeth Marie. Hailey went to her son and knelt before him.

"Honey, I'm so sorry. Robin was a sweet girl. We all loved her as I know you did." The young man hugged his mother and cried, letting down his grief for the first time since the shooting. Mark stretched his free arm around them.

"Mom, what are you going to do? I mean, poor Nick saved my life and then Ted, who I just found out was also an agent. And that Maria, wow. Agents at the hospital said she was like a machine and I thought she was just a really smart girl in my English Lit class. And the other kids. So many, all dead. A whole bunch wounded, too." Sobs and tears stole his voice. He searched her face hoping she could fix everything, knowing it was an impossible task to bring the dead back to life.

She was silent just then, cooing at the baby, but obviously deep in thought. Elizabeth Marie sensed food nearby and cried out. Hailey transitioned from grief to joy at the sight of her baby and sat beside Mark. After a few buttons came undone the infant nuzzled once more. Hailey looked down at her newborn and held Adam's hand.

Mark spoke instead. "Let her finish feeding, OK? If she doesn't relax we'll get lots of complaints from your baby sister. Your mother has had a tough day. Her labor and delivery was all hard work and then the shooting brought on extraordinary stress. You and I have to see your mom as two people: our wife and mother, and the President who must hold the country together with strong resolve." Mark hesitated and Adam hung on his calming words. "I'll say this, son. She will deal with all that has happened and continue to be the best mother and wife on the planet."

"Ladies and gentlemen," Hailey spoke with calm reserve as the TV camera and supporting lights glared at her. "Today cowardly terrorists directed from the palace of King Fassud Kalim shot innocent children to death in an attempt to assassinate my son at his school. They killed six children, a teacher, and three Secret Service Agents. Another eight students and two more agents were wounded, some seriously. My son was not seriously hurt because his girlfriend took the bullet aimed at him. She died as a result. Two agents protected my son and they also died, placing their lives in the line of fire.

"There were ten assailants and all but one was killed. The surviving assassin bragged that his orders came directly from the king for the purpose of jihad, as a call to all Arabs to kill Americans." Hailey paused and never blinked. She continued. "This was an overt act of aggression and we have retaliated in kind. Just minutes before I began this announcement, I ordered Tomahawk missiles fired directly onto King Kalim's palace. At that time, the king was celebrating the killing of innocent children, men and women with terrorist leaders for Hamas and Hezbollah. All inside the palace were killed. A nearby building housing the king's many wives was not damaged.

"I have asked Congress for a declaration of war against countries anywhere in the world that harbor or sponsor terrorists. There will be no more negotiations and appeals for cease fire. The next time an American is hurt anywhere by a terrorist, I will order the heads of state and their leadership in the sponsoring countries attacked directly.

"Citizens, terrorists do not fight by any principles of war or Geneva Conventions. Yet our country has done so in the past. From this point on, I will not accept a slap on either cheek before acting. We are at war and I will pursue that mission with vigor. As intelligence identifies targets I will direct attacks." She stopped and drank from her water glass, set it down and looked back at the red light of the camera.

"I offer my sincere condolences to the families of the victims of this heinous act. I designate the rest of this week be set aside for a national mourning period. Thank you and good night."

In the following days, President Daniel ordered attacks on targets in virtually every Middle Eastern country, and a few in Africa and Southeast

Asia. In a few cases missiles hit palaces of dictators, in others, military targets housing terrorist operations. No troops were deployed; just the powerful Tomahawk missiles. And this time the so-called Arab Street reacted differently. People took to the streets and overthrew corrupt princes and sheiks. Religious zealots were defrocked and a movement started to separate church and state, and church and education. Terrorists were corralled in a few places and an angry mob beheaded them on the spot. It was the beginning of a pan-Arab revolution by a people no longer willing to blame outsiders for all their troubles.

Epilogue

Senator Kent Kraft rammed through Burch Magnum's nomination for Vice President in a special session held immediately after President Daniel's address to the nation. He then carried her cause further by demanding a declaration of war as she had requested. A changed man, one who had regained the stature of public servant over spokesman for special interests, Kent Kraft bolted from his party later in the spring and took enough senators with him to give independents the majority control in the senate.

Speaker Nederthal resigned his position and his seat in the House. He retired to Mississippi where he continued his hobby growing orchids. His former job as Speaker was filled by a rising star in Congress, Lara Mendenhall. Mrs. Mendenhall was a Rhodes Scholar and Ph.D. graduate from Vanderbilt University where she taught French. She had served three terms representing Nashville, Tennessee and its metropolitan area. Mrs. Mendenhall had certain qualifications that gained her national attention overnight. She was smart and spoke several languages. She had served in her state's national guard as a helicopter pilot. She was married to a former All-American football player and had three children. Lara was also a knockout redhead with a gorgeous smile.

Matilda Pratterly entered a rehab center for the fifth time and disappeared from public view. Lyman Trevolt's show lost its sponsors. He is now the weatherman for a radio station in Aberdeen, South Dakota. Jocelyn Andrews continues to run her think tank and host a game show. Charles Goodenhour took on the job as head of the Public Broadcasting Corporation.

Dan Roberts won his second Pulitzer with his biography of President Conley. He continued to research the machinery of an independent White House working closely with Katlyn Arnold, President Daniel's press secretary. He asked Hailey Daniel if he could do his next book on her presidency and she laughingly agreed, saying it would be a short book because she might serve only one year if the voters tossed her out. But by the summer of that general election year though, most around the People's House understood the President was a shoe in for her own full four-year term. They also recognized Dan Roberts did more than research with Katlyn Arnold.

Katlyn, ever the pugnacious journalist, served her president with vigor and total devotion. She also got cold shivers whenever Dan Roberts spoke to her. In all, she estimated it took four years serving under two different presidents to seduce the notable *Post* reporter. To Katlyn, people could gossip all they wanted about their age differential: she was early thirties, Dan mid-fifties. She would always have fond memories of the sofa in the corner of her office, the small one right down the hall from that of the most powerful leader of the free world, the sofa where she pounced on the wily reporter, and wouldn't stop kissing him or let him up until he agreed to marry her.

Jennette and Jason Kramer, the movie-star-gorgeous couple, proved proficient producing offspring. Jason runs his marketing empire full time but has cut his traveling down considerably. Proof of the latter is the five children the randy couple generated in their first five years of marriage. Mr. and Mrs. Kramer are frequent guests in the White House, at no charge to the taxpayer. Both sit on the board of Mark's nonprofit corporation that manages the National Children's Rehab Center in Crested Butte.

Caroline Jankowski, the first women to manage the National Archives, retired in late summer of the election year and moved to Boca Raton, Florida where she and her devoted husband provide day care for their grandson and keep an enormous wine cellar.

Anatoly Tushenko rose to prominent heights in the Russian government, largely due to his personal friendship with the President of the United States. He was rumored to be the next ambassador to Washington. Fang Shau rose as well, but into domestic politics as a high party official in Beijing. Lin Tao was rumored to become the Chinese Ambassador to the United States and was a frequent participant in volleyball games on the White House south lawn. Charles Morgan became permanent liaison between Israel and Palestine in their continuing efforts at a peaceful settlement.

Wendy Tucker, Administrator of the Willows in Blue Ridge, gained national attention. Wendy spent much of her time showing visiting nursing home professionals how she managed the place. Marie continued to recognize only Adam until she died peacefully in her sleep.

Vice President Burch Magnum took on the voluminous job vacated by Hailey. He created task forces to tackle large health, education and economic issues and formed an alliance with Lara Mendenhall in drafting revolutionary legislation.

Elizabeth Conley, the popular First Lady, stayed in the White House the remainder of the year, finishing a four-year stay. She retired to Colorado Springs and took up golf. Her third great grandchild was born on the eve of the November general election. In honor of his famous great grandfather, he was named William Conley. He too had no middle name.

Elizabeth Marie Daniel was a large baby, taking characteristics for size and beauty from both parents. Her first word was ball, spoken at seven months. Hailey gave her a miniature volleyball and her doting father played with her every morning and afternoon. Adam Daniel graduated at the top of his class and applied to William and Mary, where he could be close to home. Maria Hernandez was assigned as his permanent agent and the two became close friends. Mark still jogged with his wife every morning. His time was spent caring for Elizabeth Marie and directing the rehab center back in Crested Butte where his family vacationed.

Hailey announced her candidacy for President in the spring and vowed to keep to the path set by Bill Conley. She agreed to debate opponents anywhere anytime, but would limit her travel. Again, as in her previous campaigns, she accepted no donations larger then ten dollars. In the fall, she maintained a 75 percent voter approval rating and polls showed her with a 20 point lead over all other candidates combined.

In the summer before the general elections, the states approved an amendment to the Constitution that limited the president to one six-year term and members of Congress to a maximum of twelve years service total. The Conley-Daniel administration had created the second biggest revolution in American history without firing a shot. As promised, the two leaders had turned off the old system and started a fresh one that answered directly to the voters.

Acknowledgements

Special thanks to my readers: Vivian Perdue and Mickie Davies in Virginia, and Christine Wren and Bob Svenningsen in Colorado. Vivian and Mickie forbade the characters from their "sneering" and helped update some basic grammar. Bob advised on the latest doings at our old agency and provided great advice and updates on relevant regulations.

Christine advised where my characters had abandoned their true nature. Her insight was very helpful when it came to balancing the many aspects of Hailey MacMurray, a beautiful woman who is a single mother first, and an elected official second. *Gracias, Senora.* Also, much thanks and appreciation to Richard Wren for his patient photography of a reluctant smiler.

My wife Joan inspired the plot for a woman becoming President. One night she said, "Why not elect a woman and give her a chance. She couldn't screw it up any more than the men have." Or words something like that. Thanks, honey. Also, I remember a cartoon that showed God and one of his angels sitting on a cloud watching fire consume Earth. God turns to the angel and says, "Next time I'll give the match to a woman."

Author's notes

Vivian tells me there is already a Blue Ridge, Virginia. "A nice place with old homes," she said. "But not many." *Leading Voices'* Blue Ridge is a fictional town. I like the name and use it in most everything I write about Virginia, moving it around to suit the story.

When I told my friend Lou Morton about the plot he exclaimed, "That's a fantasy. It'll never happen." Lou should know. He taught American Government at Mesa State College in Grand Junction, Colorado. Still, I'm an eternal optimist and always hope for better.

Few of the ideas for change are mine. I picked them up along the way starting with the first lecture I heard in political science at the University of North Carolina. Such ideas as term limits and giving the president one six-year term were preached that day. I thought them worthy. My professor claimed these changes would be supported by the people eventually. I'm still waiting.

I disagreed with many things I saw in my 25-year federal service career. Most had to do with inept political appointees who were running for office on the taxpayer's dime, campaigning for their boss's next election, or arranging photo opportunities. They were not managers but controllers, squelching productivity. Too many of these folks stay on, burrow into the hide of the bureaucracy, and contribute little.

The Federal purse. There have been successful, authorized tests allowing some agencies to disregard the myriad of regulations on how to buy things. I support total abandonment. A friend and salesman for a top forms printing company once told me the regs didn't matter. His company would always get their larger share. I suggest managers be held accountable: praised if they get the job done under budget; fired if cronies get contracts.

Our political leaders attempt two options to rein in our government: try to make it efficient, supposedly acting like private industry—impossible by definition; or, spend money trying to set up the mammoth federal enterprise as an example—this is called pork.

Printed in the United States
22070LVS00002B/1-39